BESTIARIUS

Also by Mayo Purnell

ROMAN ANIMAL TRAPPER

Bestiarius

by Mayo Purnell

TECHNICAL NOTE

By the third century A.D., over two hundred thousand of Rome's million inhabitants were on welfare. Depression, loneliness, and the meaninglessness of their existence had caught up with them in high-rise tenement living. Their inherited lack of self-worth was medicated by cheap sensual thrills, and the precariousness and insecurity pervading the Roman world had translated itself into their desire to see people get debased and hurt. This class was the 'Mob,' a dangerous and powerful animal whose sensibility extended well beyond the fifth of the city's population it composed, effecting the freedmen, bondsmen, slaves and servants, and a great part of the upper class as well.

But the situation in Rome was merely a symptom of the disease infecting the Empire as a whole, which was overextended, bankrupt, and composed of a widespread, multi-ethnic lower class for which it could no longer provide physically or emotionally. The first half of Western Civilization was coming to a close. Its art and literature were not only past their peak, but had begun to stale. Moreover, its traditional religious beliefs – the concept of the individual at the whims of mercurial deities that were basically larger versions of himself – were incapable of fulfilling the needs of a populace brought into increasing awareness of the scope, potential and danger of the world around them. Spending their days at the baths or watching the 'Games' in the half-a-dozen amphitheaters around the capital only furthered their need for something more to hold onto – a need which the government could no longer fulfill, and simply mollified with more and wilder spectacles.

Hence, with the Games their only emotional outlet, the Mob's thirst for the sadistic and the perverse mounted through the years. What had once been real exhibitions of skill and courage staged to inspire a budding civilization in a world of enemies out to crush it, became excuses for cruelty exhibited to appease a morally exhausted civilization with nowhere to turn but in upon itself. By the third century A.D., feats of strength and skill no longer pleased. Death and sex were the only emotions that could still keep the people in their seats.

The Games had gotten out of hand. But to have abolished them, as the philosopher-emperor Marcus Aurelius would have liked, would have been concomitant to abolishing all modern professional and collegiate sports, not to mention Reality TV. It would have thrown so many people out of work throughout the Empire that it would have threatened to collapse the Roman economy. Every city, provincial town and legionary camp from Scotland to Saudi Arabia had an amphitheater, however humble or grand. And then, as now, to have abolished the Games would have not only been to remove an industry, but a crucial emotional outlet for the common man.

The system of appeasement to which Rome had spiraled and sunk had august origins, however. As early as the first century B.C., Julius Caesar realized that whoever had the 'people' in his pocket, in a sense, had the power. Publicity and entertainment, in short, hype became the answer. Caesar has even been called the 'Father of the Games,' for he fought fifty pairs of gladiators to the death in the open square of the Roman Forum to garner popularity.

Needless to say, his successors all realized the buying power of the shows which had once been bloodless county fair-like carnivals held in the valley between the Aventine and Palatine hills until 263 B.C., when two brothers had a pair of slaves fight to the death over the grave of their father, who had been a general. Originally an Etruscan practice, it was a stylish funeral, and it started a fashion out of which an actual profession developed. A profession known as 'Gladiator,' or swordsman, deriving from the Latin 'gladius,' for sword. As the Roman commonwealth expanded, it encompassed an unending amount of criminals, misfits, and prisoners of war which aided in the development of this profession.

The shows developed as well, and the wooden bleachers lining the slopes of those two hills grew into a stone and marble stadium known as the *Circus Maximus*. After its restoration in the early second century A.D., it could hold an estimated three hundred and eighty-five thousand. Chariot racing was extremely popular, the different teams supported by particular neighborhoods of the city in a way that is surprisingly similar to today's regional Italian soccer. The spectacles, which could roughly be divided into animal hunts and gladiatorial bouts, started as intermission acts between the races. But with the construction of the 'Flavian Amphitheater' between 69 and 80 A.D. – a building known to history as the Colosseum – the spectacles were given a home of their own.

By the time the Colosseum was finished, wild animal events were already an important part of the shows. Events featuring massed hunts were nothing new, and Romans loved animals. Caesar brought African elephants to the Circus Maximus; by the third century one could see their shorter cousins from India, and even huge snakes from beyond. The expiatory blood-letting of these hunts had always been particularly fashionable with the Mob, though the upper classes still prided themselves on their preference for the gladiatorial contests.

But the patricians had never particularly been the driving force behind the games, and a special class of contestant called a 'Bestiarius' developed around the increasing popularity of the animal segments. Like the gladiators, these professionals had their own school across the street from the Colosseum, remnants of which still exist. They had their own styles, such as dodger, chaser, pole-vaulter and hunter; their own traditions, slang and dress. In fact, each new day of spectacles started in the morning with these *venationes*. These wild beast hunts.

ROME

FLAVIAN AMPHITHEATER

A.D. 222

He strode down a dark stone corridor past blinding torches burning in brackets on the wall. His name was Caius Marius Mannix and he was a powerful man, with eyes that changed color in the various shades of light like the deep volcanic lakes in the hills where he was born. He walked with a purposeful stride and a set jaw, his muscled thighs flaring with each step of his black leather boot sandals.

Dark hair framed his brow and fell in waves over his ears and down the nape of his neck. His features were pleasant though his expression was grim, his nose prominent and ridged, his mouth well set. His cheekbones were high, the skin beneath them tight, windburned, and stubbly with an oily dark growth of whiskers. He wore a sleeveless blue tunic belted tight at the waist with a wide black bronze-studded leather belt. Ruby and azure amulets glinted in the torchlight from a leather thong worn tight about his corded throat – the goodluck gift of a priestess of Isis who showed the whites of her eyes and moaned to die in his embrace.

The cavernous tunnels, passageways, cells and mechanical elevators, the underground world already reeked of the odor of human refuse emanating from the lower depths where the extras were kept. The smell always increased around

1

this time as it was about to begin, mixing with the sweet sweat smell of fear and the torch smoke, making it difficult to breathe.

The animals thrashed against the sides of their cages, the iron bars shaking and reverberating. The sounds were what really rattled an inexperienced man, the way the ovoid matrix of tunnels drew them out, echoed them, layered them, mutated them. The guttural roaring of lions, that weird, high-pitched crying of the leopards, the insane screaming laughter of the hyenas. Over it all, the constant blanket of crowd noise and music above the floor as if carried on a wind from across the Styx.

Mannix stopped and gazed through an iron grate inside the perimeter wall, taking stock of the atmosphere inside the Amphitheater. The misty sanguine glow cast by the overhead awning was penetrated by brilliant slits of sunlight thrusting through its vents to lance across the arena floor where the finely-grained white sand sparkled like a lake of diamonds. Inset with panels of purple porphyry stone, the black marble perimeter wall containing the floor rose to a height of fifteen feet, with six-foot elephant tusks arcing down and over from bronze sockets embedded atop it. For further security, a ring of ornamental masts for netting encircled the top of the wall. The netting was down now. It wouldn't be brought up until the elephants and the apes came.

He watched the ticket-holders being shown to their seats by the locarii, the first thirty-six rows reserved for the Senatorial class and the Equites. A flourish of trumpets announced the Emperor, a flash of purple and gold amidst the silver and crimson of his guard; the nineteen year-old moved toward his box with his mother and their distinguished audience, young female dancers scurrying backwards before him scattering rose petals in his path.

Ambassadors filed in, and wealthy tourists from all over the empire; visiting rulers were seated with their courts. The Vestal Virgins entered from a rose-marbled archway in the purity of their hooded white stolas, seating themselves in their private box opposite the Emperor's across the floor.

The upper class seating was divided from the lower by a horizontal band encircling the bowl of the Amphitheater, with temple-fronted niches containing statues of gods, athletes and heroes staged at intervals between segments of polychrome marbles set in geometric patterns. Above it rose the tier of seating for the Plebians and, above that, the highest level of wooden gallery seating beneath a colonnaded terrace for slaves and working poor; all of it newly restored after the lightning strike and fire of five years before.

After the Senators and the Equites were seated in the first two tiers, the Praetorians guarding the entrances outside allowed the Mob their frenzied stampede for seats in the upper levels or standing room in the gallery. Women were knocked down, children trampled; screams pierced the tumult. Fights broke out in the corridors and stairways leading to the top two tiers, and the sailors standing atop the terrace where they worked the masts and rigging to hold the awning, cursed and brandished bullwhips as they watched the crowd surge like a plague of insects up the aisles toward the wooden gallery seating beneath them.

Spanning the great oval, the awning protected the spectators from sun and rain. Wool dyed predominantly red with radiating segments of yellow, blue and green, it diffused that sanguine glow into the Amphitheater where its colors shifted gently as it undulated high above in the breeze, tinting the marbles and catching the statues in alternate tones of carmine, turquoise, peach and jade. From the horizontal band with the temple-fronted statuary niches which divided the Patrician from the Plebian seating, a second ring of huge masts rose to encircle the upper tiers and help support the vast tarp. Between them stretched a system of catwalks for the sailors, replete with cranes which could support men and animals up to the weight of a bull, and levitate them out over the arena floor.

Perfumed fountains shot colored water into the air, statues of gods urinated it, goddesses poured it from urns, huge marble dolphins spouted it between their teeth. Everywhere it gushed, cooling the vast circus and sweetening the garlic and human stink. Program sellers, vendors of sweetmeats, wine, and cushions to cover the hard marble seats, wound their way through the packed aisles displaying their wares. Bookies climbed from tier to tier shouting odds on the posted events.

A white bull and two rams wearing golden head dresses were led onto the arena floor where priests awaited them at its center by an altar to Jupiter Latista. Overfed and pampered all their lives, the animals walked bleary-eyed and blinking with the noise and confusion, but without much concern, for humans had always been their friends. When they arrived before the altar, their attendants pushed and pulled them into places a bit separate from each other and the men were handed double-bladed ceremonial axes by the priests. Their technique steeped in piety, they brought the axes smashing down into the backs of the animals' necks where the blows created visible wedges and the heads dropped forward.

The rams collapsed immediately onto their forelocks, but the old bull stayed up, his large eyes rolling in the firelight burning atop the altar. Then he gave a surprised bellow and his hindquarters began to scrunch up and hunker down beneath him like a female dog urinating. His great girth wavered and his forelocks trembled and he collapsed drunkenly with his head flopped forward to stretch the wedge in the back of his neck huge and horridly. Then his hindquarters relaxed and the old white bull settled as if into his hay mound to sleep, the blood running very easily in florid undulations caught and slivered by the firelight from the altar like burnished golden streams.

The priests wasted no time with their knives and had the entrails of the three animals out and examined over the altar, sprinkling wine and incense on the fire. Then the carcasses were drug off the floor, their golden head dresses bobbing limply and the slaves quickly raking fresh sand over the bloody furrows. The entrails showed that the gods were favorable to the games proceeding. But, with the stadium packed to bursting, they usually were; and, while the attendants removed the altar, the priests filed out, chanting hymns and swinging incense burners.

4

Stimulated by the blood and the beginning, the sound of the crowd was like the noise of the surf. But from his world came the sound of the jungle. The freshly laid, pure white sand specially ordered from Egypt sparkled with the semi-precious stones sprinkled across it, muffling the yapping of wolves, the chattering of monkeys, and the trumpeting of elephants in the bowels of the Amphitheater below. The animals smelled the blood of the sacrifice, as the scent seeped beneath the festive atmosphere into the land of shades where they lay. A shadowland created by the great skeleton of travertine piers supporting the seating, which were sunk forty feet into the earth when the Amphitheater was begun a century and a half before as a reparation for the excesses of Nero's 'House of Gold.'

Mannix knew the building, knew it like another man might know his own home. He knew from overhearing the architects who were sometimes called in for restoration work in the off seasons that the construction of the Amphitheater was originally divided into four quadrants, among four contractors, and that the work in the northeast quadrant was shoddy. He knew that the ground it was built on had still been boggy from the artificial lake that had formerly centered the pleasure pavilions of Nero's palace; and that the colossal statue of the Sun God outside was originally a depiction of the infamous emperor, but given a new face during the reorientation of the sight.

He knew that the boggy ground from the drained lake fostered the sinking of the stadium's travertine foundation piers, which in turn lent themselves to the creation of an underground world of ramps and tunnels, cells and holding pens which were fully developed in aiding the logistics of the spectacles. Condemned criminals and prisoners of war not fit for the main events were kept in lower cages than the animals. The Amphitheater had its own ecosystem and, being much less valuable, if an extra died awaiting his or her stage call, they were simply butchered and fed to the beasts.

Beneath the arena, and he knew them all like the back of his hand, an axially symmetric system of tunnels and corridors comprised of trap doors and elevator shafts allowed men, animals and props to be brought on and off the floor in a timely manner. With something akin to the technology of a prison, corridors led from a maze of cell blocks on different levels underneath the seating to the arched insets caged with iron encircling the inside of the perimeter wall beneath the arena.

Medium-sized animals such as antelopes and leopards were driven from their cells into the insets by groups of technicians – mainly slaves, but highly trained and knowledgeable – behind wooden shields that filled the corridors and locked into grooves in the walls, or simply using fire-brands and the logic of dead-ends. Other larger animals, such as bulls and rhinos, were driven up the eight tunnels beneath the stands into a concentric system of parallel chutes where a dead end awaited them in a caged elevator shaft.

The elevators were counter-weighted, or worked by men on windlasses, sometimes up to eight men on a five-hundred pound bear. There were parallel rows of elevator shafts for men and smaller animals, two rows on either side of a central line of large chutes for bringing up props and backdrops ranging from a forest of trees to large chunks of realistically-crafted plaster that could be put together to form a fairly tall mountain, a city or fort. With ramps and ladders placed inside of them, and corresponding to the elevator shafts in the floor they concealed, a mountain, landscape, city or fort, could erupt men and animals out of its own system of trap doors.

All of it soot-stained white stucco walls with torches the only lighting, the layout beneath the floor was reminiscent of a provincial Roman town, which in turn resembled the layout of the legionary camps they often grew from. The central line of panels for props and sets corresponded to the *decumanus*, the straight street providing the axis of the town. The elevator shafts flanking it were aligned like parallel side streets, with smaller 'cross streets' traversing and creating intersections between them.

Logic, axial symmetry, and functionality; the theatrical nature of the spectacles was aided by the structured symmetry beneath, which in turn lent itself to timing and communication behind the scenes, where spotters watched indications from the

'Ringmaster' in his box beside the Imperial podium. Mannix knew all of these things. And it was a knowledge which ate at his soul.

II

Mannix heard music coming from outside the Amphitheater, and watched as the inaugural procession entered the arena through the Gate of Life. Led by a contingent of the Praetorian Guard, their silver cuirasses heliographing in the strips of sunlight cast across the sand by the ventilation slits in the awning, musicians marched in playing horns, fifes and flutes to the beat of drummers and the background strains of the Amphitheater's hydraulic organs. Chariots drawn by zebras in splendid harness carried the sponsor of the series and his retinue of olive oil executives. Behind came horse-drawn floats carrying statues of gods and goddesses and groups of actors miming mythological vignettes.

Another flourish of trumpets announced the combatants, rank after rank of gladiators trooping in, the better physiques naked, their skin glistening with olive oil. The more famous carried palm branches in their hands and wore garlands of flowers on their heads. The traditional styles represented the earliest enemies of Rome – heavily armed 'Samnites,' and 'Secutors' equipped as Gauls with fish emblems on their helmets. Then *Retiarii* with nets and tridents, *Postulati* in armor with swords and lead maces, and the trainers – retired survivors of the ring themselves – the *Lanistae* in simple tunics carrying their oaken disciplinary canes.

Armor and muscle pulsed in the gold stitched amber glow as the parade became a bizarre and curious array of militaria large enough to give a fair-sized army a run of trouble – from Parthian archers and Sarmatian cavalry, Thracian peltasts and Greek hoplites, to fiery-haired Celts with double-bladed axes, Syrians with slings, Egyptians with boomerang hatchets, Essedarii with lassos and Germans with huge broadswords. Elephants emerged carrying howdahs full of

Nubian spearmen and a train of mule-drawn cages exhibited rare and exotic animals. Then came Mannix's fellow bestiarii, leading panthers on chains, dancing draped with pythons, riding giraffes, stags and antelopes, some driving light chariots drawn by ostriches.

Through the midst of it all, boys dressed as cupids with gold-dusted hair and skin ran about with toy bows shooting light shafts into the crowd attached with lottery tickets. And beautiful topless girls with garlands of flowers around their waists flashed tambourines on their hips, hands and above their heads, while dwarfs with big brightly colored phalli strapped to their loins danced around them tumbling, doing handstands and somersaults.

Mannix gazed across the stands. The crowd was keyed up to a fever pitch now – sixty thousand people, most of whom had absolutely nothing better to do. The first day of the inaugural series in which the Amphitheater had been operational since the lightning strike and fire of five years before, it was due to start off big. Graffiti advertisements in their respective slots in walls throughout the city were listing the numbers and variety of the animals without spoiling the surprise of just how they would be displayed.

For the last month, tickets had been distributed, thrown to the throngs in the streets by the Spanish olive oil conglomerate sponsoring the games. They had been sold by speculators, and used as gifts and light bribes by politicians. As for the ticketless, the norm – thousands of the Mob had been camping for the last week in the piazza of the Ampitheater; eating their free bread, scamming their free wine, fornicating in the oleander bushes and generally making life hell for the Vigiles and the city trash collectors.

The inaugural procession slowly wound out of the arena, the lagging gladiators receiving the last of their applause as they kissed their hands and waved to the crowd and the squealing girls. But beneath the misty sanguine glow cast by the awning and punctuated by brilliant slits of gold from the morning sunlight thrusting through its vents, beneath the undulative surf-noise of sixty thousand voices and the melodic strains of the hydraulic organs, beneath the continual falling of rose petals from the catwalks like red dust from the rafters of the banqueting hall of Olympus – beneath all of that lay the spring-coiled tension of high artifice.

Ring captains cursed as they ran up and down the chutes, checking readiness and shouting commands. One and a half-ton bulls, driven half mad in confinement, reared, pawed, bucked and kicked crazily, splintering thick shards of wooden grating. Leopards hissed, their eyes sparkling like diamonds in the torchlight; hyenas yipped, screamed, and urinated on the floor of their cages.

The animals smelled fear. Their primal instinct told them that today would be different from other days. The men could taste it in their mouths, that tongue-swollened copper taste. Controlled, fear could be a drug that heightened care, awareness and agility. Out of control, it could spell one's end. Experience was the difference. Sport was the venue. And staying alive was the name of the game.

As he watched the last of the gladiators depart through the Gate of Life, his aquamarine eyes scanning across the diamond-grained sand, Mannix felt a familiar slowing of his thoughts until they began their recession into reactions, and his spinal cord did the thinking for him. He turned and continued down the tunnel and left down another ramp into the darkness with the torches lighting his path and the guards edging out of his way.

In their staging area, he and his two teammates sipped the *posca*, the ceremonial mixture of vinegar and water, rinsing their mouths with it. The younger one, Demetrius, blinked too much at the rushing noise of the crowd, and flinched when something screamed. Marcellus didn't seem to hear it. Their leader simply sat on a bench against the wall, leaning forward with his corded forearms across his knees. Then his head rose with a different noise, strange in its context. The noise of silence from above.

The arena floor was finally cleared, and a hush had fallen over the stands. Sixty thousand people waited in a pregnant pause of anticipation. The awning undulated slightly

10

in the wind, rippling audibly as the air whipped through its vents.

Technicians in the catwalks and the sailors on the terrace above the gallery seating were maintaining their routine inspections, tightening certain ropes, loosening others. The two hundred and thirty-eight seamen were happy. It was a sunny spring day, with mountains of cloud tumbling slowly across the cerulean blue. Now that the season of games had begun they were able to come into the capital from its invariably duller port town of Ostia, where they were stationed. In Rome, they were quartered in the baths of Trajan on the Oppian hill across the street from the Amphitheater, and after each day of shows had a fair amount of time to spend in the 'Suburra,' the red light district behind the baths.

A massive cumulous cloud passed across the sun, increasing the poignancy of the silence. The Seven Hills of Rome were thrown into huge chunks of light and shadow, the temples topping them alternately illumined. Inside the microcosm of the Amphitheater, the myriad faces of people and statues undulated with a subtle shifting of hues as well. White togas caught indications of teal green and lemon yellow, the stands caressed by a continual array of mellow light and shade with a predominantly amber tint.

Then, amidst the forced calm came a trumpet blast. Grates began slamming open around the circumference of the perimeter wall, trapdoors opening in the floor, and animals pouring, erupting, and fanning out across the sand in every direction like creations from the mouth of God. Underneath the floor, men pushed and pulled wildly at windlass handles, ripped back safety catches on counter-weight locks, threw back grates with ropes, jabbed at animals with firebrands, screamed through the confusion, and tried desperately to stay out of the way.

Above, the crowd roar was back in a crescendo of delight as antelopes hopped and darted across the sand, deer bounded with wild flashing eyes, cheetahs slunk low and paranoid against the side of the perimeter wall, boars galloped, bears loped, bulls bucked and twisted; and ibex, jackals, panicking cranes and ostriches all melded into a patchwork quilt of confusion. And then, just for 'padding,' as they called it in bestiarii slang, a herd of wild horses was driven in from one of the axial gates, and a herd of domestic cattle from the other. The variety of animals was amazing, and as the numbers increased, and the hooves pounded, the sound ricocheted through the passageways beneath the stands becoming louder and louder until it rumbled into the stomach like thunder and the Mob gave in to the excitement that had become a need as basic as food to it.

Random fights began breaking out amongst the animals yet they were separated and swept away from each other like waves of a rippling quilt as the mad stampede tried to find some way of escape. The Mob's major concern was with the numbers. Never giving a thought to the massive amount of work going on beneath the sand, if each show wasn't bigger than the last they felt cheated. Just as sure as if the bread dole was a little light because some of the grain was going to feed the legions which protected them.

With the exception of a number of real connoisseurs, they couldn't conceive of the technical expertise that made it possible to deliver all of these different species into the arena at the same instant. In their minds it was simply a function of the architecture – when one went to a theater, one saw a magic show. As they began to lose interest in the swarming, fighting, panicking beasts, foxes with firebrands tied to their tails were set loose to dash in desperation through the packed mass, terrorizing the confused creatures, the crowd screaming with glee.

Then Parthian archers captured in the late Mesopotamian campaigns appeared at intervals atop the perimeter wall. Armed with powerful, sinew-backed bows, they knocked arrows feathered with peacock trains, drew back and rocketed shafts into the packed mass of animals while the crowd cheered them on. Tremendously skilled, they thinned the mass of beasts by a hundred within seconds.

Beneath the floor, the bestiarii had come up to their entry points, which were the same as those of the animals. Some crouched waiting on the ramps beneath the trap doors, some in elevators already primed at the top of the shafts, some on horseback in the shadows of the axial gates. Mannix, a 'Venator,' or hunter, waited in one of the insets around the perimeter wall, his eyes flickering and blinking against the sweat, his nostrils quivering with each breath. He recognized the change progressing within himself, the recession almost complete, abstractions of the hunt focusing behind his dilated pupils.

The crowd above was working itself into mass hysteria. Mutations of the roar rushed through the tunnel inside the perimeter wall like a wind carrying the greeting of Hades across the Styx toward his approach. His eyes moved now from the cattle lowing and the wild horses screaming kicking on the sand with arrows sticking out of them to the Emperor, who gestured to the Ringmaster with his jewel-bedecked hand. A trumpet blast cracked the roar and the grates began slamming open again, the trap doors sliding back, and the bestiarii rushing into the arena from the same openings that emitted the animals.

The men carried a variety of equipment – capes, swords, pikes with shields attached halfway up the shafts – some loping in through the axial gates on horseback with spears. But Mannix carried nothing at all. Wearing only the sleeveless blue tunic belted tight at the waist, he shot out across the arena, sprinting over the white sand, his legs pumping sunburnt and bare, his massive arms pistoning striated and sinewy with rope veins writhing like serpents down his biceps, across his forearms and into his hands.

The antelope hopped and leapt ahead of him, an African oryx, darting through a confusion of dust and animals forking and pawing the diamond-grained sand, its beautiful pelt of short silken hair now white, now brown, now a shadow through a blinding light slit cast stabbing down from the great sail of awning overhead, changing directions, cutting and bounding, Mannix in pursuit all eyes and feeling, peripheral vision and sixth sense. Speed refined with quickness, every nerve rippling with lightning and a heightened, cat-like awareness of what was happening around him, the swipe of a whirling bear claw came within a hair's breadth of his cheek as he sprinted past dodging

13

it in an infinite pivot, his footsteps flashing through the patches of golden sunlight littering the arena floor.

Blur of black and white stripe, a zebra rushed through his path at the last instant but the timing was still right and he leapt casting himself much as the antelope's natural hunter, pawing his way in mid-air up its back, over its collapsing hindquarters, seeing his outstretched fingers reach for the horns. For an instant he could feel the rough prickly feel of its short brown hackles on his thighs, the lock-on of his hands and the flash of its sweet brown terror-stricken eyes before the momentum carried him over the oryx's horns but he held on, twisting his torso and ducking his shoulder and flipping his body to wrench the head in an expert twist with the vertebrae in the antelope's neck rippling xylophonic through his abdomen.

On his feet in an instant, whirling in a cape of sand, he was moving, sprinting, dodging and leaping, his speed decreasing or increasing to avoid collisions, his brain wide awake like snakes in a panic. Knocked down by a big black buck deer from the forests of Germania galloping wildly past with a spear sticking from its ribs, Mannix rolled and sprung back to the pursuit. Working fast, and focusing on the antelopes, he leapt from one to another, grabbing each oryx by the horns, his feet planting, skidding, sand flying as he wrenched the neck in a textbook twist dropping the animal. Sometimes he went down with a tough one but always up, rolling and up. Energy gauged, ignited by fear, speed refined with quickness and the synapses firing just right, he killed five in rapid succession . . . then fifteen . . . then twenty, crashing his knees onto the spine of a slinking mynx that flipped and screamed and raked him with its claws before he snapped its neck with a vicious thrust of the flat of his hand on its jaw.

The Mob was on its feet in a tumult so great they couldn't even hear themselves scream. With each antelope that Mannix dropped a collective, involuntary roar crack-sounded like lightning through the Amphitheater until the crescendos formed a regular rhythm, coming like the crash of the surf in a storm. Thousands of handkerchiefs fluttered with nervous energy through the filtered amber glow, catching in the strips of sunlight penetrating the awning's ventilation slits like olive leaves tinkling silver in the breeze of a sun-patched hillside. Even the members of the Senatorial class filling the first concentric ring of platform seating, in their curule fold-out chairs with their purple-bordered white togas gathered up daintily around their crossed legs and burgundy boot sandals, applauded and smiled and turned to each other in wonder as the bestiarius killed animal after animal after animal. Graffiti on walls throughout the city named him 'The Myth.'

But the crowd of beasts was thinning now, and it was becoming harder for him to catch something. The properly-armed venators went after the more dangerous game immediately to lessen the risk to the other men, and scattered contingents of other bestiarii were finishing off cattle and horses across the floor. Half a dozen human bodies lay in a trampled mass of purple pulp in the blackening sand, and a venator drug himself toward one of the insets in the perimeter wall where he was helped off, gasping with a lung full of broken ribs.

Mannix spotted the members of his own team, Demetrius and Marcellus, who seemed uninjured. Breathing hard and bleeding, he adopted a new technique enabling himself some rest while keeping the crowd keyed up. Putting his hands behind his back, he slowly approached the animals left cowering against the perimeter wall – mainly jackals, mynxs and foxes crouching exhausted and too terrified to move. He picked one and crashed down upon it with his knees and, threw his face forward to catch it by the back of the neck, biting repetitively until he had a hold. When he was locked on, he began to shake the animal viciously as it wheeled and flipped and sunk its claws into his cheeks, chin and ears, yet still he would not use his hands, but just kept thrashing them until he bit through enough nerves and tendons and vertebrae in their necks to kill them.

The crowd was hysterical by now. Young men, primping idlers, regulars to the Amphitheater who waited all day oiling their curls in the exits for moments like these, sidled up to women lost in lust for the violence below, women they had watched for, knowing how to pick them by now, the tell-

15

tale signs – the nail-biting, the weakness in the abdomen; how easy their pheasant-greased fingers slid up the girls' smooth brown thighs. Some of alternative persuasions could be seen walking jerky and blinking down the stairways to engage the services of the plump little slave boys who went around highly painted with their tunics hitched up above their buttocks, parading through the under-the-stands world of snake dancers, astrologers and fortune-tellers.

Mannix stood, his green eyes prowling, his blood-streaked mouth sucking great draughts of the fouling air deep into his lungs. His smock was in shreds, his torso lacerated, and the blood of a variety of animals curved fanning over his cheeks and down his chin and throat. A disgruntled wildebeest trotted past switching its tail.

The first lot of animals was almost gone, the arena slaves out cleaning the sand with shovels, baskets and rakes, dragging the carcasses off with hooks. But before they could finish, the grates in front of the chutes began to creak and whine and slide upwards. The slaves panicked and raced for the exits, and Mannix yelled to alert his fellow venators as he backed against the perimeter wall.

New animals were emerging into the arena, the air pungent with the scent of singed hair from the torches used to force them up the ramps and out the concentric system of trapdoors staged across the floor. These new arrivals were not deer, foxes or antelope, neither horses nor cattle. Without taking his eyes from the field, Mannix moved his hand toward the grate in the perimeter wall through which an attendant was handing him first the 'Gladius,' the short sword, and then the curved rectangular legionary shield. Likewise the other venators were re-armed according to their personal preferences.

A cluster of three arena attendants still raking the sand sprinted dropping their rakes as they made hard for the dark arch of the Gate of Death. Looking behind them as they ran, one of them blindsided a three hundred-pound female lion, scaring the cat as much as it did the slave. His fumbling and screaming sent howls of laughter through the already drunken

Mob standing pissing under the colonnaded terrace over the topmost rim of seating.

Mannix set off at trot to the center of the arena, letting the weight of the sword and the shield settle into his body. A hyena loped toward him at an angle in that strange hop-running manner of theirs, the smell of the dirty splotched beast hitting his nose, the snubbed snout and the fangs and the craziness in its almost human eyes. The bestairius relaxed and veered toward it and then cut dodging it at the last instant as the six-foot, two hundred-pound monkey-dog rose up on its hind legs; Mannix spun in midair to the side and lashed his sword slashing for the throat but it missed and ripped through the loose skin covering the animal's shoulder.

The hyena screamed and wheeled and scurried snapping viciously at the pain and the man, thrusting with its powerful hindquarters in hop-jumps and using its clawed paws like human hands crashing down on the top edge of his shield pulling him forward off balance into its blood-frothing snapping fangs. Mannix ripped his hand out of the strap-grip at the last instant with the rancid breath and the muzzle all over his face; throwing himself backwards and letting the hyena trip forward with the shield, he brought the edge of his blade crashing down into the skull area in a messy, off-balance cut that was in part negated by the mass of the animal's neck muscle.

The wretched beast squealed like a pig, stunned and split open and lurching toward him and, as Mannix righted himself for the deathblow, he saw a quick flash out of the corner of his eye before three wolves driven crazy in confinement sprinting biting at each other smashed into his legs. His stomach drew tightening into itself as he went down on top of the hyena's back, which roared and threw its foaming head around at him. Rolling off the spine, his legs up in the air, the wolves all over him snapping at his face, the hyena and each other, the bestiarius screamed and kicked and clumsily hacked his sword like a child in a crib. With one of the wolves locked onto his leather boot sandal and the fangs beginning to break the skin of his foot, another grabbed his sword arm, their growls

17

harmonizing like a chorus of demons. The third one yelped and spun as the hyena sunk its fangs into its hind leg.

Mannix jammed his free thumb puncturing through the eye socket of the wolf on his sword arm, which contracted howling and spinning off to the side, then hacked desperately at the wolf on his foot, pulling his leg into him enough that he could smash the sword down into its spine. As the wolf collapsed onto its forelocks snapping backwards at the pain, the bestiarius kicked himself loose of the wreckage and threw his head back and roared in wounded rage. Crawling and shuffling and tripping drunkenly to pick up his shield, the hyena dead at his feet, its ear chewed off by the third wolf now whining and hopping and trailing its hind leg by a tendon, his sword arm was gnawed but not broken, blood filling the sole of his boot sandal and squishing from the open slits as he stood.

The hopping wolf snapped toward him and he decapitated it, then ran his sword through the base of the neck of the paralyzed one. Suddenly aware again of the pounding and the galloping and the yelling and smashing all around him, he leapt out of the way of an onrush over a dead zebra to find a young bestiarius trying to deal with a situation in the center of the arena. A Nubian lion and a tiger from the forestlands bordering the Caspian Sea were snarling and pacing around one another threatening a fight. Mannix could see that the cats were not trained maneaters, but rather captured beasts fresh from the wilds. Nervous of people, after long periods of confinement in caged carts and ships, their major compulsion was to escape. But there was nowhere for them to go.

Mannix motioned to stop the young venator from coming in too close. The boy was obviously out of his league with the javelins he was holding, one in his throwing hand, two more held with quick-release straps to the inside of his shield as he danced and hopped in an arc around the beasts.

"Wait until he's on me!" Mannix yelled at him. Then, closing slowly, he tried to relax, to focus all of his concentration into his wrist – tightening it, locking it – he struck for the head of the tiger but it wheeled on him at the last instant, roaring and spinning and shooting at him with its forepaws swatting roundhouse blows clonk-gonging on his shield.

The bestiarius stagger-danced backwards trying desperately to keep his feet, coiling his abdomen, butt and legs to balance him through the buffets until he could roll off to the side just as the lion jumped on the back of its striped cousin biting rabidly at its neck. The tiger thrashed its head backwards snarling in rage and desperation, and Mannix came back in with a vicious sidearm slash that split the lion's skull open, then spun off to the side.

As the kingly beast slipped limply down the back of its feline cousin leaving a wide swathe of crimson across its striped coat, the tiger struggled outward from under the carcass, hissing, backing, and watching the bestiarius. For a moment Mannix could see himself – a dark reflection in the tiger's golden eyes, green slivers sparkling – before he lowered himself for the approach.

"Get ready to take him on the side," he shouted at the young venator with barely enough time to see a quick flash out of the corner of his eyes before he could scream "No!" too late, the boy having just flung a javelin into the tiger's ribcage without nearly enough stopping power for a cat its size.

The charge hit him like a battering ram, blasting him ten feet backwards with shield and javelins cartwheeling off behind, his bronze helmet cracking sickly as a walnut as the fangs went in.

Mannix sprinted toward it but the cat was on him then with no in-between time, biting furiously at his shield, its needle-sharp claws raking strips of painted canvas off the wooden core. The quickness and ferocity of the attack staggered him, every ounce of strength concentrated through an s-curve of thigh, buttock, torso and deltoid to keep his shield aloft and stay alive within all of two seconds before he could sidearm his sword around crashing through the cat's ribs into its soft underbelly. The tiger screamed like a witch and Mannix quickly slipped the blade out and drove it deep between its shoulder blades, then pulled it clean leaving the beast twitching on the sand in its death throes.

The bestiarius was trembling uncontrollably now. He staggered once. The light seemed to be changing in the Amphitheater, shadows feathering outward as the sunlit slits through the awning retreated into a passing cloud bank. Pools of darkness across the lightness of sand marked death, things whipping through his vision all blurred. The random fights raging around him had turned into primary shapes, shifting and shaking, though he saw a face he seemed to recognize, but like a hallucination.

Its head swollen to the size of a pumpkin, ice-water flowed down the inside of his torso as he realized that it was young Demetrius, his team member, turned toward him meeting his eyes for a split second with the look of a child falling into a well as a Spanish fighting bull came scooting and butting back in for another vicious headbutt of marble-hard skull with two thousand pounds of force behind it. Mannix watched helpless and dreamlike as Demetrius was blasted and stamped like a rag doll, the bull bounding and leaping past like a spring lamb to turn back in for another charge.

The boy sat up again drunkenly on the sand, his face like a Greek theater mask of tragedy and pain. Already dead this time, his body merely reacting on nerves, he swatted at the air with his hand and then collapsed sideways and died with no dignity, a wrenching sight for Mannix, a lovely sight for the Mob, who all did the same. Enraged, the bestiarius sprinted unthinking toward the bull which was coming in for another pass at the already-dead venator. His other team member Marcellus screamed to stop him but it was too late, Mannix cutting to the side at the last instant to drive his sword behind the bull's shoulder blade but the beast cut with him just as nimbly and batted him with its head, his sword and shield flipping up into the air like a child's toys.

The bestiarius came down in a heap fifteen feet away, the bull all over him rooting and butting and scooting trying to get a horn in him. Mannix grabbed the horns and held on with everything he had as the beast tried to shake him loose, all snot and blood and raging testosterone, lifting its head and smashing him into the ground, over and over, the bestiarius screaming and

20

gurgling and kicking with his feet scooting along trying desperately not to go down under the hooves.

Marcellus, chasing, threw a spear into the bull's flank but still it kept smashing and driving Mannix into the ground. Several other venators ran up hurling spears and the bestiarius finally noticed the weight shift of the bull, how its movements slowed and strangely changed. Then it abruptly pulled up and lurched to the side once, and he saw the flicker of the sword Marcellus just tossed him land in the sand beside him.

The bestiarius dropped immediately off the bull's nose and threw his battered body to the side in the sand to grab the sword only to find twelve hundred pounds of agitated brown bear all over him roaring horribly as the bull collapsed in the background. Four-inch fangs seared into his left shoulder, lancing through the muscle fiber to settle into the sick numb feel of a scalpel on dumb bone.

As the bear slowly drug him across the arena, Mannix stabbed furiously upwards into its belly screaming like a child, his sword thrusting sloppily as a drunken wine goblet in a tavern song. He realized that he was going to die, his dwindling thoughts fragmentary, and not at all of a person, a mother, the warmth of companionship or love; but rather of changes of the light on the landscape, changes of the wind in the trees, of the force of the wind and the weather in his childhood memories.

As his vision began to cloud, he could see these things, as if through a glass and darkly, its surface consumed with the bear's huge elongated torso streaming down above him from the pink skin in the creases where its arms met its loose-muscled and heaving pectorals, the needle-like quilt of hairs changing from brown to black, smothering and close. Its forelocks rippling with each step, the smell of the beast enveloped him like the scent of sex in a closed room, its deep-crackling guttural breathing massaging into his organs, his heart and lungs. He felt the bear balk and grunt and he knew that it was taking hits, probably spears. Then it came down over him in that in-between time he could feel now, and then contracted once, spiritless.

Mannix came rushing back to the fore, kicking and jerking and throwing himself out from under the huge carcass. Marcellus and the other remaining venators tried to help him, but the berserk bestiarius threw them off. He lurched down to pick up his sword only to collapse on his hands and knees and then claw and kick and lunge himself upright again, barely able to hold onto the sword.

The crowd was delirious, drugged with the scene. A slight rippling had begun across the stands, the first syllables coming into earshot like the sound of a million branches . . . swaying in the wind as they chanted . . . "Man . . . nixxx . . . Mannnnixxxxx . . ." and then it growing to "MANNixxx . . . MANNIXXX! . . . MANNIXX!! . . . MANNIXX!!! and growing and growing into a unified frenzy coming faster and desperate and all-encompassing as the one thing they could still hold onto.

Legionaries with their shields locked together in brackets had aligned across the end of the Arena to begin their sweep, marching in a wall to drive the remaining animals back into the chutes where technicians had placed basins of water to lure them inside. Behind the legionaries came other bestiarii with lead-tipped whips in case any of the animals broke through the line of soldiers; and behind them 'andabatae,' prisoners of war in visorless helmets corralled into a group by arena attendants with long forked poles to keep them together.

When they reached the sand, the andabatae began swinging spiked balls on chains blindly around them trying by chance to hit one another. They provided a bit of slapstick between acts, for the crowd tended to behave better when there were no let-downs in the action.

A god in ruins, Mannix staggered toward the remaining animals looking for something on which to strike back at the pain, blood undulating in fresh waves over his tunic and down his leg to fill the footprints he left behind in the sand.

Marcellus grabbed him gently beneath the armpits. "Caius," he said. "It's time to leave. The crowd will let you go."

Mannix shrugged him off, kicking drunkenly at a wild dog yelping past, his face creased with rage.

The line of soldiers was almost upon them now, the centurian yelling, "Get that crazy bastard off the floor!" the remaining animals backing snarling before the steadily advancing line of spears. Most of the beasts found the chutes and rushed in to drink rabidly, though a crazed tiger from the last shipment brought up the Red Sea route from India whipped arcing across the floor in a cloud of sunshot dust to blast its way through the wall of spears, leaping through the men knocking off helmets, breaking noses, the bestiarii whipping desperately with their flails trying to get behind the cat to drive it through the Gate of Death. The roaring cat viciously blindsided one of the andabates, the blow snapping his neck like a twig.

Marcellus grabbed Mannix by the back of his belt. "The hunt's over, Caius. Come on then, settle down," he said, but the bestiarius turned on him with a roundhouse blow which his agile friend ducked, throwing him off balance to collapse on the sand. The other remaining venators rushed in and the raging bestiarius fought like a madman while they drug him off the arena floor through one of the open insets in the perimeter wall.

Beneath the stands the doctors were waiting. The orderly led them to a medical room where other venators were under treatment. Mannix, still fighting, slammed his fellow bestiarii against the stone walls of the corridor until they subdued him with the help of four big Egyptian medical attendants. The Egyptians seized the raging venator, berserk with his wounds and the bloodlust, and drug him to a wooden operating table where they threw him down and shackled his arms and legs.

The doctor grabbed his cheek, careful not to lose a finger, the Egyptians gripping fast on his head as the physician pried his jaws apart with a piece of wood and skillfully poured an herbal potion with a predominance of opium down his throat. The bestiarius choked and gasped, his body arcing wildly against the shackles.

"First day of the season," the doctor grimaced, shaking the snot and blood off his hands, Mannix all the while sobbing in great convulsive gasps.

III

The Emperor was shooting dice with a dwarf in the Imperial box. The box was a huge, blackened bronze pavilion framed by alabaster columns polished to the sheen of a snake's skin, their golden Corinthian capitals topped by white marble globes with bronze winged female figures pirouetting from their tops. Tied beneath their capitals, the columns were strung with a vast crimson canopy fringed with golden tassels. Like the banner that draped from the lip of the box over the perimeter wall into the arena, the top of the canopy was embroidered with a huge black aerolith superimposed with an imperial eagle – the sacred image of Elagabal, the 'Invincible Sun.'

Beneath it, the Emperor's courtiers lounged languidly amidst marble side tables laden with gold-trimmed green glass bowls full of fruits and eggs, cucumbers and honeycombs. There were old men in white face powder and hair nets, magicians, astrologers, famous actors, dancers, gladiators and charioteers – and a cadre of base-born profligates scoured from the public baths for their unusually large organs. Nubile female slaves in leopard-skin tunics moved amongst them bearing platters of lamprey soaked in a blue oyster sauce. Silver flagons of rich ruby wine glimmered in the shadows, and costly Indian perfumes burned in the bronze tripod braziers staged at intervals throughout the tiers of marble armchairs and cushioned dining couches, their sickly-sweet smell rising in tendrils through the crimson-canopied gloom.

The aftershock of the *Venatione* had not quite died out, but still reverberated in the upper levels of the stadium where many of the Mob continued to chant Mannix's name, lost in their fervor. The fact that the chanting had not stopped even though the opening hunt was over had begun to distract the Emperor a bit from his dice game. Reclining on a silver and pearl enlayed dining couch with the dwarf beside him in a chair with his plump little legs sticking straight out and his feet in curled-toed shoes, Elagabalus slowly looked up.

A largish, strongish young man wearing a cream-colored toga beneath his purple silk cloak, he had piercing green eyes with violent whites beneath languorously drooping lids. With his smooth, honey-colored skin and his sharp aristocratic features, he had the kind of face that teenage girls swoon over, twenty-somethings fall in love with, and older, more experienced women find suspect. Forsaking the longer hair and beard made fashionable by the Antonines and his own Severan forebears, his dark wavy hair was cut short and combed forward in the classical Roman manner, but topped by a golden diadem.

Staring up at the gallery seating where the Mob continued its chanting, his expression was one of pride, irritation, and a deep lassitudinous ennui. He knew that the bestiarius Caius Marius Mannix would never deign to be one of his courtiers, and the knowledge did not please him. For he had the very cream of the Stage, the Circus and the Amphitheater in the box with him at present, and Elagabalus liked to get what he wanted.

But, more than that, the nineteen year-old had always been obsessed with powerful men. Men who could be remembered for hundreds of years. And especially gods, who could be remembered for thousands. For he knew what the Mob did not – that the gods were all just men in their day, who had the ability to be followed.

When he made his triumphal entry into Rome two years ago, by the time the four white horses with their purple plumed head dresses had leapt and lunged and strained him in his chariot of gold up the last steep leg of the switchback ramp scaling the Capitoline Hill to arrive before the massive temple of Jupiter Optimus Maximus, the official from the Senate repetitively whispering 'remember thou art mortal' in his ear had become irritating. The hundreds of thousands of people choking the streets and thronging the porticoes and hanging from the upper-level arcades of the basilicas in the marble-sparkling Forum he had just pranced the horses through down the Sacred Way beneath a continual rain of roses past the Praetorians in their red capes holding back the screaming bodice-clawing girls offering him their bodies for endless nights – were all still chanting 'Hail Caesar! Hail Caesar! Hail Caesar!' And here was this onion-breathed twit beside him whispering 'remember thou art mortal' in his ear.

Beaming at the priests descending the steps of the temple to greet him, he had brushed past that official who had ridden with him in the chariot as he stepped down from it, discreetly grabbing the man's testicles and squeezing and feeling the thrill of his scream as it was drowned in the vast uproar of the Roman populace. And then he climbed the tremendous marble staircase of the temple flowing down around him like butter in that luminous fall afternoon, climbed it as if he owned it, nodding only cursorily at the priests in their hooded black robes while wearing his own of purple and gold, the best Phoenician weave. His arms and head were studded with jewels the same as he wore when the officers of the defected Legions found him in the Temple of the Sun at Emesa the year before, dancing to the sound of flutes and tambourines around the monumental altar bearing the figures of the many gods subordinate to his own – the 'Jupiter of the East,' they claimed. And those pompous praetors with their taciturn tribunes declared him as handsome as Bacchus, proclaimed their allegiance, and turned a blind eye from their tents later that night as he buggered their grooms.

A year afterwards and one ago, while striding beneath that portico of seventy-two foot columns through the incense smoke rising from the huge bronze cauldron braziers into the vast velvety shadows of the Capitoline temple in Rome, Elagabalus had smiled as he walked. Smiled at that hundred-foot statue of Jupiter in marble, ivory and gold hovering staring sternly down at him as he walked alone through the dim shade over the long space of the richly marbled nave past the ranks of black palm-tree candelabra beneath the gilt-bronzed Lebanese cedar beams; smiled his brilliant white smile only slightly evident of an adolescent thumb-sucking diastema as he walked across that hundred yards of space to finally arrive beneath

27

those huge fat white marble toes atop the marble plinth inscribed in gold, 'IOVIS OPTIMO MAXIMO.'

And instead of sacrificing those poor little wing-clipped wrens, he had simply popped their silly little heads off between his thumb and forefinger and he laughed then, and looked up at that statue and said, 'Out of the way, old-un.' For from the first moment he saw that huge old cold stone statue, Elagabalus knew he had him beat.

But from the first time he saw Caius Marius Mannix, he knew he was of a different breed. And he had seen the bestiarius for the first time eight years before becoming Emperor and a full ten years ago, when he walked into a marbled bedchamber after playing in the green grass outside and hearing a disconcerting sound emitting from its gloom.

And he had no sooner walked into that chamber than he had run out again, run out of his mother's room with a gaping hole in his ten year-old breast already devoid of her attention. An attention which was later replaced by that of the masses after his grandmother had him assume the hereditary priesthood of his line and began to push him towards the throne.

And now it was this, more than long life, that Elagabalus craved. For ever since that glimpse in his mother's bedchamber he had been afraid, afraid of his class, and of his kind. A fear that only attention could assuage – the attention of the masses, their adulation. Their affection, even.

To a great extent he had achieved this adulation, however, and at the expense of the upper classes, not to mention the Roman treasury. For, as a supplement to the sense of socio-religious inclusion he offered the rabble with his sun god festivals, he liked to play with them, to banquet them, and throw great drinking bouts for them. Often referring to the Senate as 'slaves in togas,' and the Equestrian order as 'nothing at all,' Elagabalus was in need of the Mob; and they of him. And thus he purposefully collected their heroes, and surrounded himself with them.

But Mannix was not simply a hero to the people but an institution for Rome. Elagabalus knew this. He also knew that the bestiarius would have perhaps given his support to the right type of man, the right type of leader; and the knowledge of this unnerved him. But, moreover, the Emperor knew that Mannix's status with the Mob was a status much deeper than the cheerful adulation he himself had achieved. For it was a following which could not be bought, but which was based on courage, character and deed.

The Games at the Amphitheater were traditionally held through the fall and winter, though by Elagabalus' childhood they were beginning to extend into the spring, with even 'pre-season' exhibitions in the summer. When he watched him in the arena, he saw that Mannix fought without hesitation, and with a concentration and a fixedness of purpose that lent itself to his survival. Through the years, the bestiarius had developed a brutal technique which, combined with his often dazzling feats of skill, had secured him a tremendous following amongst the Mob.

Elagabalus knew that, while only a novice at the school and not even his own age, Mannix's name had begun to appear on advertisements for particular series of Games – frames in the corner of walls at street intersections rented by the editors, who paid sign painters to list the venues. By now it had seeped like a ghost into the consciousness of the city in the form of graffiti scrawled across alley walls, etched into the stuccoed columns of streetside porticoes, and painted hastily across the podiums of old temples. With his brutal technique punctuated by flourishes of bravado, not to mention his knack for survival, through the years Mannix had come to represent something for the people. Something they'd lost.

He was a throwback, hearkening back to a time when the Romans lived their Empire. When every Roman was a fighting man, and every Roman tough. And when the Games encouraged the manly virtue necessary to that budding civilization on the rise in a world of enemies out to crush it.

Whether they were aware of it or not, Elagabalus knew that, for the Mob Mannix represented the best of 'Romanitas,' of Roman-ness. Their generals and politicians were corrupt, their arts and letters stale. And each bad Emperor served to undo more and more the work of the good ones. In short, they had no one to trust.

But Mannix facing death crouching in a variety of inglorious forms in the arena they could trust. There was nothing to hide out there. And as the Games were still thrown under the auspices of a religious ceremony – and hence the expiatory bloodletting of the venationes was metaphorically a propitiatory sacrifice for the people and not just a deep release – Mannix, whether they realized it or not, functioned in their collective subconscious as both a kind of sacrificial lamb and a high priest.

When only a child, Elagabalus had heard of fans throwing themselves on the funeral pyres of favorite gladiators and charioteers. All of this had created an obsession with the nineteen year-old to the extent that, in a darker and more fearful-than-usual moment a year before, his mother and grandmother discovered that he was interviewing potential assassins to have the bestiarius disposed of.

The two women had shown unnatural alarm. The power that Mannix had come to hold with the Mob was too great, they said; their own position with the Senate and the aristocracy too precarious. The assassins that Elagabalus had hired on a whim would never walk again; and with no effective way to stack the odds against Mannix in the Amphitheater – for the *venationes* were chaos anyway – the young Emperor had watched the bestiarius in the form of policeman in bars, the Praetorian Guard, and private detectives out to discover an angle from which to subvert his standing with the Mob. But to no avail.

Elagabalus leaned back on the couch and looked up at the champion gladiator Prixus sitting in a porphyry arm chair a level above. Prixus was also quite popular with the Mob, and he was moreover known to be the Emperor's favorite. Elagabalus cocked his head slightly and, with a sneer on his face, said, "It seems they know who the first man in the Arena is, anyway."

The huge-muscled gladiator's smile faded and he reddened with shame.

Turning back, Elagabalus' eyes ran again across the rabble in the gallery seating still chanting Mannix's name. Then his nostrils quivered and he turned to the dwarf beside him and casually leaned over and ripped a lock of his hair out.

The dwarf squealed and screamed and pounded his fists into his plump little thighs and Elagabalus, after examining the tuft of hair between his silver-painted fingernails, looked back at him and smiled.

IIII

Sea on one side, mountains on the other, springtime is capricious in Rome. High above the Colosseum, a tiny speck weaved amidst the darkening clouds, pregnant with rain, that had accumulated across the noonday sky. The hawk cocked its head as it circled, and stared down through the oculus in the awning at the pale sand of the arena, watching as the two-legged creatures darted and ran. It wondered why some fell and lay so still.

The sweet smell of congealing blood held by the humidity spoke of food. But the bird had lived long enough around Rome to know that the meat below would soon vanish. It dipped a wing and turned on an air current and pointed its beak toward its home in the Alban hills.

Five hundred feet below, the andabatae were still slugging it out. Condemned criminals and prisoners of war not fit for the main events, their only chance was to live to fight in another intermission act. Still, they fought with the mad bravery of desperation, hanging on to the concept of another day.

The crowd roared with laughter at the men's clumsy swings, the arena slaves corralling them and pushing them together with their long forked poles. Meanwhile set technicians were busy constructing a mock landscape across the arena, rolling out huge chunks of plaster from the axial gates, and bringing up trees and shrubs from the central row of large trapdoor panels staged across the floor.

Standing in the Gate of Death directing traffic, and screaming occasionally at the slaves corralling the andabatae, the Ringmaster bit his nails anxiously. "Get them over to the side, you stupid bastards! Or by the gods I'll have you out there in their place!" He shook his head disgustedly, "Slaves . . ."

muttering to his assistant, "to think we actually pay these people."

The slaves used their long forked poles to shift the sideshow over to one corner of the arena against the black marble perimeter wall to give the set technicians more room to work on the floor, the Mob all the while heckling the andabatae and shouting advice. The Senators in the lowest tier of seating had turned in their seats, and sat fanning themselves and gossiping, the favored subject Elagabalus' recent assassination plot on his cousin Alexianus, and the grand banquet at week's end designed to make amends. Though they didn't deign to watch the pointless struggles happening below them, the Mob loved it, roaring with glee at the desperate whirling and the messy hits.

"He's on your left!" a random voice screamed. "No! Now he's behind you!"

Meanwhile a ring technician on the scene dressed as Charon, boatman of the Styx, replete with a white skull mask and a black flowing robe, performed a strange, witchdoctor-style dance around the group while adroitly juggling hot irons. Plunging the irons into a brazier of glowing coals occasionally, when one of the andabatae fell, he ran up twirling the molten prongs and flamboyantly gripped a calf or an arm with them. If the downed man twitched, an arena attendant dressed as Hermes, another underworld god, cut the rawhide straps that kept the visorless helmet in place, kicked it off and brained the wretch with a mallet. Then slaves immediately hooked the body through the achilles tendon behind the ankle, and drug it through the Gate of Death down to the Spolarium, where they stripped the armor and turned the carcass over to the butchers who cut it up to feed the animals.

The Ringmaster turned away from the scene and hurried down a corridor scowling in frustration. He cuffed and kicked two slaves blocking his way with a basket of andabatae meat heading for the animal pens. The kick ripped a hem of his robe, which further infuriated him, the robe specially made of blue satin embroidered with gold stars, suns and moons like a wizard's get-up. He hurried down a grungy white corridor

33

bordered in a four-foot strip of flaking red fresco and flickering with the light of oil lanterns to arrive at the clinic.

"May all the gods damn you, Mannix!" he yelled at the prostrate bestiarius, who lay on the thick oaken table with his eyes closed, breathing raggedly. Tiger blood streaked in slivers from both sides of his mouth where the doctor made him drink it from a bronze goblet after the stitching, and a medic was pouring cool water over his torso with a ladle.

The room was large and cavernous, and half a dozen other venators lay about moaning with medics in attendance. The Egyptians worked in the background, cauterizing the operating saws and scalpels in a brazier of hot coals. Others fanned ostrich plumes across the room toward the ventilation grills, or threw buckets of water over the floor to wash the blood into a shallow trench running along one of the walls. The trench linked with its constituent branches running throughout the underground world to empty into the main conduit of the sewer system of Rome; and oil lamps dangling from chains cast the entire scene in an eerie orange glow.

Most of the bestiarius' blue-gray tunic had been cut away by the doctors, leaving only the short-skirt bottom half and the broad, black, bronze-studded leather belt. His legs stretched outward across the bloodstained planks of the table, veins running down the meat of each calf into his thick-banded boot sandals. His arms lay flat, the palms of his hands facing upwards, his corded forearms flaring back from the leather bands that lent support to his wrists. The veins in his forearms snaked over his biceps to disappear in the deltoids, one of which glowed in the lamplight like the cranium of an ivory elephant. The other was busied by the doctor's hands, which were removing the sphagnum used to disinfect the wounds and ooze in its own subtle anesthetic, while another stood by with a compress of myrrh to swathe the stitched gashes.

When the bestiarius' eyelids cracked open, the room was unfamiliar, and glimpses from his childhood still swam in his vision.

Adrift on waves of opium and fatigue, he struggled to remain in those autumnal seas, and give vent to his subconscious longing, especially of late, for the dun-colored hills and the deep green trees, and the azure blue of the sky. For the mist-shrouded mornings and the witch-haunted evenings, and the lance-thrusts of sunlight penetrating the pines. For the contentment he had felt as a boy, for a fleeting period of time, with a dog and a stick and an aloneness he loved, which did not bleed him like his later loneliness in a soul-less city of a million.

"Bloody show-off!" the Ringmaster spit. "Can he function?"

The doctor smiled grimly. "The penetrations are fairly clean, not much tissue damage. He should be all right in a few weeks."

"A few weeks! We need him up right now to get those whores ready for the jackasses!," the Ringmaster screamed.

"I'll get you ready for those jackasses, Apicius," croaked a weary voice from the table.

"Watch your tongue, Mannix, or I'll have you back out there this afternoon," the Ringmaster fired back. "Now get your ass up and let's go. Northwest quadrant, third cell block; we don't have much time."

The stage-set outside was nearing completion, and the mid-day pageant was on schedule. But another novelty act was necessary to keep things tight while the elevator shafts were re-loaded and linked by ramps to trapdoors inside the landscape. The contents of a whorehouse operating in Trastevere without a permit would serve its purpose.

"Marcellus knows what to do," Mannix replied. "Get him."

"Marcellus couldn't fuck a goat," Apicius yelled back. "This thing has to be done right, or the Editor will have my ass. And shit rolls downhill, Mannix. You get me?"

The bestiarius leaned and twisted his body upright groaning with pain. With both hands on the ledge of the operating table, he waited a minute glowering at the Ringmaster until the blood righted itself in his brain. "I'm not doing it."

"What do you mean 'you're not doing it'!? You'll do whatever the fuck I say!"

35

Mannix chuckled and shook his head grimly. "I'm a hunter, Apicius. A bestiarius," he growled, the opium fog thick in his brain. The wound had settled into a deep, dull, nerve-gnawing pain that he tried to fool himself was just an ache, though it was worse. "Get your bullies and your scum to do your dirty work for you."

"COCKsucker!" Apicius shook with rage. He whirled to face the Egyptians, "You you and you," he pointed, "come with me now!," he shouted, turning in a brief whirl of robes and stalking off ahead.

The big bald Egyptians followed Apicius the Ringmaster down a tunnel undulating in the light of torches, turning corners and moving down declines that leveled off, Apicius rushing ahead hurrying them, nervous as a child, and cursing Mannix all the while.

They soon found themselves in the unbroken space of a curving corridor exemplary of the concrete vaulting solutions perfected by architects of the early Empire. The noise of the crowd sounded like a hard rainstorm on a rooftop high above, Charon hurrying past coming from the other direction in his white skull mask through the flickering light still holding his hot irons and complaining about the arena slaves with the long forked poles not being able to control the andabatae well enough.

In an intersection with an animal cell block they were suddenly stopped by a shrill whistle blast from a technician with his hands outstretched, while another behind him pulled a heavy iron gate sliding shut across the arched opening and locked it into the wall. On the other side of the intersection they could see the same procedure as the opposite gate was secured. After a brief pause and some shouting and cursing from back down the corridor, four cheetahs slunk angry and hissing past the grated intersection, turning back to look at the object of their torment as a huge wooden shield that filled the entire corridor came steadily after them sliding through grooves in the walls. The shield wobbled a bit under the groin vault of the intersection, but its axels continued through slots in the gate, the three men behind it belted into a tripod apparatus harnessed around their necks and waists to keep the shield balanced using their centers of gravity. Apicius chafing impatiently, the gates were quickly unlocked and slid back and the officious traffic director blew another shrill blast on his whistle and motioned them past.

Marcellus and some of the cell-block guards were arguing loudly at the end of the corridor up ahead. As the Ringmaster arrived, the guards at the door of cell block three in the northwest quadrant slid the heavy bolts back and pushed the oaken door creaking inward on its rusty iron hinges.

The smell that hit Apicius' nose actually startled him a bit, such a dramatic contrast it provided to the scent he had become accustomed to over the last four hours. A pitiful little island of perfume in a sea of stink, the whores sat in their cell, garishly painted and huddled trembling like little baby peacocks in a sleeping cyclops' den.

"All right you whores, listen up," said the Ringmaster, "and we'll get this thing over with as quickly as possible. He turned and gestured to Marcellus. "You got the cloths?"

Marcellus handed him a terracotta jar.

Apicius drew back wide-eyed and flinching. "I don't want that shit." He turned to one of the Egyptians. "Here, you! Get in there!"

The Egyptians entered the cell, the whores drawing back in fear.

"Watch the dresses!" yelled Apicius. "They can't look raped before they even get out there!"

The six young prostitutes wore diaphanous dresses embroidered with jewels that came conveniently just past their privates. By far the most precious clothes they'd ever worn in their lives, they'd obviously been drugged, but the knowledge of their position drove them frantic. They fluttered into the corner like a covey of terrified pigeons as an Egyptian approached with one of a dozen rags soaked in the uteral fluids and blood of female donkeys, the smell of wet rust and burnt leaves filling the cell.

The Egyptian lunged and grabbed one of the girls around the waist, pulling her up off her feet and rubbing the cloth into her naked crotch as she frantically kicked and screamed, Apicius all the while shouting, "The dresses! Watch the dresses!" with his fingers tugging at his hair.

All of the whores were screaming now, but without any hope against the big muscled automatons.

"Grab them!" Apicius gestured disgustedly, sickened by the task. He shook his head. "Nothing can save you now. Might as well go out with a bang," all the while resenting this aspect of his job.

The Egyptians subdued the whores one by one, spreading their legs for another to rub the scent of a female donkey in heat into their crotches.

"Get them to the elevator shafts," growled Apicius, and the troop set off out the door and up the corridor, the Egyptians half-carrying, half prodding the pitiful little group of misunderstood girls toward their stage call.

The corridor was one of eight that entered the central area beneath the arena floor. Run with grunge and torch smoke and rife with the smell of beast and blood, beds in the form of giant oyster shells were affixed to the platform lifts of the six elevator shafts normally used for large animals – three each staggered down the concentric aisles on either side of the underground tunnel running the length of the Arena from the Gate of Life to the Gate of Death. Three of the whores were taken through the narrow crossing aisle running perpendicular to the axis tunnel into the concentric aisle on the other side. The grizzled Ringmaster grimaced as he watched the three on his own side strapped spread-eagled and screaming to the giant oyster shell beds draped with gorgeous satin sheets.

V

Mannix was alert, morose and surly, the short-skirt bottom half of his sweat-soaked tunic glistening blackly with blood. He strained upward on the oaken operating table testing his breath and his ribcage. The pain caught him up short and he smarted and leaned forward with the instinctual knowledge that at least two of his ribs were broken. He leaned over, and rested his forearms across his knees, his loose-muscled shoulders sloping wearily into his snake-veined biceps. A medic steadied a myrrh compress while the doctor wrapped bandaging over it and beneath his armpit several times and then around the great slabs of his chest and back.

When finished tying off the bandages, the doctor handed the bestiarius a note, raising a gray eyebrow.

"A runner from upstairs left this for you."

Mannix's eyes, piercing green now and blood-shot around the whites, looked up from beneath the deep red-line furrows in his brow. His ear and part of the skin of the side of his head was raw, and matted sticky with his hair. He took the small scroll, curling his lip at its scent. The doctor walked across the room to wash his hands in a cauldron of scalding water, and the bestiarius picked at the gold-threaded tie and unwound the little perfumed parchment.

As he read it a coldness settled across his face. He stood shakily and shuffled toward the hall. Through the archway leading into the clinic, he dropped the scroll into a glowing brazier of cauterizing coals on his way out, where it crumpled and curled into blackened oblivion.

"Where are you going!?" the doctor shouted after him, but Mannix waved him off.

Down the hall, he stopped to rest for a moment with his good hand on the wall, then continued on, making his way into the corridor ringing the inside of the perimeter wall. He gazed into the Arena through a grated inset, his pupils dilated with the opium. Seventy yards across the sand, past the random bodies of andabatae being drug out with hooks through their ankles, his eyes came to rest on the Imperial box, where she sat in a marble armchair a level above the wide platform podium where her son and his courtiers reclined.

A well-preserved forty-one year-old with buttermilk brown skin, big black hair, and big almond eyes – her breasts about to burst from the black leather bodice which squeezed them into obscenely round balls beneath the necklace of gold draping her husky throat – Julia Soaemias, formally entitled 'Empress,' popped a purple grape between her vilely red lips and ran her hand across the muscled thigh of Prixus, champion gladiator and personal favorite of her son.

Her own mother, the sixty year-old Julia Maesa – also entitled 'Augusta,' and the controlling influence of the regime – sat a bit above and to the side in a peach-colored stola draped with a shawl of Syrian weave. The courtiers of her grandson knew to give this woman a wide berth, and she sat apart beside her other daughter, Julia Mamaea, with her other grandson between. Mannix glanced at the young Alexianus, thirteen year-old son of Mamaea; a quiet, sandy-blond boy reputed to be of a rare, excellent and chaste character nothing like that of his cousin, the Emperor.

It was the first time that the members of the Imperial family had been together for several months, and it was no secret that things had run amiss. The occasion for their reunion was the restoration of the Amphitheater, which they financed, after the lightning strike and fire under Caracalla. Their dutiful appearance for the inaugural ceremonies finished, Mannix watched as Julia Maesa and her daughter Mamaea rose and escorted Alexianus out; and the bestiarius was faintly glad that the boy would not be witness to the next act.

Then his eyes moved to the voluptuous woman in black, who had haunted him for half of his life. He watched as she took her leave as well, before his gaze moved from her to her son, the Emperor. And his hand gripped the iron grate until his knuckles turned white.

For every inch of love an inch of shadow, as the poet said; it all started thirty-four years before when Septimius Severus, a Roman from North Africa and former military governor of Pannonia, married Julia Domna, the Syro-Roman daughter of the hereditary high priest of Elagabal. A Syrian 'god of the mountain,' also known as the 'Invincible Sun,' Elagabal was identified with both Jupiter and Helios in the Roman pantheon.

During the civil war which followed Commodus' assassination, Severus was subsequently proclaimed emperor by the Eastern Legions, defeating Didius Julianus and Pescennius Niger to legitimize his accession to the throne. He soon after brought his wife and their two young sons, Geta and Caracalla, to Rome where, by an ingenious procedure of retrospective auto-adoption, he presented himself to the world as the legitimate heir and successor of the Antonine emperors.

They did not come alone, however, for Julia Domna brought a cadre of her rather suspect friends and family members along in train when Severus entered the capital. Intermarried provincials, Romans of Syrian extraction or vice-versa, the most competent amongst these courtiers was Domna's sister, Julia Maesa, who brought with her two daughters, Julia Soaemias and Julia Mamaea.

Maesa played court life skillfully to her advantage, enriching herself, her family and her supporters in every way possible while her daughters, Severus' nieces, took entirely different paths in their hyper-privileged youths. Julia Soeamias was fifteen at the time of her arrival in Rome, where she soon enough came into her own as a brood mare with no one tell her 'no,' while Mamaea, her bewildered and unattractive younger sister, stayed mostly in the background.

By the time Soeamias was twenty-three and often present in the Imperial box at the Amphitheater, Mannix was eighteen and had already begun to make a name for himself for his feats in the arena. But the sad wings of destiny did not fail to dictate that this young Imperial trollop would take notice of

41

his dark wavy hair, his blue-green eyes, his rugged good looks and his lithe, tigrous body. And that's when the trouble began. And began when Mannix was just eighteen, and still a novice legally bound to Lepidus, who came into his cell one day to inform him that he and Marcellus were to perform an exhibition in the Palace Stadium on the Palatine Hill that evening.

VI

The structure wasn't a stadium at all, properly speaking; rather a sunken garden in the shape of a circus racetrack surrounded by a two-storied portico – arcaded on the ground floor, columnar on the upper level – which allowed visitors a sheltered participation with nature. It was built adjacent the palace proper which, save the newly completed Severan wing, was constructed for Domitian over a century before by his flamboyant architect Rabirius – who turned almost half of the land mass of the Palatine hill into a multi-leveled symphony of water and colored marbles replete with a basilica, a throne room, a colossal dining room, five fountain courts and, of course, the stadium. Like the sunken fountain court on the southern side of the hill, the stadium was not really sunken at all, but created by cutting back the slope and building up the opposite three sides to utilize what would otherwise be space lost to the fall-off of the hill.

Glossy green acanthus bordered the bases of the statues ranked before the pink Chian marble half-columns projecting from the piers of the ground-floor arcade. Towering from the racetrack-shaped garden beneath to well above the roof of the upper level peristyle, plane trees in flaming autumn leaf rose amongst the orange trees, cypress and bay. At either end stood semicircular fountains into the basins of which water gurgled sonorously out of the mouths of Greek herms.

The banquet guests were in arrival; Mannix and Marcellus could see them trailing their long robes like peacocks on the opposite side of the upper-level peristyle, as they promenaded the balconied course before the rich red, black and orange fields of fresco coloring its back wall. Escorted by two bald ear-ringed Egyptian eunuchs replete with white skirts and black eye mascara, the boys walked down the peristyle toward where it broke at the mid-point of the longitudinal axis of the garden and forfeited its shelter to a huge apsed semi-dome – like the bandstand of an outdoor concert hall – which afforded a terraced view of the entire expanse.

Facing west, the Parnassian sunset shot a wedge of rich apricot arcing down the inside of the vault and rippling in its octagonal coffers. Before the vault spread a throned dais, which overlooked the balconied marble railing into the garden. The two novices felt as if in a dream as they watched, between the bald heads and brown shoulders of the eunuchs walking in front, the gray-haired, gray-bearded man with the delicate golden laurel-leaf crown turn as if in slow-motion at their approach.

With all the ease of royalty playing the host, Septimius Severus, Emperor of Rome, descended the two steps of the dais toward them, a silver goblet poised in hand. His large, dignified frame was draped in a deep burgundy robe with tracings of saffron embroidery, a tuft of gray chest hair rising from its neck. With his cloak of Imperial purple with the golden eagle medallion clasp tossed carelessly over a simple but gorgeously-carved chair of Pentellic marble, here was a man at home in the camps or the court, and ready to tell you about it.

The Egyptian eunuchs parted for his approach, and the two boys lowered their heads.

"Ah," he said, holding out his hand, the other supporting his goblet of wine, "my two young huntsmen."

"Dominus," they said in unison.

The Emperor was in his 'we don't stand on ceremony here' mood and, as the novice bestiarii shook his curly-gray-haired forearm above its silver wrist clasp, Mannix was a bit surprised to notice that the man who had marched on Rome eleven years before with sixteen Legions backing him had affected just the slightest broadening of his shoulders as he stood before them.

"My niece and her friends tell me you two are the most promising bestiarii at the school," he continued, raising an eyebrow. And then he smiled. "But old Lepidus assures me it's true." He nodded. "My compliments."

"Right, well," he said, "it's her birthday today," rolling his eyes. "And if I don't keep those girls happy they run me out of money."

Mannix and Marcellus didn't know whether he was joking or not, nor how to respond.

Raising his commanding voice to the family members who sat, stood or reclined about the space beneath the huge semi-dome, "We've got the cooks," Severus said over his shoulder, "now we've got a pair of fine young huntsmen to catch our dinner." He smiled, turning his head back to Mannix and Marcellus as several random claps and half-hearted girlish whoops emerged from behind. "And yours too, boys. And yours too," he added with a conspiratorial wink, ushering them up onto the dais where his wife was seated in a gray-veined marble chair beside his.

In a tastefully exquisite, golden-green shawled stola, the Empress Julia Domna smiled at the two boys with just the right amount of bored pleasantry, as if warming up for the peacocks now rounding the corner of the upper-level peristyle and starting toward them from its opposite end.

The white marble platform on which she sat was framed by polished, Thessalian green marble columns with gilt bases and gilt-bronze victories pirouetting from white-marble globes atop their gilt Ionic capitals, the columns strung between with thick drooping bunches of pink and white roses. Draped with tiger skin rugs, the raised dais was large enough to accommodate a dozen choice guests on the gilt-wood curule fold-out chairs which a pair of young, quietly practiced female slaves in white silk smocks was situating in an arc to either side of the royal couple.

The girls shot shy glances at the boys as they replenished the two silver braziers at either end smoking with incense of cinnabar rising in tendrils through the horizontal sunlight. And Severus beckoned for the pair to help themselves to the devilled eggs, grapes and cheese in the silver platters gleaming atop the random marble side tables spaced about the tiger skin rugs and supported by sculpted griffons.

45

"Ballast up," he said with a chuckle. "And then there are a few who I'm sure would like to get a closer look at you."

The boys' eyes sparkled at the delicacies. Afraid to touch them but commanded by the master of the known world to do so, Mannix raised a devilled egg slowly to his mouth and stuffed it in with one bite, Marcellus a handful of cheese. As the Emperor's Gallic-style burgundy boots descended the back steps of the dais, the boys crammed several more eggs and handfuls of cheese into their mouths before following him onto the rich expanse of Numidian orange marble inset with large purple porphyry disks paving the space below the coffered curve of the semi-dome.

Below it, before the concave wall inset with white-marble statues in niches framed by pairs of outlandishly-speckled red and black Lucullan marble columns upholding alternating bow and triangular-shaped white Luna pediments, a cast of rather dissipated youths sat or lay scattered about on dining couches – half a dozen girls and boys and some strange, foreign-looking token guardian-types who seemed hapless and put-upon.

"I think some of you know these two young men," smiled the Emperor. "If not formally, then by sight," he added, now the conspiratorial uncle with the best birthday gifts.

And indeed, the birthday girl lounged with her leg draped over the ram's-headed marble arm rest of her chair, her pink silk stola caught up around her crotch to reveal a fair expanse of brown meaty thigh, her other leg pulled inwards atop the flattened head and arm of the cheetah skin spilling off the ledge of the seat.

Her shapely calves tapered into a pair of unlaced legionary boot sandals, and her gold-embroidered shawl drooped languidly over one shoulder to fall beneath a youthful protuberance of smooth tanned bosom accentuated by the tight string of garishly large pearls around her throat. With her black mass of hair a-riot with red roses, the twenty three year-old Julia Soaemias gave a short sigh as Mannix bashfully met her large almond eyes.

46

Several of her friends loitered with their effeminate boyfriends on the dining couches about, the boys wearing slender little diadems in their hair and trying to distract the girls' interest in Mannix and Marcellus with snide statements on the preclusion of brains with brawn. Soaemias' sister Julia Mamaea, a rather endearingly unattractive girl with wiry black hair, sat with her aged tutor across the space. She tried to smile politely at the novice bestiarii but made a mess of it.

Their cousin, Severus' son – the sixteen year-old Marcus Aurelius Antoninus – stood sullenly in a white toga leaning against the marble veneer of the apse in the shadows outside the swathe of sunset now turning a pale rose and beginning to fade. Later known as 'Caracalla' for his affected preference for the 'Caracallus' – the hooded cape worn by soldiers stationed in Germany – the future emperor stared moodily at his younger brother Geta shooting dice with three of his friends across the way within the perimeter of one of the large porphyry paving disks. He cast a self-involved glance at the two bestiarii, noting their muscular arms and legs with irritation, as if at something his father couldn't buy for him. Then he returned to his brooding in typical neglect of his wife of two years, the daughter of his father's Praetorian Prefect.

The peacocks had arrived – several princes of Characene Arabia with a contingent of their women escorted by Julia Maesa, her gracious hostess routine only thinly veiling her politicking, busy-body nature.

"Put your leg down, Julia Soaemias," she said without looking at her daughter, her smile all the while fixed on the guests she was presenting to her sister, the Empress, who had risen cordially to receive them.

Severus wheeled, and stepped briskly back up onto the dais with a "Well hello there!," to the fat Arab princes he was trying to restore the trade connections with after the recent brutal war in Mesopotamia, leaving Mannix and Marcellus to an awkward moment standing alone before the royal creatures in the semi-dome.

Julia Soaemias, who hadn't so much as registered her mother's command to put her leg down, capitalized on the distraction by hopping nimbly to her feet, purposefully bouncing her rather large tight breasts. With her pink silk stola still caught up around her upper thigh, she shuffle-clunked in her unlaced legionary boot sandals up to Mannix and looked him straight in the eye. A look which the novice bestiarius returned without bashfulness this time, though inside he was all nerves and aching groin.

Young, strong, his face eager and intent, Mannix's dark hair shone streaked with gold in the sunset as it fell to frame his finely sculpted throat. His belted blue tunic pleasantly revealed his tanned, lithely muscled arms and legs, not yet knotted with the scar tissue awaiting him from future wounds, but just enough to make him interesting.

Soaemias looked him up and down, and even had the impeccably bad taste – which made her sister bring a hand to her forehead – to walk around behind him as if examining a horse.

Marcellus stood shorter but gracefully muscled as well, with his sandy-blond good looks and his olive skin oiled for the evening's performance. Soaemias came around the side of him as if swinging around a column, liking his body but frowning at his smile. Then she abruptly walked through the narrow space between the two, jarring both of them and yelling "Who's winning?" at Geta's game of dice.

"Where are my hunters!" exclaimed Severus from the dais, and the two boys bounded up the steps, still registering the feel of Julia Soeamias' hands on their genitalia.

Everyone was standing on the dais, a combination of delicate golden sandals, polished boots and strange shoes with curling toes that got caught in the tiger skins, all protruding from robes, togas and stolas that were each worth more than the pretty and professional slave girls who were filling their wearer's wine goblets. With their bodily grace unsullied by excess, Mannix and Marcellus stood out like stallions amidst the pomp and squalor. They were each surprised to be handed a silver goblet of wine by Severus himself, who'd already had a few by the look of him. He took up his own and raised his voice above the chatter of the princes, queens and prelates, for the education of whom he was about to show how real Romans behaved.

"These two young men will catch our dinner below," he said. "For our pleasure." Then he turned to Mannix and Marcellus. "We salute you for it."

The corpulent Arab ephebes raised their eyebrows as slightly as their goblets, then turned back to their conversations with the matriarch, Julia Domna, and several Roman industry moguls representing offices in Palmyra, Tyre and Alexandria. Her sister Julia Maesa buzzed around like a bee, listening, gathering information, and schmoozing away.

"Well, boys," said the Emperor. "Have some fun for me. It won't be as good as hunting lions in Mauretania, but it's the best we can do," he chuckled. Then he turned back to his guests.

Knowing they were dismissed, Mannix and Marcellus still had a decent amount of wine in their goblets after the toast, for Severus didn't pour lightly. They tossed it off in several gulps, not used to its strong, un-cut quality; for Lepidus had their weekly wine allotment cut with water to save money. Then, faintly confused as how they were to get down to the garden, they turned to find the pair of incongruous Egyptian eunuchs awaiting them at the foot of the dais. A slave girl appeared at their side holding out her hands for the goblets as if they had intended to steal them. After handing them over, they were led by the Egyptians back down the way they had come.

The eunuchs had a sickly-sweet smell to them which the boys couldn't help but curl their noses at as they followed, glancing through the Parian marble columns of the portico at the arcades of the ground-floor peristyle being blockaded with strong wooden fencing by a seemingly inexhaustible supply of palace slaves. The sky had turned to lime-blue twilight and, as they turned a corner, they noticed torches being lit in brackets on the piers of the arcade below. Through a doorway in the red-black-and-orange frescoed back wall, they followed the Egyptians down a flight of shadowy stairs through an arch into the ground-floor peristyle where they were turned over to a Praetorian Guardsman.

The gold signet ring indicative of the guardsman's promotion to Equestrian rank glinted in the torchlight as he pointed out a rack of assorted weapons against the back wall of the arcade. "Take your pick," he said. "There won't be much in the way of dangerous game, no man-eaters. Stags, ibex, some Tuscan boar; nothing you couldn't handle with your eyes closed. Anyway, you two know better than me."

The novices wondered vaguely how many animals they would be required to kill, but decided against asking. The adrenaline that had started when they were dismissed by the Emperor was beginning to build, and they were ready to get started, to get back to their own field in which they were superior to the people above them.

Mannix selected a boar spear with a round disk halfway up its haft to keep the animal from getting to him after it had been penetrated, and also gathered half a dozen casting spears. He slung a leather cup harness full of light javelins around his torso and hooked a Spanish dagger to his bronze-studded leather belt. Marcellus picked a Scythian bow with a rather nice, silver-plated gorytos full of arrows which he wondered faintly if they'd let him keep, or how he could steal, both of which he slung over his shoulder. He hooked a dagger onto his belt as well, cradled a bundle of casting spears and nodded at Mannix.

The boys glanced up at the dais across and above the stadium-garden. Lit by oil braziers, the balconied platform had become a centrally-positioned circus box behind which the huge apsed semi-dome towered, its coffers rippling and buckling in the torchlight with the smoke of incense trailing and the bunched strings of rose petals bowing between the columns bordering the dais. The figures up there were becoming enlivened with the wine and Severus was back to holding court, a man all about the action of the moment, whether business, pleasure, or war. The slower aspects leading up to that action were better left to others, as far as he was concerned.

"If you want to eat tonight, I'd get your gear set up out there and get ready," said the tough Praetorian behind them, "we're about to let the animals in."

The smocked slaves in front of them opened one of the wooden barrier fences between the ground-floor arcades enough for the two to slip through. From the ground, visibility through the garden was vastly reduced, and it became a kind of strangely mysterious fantasy-land of torchlight and trees.

"You take that end and I'll take this other," said Mannix, walking toward the far fountain.

"Right."

"And be careful with those arrows."

The two moved toward either end with their equipment, each feeling the loss of the other and the recession into his own, cell-wall-gazing self. The first stars began to appear above as they walked through the haphazardly planted oleander bushes, their boot sandals crunching atop the huge red and orange leaves of the plane trees fallen for autumn. They took up positions at each of the semi-circular fountains, Mannix laying his spears around the basin, stretching his shoulders, arms and legs.

Within minutes they began to hear the sound of hooves loping across the grass and things rustling through the bushes over the sonorous gurgling of the water-spouting herms. Mannix took up a casting spear and started in, wasting no time, the spear held at his hip, his legs bent, his steps light. He rounded a cypress and startled an Umbrian buck with a fine rack, the animal side-stepping wildly and thrusting off with a snort. With the power and the sound of the beast in his gut, Mannix sprinted after it bringing the spear to his shoulder.

The torchlight made visibility terrible from below but quite good from above and, as Mannix slowed his sprint through the wavering sanguine light cut up by the bushes and trees to blind and then recede, the party on the podium could watch Marcellus at the other end of the hundred meters of space, moving low to the ground with his spear and listening carefully to the rooting, whickering sound coming through the oleanders all around. Severus kept his eyes on the garden and his ears on the conversation going on around him which, after the preliminary niceties, had moved to the recent peace suit in which the Parthians' chief concern was the reopening of the

51

trade routes between the West and India, and the Land of Silk beyond.

Mannix switched the casting spear to his left shoulder and pulled a light javelin out of the leather cup harness on his back. The buck had loped thirty meters down the side of the fenced arcade and then lost his smell. Coming up on its flank twenty meters out, the young bestiarius slowed to a walk, rose up on his toes, stutter-stepped and side-armed the javelin into the big deer. Aiming for behind and beneath the shoulder, the wine had thrown him off and the javelin penetrated the side of the buck's stomach behind and beneath the rib cage. The deer grunted and thrust off and Mannix cursed and sprinted after it, disgusted with himself at making a mess of such a beautiful animal.

Julia Soaemias trailed her hand lightly upon the balustrade above, away from her friends and boyfriends who had all risen and begun to walk with their wine goblets for a better view. Caracalla was leaning on the balustrade a ways behind, casting hopeful glances at her. Though his cousin had used her hand on him before he'd ever learned to do it himself – and done a few other things to him through the years – her interest was directed below, where Marcellus had speared an ibex and then mercifully cut its throat.

Mannix put another javelin through the flank of the Umbrian buck, which bounded into one of the wooden barriers at the end of the peristyle shattering its boards. Slaves running from either end hesitated as they got close to the buck rearing and pawing crazily at the splintering barricade. The Emperor had leaned forward in his seat with his elbow on the marble arm rest, fingers beneath his chin, watching as Mannix moved in. His wife, who had much better business sense than he, was elaborating on the restoration of the trade routes.

Two Praetorian Guardsmen were jogging down the peristyle toward where the Umbrian buck was caught up and tearing through, but Mannix rushed up from the side and solved the situation by running the casting spear into the frothing deer's chest sending a bright torchlit ejaculation of arterial blood into his face and mouth. As the buck collapsed, Julia

Soaemias let out a whoop of approval which startled the bestiarius and caused him to look up, where he caught a glimpse of her breasts squeezed almost to bursting between her crossed arms as she leaned over the railing of the balcony smiling lewdly down at him. He wheeled and vomited a great gob of the deer's blood, then started back into the garden, where he and Marcellus went on to perform thirty minute's worth of textbook technique as Julia Soaemias and her friends ran about the upper peristyle chasing themselves and, on the dais, the Empress and her sister worked on the merchant princes who held the franchise for the Mesopotamian roads and the ports of the Persian Gulf.

The Romans and Parthians had been at war on and off for two and a half centuries. And, after each one of them, the real peace treaties were conducted at tables lined with Arabs in head dresses and Jews in black robes, the issue always trade routes and commerce. Daughters of the hereditary high priest of the Ba'al at Emesa in Syria, Domna and Maesa could play that card when need be, for the town on the Orontes was two hundred miles due east of Dura-Europus on the Euphrates, one of the major caravan routes stretching between.

Since the end of the Seleucids' reign two hundred and eighty years before, the dynasty of priest-kings had ruled at Emesa, gaining autonomy through the god worshipped from an unknown time – a mysterious black stone supposedly fallen from the sky. Acquiring Roman citizenship by virtue of their loyalty and services rendered during Corbulo's war against the Parthians, then Vespasian and Titus' war against the Jews, the temple and its clergy were filthy rich, preying off the superstitions of the bedouin caravaners who all paid homage to Elagabal on their passages through.

Severus had stayed in Syria when in command of a legion there and, like many others, had made the pilgrimage to Emesa as a tourist. Wined and dined by Domna and Maesa's father, and catching the eye of his elder daughter, the Roman from Africa was already fascinated by Egyptian gods, and not immune from Eastern cults. His accession as Imperator made an empress of Julia Domna, who with her sister Maesa was heiress to this extremely wealthy priestly dynasty.

The animals were gradually thinning in the garden below. Marcellus had taken a wild boar at the expense of a nasty gore through his calf muscle, and Mannix caught an ibex from behind with his dagger en route back to his weapons at the far fountain. When he arrived, he took up his own boar spear, keeping his leather cup harness of javelins over his back. The torchlight was nerve-racking, pulsing and quivering in the light breeze and, as he moved back in through the trees beneath the light rustling of their leaves, a tell-tale angry grunt-squeal and gallop made him drop to a knee.

The boar had come from an angle, and Mannix couldn't see it until the hundred and fifty-pound black mass was on him and a curved tusk seared up his quadricep muscle, the beast rooting and butting and biting at him with rabid quickness. Yelling with the pain, he drew the long Spanish dagger and thrust it into the pig's mouth crashing through its incisors and lacerating its tongue. The boar balked and squealed and he quickly drove the blade through the side of its throat, silencing it.

As he rose and began to limp quickly to the side of the barricaded peristyle to try and take stock of what was left, something light and perfumed hit him in the side of the face. He looked up quickly to find Julia Soaemias lowering her pink silk stola, her undergarment on the ground at his feet. Mannix grimaced and looked for Marcellus and the Emperor stood clapping from the dais.

At his command – for the fat Arab ephebes were growing hungry – the several remaining deer and one wild boar were driven out of the garden into off-stage holding pens by a contingent of waiting Praetorian Guardsmen brandishing torches. The palace cooks were sent in, and the animals quickly and efficiently butchered. While one of the deer and one of the boar were spitted and beginning to roast in the garden below, the two bestiarii were patched up by several Palace physicians beneath the ground-floor peristyle.

Generally slaves, bondsmen, or simply freebooting adventurers, gladiators and bestiarii were technically of a lesser social stratum than even the Plebians. Yet they often found themselves in strange social situations, scenarios which members of the Equestrian and even the Senatorial class would never by privy to. For they held that mystique that entertainers and, particularly, sportsmen have throughout the centuries, often gracing the courts of kings and emperors.

Hence the two novice bestiarii were subsequently beckoned to the dais by Severus, toasted again formally, and then invited to dine in the apse with the birthday girl and her friends. The Emperor gravitated toward Mannix and Marcellus over the party guests, especially with half-a-dozen goblets of finely aged Falernian in him. For the military ruler was in a middle ground between the two poles, knowing instinctively with the Greek Classics that body was form which was made by the soul. And just as sloth, greed and corruption found their way sooner or later into the physiognomy of their owner, so did mind, effort and will. Hence the purpose of Sport.

He discoursed a bit on these topics with the novice bestiarii on the dais while Julia Soaemias and her nubile friends buzzed around like bees, and was impressed with their erudition on the philosophy behind their profession, which they considered the very pinnacle of sport because it was not about man versus man, but about man versus Nature. And that was always a losing battle; yet one which every man was born to fight.

A troop of acrobats, jugglers and musicians had taken the place of the hunt below, and as the party became enlivened and business gave way to pleasure, the birthday girl found her prize. Having strategically sent one of her friends to involve Marcellus in a game of dice, Julia Soaemias was able to corner Mannix on his own leaning on the peristyle down the way with a goblet of wine and a haunch of venison watching the festivities below. His thigh was swathed in white linen bandaging and he was in obvious pain, which made him infinitely more desirable in her esteem.

"I see you left my little token on the ground down there," she said.

"What did you expect me to do," he replied, not looking at her, "put it on my head and wear it to dinner?"

She tried to seem offended. "You're pretty fresh," she said.

"And you're not," he smiled thinly, his gaze still on the garden.

"You're not stupid, are you," she stated, again examining him like a horse.

Mannix didn't respond.

"You might even be intelligent," she went on, tilting her head to the side. "And that's dangerous for slaves."

"I'm not a slave," he said, still not looking at her. "I'm a bestiarius."

"Oh," she smiled, trying to be cool. "Like to show me some of your handling techniques?"

"Maybe I would," he said softly, gazing at the confusion of acrobats and jugglers in the torchlit garden below. "And maybe I wouldn't," he turned his head and looked at her then, and the feeling of fear and desire it elicited stung in her bowels.

VII

The crowd was growing restless, a bad sign. The last of the andabatae had already finished off, the winners flailed back into the tunnels and down to their cells where some would suffocate or smash their heads against the walls until they died in the darkness before tomorrow's act. The Mob busied itself singing bawdy songs and throwing chicken bones and rotten fruit at the arena attendants finishing the stage design of huge plaster rock escarpments replete with bushes and trees. They finally quieted down when a trumpet blast signaled the next segment of the show.

Apicius had made his way back to the editor's podium beside the Imperial box where, out of breath, he made the introduction for the next act.

"Ladies and gentlemen!" he shouted, huffing and puffing. "From the reverend Annals of History! From the sacred mists of Mythology!" he threw his arm up dramatically in its fat fluttering sleeve. "We proudly bring you ... the Six Golden Asses of the Phrygian Earth Mother Goddess!"

Mannix gently ran his fingers across the stitched punctures in his shoulder, watching through the grated inset in the perimeter wall as the trapdoors opened and slipped back into their grooves. Six squares of shadow appeared in the white sand of the arena floor staged in an elliptical arrangement belying the form of the Amphitheater. To the macabre accompaniment of the hydraulic organs playing weird strains of mystical music, the six large platform elevators began to levitate, first the outline of the oyster shells breaking the ground, then their helpless wriggling occupants becoming apparent, strapped spread-eagled on top of the satin bedsheets. The Mob let out a roar that startled the priests on the Palatine.

The hydraulic organs playing all the while, with another flourish of trumpets, three jackasses in magnificent golden harness loped out from the Gate of Life, another three from the Gate of Death. The bestiarius watched with disdain, hoping for a quick end to this misery. For he knew what the Mob did not. The donkeys were belligerent and well-trained, their sexual instincts, like that of all animals, controlled exclusively by scent. From birth, they had never been allowed sexual contact with one of their own kind; but had been whetted on old beat-up whores that disappeared at night from the dark river walks of the Tiber, or young girls gathered in cavalry raids on the Danubian frontier.

The jackasses loped around the arena snuffling and whickering and shaking their toothy heads against the irritating and unfamiliar feel of the decorative harnesses. The crowd noise and the confusion of stage technicians working on the plaster rock escarpments around the perimeter wall occupied their nervous systems for a while as they stamped and whinnied about the oyster shell beds. But without the appearance of an immediate threat, soon enough the heat-scent rubbed into the girls' crotches began to penetrate their whiskered nostrils and start the electrical impulses moving in their brains; and one of them moved closer and closer in, stopping and backing and sidestepping around one of the shells. He took a precautionary bite at the epicenter of the scent attracting him and the girl arced her spine and gave a piercing scream that sent a flock of pigeons lighting off the caldarium of the baths of Trajan across the street, startling the jackass enough that he backed away pulling with him her flimsy jeweled dress in his big blocky teeth.

The crowd went wild at the sight of the smooth squirming skin and erect brown nipples and the donkey's sex organ dropping from its sheath like a sleepy python from the hollow eye of a stone Buddha. Fistfights broke out in the top tier of wooden seating. At the Emperor's bidding, the Parthian archer nearest him rocketed deadly shafts into two men who had torn the dress off a woman in the stands. But before things could get any more out of control, the jackass reared up with a

58

great guttural 'Haw-Hee!' and flopped his girth down on top of the screaming whore, breaking her shoulder with his hoof.

The oyster shell beds were designed to facilitate the asses, who were familiar with them; and his paws collapsed to where his knee joints slid into the grooves on either side, his flanks lowering, scrunching down to where his parallel organ could thwap and slip clumsily up the inside of the girl's thigh. Meanwhile three other asses had initiated the procedure, and the hydraulic organs played backup to the piercing screams of the whores and the continual roaring of the crowd. Mannix lowered his head and turned away from the awful reddening scene, casting a malevolent glance at the Imperial box.

The day threatened rain, but the clouds were capricious. They broke up like a patchwork quilt in the wind, and a huge raking shaft of sunlight penetrated the shadowy atmosphere inside the Amphitheater. The oculus in the awning cast the solar disc on the western stands, brilliantly illumining the togas and faces of the thousands it passed across while plunging the rest of the interior into a deeper mist of shadow until eyesight could aright itself again to the warm sanguine glow redifused with slight color shifts as the disc began its slow revolution around the inside of the oval. It was noon in spring, and the sun was still below its zenith.

The next act scheduled was a recreation of Ulysses and his mariners having to sail through Hades. The plaster landscape hugged the perimeter walls, the jackasses finishing up with the whores. Two of the beasts wouldn't perform, but just clopped around switching their tails and irritatedly watching their stable-fellows scrunch and hunker and snort, muffling the fading screams of the girls with their great girths. The donkeys were finally driven out and the four cheetahs Apicius and the Egyptians were stopped by earlier at the intersection were let out to put an end to the whimpering misery of the whores. Seen from the topmost rim of seating, four of the oyster shell beds were a muddy mixture of blood and slickened satin, two of the others still fresh.

The cheetahs were mankillers trained on the same principle as the donkeys, by never letting them feed on anything but human meat, and always letting them win attacks against padded bestiarii, who never struck or disciplined them in any way. The blood scent, and the obviety of trapped and wounded prey would make their performance all the smoother. They were led up the ramps leading to the half-moon arches around the inside of the perimeter wall, which opened into the plaster rock escarpments, and they appeared as if in their natural habitat, suddenly perched on the rocks surrounding the arena floor, their long tails curled and slowly undulating.

Two of the whores were already dead, the others lying in shock staring up through the oculus in the awning at the shifting tapestry of cumulous clouds. The cheetahs hopped down from the rocks and loped playfully to pounce up on the shell beds and begin feeding placidly on the girls. They avoided the dead meat, but only went for the live ones, which pleased Apicius the Ringmaster to no end, for the act was pulled off without a hitch – all of the deaths occurring on stage. If one of the girls screamed or moved too much, the cheetahs simply sank their teeth into her throat and shook, loosening the jugular enough that it was soon over. The surf noise of the Mob was at a continual low moaning; their expiatory need satisfied predominantly by the sex-death aspect.

As the cheetahs were feeding, the six platforms began slowly to descend, Apicius crossing his fingers that the cats wouldn't balk and have to be driven or lured from the arena. And indeed they did not; one of them merely raised his short bloody snout to have a look around. The cats were used to the multi-leveled movement and the meat was tasty. When the last of the shells disappeared below the floor-line, the technicians below pulled the counterweight ropes that closed the trapdoors, which shifted back into their slots, and slaves came out and spread fresh sand across the six shallow spots. The cheetahs were controlled inside the elevator shafts until proper clearance for the route back to their pens was secured.

VIII

Within a month of leading him off to an out-of-the-way corner in the bath complex of the newly-completed Severan wing that night, some in the know – mainly the Isaic priestesses with the painted eyes and the mystic intuition who used to dress her hair every day – said that Julia Soaemias had fallen in love with the novice bestiarius. And had fallen in love with him at just that time in her life when that love and, perhaps, only that love, could have saved her from her self.

She smiled.

Staring absently through the Numidian orange marble columns of the first fountain court of the Imperial Palace, she sat on a bench beneath the shade of its peristyle promenade. In a white stola which took a slave woman some time of her life to make, her body, at age forty-one, was only slightly the worse for the bed and the drink. The laxity of her posture was still much the same, with the heel of one of her gold-laced sandals posted on the ledge of the bench, and one of her thighs subsequently splayed.

The thigh was still smooth and meaty. But, upon close inspection, the honey-colored skin of its inside was beginning to reveal the stretch-marks which preclude flaccidness. And though her breasts – which the bodices she wore in public pushed up into seemingly firm round balls – were still smooth and brown, they sagged like wineskins in the plain casual dress she had changed into, with the tiny white squiggles beginning to streak along their sides as well.

Her position on the bench, with one thigh raised, unconsciously revealed the blue silk pouch of underwear beneath her stola, from the sides of which protruded tiny tufts of wiry black hair. And, indeed, she had been negligent with her looks of late; very tired. Having to be present at the inaugural

61

ceremonies of the newly restored Amphitheater this morning exhausted her; not to mention her 'ornatrice.' With her son and his courtiers there for the rest of the day, she had a bit of peace.

Yet they would all return tonight, drunk and squealing and urinating on the marble-paneled walls.

Sometimes the drugs helped. Prescribed by her doctors, and transported from India at tremendous cost, they helped her sleep at night. But they were worthless without a carafe of Falernian at dinner, all of which made her sweat so in the daytime.

The bath helped; the complex terraced out from the hill amidst birdsong and cypress trees. But it brought confusing memories. For when the right blade of afternoon sunlight through the glazed windows cleaved the velvet shade of its deeply-marbled apodyterium, she could see two ghostly phantoms behind the shelter of a waterfall cascading from the urn of a marble sea nymph. Two bodies, each of them in their youth one of those impossibly rare, god-like creatures for whom balance and timing were always perfect, whose physical capability always seemed the unconscious blooming of a reflexive intellectuality, of physics calculated neurologically. But now the bath was too often filled with her son's equine courtiers, whose oversized organs belied neither bodily grace nor bodily charm; and Julia Soaemias mostly just wanted to be alone.

She raised the green-glass beaker with its cool, clear liquid by her side and drank. Sighing softly with the burn, she set the glass back down and ran her tongue over her dry, slightly puffy lips rubbed clean of the vilely red lipstick she had worn at the Amphitheater that morning. Today was the first time that she had watched Mannix in the Arena since becoming Empress three years ago. It was also the first time that she had felt that old sting of aliveness in her bowels felt only otherwise in his arms. A combination of love and hate, loss and gain, seeing him started her remembering it all again.

She had been able to avoid it over the past several years due to the fire damage to the Amphitheater, and the bestiarius being on exhibition in Germania for a year, and afterwards only performing several times in smaller venues around the city. But now that the restoration funded by family money had rendered the Amphitheater fully functional, the morning's inaugural ceremonies dictated that she be present. For it had always been the obligation of a Roman emperor to architecturally embellish, aggrand, or further functionalize a city which had, for over a century, been called 'eternal.' The final touches on her cousin Caracalla's baths were still in the works; and, of course, her uncle built his new wing of the Palace with its own baths where it had all begun on her birthday night eighteen years before.

She remembered – it seemed important to remember now, to have it clear in her mind – that, after that night with its hunt and its heady wine, Mannix went on to distinguish himself in the Secular Games thrown by her uncle that year, who left thereafter for the Rhine. In spending most of his reign on campaign or in the provinces supervising the defensive works of the contracting frontiers, much of the administrative duties of the Empire – and especially of the treacherous Roman political scene – were left to her aunt.

Julia Domna proved able at the task, however, playing one powerful general or senator against another while adroitly keeping herself and her husband from falling into the many traps set by political enemies in the capital. Severus often sought her advice, and she was the only empress since Marcus Aurelius' wife to be given the affectionate appellation 'Mater Castrorum,' Mother of the Camp, by the Legions.

Julia Soaemias respected her aunt. Though daughter of the hereditary high priest of Elagabal at Emesa in Syria, in sensitivity to the religious conservatism of the upper classes in Rome – and regardless of how she might have capitalized upon it with the lower – Julia Domna was not seen to encourage the cultural aspects of her lineage while empress. Despite how indelibly her line was subsequently stamped with them. She had the good taste to restore the Vestal Complex, and to patronize the traditional Greco-Roman arts, inviting the most brilliant philosophers, writers and other artists in the Roman world to grace her court. In so doing, she had kept learning and culture alive in a world that had fallen into chaos within less than a generation.

For though a tough, able soldier by nature – and though she loved her uncle dearly – Julia Soaemias had to admit that Septimius Severus was something of a dotard to his women, through whose subsequent machinations the flavor of his court was gradually changed. And as the family approached a matriarchy in a way that no prior dynasty had – with her aunt working effectively to handle the administrative and political affairs of the Empire on the surface – behind the scenes, her rather suspect friends and family members were working their own wiles in the back corridors of power in the capital, which had long before and sadly enough become more dependent upon nepotism and simony than upon function and ability. The most successful and intelligent amongst these machinators was, of course, her mother Julia Maesa, who did whatever was necessary to ensure the continuation of her line in the world power structure.

But while her mother busied herself securing the political scene with her sister the empress, Julia Soaemias played her own games. And as Mannix was a bondsman and not entirely free, she could get to him and she did. Without Severus there to appeal to, if he had refused she could have caused Lepidus some trouble, and Mannix was loyal to the school. So, despite his distaste for her burrowing sicknesses, the bestiarius was often enough a backdoor feature at the Severan court, with the Praetorians waving him through the checkpoints and the sickly-sweet-smelling eunuchs letting him in through the servants' quarters.

But the sex was reassuring and life was short. And, for them, probably shorter than for most. For Julia Soaemias had her own arena of death surrounding her. An arena of power shifts she never knew which side of she was going to wake up on in the morning. An arena of purges and assassinations, and almost constant civil war.

At the age of thirteen, for their loyalty to Didius Julianus, she had watched her uncle Severus execute most of the Praetorian Guard's entire officer corps. Subsequently replacing them with men hand-picked from his Legions, the purges had gone on; and she had more than once spied with her sister and her cousins from behind a heavy gilt tapestry in the curvilinear library of the office wing – its walls paneled with disturbingly appropriate burgundy-wine Tenarian marble – as her aunt and her mother signed the death warrants for hundreds in the ongoing process of elimination.

Yet, like Mannix, Julia Soaemias had not feared death. Quite the opposite. Beings as afire with life as they could not even have foreseen death coming. With lips, hands, tongues and toes, they denied that death existed. If it had taken either of them in those early years, they would have surely been unaware of the fact. Death would have amounted to no more for them than a faintly humorous spasm.

Mannix had the fearlessness of the beginner, and was just becoming familiar with that Olympian Zone which made him both different from, and special to, all of those unlucky normal people. Having only just become acquainted with the taste of that dreadful thrill, he was like the youth who first begins to imbibe in wine, the intoxication of which opens his perspective on a higher plane of which the slothful and ignorant surrounding him in safety in the Amphitheater and the Palace could never perceive. After all, what could a woman do to him?

Julia Soaemias knew this instinctively and she both loved and hated him for it. Because, for her, what had started as an obsession with the conquest and possession of a thoroughbred, progressed into a deep-seated need. A need to touch Mannix's skin and to smell his smell. A need to hear his voice as he talked about the hills. It soon reached the point where she was only calm when he was by her side, and she even begged him on her knees to go into exile with her to Crete, where they could live in a restored Minoan palace together, just the two of them, and be left-alone normal people.

If pressed – and at times she would have liked to have burned it out of him over a bed of hot coals – she knew that the Bestiarius would admit that there had been moments of tenderness between them. Before she realized that he did not love her, nor ever would; for a man in his business was, at best, frugal with his loves. Still, and perhaps just because of this, his was a tenderness which she had never felt before, but which was registered in such moments as when they would seek that out-of-the-way corner in the apodyterium, the white of her gown turning to gray at the waterline as she moved softly with the shifting of the element, maintaining a delicate balance.

She could remember how he would pull her hair up from the back of her milk-white neck for the wavy black curls to tumble out of his hand, and with his other move the strap of the stola off her shoulder to reveal one ripe breast, its nipple gorged and protruding and the blood beginning to fill him as well, bringing sensation to an organ that generally had none.

She could remember a night when he placed her body between his and the balustrade of the vast rose-marbled terrace overlooking the Circus Maximus, both of them content just to look and to feel, and to take in the city from that strange, luxuriant vantage. Relishing his iron and leather smell and the wine and boar on his breath, she had backed into him then, pressing and close; and he moved her hair to the side and slowly kissed the soft, smooth, sickly-sweet skin of her neck up to the base of her ear.

But mostly what she remembered now, looking back upon it all, was the blank, vacuous, lost feeling – the dull, dim-witted shock – each time that she realized it was not to be.

For when her mother got wind of the rumors being whispered throughout the corridors of the Palace (and threatening to leak out into the city) concerning her daughter's lascivious ennui over a young novice bestiarius, Julia Maesa was not pleased, to say the least. And within three months of their first tryst on her birthday night, Julia Soaemias was married off to a member of the Equestrian order in a quickly arranged political ploy of her mother's.

Needless to say there was no love lost between the couple, the arranged husband one of those suspect Syro-Romans elevated when Severus came to the throne – a political climber more married to her mother than to her. But it was thus that a pining and pregnant Julia Soaemias was packed up and sent back to Syria, where her husband was given a minor magistracy.

She set the green glass beaker down by her side and frowned slightly at the thought of Antioch. At the memory of those jasmine-smelling Syrian evenings when the great bloody gas ruin of the sunset stretched languorously across the sky, and the only possibility to escape her husband and kill the void for an hour was in a vaulted storeroom with some rank-smelling negro palace slave. When they had to be there they always lived in the palace of the old Seleucid kings, the stones from which her mother said she drew strength. But, for Julia Soaemias, the whole province was a budget inn.

Her frown stayed in place with the thought of her mother, who had betaken herself to the Gardens of Sallust to live. Her younger sister, Julia Mamaea, with her son Alexianus, had gone there as well. Yet they would all be here tomorrow night for the banquet. Her mother always was one for keeping up appearances.

Julia Soaemias smiled again. She did not love her mother. Or did she? She could not remember any more; nor did she much care. Throughout her childhood, her mother had humored or ignored her as the situation dictated.

And though there had been moments of closeness – particularly while conspiring against Macrinus four years before – it was mainly her mother expecting her to play the role that she had always played – the role of whore. For her mother knew that if they could convince the world that Soaemias' son was the product of an affair with Caracalla and not her lawful husband, it would appeal to the Senate and the Roman aristocracy's preference for keeping things in the blood. Of course he wasn't.

But the role of whore had come easy to her. For, from a young age, Julia Soaemias was endowed with Body. Her sister Mamaea wasn't, so there was never any question of her breaking free. She only had to use her mind and her silence to stay in the background and wait. But Julia Soaemias was a brood mare. And she grew up without fear. Without fear of man, beast, nor devils; the gods she had never known.

Body was what she was, and Body is what she had always been. It was what she learned how to use in a world in which she was never required to do, but simply to be. Be a niece, be a daughter, be an Empress, be a Name.

And thus she had learned how to use Body to get what Name wanted when Name could not get it. And she had learned how to use Name to get what Body wanted when Body could not get it. And now her body was full-blown like a rose, with loosening petals.

IX

Mannix had made his way back to the clinic, where they gave him a maroon wool 'paenula' – a hooded cloak which fell to the level of the knees – in place of his shredded tunic. He staggered back down the corridor which funneled into the large tunnel connecting the Amphitheater with the four gladiatorial schools across the street. Shuffling down a central colonnaded aisle, a huge warehouse space of storage areas for props and offices for stage managers widened on either side. Crews clustered around tables beneath candle chandeliers pouring over venue charts for the series of Games, which was scheduled to run for thirty straight days – the inaugural series of the newly restored Flavian Amphitheater.

Keeping checks on shipping contracts, to make sure they were properly handled, he could hear concern over whether a group of Indian rhino would arrive on schedule for the grand finale. Other managers were making sure that the sand supply was adequate, the water systems working beneath the Amphitheater, the sewage tunnels kept clear, and the burial contractors keeping a timely schedule in removing the excess bodies at night via wagon train over the Esquiline hill and outside the walls where they were burned in pits to avoid plague. Others still were seeing that the show was working on schedule, consulting with the lead technicians on choreography and rehearsals, and so on. The men worked hard, their white tunics soaked with sweat, their hands dirty. They thought, like all men did, of their baths at the end of the day, and of joining their wives and children at home.

Mannix had no such thoughts as he walked on through the underground colonnade hung with oil lanterns running beneath the street towards the 'Ludus Magnus,' the main gladiatorial school, and turned right into the branch tunnel to the

'Ludus Matutinus,' the school where he trained as a bestiarius. So named the 'Morning School' for the bestiarii events opened each day of games, he emerged from the ramp into the large rectangular courtyard and made his way to the communal hall, where he piled a lunch plate full of pheasant legs and fresh bread, and grabbed a goblet of frothy barley meade.

He slid onto a bench before an oaken table. Other bestiarii were scattered about eating or lying on the benches. Kitchen slaves hustled behind the scenes. Several passed by and nodded or placed their hands on his good shoulder.

Marcellus sidled up with a plate of food and ate with him. "Bad about Demetrius today," he said, his eyes on his food.

Mannix nodded, not wanting to talk about it. Despite himself, memories rushed through him like the first ray of morning sun over a ridge of hillside, painful to behold. Demetrius was a novice still living at the school serving his time as legally bound to the director. Five years and three emperors before, Mannix had found the boy in the hellish chaos of the Imperial household where Julia Soaemias sometimes called for his services and who he didn't mind obliging until she brought the boy into the bedroom one day and Mannix said 'enough' and had a revelation of what the kid was going through from everyone in the Palace including the cooks.

He got him out of there, promising her, and moreover her mother, that the Senate and People of Rome would never hear the end of certain things if she so much as breathed a word. For lack of a better place to put him, he had turned Demetrius over to the rough care of the Ludus Matutinus, where he himself grew into manhood. In time he had taken a rare liking to the boy, and an interest in his training. He thought Demetrius was ready for the arena, but that didn't matter now. And the bestiarius didn't let attachments sink in.

"The whores went off well," Marcellus continued, trying to make small talk.

"I'm not sure they would have agreed," Mannix replied, wanting even less to talk about the whores. He wiped grease from the corner of his mouth with the back of his hand to hide his involuntary grimace.

Though he could still hear toothless bestiarii from Marcus Aurelius' time waxing poetic of an evening in Milo's Tavern out the Via Praenestina about how their predecessors used to train stags to pull chariots – an extremely hard feat due to the fact that stags are very nervous animals and only a few bestiarii had ever pulled it off – the sad fact of the matter was that the people didn't give a damn about stags pulling chariots, nor did they have any idea of, or appreciation for, how hard it might be to train them.

Yet he had to admit that training jackasses, bulls and big cats to rape women was no small feat either. Bestiarii had worked on the project as far back as the reign of Nero, who had actors dressed as animals fornicate while performing mythological pageants. But the acts had nearly always failed with real animals, so for whole half-centuries at a time the experiment had been shelved, to be revitalized only under forward-thinking animal men with a lot of talent and drive.

Firstly it was necessary to procure a woman who was willing, one who would cooperate through the procedure. Then one had to find an animal that would perform on schedule before a raving crowd. A jackass, or even a large dog that would voluntarily mount a woman under those circumstances was a rare animal. And, of course, the fact that the woman was willing was no fun for the Mob. So bestiarii in different periods had experimented with training animals to rape women, covering them with hides or even building wooden mockups of cows or lionesses and putting the woman inside. But to no real end.

Any old farmer could have told them what the problem was, however, and one of them probably did. An animal's sex drive is not controlled by sight, but by scent. And so it just became a matter of keeping watch on all the female animals in the stockyards at Laurentum, and when they came into season, collecting their blood on cloths. The cloths were then kept sealed in labeled jars.

71

Sitting at the table staring into his meade, Mannix could remember his first exposure to the procedure as an apprentice bestiarius turned out with his colleagues in the open peristyle courtyard of the Ludus Matutinus one night to provide noise and confusion for a torchlit scene of wickedness. The director of the school had procured old Delila – a whore from under the stands with whom many of the novices had in fact become regulars. Delila had been wined and warmed up to the idea over dinner, where an agreed payment for her services was settled upon. And then the director had escorted her very gentilely out into the peristyle courtyard – a large rectangular space surrounded on two levels by colonnaded walkways running before the quarters of the novices.

Delila was all tits and giggles and flirting with the trainers as she got down on all fours and pulled up her dress and they draped the scent-cloths over her back. A young male leopard was tied by a leash to a stake in the courtyard, and the novices were standing about talking and moving around, providing noise and confusion – an important aspect of the animal's training. When they had Delila situated with the cloths, the leopard's trainer brought the cat over and began to encourage him to mount her. The leopard took one look at Delila's big rump and turned the other way, but they kept working very patiently with it, all the while telling Delila to stop her giggling and be still.

Born in captivity at the government stockyards in Laurentum, the leopard basically thought its trainer was its mother, the bestiarius having handled it from the time of its birth. So it had no problem with him helping it and guiding it and positioning it on Delila's rump. Pretty soon it gave a few tentative hunches, but what with the trainer moving its arms to where it hugged her around the waist, it was still too uncomfortable being in such close physical contact with the woman to really get going. At a certain point the trainer said 'that's enough for tonight.' Then he steadied the leopard and had Delila use her hand on it from the side while the cat licked its chops and snorted. Then its haunches started trembling and Delila giggled and squealed and that was that.

The next night went a bit better. They had some trouble mounting the cat, but once it got in there it hunched away. The noise and confusion among the novices died down a bit as they watched, sickened and mystified as Delila's face went from drunken giggles to pensiveness and then back again as she caught herself and realized her situation.

The third night, when that leopard saw old Delila out there on all fours with the scent rags over her he was love-struck. He reared up on his leash and when the trainer took it off the stake, the cat pulled so hard that he was jerked along with it as it clawed across the sand to pounce right up on that old whore and start humping. Only Delila didn't like it so much this time, for in its fervor, the leopard's dew-claws were beginning to sink through her dress into her back. She began screaming for them to stop it but the trainers wouldn't. Mannix and Marcellus and the rest of the novices stopped making noise and confusion, which was mainly nervous laughter anyway, and began to shift on the sand and look at one another as Delila screamed in obvious pain and the trainers motioned not to stop it.

When the old whore began frantically trying to get away from the animal, the leopard grabbed her by the back of the neck with its teeth and shook her into submission, then settled back to hunching. But the pain was too much for Delila and she kept struggling and the leopard grabbed her again and started shaking only this time it opened up enough of her jugular that she collapsed on the sand with a pool of glistening black spreading out around her head. When the leopard was finished, so was old Delila, and two of the school's slaves loaded her onto the back of a cart and went and dumped her in the river.

Mannix didn't sleep that night. He just sat on the straw-filled mattress on the stone shelf that served as a bed, his back to the corner of his cell, staring at the grungy, age-stained stucco walls with the faded names of loves quivering across it in the light of the small candle he was allowed. Affordable, surrogate loves, the peeling graffiti of two hundred years of loneliness in delicate fleckings of terra rosa amidst the dusty scratchings of fight outcomes and win-loss records ripped

73

through with cracks fissuring back to crevices that split like wounds over the rusty skeleton of Flavian masonry.

Still, using the same principle as in training cats to become maneaters, a habit pattern was established with the leopard – and indeed a wide variety of other animals – by never allowing it to come into contact with a female of its own species. With a bull or a jackass the woman rarely survived the training phase, but the System always provided more brokendown bags from the provinces who did not fully realize what they were in for until it was too late. In the arena, though, all of it had to be done up, without any coaching or intervention whatsoever. The Mob was spoiled, and the novelty itself was not enough.

Mythology generally provided the dramatic context; since Jupiter, father of the gods, often abducted girls and boys in the guise of various animals. The stockyards had a prize bull whose sole purpose was for the 'Rape of Europa' acts, always a great crowd-pleaser. One time, for a special event centered around the concubines of the surrogate king of Bithynia – who had poisoned him to get his money – the women were tied down on all fours and a troupe of chimpanzees made drunk with wine and set loose. It worked perfectly, because chimpanzees closely resembled the sculptors' renditions of satyrs, and many people actually believed they were real satyrs found in 'the deep dark forests,' as advertised.

The principle behind training maneaters was much the same as in manipulating an animal's sex drive. Both were greatly dependent upon breeding, and overcoming a wild beast's instinctive dread of humans. Mannix spent a good deal of his novitiate in the government stockyards at Laurentum outside the walls of Rome being familiarized with the psychological procedure. A lion, tiger, leopard or bear cub born in captivity who never learned to fear people was far preferable to an animal caught wild. So trainers would take a cub and begin to roughhouse with it, constantly feigning injury and letting it get the better of them. By the time the cub was half grown it was already aggressive, and Mannix himself had taken place more than a few times in the next phase of its training.

74

Wrapped in heavy padding, he would have to enter the cage and tentatively approach the animal while acting nervous. As soon as it struck out at him, he would fall on the floor seeming badly hurt. The sight of a wounded victim would generally encourage any aggressive animal to attack, and the trainer would often tie bits of meat to his padding to increase the stakes. The animals always won in these scenarios, and the trainers were careful never to strike or discipline them in any way, merely restrain them or pour buckets of water on the pair to break it up. With typical Roman pragmatism, the process served not only to train the animal, but to get Mannix and his colleagues familiar with the feel of its charge and attack.

Prospective maneaters were fed only human meat. And there was always plenty of that on hand. Later in their training, they were encouraged to attack slaves, who had their arms broken and their teeth knocked out so they could not injure it. But even if women or children were used, the animal had to be convinced that it could always win without trouble. If a slave put up too much of a fight, he was taken out with a quick spear thrust.

In these and other various ways, a trainer would get an animal perfectly conditioned to a 'habit pattern' which made it completely harmless to himself or any other person save one exposed to the specific conditions under which it was used to killing and eating prey. The better trainers prided themselves on being able to take their lions or leopards for walks past the antelope herds, or into butcher shops, without any reaction at all from the beasts. Some claimed that they would starve to death if they left them there because the cats would not recognize the meat as edible.

In truth, Mannix knew training stags to pull chariots was probably a harder feat than training a maneater, due to the different brain-electrical makeup of animals that eat meat in general; and as a carnivore grows more confident, it also grows more aggressive. But he also knew that the old-time bestiarii, in their cups of an evening, denigrating the newcomers for degrading their noble profession by training animals to rape women, were simply forgetting that they themselves had been criticized in much the same way by the still-earlier generations of bestiarii for training maneaters.

X

The lines around her mouth were dug in further, the little bitterness cracks starting around her lips. The skin across her cheekbones and nose had grown porous with the sun, and the crow's feet digging in beneath her big almond eyes, without makeup, painfully showed. Picking absently at a strand of curiously un-dyed gray before her crossed eyes, Julia Soaemias reminded herself to reprimand Omphale; perhaps have her whipped. And yet she wasn't cruel as a general rule, except perhaps to herself.

But she was still magnificent. Perhaps even moreso now. With her smells turned from lavender and yeast to velvet and musk.

She squinted up into the sky, gigantic icebergs of cloud jostling slowly overhead across a delicate field of deep blue celeste. Sunlight and shadow osmotized and receded around the court, its blue-veined Pentelic paving alternately warm yellow and cold gray with their passing. Staged with palms planted in great bronze pots, their fronds rustled in the breeze, and the pink and white oleanders in the vases about the peristyle gave off their fresh scent.

Her gaze wandered across the vast square, the fountain in its center an amazing confusion of white marble figures with Odysseus and his mariners in the act of blinding Polyphemus – the sailors just over life-size, the cyclops twenty feet long. The peristyle surrounding the space was contained by a surge of great buildings. To her left through its Numidian orange marble columns, instead of a back wall, a second portico of thirty-foot gray Egyptian granite monoliths led into the colossal banquet hall, the pediment of its smooth-faced, gabled bulk rising one hundred and twenty feet above the roof of the peristyle with a line of bronze-latticed windows spaced high across. Over the soft rasping whisper of the whisk brooms in the square and the occasional cry of a gull arcing off overhead, she could hear the busy clatter of silver and the distance-hushed voices of the slaves through the open portico leading into the hall as they made ready for the coming banquet.

To her right, the rear face of the throne room rose a hundred and fifty feet, flanked on either side by the basilica and the 'lararium' – the chapel of the household gods – to form the tripartite block of the official public wing of the Palace fronting onto the Forum in the valley below. Behind her stretched the two-storied flank of the office wing with passage through to the second fountain court with its temple-graced island and its fat old swans, some of whose predecessors were not only given names but state funerals. Beyond it stretched the stadium garden terraced out from the hill slope.

But over the roof of the long block of waiting rooms lining the peristyle on the side of the square straight ahead of her, she could see what pleased her the most – the canopy tops of the tremendous umbrella pines hovering frosty lime in the sunshine from the old garden behind the Temple of Apollo outside the Palace grounds. As any good Roman would, she liked order and axial symmetry, but she also had a fondness for gardens gone to seed – that slow revenge of nature upon the hand which tried to control it. She smiled at a magpie perched warbling in one of the trees. Staring at the temple's handsome rear entablature and one of the old bronze griffons perched on the corner of its sun-warmed terracotta-tiled roof, she lifted the beaker to her lips, and recalled the prayer of the poet upon Augustus' dedication of the building two and a half centuries ago . . .

'Grant, son of Latona, that I may enjoy what I have with good health and, I pray, with sound mind, and that my old age may not be squalid and not without the lyre.'

Rome . . . she'd spent the best years of her life here. Not only in this city but here, in the Domus Augustiana. Reflecting upon the verse, she appreciated Horace's use of the lyre as a metaphor for the poetry of love. For if her last years had been devoid of love, she would ensure that their ending be not devoid of its poetry.

She looked up again into the clouds tumbling volcanic in mute, slow-motion eruptions above, coming together to threaten rain. Mannix had taught her about clouds. About clouds and the way a herd of sheep trickling down a yellow-grass hillside could transport one a thousand years back in time to where the pipes of Pan were audible in the leaves of the poplar trees. He had taught her about clouds and trees and the way sunlight danced across the rocks in a river. And he had held her and kissed her and made her thighs turn to butter but she had taught him a thing or two as well.

But had she ever told him about the real things, the true things for her? About the way sunlight spills off of the greave of a particularly pleasing piece of architecture. Or the reassuring curve of a hamstring on a refined Greek bronze.

When she watched him this morning, when the bear had him by the shoulder she put her fingernails into the thigh of Prixus so that they drew blood and the champion gladiator winced in pain. And through her drink dulled senses at present, the feeling of fear and desire the thought of him elicited still stung in her bowels just as his eyes did eighteen years before – the day her fear of neither man, beast, nor devils gave way to a birthday present who was all three.

When he left her that last time over an inconsequential little slave boy who wasn't at all being hurt and now would never be hurt again – but no, she had not wanted that. Would never have wished for that. And he didn't leave her over him, anyway. It wasn't that. It couldn't have been that.

For a brood mare like Julia Soaemias, not to mention a bestiarius, that was a bit hard to swallow. Beyond the simple feel and orgasming of it, sex was a game, an athletic contest, an arena. An outlet for the demons in her smooth meaty thighs and her firm, prominent breasts. And little Demetrius was no innocent himself. He'd spilled his seed as well as his stupidly-smiling gasps over her skin after his whippings time and again.

But Mannix had taken a ridiculous, prudish dislike to it. And she'd held her tongue to keep from accusing him of a weakness for lithesome youths. But no, it wasn't that either. It was just that he didn't want her anymore. That he'd tired of her. When their exile added insult to his injury, she was forced to let him go. And when she returned with the regime three years before, her pride forced her to leave him alone.

But it was really none of those things. It was before all of that. Long before. He left her from the start. He didn't leave her; he was never with her. He never loved her. And that still stung with the fear and the desire in her stomach. And it still caused her to do things that hurt herself.

For, through it all, she had reached a point where she could no more trust or control her emotions than she could the thoughts that raced and spun through her mind each night. She had been through the drink and the drugs and the countless lovers, but none of it had helped. And she had been through the police reports and the private detectives and she knew about his little whore in Trastevere and she'd dreamed up so many ways of killing her but she knew that that wouldn't help either. Her mind and her heart and her body had become a battleground of confusion, where love and hate, loss and gain, osmotized and receded like the sunlight and shadow in the marbled court before her.

Perhaps it was her blood. Some kind of Romano-Syriac confusion she was always destined for while growing up in a world of concessions, half-measures, dubieties and compromise. A world of political brokering, arranged marriages, and people who didn't believe in anything except their endless need to play the power game. A world that, from birth, rendered her less and less able to trust, seized in the game's unending lies, its daily criticism, its demands for total attention. A world that, by now, had rendered her chronically drunk or opiated for getting through the day's reverses – its losses – by inches, of whatever it was she ever had or was.

Her parents had not loved each other. Her late father, Julius Avitus, was Roman. Her mother, Julia Maesa, Syro-Roman. Her grandfather, Julius Bassianus, was high priest of the Syrian sun god. But Bassianus no more believed in his god than in the man in the moon he used to laugh about while fondling her in his lap on those nights when she tried to endure what she could not forgive . . . the slat-shades going down, the painted little-girl room, the hand she held the hand that held her down. But religion was all politics to him – keep the Bedouins under control and the trade routes secure.

But Mannix was of ancient Latin stock. And he had the darkness and the strangeness in his blood which was much darker and much stranger than any hoax sham behavior her grandfather, the high priest of the Ba'al, could cook up. There were no concessions, half-measures, dubieties or compromises with him. Mannix received his Being from his Doing. And, as the poet said, love was the shadow that ripened the wine.

But she was beyond all of that now. Had been for years, really.

Oh, perhaps she could still find herself – when the drugs or the drink put her in the rare mood for it – find herself in some casual, athletic way liking the ride up and down some random, stubborn, marble-hard member until she softened it into the flaccid, faintly ridiculous and repulsive thing she had always held them to be. Something rather like what one of the Palace stable hands might feel upon exercising a stallion until it's frothing and docile. But real joy in life was something she had felt only once, and only for a short while.

Yet there was this place on Crete that she remembered from a girlhood trip there. An old Minoan Palace crumbling in the sun, pines on long slanted mountains all around. Autumn sunlight and cold, purple rainclouds; mid-afternoon. Her face had suddenly emptied and became hopeful as she gazed with melancholy joy upon those flaking frescoes of high-breasted girls and thick-thighed boys, their strong, lithe, charming bodies tempered in direct contact with the bull over which they leapt and tumbled in simple, certain and graceful movements.

One panel in particular caught her eye, a fishing scene, youths in a barque with the fish below. Out of nowhere one of the fish took wing and leapt from the water in total disregard of the bounds of its nature. Casting it off, striving to break the bonds of its fate and to take flight; upon seeing it, Julia Soaemias had for the first time caught a glimpse of the light.

81

But her mother's voice had called her away. And the glimpse had flickered, and no sooner begun to fade.

Her mother was always calling her away, she smiled to herself. Just as she would soon again, with the assassin's blade. Or would it perhaps be poison? An arranged accident? She frowned at the thought of her body burst open like a pomegranate like so many she'd seen on the sand of the arena. Poison might be prettier. An accident might be an interesting surprise. Or she could do it the old Roman way, do it herself in the bath with her own blade. She could starve herself in a chair overlooking the stadium garden as her aunt had. It would have a certain symbolic touch to it, seeing as they had met there, and he would be certain to hear about it. But she was not melodramatic as a general rule.

She could overdose on the drugs her doctors gave her. She almost had several times, and had felt herself slipping into a not-entirely unpleasant middle ground between life and death. But it would be unsporting. And, whatever else she might be, Julia Soaemias was no coward.

Essentially she found that it didn't much matter to her either way. She had already done it herself – simply orchestrated it like a play, and left the final act open. For Stoicism was a religion with only one sacrament. The clouds were closing above and she felt the first drops of rain.

XI

Across the street at the Amphitheater, the base of the plaster rock escarpments had been sealed with pitch on the inside by the stage technicians, as had the central row of trapdoor panels and the platform elevator shafts left exposed after the remains of the whores had been brought down. The pitch was a temporary measure that would suffice for the duration of the next act, as were the flood gates that had been established across the Gates of Life and Death. For pipes in the perimeter wall had been opened and were currently gushing water that was gradually filling the snaking ravine of sand winding through the center of the rock escarpments up to about ten feet – more than sufficient to float a decent-sized boat down it.

After lunch, Mannix walked back through the tunnel under the street and up the ramps to floor level. The barley meade had kicked the opium back up in his system, and he stepped up wobbly on a bench to get a look at the show over the flood gate secured across the Gate of Death.

The boat was being assembled with pegs by stage technicians while the water slowly filled up around them, gushing around their knees, their waists, then floating them along with the developing barque until they had it together and steadied for 'Ulysses' and his mariners, twelve in all, to jump in. Others tossed in oars, and the boat got rockingly underway shortly before the Bestiarius arrived. Mannix shook his head in admiration for the stage technicians, some standing on the bench beside him dripping wet, their chests still heaving with the effort of making ready the barque. He looked up with contempt at the stands and the Mob swaying and singing and laughing without a thought in their heads for the effort and ingenuity just displayed.

The clouds had finished closing above, and springtime thunder rumbled across the sky. The boat had made it about a third of the way across the arena without anything happening. The crowd was growing quiet, the tension beginning to mount. Ulysses and his men were Thracians, prisoners of war from a recent uprising against the heavy taxation of the Black Sea ports. Good fighters all, whatever awaited them would be no easy matter.

Suddenly a murmur started across the stands as ghastly apparitions began appearing on the rock escarpments – figures in white skull masks such as the Charons wore, but also in diaphanous white robes. The darkening sky above lent itself to the ghostly topic, the atmosphere inside the Amphitheater providing a shadowy contrast to these white skull-headed figures on the rocks who began lifting their arms in slow motion and waving dreamily at the sailors.

Out of nowhere something swooped down fast over the barque in a high-pitched scream that shattered the hypnotic quality of the scene, startling the crowd. Then other figures came suddenly screaming down through the blue mist of atmosphere above the arena. The crowd gave a gasp of surprise as they beheld flying shades in fluttering white robes which obscured the harnesses and cables by which they were being swung from cranes that had arced out from the catwalks where technicians were manipulating them.

The mariners began rowing for their lives, Ulysses shouting commands, drawing his sword. The flying figures had produced daggers from their rippling robes and were swiping and slashing at the men as they swooped screaming by. Within seconds the sail of the boat with its huge green eye motif was in tatters and falling down around the Thracians, draping over their shoulders and heads, blinding them. One of them arced with a shout and pitched into a reddening swirl in the water. The ghouls on the rocks were still swinging their arms in slow motion, swaying and moaning to the sounds of the hydraulic organs playing strange strains of Hadean music which echoed throughout the Amphitheatre.

At their captain's command, three of the sailors on either side dropped their oars and picked up bows, one of them just as quickly dropping it and backing, clutching his slit throat as he flipped over the side of the barque to join his comrade floating face down in the river. But then the Mob went wild as Ulysses got a lucky shot up through the lower abdomen of one of the harpies sweeping in fast, its momentum impaling itself on his sword up to the hilt, knocking him down and ripping the blade out of his hand as it swung on past and out over the stands in a shrill piercing scream and an arc of bloodspray that speckled faces and white togas in thousands of droplets and then began convulsing in its death throes shaking and rattling the harness and jerking the cable out of the technicians' control. The point of the sword protruding from its lower back, the figure sailed low over the Patrician section pinwheeling on the cable, its robe all caught up in the harness revealing it to be female. All of them were females.

Meanwhile all hell had broken loose. The boat was careening in the water, its bow scraping along the plaster rock escarpments. Two of the ghouls on shore ran up and tied it fast, one of them at the expense of an arrow shot at point blank range through an eye socket of his skull mask. He spun and fell with a jerky reflexive movement and then slid and bumped down the rocks into the water where he disappeared in a gentle billowing of white robes. The ghouls on the rocks, all males, started throwing lassoes at the sailors, trying to pull their 'souls' into the land of the Shades.

Ulysses unbound a bundle of light javelins and, with a fistful in one hand, took aim at anything wearing a white robe. Thracians were experts with the javelin, and his peltast ancestors doubtless harried Pompey's Legions. His first cast at one of the harpies missed, arcing to deflect off of the double layer of netting that had been pulled up around the perimeter wall masts. The next crashed through the ribcage of one of the females who convulsed and fell limp in the harness dripping a long-falling red gloop.

There was quite a fight on, the harpies still sweeping in fast; the mariners were outnumbered but getting kills. Ulysses concentrated urgently on the ghouls, flinging the javelins quickly and accurately to both sides of the barque. The rock escarpments provided cover, however, and the ghouls raced to and fro, their robes rippling as they ducked and dove like demons behind the realistic chunks of painted plaster.

A lucky lasso cast landed around one of the sailors' necks, the man's eyes bulging with a gasp as two skull-masked ghouls sprang jumping from rock to rock to grab the rope end with the lasso thrower and dig their heels in, jerking and scraping and throwing their bodies backwards as they pulled on the rope. The sailor was yanked tripping over the side of the boat to land with a crash on the rock escarpment, Ulysses lunging madly for the rope with a sword, one foot in the boat, the other out. A harpie screamed down and lacerated his back on the fly-by and he arced with pain but still managed to cut the rope. He couldn't get the mariner back into the boat, however, and the unconscious man slipped limply into the water.

The barque was now out of control bumping in circles down the ravine. There were only five sailors left, but the ghouls on the rocks were considerably thinned, many lying scattered about with arrows protruding from their white robes and long blood trails streaming down over the dusty yellow rocks into the darkening water. The sailors were fast and accurate; good fighters imbued with the urgency of their situation. Their heads turned furiously in every direction with bows at the ready, for they knew that if they survived they had a decent chance to get hired on permanently. A few persistent harpies were still coming, half a dozen others drifting limply in circles over the grandstands, their arms and legs dangling lifelessly. One of them started her arc around the bowl of the Amphitheater to gather momentum.

Ulysses kept an eye on her as he grabbed a bow and knocked a shaft, his back streaming blood. As she turned in and started her banshee screaming dive, he slowly drew back, hearing in his ear the creaking of the bow as he stretched with concentrated strength, then the whining of the string over the crowd noise, buzzing in his ear like a bee as it was pulled to the utmost ounce of its taughtness and he waited . . . waiting . . . the harpie closing fast, her face white with makeup changing its expression as she realized what had happened, the scream changing from one of attack to one of horror until . . . ten feet out . . . he whispered . . . "Eat this bitch" and rocketed the shaft with all of his might into her open mouth crashing through her teeth and out the back of her throat throwing himself to the deck as she screamed past overhead in a doppler of horrid guttural roaring.

The arrow gave a little hop in the mist of blood left behind, and then clattered onto the deck beside his ear. The crowd went insane. People tore at their clothes, midgets danced in the aisles. Patricians turned open-mouthed and goggle-eyed at each other, Senators politely applauding and even the Emperor, slumped in his seat, clapped languidly.

Ulysses lifted his sword and gave a victory shout and, with two of his mariners, jumped onto the rocks in pursuit of the remaining ghouls. The other three mariners went ashore on the opposite side of the ravine to complete the rout. The scattered few ghouls on either side were running in a panic trying to claw their way back into the trapdoors in the plaster rock escarpments, but the doors remained closed; and Ulysses and his sailors hacked them down without mercy.

The entire Amphitheater was quaking with the continual roaring of the crowd, none of whom could hear themselves scream, but would go home hoarse and just as drained and exhausted at the end of the day as if they'd worked for their bread, their stomach muscles knotted and aching, in their ears the continual noise of the sea. Ulysses and his five remaining mariners stood on the rocks, their swords raised and streaming, the harpies above dangling limp and dripping like rain-doused dandelions. The barque slowly shifted in the water, funeral barge of six of his men who lay in pools of arterial blood, one with his neck grinning from ear to ear, another bobbing open-eyed in the river around the billowing robes of the ghouls floating like gigantic water lilies.

XII

Standing atop the bench in the Gate of Death, Mannix whistled through his teeth, glad to see that courage and resourcefulness still sold. He knew the Thracians were assured a job, with better odds, for as long as they lasted. And well-deserved, as far as he was concerned.

"Bravo!" he shouted, before stepping stiffly down from the bench.

The stage technicians were motioning him and the other backstage spectators – mainly arena attendants and third-string gladiators – into the lateral arches, across which they established smaller flood gates. Then they pulled the beams holding the large barriers across the Gates of Death and Life opposite, and Mannix watched behind the lower barrier of a lateral arch as a great mouth of water rushed through the corridor and into the piazza outside the Amphitheater where it began swirling in the myriad system of drains set in the travertine pavement.

One of the dead ghouls came rushing out with the water, bobbing and bouncing helplessly as a child on a wave in a billowing of diaphanous white robes all caught up in and around and molded to his skull face until he was simply plopped onto the pavement and the water retreated into the drain holes and an old fruit vendor across the street shielded her eyes and gives a cry.

On the arena floor, attendants worked in the sucking mire of wet sand disassembling the plaster rock escarpments. Others took apart the boat and carted off the dead Thracians to the butchers in the Spolarium, and unharnessed the limp harpies from the cables the sailors had lowered. Beneath the floor, technicians scraped and gouged away the pitch sealing the seams of the central panel of trapdoors and concentric elevator platforms. The water had been dripping and, in some places, pouring continually; but it drained efficiently enough through the moats and sewage channels beneath the stands. Though it helped clean and cool the underground world to an extent, the humidity it brought intensified the smell down there and lent itself to the mosquitoes and flies that bred in the animal pens.

It was raining now, a continual shaft contained by the oculus seeming to fall in slow motion, like ice, into the atmosphere of the Amphitheater. The Senatorial Class and most of the Patricians were filing out of the stands on their way home or to taverns for lunch, Indian umbrella sellers crowding the exits for easy sells. Only the Mob remained in the stands, due mainly to the fact that their seating was an unticketed free-for-all, and easy to lose. Baskets of food were opened, flasks of wine produced, and more andabatae herded back out onto the floor. The plebs would picnic and watch third-string gladiators fight it out during the mid-day break, booing and catcalling and pelting them with chicken bones.

Beneath the stands, a cluster of Jews huddled in a corner around the emaciated figure of their Rabbi mumbling lamentations, his rheumy eyes searching the blackened stones of the ceiling for Gabriel to come fluttering down. Part of a sect that fomented a recent uprising in Palestine, the men had all been slotted for more important events throughout the series, but the women, children and old would serve as fodder for the novelty acts between events. The room stank of human refuse, blood and torch smoke.

Other men, wounded prisoners of war or condemned criminals, sat or lay scattered about. There were no toilet facilities and the crowd of victims had been kept there for over a week. With the lack of oxygen in the room and the sickening stink, most were close to unconsciousness, their heads wobbling and jerking drunkenly, suffocation a blink away in the battered state of hunger and dehydration they were in.

Their heads snapped up as the heavy bolts slid back on the door and the brutal cell-block guards came rushing into the room, loud and violent, yelling, snarling, kicking people on the floor and slapping them with the flat of their sword blades.

Their leader – a hardened, veteran employee of the Flavian Amphitheater – motioned to the prisoners of war and the criminals, his fingers beckoning, his voice bored.

"Get your filthy asses up. Form a line, single file, and follow me."

The Jews would have to wait. If they died before their stage call tomorrow, they would simply be cut up and fed to the beasts.

The men stood groggily, eyeing each other with suspicion. Most were hurt with wounds not yet healed from a month of bewildered travel over the Alps. Taken from a world of wood to one of blood-stained marble, their brows had furrowed with the continual widening of their eyes, their gibberish of language trickled down to the silence of ultimate acceptance. They filed out past the guards prodding them with drawn swords that pricked skin and drew blood, moving up the ramps guided by the torches burning in brackets along the walls.

Above, in an assembly area, a long oaken table stood strewn with weapons. The prisoners of war and criminals that were herded from the cell below were instructed to strip naked, those hesitating quickly lashed into submission.

"You will oil your bodies and arm yourselves with the light javelin," said the chief of guards, as he paced in front of them.

A blade flashed in torchlight and an arm thunked sickeningly onto the table, the petty thief backing horrified as the spurting stump sprayed across the faces and chests of the line of men who jerked, flinched and yelled cringing away from the crimson fount, the chief raising his finger and wagging it back and forth, smiling softly.

"Do not pick up the weapons . . . until you are instructed to do so."

The thief was quickly drug out of the room and up the ramps where he and his tormenters almost knocked down Apicius the Ringmaster, who yelled "COCKsuckers!" at the troop as they lashed the poor wretch out onto the sand into a group of blindfolded andabatae swinging maces at each other. As the thief ran out, screaming and spurting blood from the stump of his arm, one of the spiked iron balls immediately caught him in the side of the head, knocking him off of his feet and out of his misery.

The Mob choked on fig pits, wine spraying from their nostrils as they laughed convulsively. Delighted by the eccentric surprise, they found it exceedingly funny. Apicius, sneering, snorted self-contentedly at this piece of unplanned showmanship and continued his walk. It would make him look only the better. For who, after all, was the Ringmaster, who the dramaturgue responsible for such a surprise?

Spotting Mannix down the corridor making his way through a congestion of circus freaks and falconers flapping with birds at their wrists, he stopped at his side. "How are you holding up?" he asked, glancing at the mass of bloody bandages protruding from the neck of the venator's paenula from where they were swathed across his shoulder and collar bone.

"I'm all right," the Bestiarius growled, irritated that any animals, even a bull and a bear, could get the better of him.

"You should get some rest, see about some fresh bandages," Apicius continued. "I have to have lunch with the Editor, the little prick. I'll see you later."

Mannix nodded, and headed down the ramp between the red fresco borders under the flickering oil braziers to the clinic, where Ulysses was lying on his stomach having his back sewn up. The surviving mariners were being tended to as well, one of them with a slit running from the corner of his mouth to his ear making the side of his face look like a dog with its fangs bared.

"You fellows put on a hell of a show," said the Bestiarius, removing his paenula with one hand and smarting at the pain. "Those harpies were hell."

A couple of groans greeted him in reply and he sat up on a table. The doctor came over and checked the movement of his shoulder, asking him if he could feel certain things, keep his arm raised under its own power and so on and so forth. Mannix winced and cursed all the while, but the doctor was under no illusion as to the amount of damage a man could take and still keep going. Satisfied with his test, he removed the blood-soaked bandages, washed the wound, and applied a fresh myrrh compress.

"You can thank your gods there's no broken bones."

"What gods?" Mannix hissed.

"Doesn't seem to be much nerve damage," the doctor continued. "The way you were kicking and scooting along with that bear when he drug you kept the puncture wounds from getting too messy. They're deep, but they'll close up quickly. Just try not to jack off too much," he said, as he re-swathed the swollen wound with new bandages. And then, raising a gray eyebrow, "Would've been better if you hadn't kicked and fought like an asshole there toward the end. Just been happy to be alive."

The Bestiarius grunted and cast a sullen look at the big Egyptians who had finally restrained him, making a mental note to catch each one of them in a dark corridor when he got well.

"Go over to the school and get some rest," the doctor continued, placing the bloody cloth bandages in the cauldron of fire burning across the room. "Sleep is the best thing right now."

Mannix nodded and the doctor slipped the paenula back over his head like a child on the way to school on a rainy day.

"Doc, give me another shot of that opium, will you?"

The doctor shook his head but complied. Walking to the cabinet, he poured a small draught of the herbal concoction into a clay cup.

The Bestiarius drained it in a gulp and shivered. "Thanks."

"And report back before the end of the day," the doctor called after him as he shuffled off down the wavering orange light of the corridor into the umber shadows.

XIII

Across the street at the Ludus Matutinus, Mannix climbed the stairwell to the third floor and walked down the colonnaded peristyle with the rain falling off to his right in the large rectangular courtyard where he trained as a novice. It was empty now. Most of the current novices were at the Amphitheater, where their jobs entailed helping with the animals and assisting the stage technicians. He stood with his hands on the balustrade feeling the strangeness of the opium and the emptiness in the rain. Memories touched him like ghosts, Delila and the leopard, too many others to count.

Born in the hills south of Rome during the reign of Commodus, his father was a centurian who died on the Danube when he was just a child. His first real memory of his father was the last time he saw him, but he still had the watery image of the huge silver breastplate shining in the sun, the smell of the woolen scarf tied tight about his father's neck, and the feel of his beard on his cheek after he lifted him high above his head. His mother was frail, and died shortly thereafter of influenza, leaving him to the hard-boned hands of his grandfather, whose farm was in the region.

They were good hands, however. For his grandfather taught him animals, and his grandmother taught him to read. And it was on their farm that he learned to love the elements of earth and air, sun and rain.

He spent most of his boyhood days in the pine forests of the Alban Hills, or helping his grandfather with the cattle and sheep. He grew up on meat and barley, fish from the streams, and the occasional wild boar they hunted in the woods – always a great occasion. He ate well, and he grew up strong.

At the age of ten, while out one day shepherding his grandfather's flock, a mountain cat pounced on one of the lambs. The sixty pound cat had sprung from a tree, and sunk its teeth into the back of the lamb's neck, and he had heard its desperate bleating.   Shot through with adrenaline, the young boy charged without thinking to throw his full weight crashing on top of the cat, which arced and flipped and grabbed his forearm with its teeth, ripping his tunic to shreds with its claws before loping away. The feel of the strength and the lightning quickness of the beast was his first lesson in technique, and he escaped with a broken arm and a bloody stomach, and a curious desire.

But the main characteristic of these years was that he grew up without any fear or preoccupation about animals. They were as natural to him from birth as the grass, fields, trees and hills that he loved. And they always remained more real to him than the humans in his life, who all left him at an early age.

His twelfth year was a trying one for the boy.   His grandmother died first, leaving the hearth a lonely winter place with his grandfather sitting by the fireside staring into its embers, and the young boy carving wood in the form of bears and deer in the corner. And then he found his grandfather one day, sitting beneath a tree with the squirrels all gathered around him. The crows had pecked his eyes out, and he drove them with a flail away from the big lifeless hulk. He burned his grandfather in a clearing in the woods, and sat staring at the fire late into the night, watching the flames rise and disappear above the towering pines into the black starry sky.

After his grandfather's death he began to wander, much of the time at night, walking softly through the mist curling around the treetrunks in the halflight. And he was afraid until he learned how not to be afraid, and came to understand the darkness and find in it a kind of light.

In those years he grew wild, his hair long, and the animals he fed on he often caught with his bare hands. One day a county tribune rode by in passing with a contingent of surveyors who were dividing up land for legionary pension allotments. A tax collector and minor civil servant, the tribune saw the condition of the farm and the boy that lived there. He saw the skulls of the animals strewn about the clearing, and the pelts the boy wore. He saw how the boy caught fish with his bare hands and strangled small game. But he saw something else in the boy, as well. Something of quality forged by hardship.

"How would you like to hunt animals for money?" the tribune asked. "For glory," he added. "In Rome." And then, raising an eyebrow, "In the Arena."

As his aquamarine eyes gazed down into the large courtyard beneath him where the rain was rippling across puddles in the sand, Mannix remembered his first sight of the city. It seemed but yesterday, though it was twenty years ago. From a distance nothing but temple-clad hills and a maze of terracotta rooftops, on the Via Tusculana he was funneled into a flood of disparate humanity and, once through the old Republican arch of the Porta Querquetulana, it was as if Pandora's Box had exploded all around him. Taken from a world of wood and hearth-smoke to one of brick, marble and madness, he reared like a wild horse on the cart and had to be restrained by the contingent of surveyors. But the tribune, whom the boy had come to trust, assured him that it was Rome, and all was as it should be.

That night he spent in the modest atrium-style house of the civil servant in the vast garden zone of the Pincian hill, amidst the little-known familial atmosphere of the man, his wife and daughter. But it was not to last. The next morning, the tribune took him on foot through the madcap city to arrive at the piazza of the great Flavian Amphitheater. Rising vast and huge, its weathered white travertine jagged with the sunlight and shadow of late afternoon, the stadium's upper arcades were ranked with hundreds of statues, its attic story sparkling with the gigantic bronze ornamental shields staged around it.

Throngs of people packed its entrances and spilled out into the surrounding square, where the colossal bronze statue of Helios rose a hundred and twenty feet into the cerulean blue, with seagulls cruising playfully about its head. Behind it, the smoke of incense drifted from iron braziers spaced at intervals across the high podium of the temple of Venus and Rome, weaving gently on a light breeze through the forest of fluted columns standing sixty feet and shimmering like pillars of carved sugar in the raking sunlight.

The boy had never seen such things, nor imagined they could exist. And neither had he seen such a crowd. Everywhere people, coming and going, chattering and chirping. They coagulated around the base of the colossal statue where the tents of merchants selling wine and sweetmeats lay bunched around its feet like the Sun God's discarded undergarments. And then streams of them trickled out again and lunched under multi-colored umbrellas, amused by tumblers, musicians and dancers hoping to be tossed a few coppers. A constant ebb and flow of humanity, they thronged about the basin of the conical marble fountain of the Meta Sudans at the intersection of the Via Triumphalis and the Via Sacra, the water sparkling and frothing as it cascaded down the sides of the giant cone fashioned after those around which the chariots raced in the Circus Maximus.

A woman in a slave-borne litter eyed him beneath her bronze-colored eyelids, a soft, sultry smile curving her lips at the fineness of his form. And, as if a strange omen which the boy could not possibly perceive, a lone priest stood before a sacrificial altar amongst the towering columns of the Temple of Venus and Rome, his hands raised palms-upward in salute. The tribune walked him across the piazza to the Ludus Matutinus, the Bestiarii School, where an acquaintance of his named Avidius Lepidus was the director.

A hard-boned, hard-drinking man who had been a top-knotch bestiarius in the arena under Antoninus Pius, Lepidus had a talk with the young Mannix and told him that he would send him through the school if he would agree to serve him as a bondsman for the next ten years. If he survived, he would begin to receive wages based on his performance.

The boy spent the first four years learning how to handle everything from elephants to foxes. He learned how to dodge and pole-vault, and was sent out against leopards tied to bulls by long ropes to sharpen his agility and peripheral vision. Acrobatics were no small part of his training, and he was often made to lay down in the sand while a boar or a bull was set upon him, learning how to kip to his feet at the last instant. His instructors used him to irritate wild animals by having him almost let them catch him and then vault over a low fence or behind a wooden shield. With typical Roman pragmatism, the repetitive stunt served the dual purpose of making the animals mean for the criminals in the arena, as well as training the novice.

In time, his real talent began to show through – the strength and quickness, the violent technique – and on selection day he was made a 'Venator,' a hunter. At this stage, his training progressed to fighting animals bare-handed, learning the best techniques to strangle them or break their necks. He learned how to blind big cats with a cape and then crack their backs with a hammer blow from his fist. He fought bears with a cape in one hand to distract them and a sword in his other. His interest in, and experience of the beasts grew with the matrix of scars across his body, and his skill was put to use in training them as well.

But every bit as important as the training of the mind and the development of skill through technique – the hundreds of hours spent on acrobatics, dodging, vaulting and kipping – the study of animals, their breeding and behavioral traits – the weaponry training with swords, shields, spears and capes – there was always the gut-wrenching discipline of the physical workout. Lepidus shouted them through hundreds of pushups, pull-ups and leg raises every day save the one day in the classroom and one full rest day each week they were allowed with a small allotment of wine (which the director rationed to them with miserly thrift, despite reserving a liter of the better vintages in the school's cellar for himself each night).

Lepidus believed in keeping his bestiarii slim and tough, prizing quickness, agility and the well-placed killing blow over raw power. For no matter how strong a man is or becomes, he will never be a match for an animal of even his own weight. And Lepidus knew from experience that diet mixed with training was a key ingredient.

Gladiators were fed tremendous amounts of barley and meat. Meat for strength, and barley to develop a layer of fat around the organs which would provide some protection from the puncture and laceration wounds of blades. As such they were strong, but sometimes unwieldy creatures, especially as they slowed a bit with age and their wounds. Often heavily armored, they needed power, a certain amount of quickness, but mainly technique within something like a three-meter radius. For with even the lightly-armed Retiarius or Thracian, their field of play was much less than that of a bestiarius, who might cover the entire floor of the amphitheater multiple times in a morning's venatione, fighting all the way.

So Lepidus reduced their amounts of bread and barley, supplementing with fruits and vegetables, meanwhile keeping their meat intake at a decent rate, but feeding them more chicken, fish and lean pork than beef. He also ran them until their tongues drug the ground, jogging them down the 'Via Triumphalis' to the Circus Maximus each morning. Singing school songs while passing the throngs coming in off the 'Via Appia' on their way to work, amidst the strange spectacle of the vast empty stadium which held a capacity crowd of four hundred thousand, they would continue their jog around the richly ornamented Spina – the long 'spine' running down the center of the track encrusted with colossal statues, columns, fountains and even a small temple dedicated to Venus, patron goddess of charioteers.

Roughly eight hundred meters around each of the 'Metae' – the thirty-foot marble-veneered cones which kept the Spina from being damaged by chariot smash-ups on the turns – Lepidus jogged along with them, singing in his grandmother's Oscan dialect and denigrating slow, fat-assed gladiators and how they always lost in bar fights to bestiarii.

On the brilliant sand of summer mornings soon to turn rabid with Roman heat, he made his novices run windsprints, sprint backwards and side to side. He made them perform agility drills where they ran in place with high knees and then hit the ground at his command, then popped back up, and then down; running in place all the while with their knees at the level of their waists, up, down, the sweat running in streams over their faces into their eyes, blinding them with the glare of the summer sun on the torturous white marble and glinting bronze, everything heat and misery, the novices vomiting and collapsing, Lepidus' harsh voice echoing through the caverns of the empty stadium as he made them fast-crawl forwards and side-to-side, and then crawl backwards in a line the entire five hundred and forty-meter length of one of the track sides until their hamstrings cramped up and their guts tied in knots and they collapsed and rolled onto their backs.

Sometimes the emperor's teenage nieces and their little nubile friends would watch the sunburned boys, often wearing no more than loincloths, suffering in the Circus below. From the shade of the rose-marbled hemicyclical terrace of the Palatine Palace looming above the northern stands, they would drink iced lemonades and giggle as one of them vomited or collapsed on the sand. They particularly watched the tall one with the dark wavy hair that shone streaked with gold in the sun, and his blond, olive-skinned friend.

But the two boys watched them as well, particularly the little Julia Soaemias, the Emperor's niece, whom they snuck glances at through a grate in the perimeter wall of the Amphitheater when they could get away from their tasks for a moment – the memory of whom they subsequently stroked in their cells at night.

And, indeed, Mannix learned more than how to dodge, pole-vault and kip to his feet at the last instant to avoid an animal's rush at the Ludus Matutinus. And he learned more than simply how to hunt and how to kill. He also learned how to love, or at least a surrogate version, with the slave girls that were brought into the school once a fortnight for the novices. But he also occasionally found himself on the obligatory end of that not-always unpleasant form of bondage.

Though his personality never quite recovered from the years of loneliness and wildness spent as a boy, it was just that particular quality of prowess and shyness that made Patrician women seek his company. But when one of them with buttermilk brown skin, big black hair and big almond eyes took a liking to him, the trouble began.

XIV

The thoughts sickened him, and he let his memories fade like tears in the rain. For though he had learned many things down in that courtyard below him – many things about animals and people and how to stay alive – over and above it all, what had he learned down there was how to die. He had learned how to deal lightly with death, giving it no chance ever and denying its importance so that it had no status, shape nor dignity. He had learned how to treat death like an old entrusted friend so that, when she touched him, she would never know that she'd scored. But mostly what he had learned was that there were many things that could kill a man, and that death was only one of them.

He raised his eyes from the courtyard where the rain rippled in the puddles across the wet-darkened sand. Over the sloping roof of the opposite peristyle, he could see the Temple of Claudius looming above the black-green cypresses on the Caelian Hill behind the school, its marble pediment run with wet streaks. He lifted his hands from the balustrade and walked down to the end of the long barracks block to the urinal where he stopped to use the facilities, his eyes wandering across the graffiti scrawled on the wall about the school director's sexual preferences.

Then he took some time, and finally found his old cell, its current occupant, like all the rest, at the Amphitheater. He sat wearily on the straw mattress atop the stone bench that served as a bed. Not being the sentimental type, he wondered if he was getting soft with age, for he hadn't been in this room or even thought about being in this room for ten years.

The crude little wooden statuettes of the Lares and Penates in their niche in the wall reminded him dimly of his childhood, the wax-dripped stub of candle, ashes of incense breeze-scattered about their feet. Traceries of spiderwebs draped the back of the niche, microcosmic mysteries, mandalas of infinity, tiny lattice-work windows wavering in his opium-dilated pupils.

His eyelids drooping, he looked about the room. The stucco walls were still grungy, and stained with age, white above the typical four-foot red border. They were still painted with the pathetic graffiti of loneliness, and still ripped through with cracks and fissures.

He put the hood of his paenula over his head with his good hand, and groaned as he lay down. Adjusting his arms beneath the cloak, a slight chill passed over him. A stillness filled the room, and his flesh stirred in the shadows. He remembered the girls who had come and gone, and a Celt named Rhiannon who had sung as he lay with her. He thought of Julia Soaemias and the note she sent, which started him remembering it all again.

Why now? Had she thought he was going to die? And, if so, still why? After all these years.

Despite himself, his thoughts traveled back over those years. After meeting on her birthday that night and their subsequent several months' affair, she was married and sent off to Syria. Four years went by during which he grew in both fame and stature. When he was twenty-two and his years of bondage dwindling at the school, Septimius Severus took his wife and two sons on campaign in Britain, where there was trouble with the Caledonians. The real reason behind the move was to stop Caracalla and Geta constantly quarrelling; for it was well-known that they were to become joint emperors upon their father's death, and the two hated each other for it.

But it was then, after those four years of separation, that Julia Soaemias returned to Rome, where her mother Julia Maesa had assumed the surrogate matriarchy over the capital. She came with her son but devoid of her husband, who had died, some say by poison, in his post. By this time, Mannix no longer lived at the school. As his years of bondage drew to a close and Lepidus groomed him for his independence, he had begun to receive wages which increased with his success and popularity.

He soon thereafter began supplementing his income by placing bets on himself with the bookies that thrived on the chariot racing and the spectacles, allowing him to finance the apartment on the Argiletum. And it was on one windy misty rainy afternoon that Julia Soaemias stood at his door in a drab hooded cloak which obscured a desirably revealing stola beneath.

Hungover and hurt, Mannix let her in the door, for Erithrea was watching from her usual post across the hall, and Romans were terrible gossips. As she crossed the threshold and he closed the door behind her, Julia Soaemias remained standing in the shadowy alcove where a small candle burned before his small votive statues of the Lares and Penates in their niche in the wall. She smiled at him with her mouth but not with her eyes. For the light had gone out of them and whatever twisted tenderness had been there before was there no longer.

At age twenty-eight, she had lost neither her voluptuous appeal, nor her lavender and yeast smell. Yet something had changed, as if that blankly vacuous, lost look he'd registered in her face four years before each time that she realized it was not to be, had hardened with the lines around her mouth. And it was then that Mannix first began to realize that he had a problem on his hands.

All that afternoon, his apartment rattled with the rain and the grinding of their bodies which in the evening gave way to candlelight and lost staring after she implored him once more to go away. The next morning she was gone, returned to Syria where she turned her obsessiveness on her son.

Within three years Severus was dead and his wife and her two sons – now co-emperors – returned to Rome, where Caracalla proceeded to stab his brother Geta to death in the Palace as he sought refuge in their mother's arms. Increasingly dangerous and paranoid, Caracalla went on to undertake a series of frontier wars with the fixation that he was Alexander the Great. Four years later, in the midst of this chaos, Julia Soaemias came back to Rome with her ten year-old son.

Aged thirty-five then, the light had further changed, and the sicknesses burrowed in with the lines around her mouth. Yet, though she had thickened slightly with age, her smooth, meaty thighs, her prominent breasts, and her heart-shaped buttocks were all still there. In the ensuing months, their meetings were orchestrated away from the Palace, often in the Gardens of Sallust, or other imperial properties on the outskirts of the city. They swam in the sea off Capri, and Mannix spent an offseason growing sick with nightlife and parties.

As to be expected, her son was a spoiled little brat whom the Bestiarius curled his lip at as he watched him gravitating to the plethora of cosmetic subterfuge littering the carts of the Isaic priestesses who raised him. An aged Julia Domna was still empress, for Caracalla had had his wife, still in Britain, murdered shortly after taking the purple. But his mother sat and stared a lot, and her sister Julia Maesa was mainly running the show, setting the stage to have one of her two grandsons inherit the throne. For Julia Mamaea, the shy, bewildered and unattractive younger sister of Soaemias, was married and had a son as well – the four year-old Alexianus.

Temptation and deceit the order of the day, it was then that the country boy Mannix began to learn that the pitfalls of the city were extremely real. Yet, even so, he did not allow himself to take Julia Soaemias seriously. Like death, he thought she could not touch him. And, anyway, she did not appeal to him much beyond the bed. When she brought a young Greek slave named Demetrius into it one afternoon in hopes of livening things up, Mannix finally said 'Enough.' Within a month, Caracalla – who had lasted for five years – dismounted from his horse and was stabbed by a page in a ditch while urinating aside a dusty Mesopotamian road.

Opellius Macrinus – his powerful Praetorian Prefect who had orchestrated the assassination – took the purple. As the remainder of the Severan court were to be allowed to return to Syria with most of their wealth intact, amid the chaotic atmosphere of the Palatine undergoing a change of the guard – and with Julia Domna starving herself to death in a chair on the dais overlooking the garden where she'd casually watched him and Marcellus hunt thirteen years before – Mannix was summoned to the Palace one day, where a contrite Julia Soaemias tried to hold sway.

That last time she begged him to go away with her she sat in a half-naked heap of defeat and richly embroidered silk, amidst the three hundred thousand sesterces she'd offered him outright, which lay scattered and rippling with evening sunlight over the tiny white tesserae of a mosaic floor. Her makeup tear-streaked, red lipstick smeared all over her mouth, her face changed with his refusal, and she'd sworn to have him killed.

He laughed, then. For he not only knew that she did not mean it, but didn't care if she did. With as many other things as were trying to kill him six months a year, what was one more?

But it would have been a tricky business at best. For Mannix had assumed the role of larger-than-life Anti-Hero among the Mob. Having tasted the dreadful thrill of walking in that Olympian Zone above the sloth and ignorance that surrounded him in safety in the stands, he had become a member of an elite fraternity that formed the axis between the poles of the ruling elite and the common man.

Lying in his old cell in the Bestiarii School, Mannix shielded his mind of these memories. His lids closed, and he fell into an exhausted, fitful sleep during which the sound of the rain on the roof above sent him tunneling down a cavernous black well through the cobwebbed honeycombs of memory in his mind until he suddenly emerged crashing into sunlight . . . a boy again . . . running in the Alban Hills through the vineyards and olive groves glinting warm October sunshine. And then down under the huge umbrella pines through the trails softly tapestried with brown rotten pine needles, sweet overripe sap smell and dappled sunlight, kicking pine cones and leaping laughingly over the shadows trying to step down only in the patches of gold. And the mysticism of light and shade, the spirits of the trees and the animals in the forests of his ancestors where the wood nymphs and their huntress once roamed . . .

The red and gold leaves began to stir on the forest floor one day as the pines above rippled and billowed like the great sails of ships on stormy seas, their cones dropping amidst the small deer darting and leaping with the scent of change. He arrived at the gate of his grandfather's farm to find the gnarled

104

old man awaiting him with a towering staff. His grandfather was a man very close to the natural world, to the architecture of hill and stream, the dome of the sky and the movements of the clouds. Like the soothsayers of his Etruscan ancestors, he would read unrevealed patterns in the flight of birds, the flow of sunlight across a hillside, or the gradual deepening of the sky in autumn. An unseen matrix of questions and answers connected to an earlier, more spiritual time, he spoke to animals in grunts and whispers, this man of bone and gristle, hard and ancient as the gnarled oak tree he used to sit under for hours at a time until he had the squirrels hypnotized and gathered all around him.

That day, his grandfather had wrapped him in a coarse woolen tunic and, taking his hand, led him out the gate of his farm and into his vineyards. The young boy could see the huge, gray-green stormclouds tumbling across the heavens through the vine-clad lattice above his head and he clung in fear to the hard-boned, leather-skinned hand. Leaving the cultivation behind, they struck an ancient trail, overgrown and invisible to all save his grandfather, winding gradually upwards through trees shadow-clad and foreboding.

Their climb was hastened partway by steps all but reclaimed by the stone from which they were hewn, invisibly green save the rhythm of their ascent. The steps were punctuated in places by roots thick around as galley masts winching the ancient lichen-frosted slabs from the millennial detritus of the forest floor. His grandfather pulled him up off his feet and over them in haste, for the boy had neither the length of leg nor the stride of the man and he was exhausted and breathing heavily when they finally arrived at a clearing, his damp flaxen child's hair clinging to a pasty face fraught with fear-widened, darting eyes. From the clearing they looked back down the valley just as the deep, guttural rumbling began to roll up its entire length toward them ever closer until he could feel it enter the pit of his stomach and then down, icy and uncontrollable, to be winced back at the tip of his penis but for a drop, and then play itself out in the slight trembling of his skinned, bleeding little knees. The trees around them waved and danced in the buffets of a wild Aeolus, and as he looked about the clearing he could see the shadowy features of moss-covered herms of satyrs with horns and pointed ears, flaring nostrils and ivy-sprouting grins. Bacchantes all, in a ring long forgotten, their Dionysian altar snaked with blossoming roots and the old chaos, the whole of the place, began to reawaken with the coming tempest. He glanced up into the face of his grandfather, long white hair flaring back from his chiseled temples, his gaze enraptured, the underside of the pregnant clouds above him a veil intermittently aburst with the silent glowing of titan fireflies.

Then suddenly Jupiter the Thunderer began to walk up the valley his winds had flown through, hurling his angry bolts crashing to the ground with a force that shook the very back of Atlas, and little Mannix felt the giving in to the terror which beckoned him from the other side of such wonder as the first fat drops hid the beginning of his tears. The carved marble altar lit up eerily in the lightning flares, quick stone glimpses of dancing maidens and drunken centaurs and goats and tambourines and flutes and axes and horny satyrs. Then Jupiter was upon them and the Hammer of the Gods descended with a violence that cleft a near oak to its roots, the crack so loud it left them shocked and deafened in a daze on the ground.

XV

His eyelids ripped open to the aftershock of the lightning thundering off over the rooftops. The ruby and azure amulets glowed in the rainlight on his throat. The pain in his shoulder throbbed, and he found to his surprise that he'd been crying in his sleep, wet tears running down his stubbled cheeks, no longer those of a boy's, but a man of thirty-six years, as far as he could reckon.

He groaned creakily into a sitting position on the bed and slid his legs off to where his feet hit the floor. The opium hangover pounded in his head and his legs felt heavy and lifeless. Through the small high window he could see veins of lightning dancing among the darkening clouds. He stood woozily, bracing himself with his outstretched hand on the wall as the blood rushed from his head, dizzying him. Growling against the pain throbbing in his shoulder, he staggered out of the room.

He walked stiffly down the four flights of stairs at the end of the peristyle and into the communal hall, where he grabbed a full pitcher of water off a table and brought it to his cracked lips. He didn't set the pitcher down until he'd drained it, the water running in rivulets down his cheeks and chin to dampen his maroon paenula. A few scattered clusters of bestiarii sat around the tables, others lay prostrate on benches with their hands folded across their chests. The candle chandeliers had been lit by the cooks, and the warm light glowed across the exhausted faces that stared up at him. A few of them hailed him. "Ave, Mannix."

He nodded back. "Boys."

Marcellus appeared at his side. "How are you feeling?"

"How it looks," the Bestiarius smiled softly, his dry, scabbed lips cracking painfully.

107

"Up to watching the main event?"

"Let's go," Mannix nodded.

They shuffled down the ramp into the tunnel running beneath the street, through the colonnaded central aisle of the warehouse area abuzz with stage managers and Apicius raising his arms and exclaiming in gestures of frustration, "What the fuck are you telling me we can't get the Essedarii next week! We'll have to change the whole venue. Why in Mithra's name didn't you let me know sooner?"

"The channel between Brittannia and Gaul has been under gale force winds for a week," the stage manager answered coolly. "It's too rough right now for the barges to cross. We just found out this afternoon. If it opens, the Brits should arrive with their chariots in three to four weeks."

"Oh fuck me!" Apicius threw up his hands and stormed off in a swirl of wizard robes.

Mannix and Marcellus looked at each other and laughed, the Ringmaster throwing a finger at them as he hurried up the ramp toward the Amphitheater. "You two assholes are on my shitlist too!"

They laughed harder. Conspirators in whatever life chose to throw at them, whether tragedy or humor, the two venators loved each other like brothers, and like more than brothers. For both had suffered the hell of fire together, and both shared the life of the professional bestiaries – which came with living to fight another day. With pitting themselves, weaker human beings helpless for years after birth, against something like a Rhino, which weighed three hundred pounds at birth and could kill a grown man, with nothing left in the balance but their wits, and how they brought them to bear upon their bodies.

They had both understood that to endure and to play such a dangerous game, one needed great physical and mental training, and a sleepless discipline of nerves. But they had also come early on to feel that – through training and becoming skillful in the game – something of their souls was affirmed. That they became more simple, certain and graceful, as they grew daily less and less accessible to fear.

An orphan who grew up under the stands of the Circus Maximus, Marcellus had lost any illusions he might have had about life, or about people, at an early age, awakening to the realization that the world was much like the Arena itself – a place without justice or mercy, where only the smart and ruthless could survive. Prostitutes were the only mother-figures he'd known, or the Asiatic women who did obscene dances under the dark alcoves to the music of flutes and castanets, cymbals and drums. They held him when he trembled as a boy, and shared their tears with him after being beaten or hurt by a rowdy drunken customer. Later they allowed him half-priced discoveries of his own.

The young Marcellus knew all of the inhabitants of that weird 'under the stands' world – which to avoid, which to befriend, which to serve – that motley crew of fortune tellers, astrologers, fruit and amulet sellers, sausage and sweetmeat vendors, all of whom formed a kind of twisted family, making a living as they did off the crowds going to see the shows, many of whom were always bored and leaving their seats to stroll down into this macabre world where they could buy eastern dishes at the various concession stands, get a skin of wine, watch women do obscene dances, and spill their lust under a dark arch. But mainly he just remembered those dark arches. Hundreds of them hovering heavily over his childhood, supporting the tiers of seats and forming a maze of interlocking passages, holes, runways and narrow slits, where he could crawl to be alone with his sadness.

He reached a point where he envied the gladiators and charioteers their game of death upon the openness of sun-drenched sand, and his thoughts began to turn in that direction. Toward death and light and openness. Where everybody knew your name. And if you were good enough they would scream it. Thousands of them screaming it. And when you walked down the street they would know who you were. Thus the dream began to unfold its great buzzard wings in his mind. The dream of becoming a famous gladiator or a great charioteer.

But his real talent lay with animals. For, like all who learned to mistrust people from a young age, he had a way with them. And so he acquired a train of stray dogs that became his best friends and that followed him around everywhere he went, imparting a kind of strangely beautiful, innocent sense of power to the young boy that he'd never had before – the ability to control other life, other creatures; to impose his will upon them. It was imperial; godlike, even.

In time he taught his mongrels to dance on their hind legs, walk a tightrope, and react to different questions posed about the chariot teams, and what a spectator thought of the reds, the blues, the whites or the greens. The different colors represented different neighborhoods of the city, and since the Circus was its own world, and the Mob lived and died by their color, their neighborhood, and the memories of its former, current, and surely future greatness – as if their charioteers were the great generals of old themselves – the young Marcellus found his place.

For if a particular spectator was wearing a blue smock, scarf or piece of ribbon, when asked about the reds, his mutts would howl, growl, lower their heads and put their tails between their legs. When asked about the 'blues,' however, they would spin in circles barking enthusiastically. The spectator was delightedly deceived of the fact that the dogs were reacting to hand signals held behind their back, and the young entrepreneur would often get tossed as much as a denarius for this display, opening the door on a world of commerce and civilization. For Marcellus, animals were the key.

He grew in confidence as he grew in stature, and soon was helping out with the venues, picking up odds-and-ends jobs such as carrying buckets of water for the animals, cleaning out cages, polishing the gladiators' armor and brushing the horses of the chariot teams. When he was about fifteen, the director of the Ludus Matutinus was putting on a show at the autumn opening of the Circus Maximus. One of the novices got in trouble with a bull and the boy grabbed a torch and sprinted in and diffused the beast enough that they could get the bestiarius out alive. The director was always one to recognize courage and talent, and he saw in the incident something in the wiry, sandy-blond, olive-skinned boy worthy of saving. So he took him in like young Mannix, and he began to teach him techniques in handling wild animals.

Marcellus was about the same age as the bigger young novice and the two boys took to each other in the way that misfits will at about that time in their lives when physical prowess and sex are their chief concerns. Their difference was that Mannix as a boy had trees and birds to minister to his loss and sadness, and Marcellus had dark arches. And he still carried scars on his heart and on his soul and in his guts for the things he'd seen or had to participate in to survive or which had been forced upon him during his formative period beneath them. Scars that were much deeper than any he'd subsequently received as a bestiarius.

XVI

Starting down the ramp into the underground world of the stadium, the smell hit them like a wave. By this time many of the patricians in the stands were repeatedly soaking their handkerchiefs in the perfumed fountains and holding them over their noses to breathe through. Mannix and Marcellus moved up the ramp system and into the low-ceilinged tunnel inside the perimeter wall. They found a choice spot inside the wall at an oblique angle to the arena where they had a good field of vision through a grated archway. Since the main event wouldn't be utilizing the grates or the trapdoor systems, their status gave them leave to take a seat and watch the show. Marcellus brought a jug of pretty decent Falernian from the school, and they kicked a few novice bestiarii out of the spot and pulled a bench up to the grated archway.

The last of the midday intermission acts was finishing up – criminals on giant see-saws spread across the arena floor trying desperately to out see-saw each other in the midst of a variety of animals including half a dozen lions, aurochs, wild boars, leopards and a few bulls. Their see-sawing agitated the animals, whose random rushes increased into a dreadful fiasco, the ridiculous antics sending howls through the drunken Mob. Before that, a troop of naked pygmies with blow-darts fought fat German women with oversized swords, prodded on by arena slaves with hot irons. Death blows were clumsy and took a while to finish.

"Really scraping the barrel with this trash," said Mannix, taking a healthy draught of the deep red wine.

Marcellus nodded grimly. "They say they used to actually have two-hour breaks between the three acts, sometimes senators speaking or public interest groups lobbying. These new ringmasters just pride themselves on keeping a continual flow of stuff going." He took the jug Mannix passed him. "Most of it crap."

Both men knew that death and torture were the only spectacles that could really gratify the people's longing – that could stultify their dread. As the novelty acts came to a close and the arena floor was cleared for the main event, Mannix could see throngs of the Mob trickling down the aisles. Bored by the sterile athletic contests of the main events, which were usually gladiatorial, they were off to wallow in the muck of the dark arches beneath the stands. But some of the older, traditional Romans stilled enjoyed a fine kill, and for them the coming of the gladiatorial contests held a virile, evocative excitement.

The rain had stopped, and water dripped from the awning in a circle around the arena floor. The sailors crawled like ants up in the catwalks, unhooking ropes, retying others, tightening in places, loosening in more; and suddenly the gigantic awning slid backwards in every direction around the oval, its folds closing in on themselves like a Chinese sail. The huge zipping sound above the crowd's head was accompanied by a great collective sigh of relief as an almost tactile funnel of stench and humidity rushed upward to escape, sucking with it a cool rippling draft into the Amphitheater through the outer arcades. Togas were loosened, arms raised.

Daylight was fading and lightning flared soundlessly among the clouds. Arena attendants were placing torches sprinkled with incense in the bronze brackets between the statuary niches around the horizontal band of colored marbles dividing the patricians from the plebs. The different kinds of incense caused the torches to burn yellow, blue, green and red. Likewise, a myriad of silver stars dropped from the catwalks and dangled twinkling in the multi-colored firelight.

On the floor, other attendants were spreading fresh dry sand and raking it smooth behind the catapults being slave-drawn across. The catapults flung roast pheasants, figs, dates, nuts, cakes and plums into the crowd. Free wine was distributed. The Editor of the Games was going all out on this first day of the series, and the spectators knew they couldn't

113

count on this liberality every day. Mannix and Marcellus whistled to old Flacca – one of the arena slaves who'd been working the Amphitheater for years and who were actually paid a small wage.

"Here you are, boys," he said, slipping them a roast pheasant and a few handfulls of dates through the grated entryway behind which they sat.

"Thanks, Flax."

Then, without further ado, large carts drawn by oxen began emerging from the Gate of Life as the catapults disappeared into the Gate of Death. Stacked full of heavy wooden crosses, a group of Christians was lashed and herded out behind the carts by brutal, leather-clad cell-block guards. As the crosses were unloaded at intervals around the perimeter wall, the Christians were thrown down, stretched atop them, and nailed to the dead trees amidst the great jeering roar of the crowd.

As hereditary high priest of the Syrian sun god Elagabal, a recent refusal from the Christian community to recognize his god's superiority over theirs had particularly irritated the Emperor, who'd had the city scoured of Jesus freaks for the series of Games. As outrageous and offensive as Elagabalus' continuation of his priestly 'duties' to the Ba'al had been to the Roman Senate and upper classes – for whom he should have left them well behind before assuming the purple – the Christian cult was also more than a little nuisance. It was an idea that had grown inexplicably throughout the Empire, threatening to overturn the historic conception of the Universe – which was based upon the fact that people are either born to rule, born to serve, or born to die. To think that they were equal and that they all had God inside was a dangerous absurdity.

Yet, if the truth had been known, deep down inside the nineteen year-old Emperor was not a little attracted to the man-god Jesus, this carpenter from nowhere who not only had the power to be remembered and worshipped, but to have people go to their deaths for him two hundred years after his own. Luckily, for Marcellus and Mannix, the two crucifixes on either

114

side of them were staged far enough down not to bother their field of vision.

Apicius the Ringmaster took the podium, raising his hands to silence the crowd. Around the perimeter wall, attendants on ladders were painting the crucified Christians with pitch. The crowd was as much silenced by mouthfuls of wine and pheasant as the Ringmaster, who with great fanfare announced, "Ladies and Gentlemen! Your attention please. The moment you've all been awaiting has arrived. The main event is about to begin!"

Music started up, horns and flutes harmonizing over the ominous background strains of the hydraulic organs. Mannix felt that familiar coldness rise up and shield his insides as the crucified Christians began going up in flames around the perimeter wall, one by one, their pitch-covered bodies, when put to the torch, exploding in fiery conflagrations that receded into black shadows in the hearts of the fire leaping and arcing on the crosses. Those waiting their turn screamed or mumbled prayers. The Mob roared with glee as each cross went up, and soon a hellish glow defined the arena while plunging the stands into black shadow. The flames settled into a steady burning, the figures inside drawing up like dead spiders, the stench of roasting flesh carried heavy on the moist night air. Mannix pulled the jug gently out of Marcellus' hands and took a long numbing pull.

The crowd noise gradually dropped to a subdued murmur as a prehistoric screaming sound filtered into the Amphitheater from outside. Louder as it came, the sound was something like the horrible gurgling notes of a gigantic wounded trumpeter. Suddenly tremendous creatures began emerging onto the arena floor, their forms obscured by the crazy orange glow and the wavering shadows thrown across the sand by the crucified human torches. Then it became clear, and the hypnotized Mob rushed back to the fore in a collective roar as they beheld Indian elephants, with howdahs full of armed men shifting on their backs, emerging from the Gate of Life. Before their attention was fully cognizant, however, huge African bulls

115

began trumpeting out of the Gate of Death opposite, the castles on their backs undulating with Numidian spearmen.

Mannix and Marcellus perked up and began eating faster, tearing great chunks off the bird halves with their glistening teeth. At last something worth watching. A pitched battle between two different strains of the same species. The African bulls were bigger, with longer tusks and more power. But the Indian variants were mean and notoriously aggressive, and their mahouts were better at controlling them. Mannix judged that the editor had put a fair dent in the current stock of the government herds in Laurentum, but he knew that more were already en route.

Yet it was as much the sound of the elephants as the sight of them that was incredible – the trumpeting, and the way their hooves thundered across the sand. Mannix and Marcellus could feel it in their guts; and, beneath the timber, iron and concrete floor, even with its huge travertine piers as supports, the pounding above was such that some of the inexperienced arena hands balked, and raced for shelter beneath the stands for fear that it would collapse.

Twelve to a side, the elephants were heavily padded for protection, for they tended to be popular animals even among the depraved Mob, and they were also often used in the city's various construction projects. The Indian bulls were draped with rich carpets dangling red tassles, the Africans with zebra skins and with lions' teeth clattering on strings from their tusks. The men on their backs, five to a howdah, were of the same nationality as the elephants – the short, tenacious mahouts from India versus the tall, sleek Africans from Numidia. They were armed with a variety of weapons, ranging from bows and thick-headed African spears, to the curved Sikh throwing knives; and the double-layered protective netting was zipping up on its masts around the perimeter wall.

When all of the elephants from both sides were on the floor, their controllers began reining the huge beasts into line with their elaborate bridle goads and starting a chaotic straggling advance across the arena toward each other, the elephants screaming and curling their trunks beneath their tusks for the coming conflict. Mannix popped a handful of oily dates into his mouth and gazed fascinated through the grating at the huge calloused flanks crumpling past at an oblique angle. The Numidians stretched up above their howdah walls and cast their spears first, their muscled backs glistening like carved ebony in the light of the human torches. An impetuous move, most of the spears fell short, or lost their accuracy with the distance; yet one lucky shot arced right into the eye of an Indian bull, penetrating deep into the socket to kill the beast immediately. It stood stock still for a second, wavered once, and then fell straight-legged to the side in a thundering crash of fresh sand that dusted up into the torchlit atmosphere.

All hell broke loose. The nimble mahouts that jumped free of the dead elephant drew their daggers and spread out sprinting across the sand like ants. A phalanx of Indian arrows whistled through the African continent, catching a dozen Numidians pressing the attack before they had time to release their own drawn bows, upending them gasping over their howdahs to fall in dust-puff impacts on the floor clutching lifelessly at the shafts in their chests. The elephants were mixed in now, bumping, jostling, butting and tusking each other, making it difficult for the men in the howdahs to get accurate shots with either spear or bow.

Two of the unmounted Indian mahouts had an African bull hamstrung with their daggers. As it crumpled heavily to its knees with a yodeling trumpet, it cast its long trunk behind it and thwapped it around one of the little men, whipping him back and over to impale him on its tusk with a sickly thunk. With four feet of gore-dripping ivory emerging from his back, the Indian threw his head back and vomited blood in a horrible gargling scream before going limp on the tusk.

Mannix and Marcellus scurried backwards reflexively as a huge gray flank smashed into the perimeter wall jarring the grate through which they watched. Their view completely blocked, the elephant began to move, and light penetrated back in for a second; but then its veined flank came crashing back against the grate again. Its trumpeting screams sounded huge and brassy and unnatural, and they could feel the massive

117

driving pressure as it was smashed again into the wall hard enough that its patchy-haired, cross-hatched skin bubbled through the openings in the grate.

Then suddenly it took off, running at an angle through the melee. Unmercifully butted and gored by its smaller but better-trained Indian cousin, the young African bull dashed crazily across the arena until the howdah came loose from its back strewing five big Numidians across the sand. Reined in by its driver, the Indian elephant began going for the men, trampling the screaming Africans, their white teeth gleaming in terror. It picked one of them up with its trunk and thrashed him into a burning cross, knocking it back against the perimeter wall to slide over and fall to the ground where the Numidian died in the crackling flames atop a roasted Christian.

Dust swirled up into the atmosphere above the melee as the huge beasts barged and turned like storm-tossed ships, stamping and kicking and shifting the fresh-laid mounds of dry sand whirling and billowing up through the oculus in the awning into the starry night in clouds of torchlit orange mist. The priests of Jupiter on the Capitoline Hill stood watching from the porch of their temple in the forest of seventy-two-foot columns as, a mile away, the arcades of the Flavian Amphitheater pulsed with firelight like a witches' den, and the sound of the crowd ebbed and flowed to the accompaniment of the macabre dance they surrounded.

Their mouths greasy with roast pheasant, Mannix and Marcellus watched as the wounded African bull that suffered the vicious attack by its Indian counterpart collapsed in a heap of blood and foam, raising its trunk to the crowd in a pitiful gesture reminiscent of a wounded gladiator. Tens of thousands of the depraved Mob shouted for mercy to be granted but the elephant was already finished and an Indian spear thrust behind its ear put it down for good. Meanwhile the other mastodons were fighting in close array, and a courageous little turban-clad mahout scurried out along the flank of his mount to jump screaming and dagger-drawn into a howdah full of spear-clad Numidians, his blade flashing and winking like the stars in the catwalks above as he slashed and stabbed in close-range confusion before the Africans could turn their spears on him. Three went down in great gouts of arterial blood before the Indian was knocked backwards over the side and trampled into a shapeless glob by the mass of elephants shifting flank to flank.

Some of the Numidians had slid off the backs of their elephants as well, and were fighting under cover of their beasts' great girths, stabbing up into the bellies of the Indian mounts; high-pitched trumpeting filled the sky. One of the Indian bulls reared up with its trunk writhing like a huge serpent, the men in its howdah thrown backwards against the side like dice, two upended and over. Then the elephant came down in a crazy charge that scattered a group of Numidians against the perimeter wall, crushing two and slinging its howdah slanting far into the double layer of protective netting. A dozen members of the Senatorial Class clambered over each other trying to get out of the way, the Mob roaring with laughter. The elephant stood for a moment flapping its ears contentedly and then crumpled to the sand, lay over on its side, and died.

Four of the African and three of the Indian elephants were down, and several more had either lost their howdahs or their crews. Handlers from the government herds in Laurentum had come out onto the arena floor trying desperately to drive the unmanned survivors back through the axial gates while the battle raged all around them. Some were caught up in the confusion and killed. An unenviable job; Mannix was proud of them for trying to save the animals.

The crosses were burning low now, and the crowd sat drugged and mystified. Several dozen bodies lay unrecognizably trampled across the floor amidst the huge shadowy islands of dead elephants. The unmounted Numidians were using their quickness and agility to attack the Indian bulls, their muscled ebony bodies darting through the wavering shadows, their comrades still in the howdahs tossing them down bows and quivers of arrows. The Indian mahouts, who had greater control over their mounts than did the Numidians, reined them back into a snaking line of retreat around the perimeter wall. With the African bulls still in a cluster, the Indian archers sent an arc of arrows into the epicenter, killing six more of the

Numidians diving over the side of the howdahs, and plunging their mounts into disarray. Their elephants, without controllers, began to retreat, looking for a way out of the arena; and the handlers quickly seized the situation and got charge of them, leading them out with their special calls.

The four remaining Indian elephants charged now, the men in their howdahs screaming above the din, elephants trumpeting away. A group of their dismounted comrades formed cover against the Numidian spearmen. Though no match for them in hand-to-hand combat, their strategy divided and stalled them as the charging elephants closed in on the last remaining African bulls with men in their howdahs, the others either dead or driven out through the axial gates.

The Numidians fought like tigers, slashing and lunging out over their howdahs with their spears, their comrades on foot driving to their aid through the Indians providing cover. But too late. The last remaining Africans on their elephants were killed with throwing knives or arrows, and the Indian mahouts reined their mounts desperately around and charged to the rescue of their brothers on the ground suffering the worst for it among the bigger stronger Numidians.

The remaining Indians on the ground scattered at the last minute to let the elephants take over, and the Africans ran for the hills, two of them smashed and goared against the perimeter wall, one of them tossed thirty feet up into the air along the protective layer of netting where, with amazing finesse, he gripped the heavy cords, catching himself.

The entire Amphitheater stopped in a pregnant pause, the Senators staring up at the dangling Numidian in amazement. Then the crowd came back to life roaring with applause at the acrobatic feat, and shouting immediately for mercy. But the Indian elephant began batting the netting hard with its trunk, and the man's wounds were such that he lost his grip and fell sliding and screaming the thirty feet back down the netting, his plummeting body bulging out over the toga-clad Senators drawing back in alarm, the elephant curling its trunk beneath its mouth, the African twisting with just enough time to see his own screaming reflection in the great black watery eye of the beast before he was impaled to the hilt on both tusks.

The crowd went wild, fistfights broke out in the lower class seating, a Patrician woman ripped all of her jewelry off and threw it into the arena, and the Praetorians entered the stands. Mannix and Marcellus looked at each other and shook their heads. Arena attendants began extinguishing every other torch around the horizontal band of niched statuary and colored marbles, bringing the lights down. The remaining elephants walked in a train out of the arena; the survivors, both African and Indian, being assisted out as well.

The Emperor stood up, a rare gesture, and raised his hands. By the look on his face, Mannix could tell that Elagabalus was enjoying the frenzied Mob. Sometimes he had sacks full of gold, silver or jewels flung by catapult to them in the Circus Maximus. But he was also given to whims – once in the Circus Maximus those sacks were full of Egyptian Asps – and he was just liable to have the whole place burned down, with them in it, just for the fun of it. Even after, or perfectly because of, its new restoration paid for with his family's money. He raised his hands higher now, and the crowd noise trickled down to silence.

"What did I teach you?," he shouted with a brilliant smile and a flourish of his arms.

The Mob broke out in a cacophony of laughter, the Senators, Equites and Patricians looking nervously up at the gallery seating as the chanting started. It took several minutes for their voices to finally lock as one . . . "You are the Sun of New Rome . . . you are Alpha Number One. The Senate are Slaves in Togas and the Patricians and Equites a joke! You are the Sun of New Rome . . . you are Alpha Number One. The Senate are Slaves in Togas and the Patricians and Equites a Joke!" And faster and faster, "You are the Sun of New Rome . . . you are Alpha Number One . . . the Senate are Slaves in Togas and the Patricians and Equites a Joke! You are the Sun of New Rome . . . you are Alpha Number One . . . the Senate are Slaves in Togas and the Patricians and Equites a Joke!"

And so, with the lights coming down in a ring around the Amphitheater, a contingent of the Praetorian Guard sealing off the upper class seating, and the nineteen year-old Emperor beaming and patting his raised hands to quiet the Mob . . . Day One of the series of Games came to a close.

XVII

The people funneled slowly out of the Amphitheater, drained of emotion and spent with the bloodlust. They made their way home through the arterial network of tight streets under the watchful eyes of the city garrison staged at key points throughout the squares. Hardened veterans of the foreign wars, they were able at quick notice to barricade streets, isolate neighborhoods, and bring heavy cavalry charging down on belligerent offenders.

Inside the Amphitheater, arena slaves scuttled through the empty seats, sweeping and cleaning the refuse of the unruly Mob – broken wine jars and chicken bones, dirty underwear and passed-out drunks. Others had the thankless task of butchering the dead elephants lying in dark islands across the shadowy white sand. What wouldn't go to feed the lions, tigers, leopards and bears would be loaded onto platform carts and transported outside of the city, where huge craniums, legs and shoulder sockets would be dumped into the Tiber downstream. The magistrates at Ostia, the port town fifteen miles downriver where the Tiber emptied into the sea, would be complaining over the next few days that some of the carcass remnants had washed ashore, or gotten caught in the wharves at low tide. They would be politely instructed by the Senate to 'Well, push them on out to sea, boys.'

Mannix and Marcellus wound their way down through the curving corridors into the cell blocks. The animals were as subdued by the silence above as by their instinctive knowledge of the earth's revolution, and the entire underground world echoed with the soft collective purring sound of the jungle at night, broken only by a hyena, which cast an invective of high-pitched laughter at the two bestiarii as they passed, its eyes sparkling from the shadows of its cage. They set about checking the pens, overseeing their maintenance and cleaning. They made sure the beasts were fed and watered for the night, and took reports from the novices and technicians on which ones weren't eating or needed medical attention.

When their day was finally done, they traveled back up the ramps and exited the Gate of Death into the wonder of the cool, rain-freshened evening air. After collecting their coin purses and personal belongings, and securing another jug of Falernian from the storerooms of the Ludus Matutinus, they crossed the piazza between the tremendous eastern curve of the Amphitheater and the facade walls of the three gladiatorial schools on their right – the Ludi Magnus, Dacicus and Gallicus. They climbed a staircase scaling the Oppian Hill aside the smaller Baths of Titus to the much larger complex of the Baths of Trajan – kept open for arena employees, gladiators and bestiarii, to wash and relax after the day's events. The staircase ascended through an arcade in its huge hemicyclical terrace, upon which they arrived, and Mannix walked slowly toward the look-out point on its western side.

Marcellus followed. He could smell his friend. Above the smell of the rain-freshened air and the greens of cypress and pine, he could smell Mannix, the raw stink of him, sweat and leather, the wet wool of his paenula and the rank rusty afterburn of dried blood. Despite himself he couldn't help but drink it in, quietly, through his nose as he walked, and let it burn inside his chest like fire.

The Bestiarius stopped at the balustrade of the look-out point. The Amphitheater hovered ghostly gray in the darkness before them. The huge bronze ornamental shields lining its attic story glowed silver in the rain-light, the two hundred and forty awning masts rising above its rim like a rank of spears before the backdrop of broken gray drifting clouds. The white travertine of its arcades was still blackened in places and scaled by restorative scaffolding after the lightning strike and subsequent fire under Caracalla five years ago, which many took to be a bad omen of a reign grown increasingly insane.

The fire severely damaged all of the gallery seating as well as the heavy timber of the arena floor. As it was to be out of commission indefinitely, Mannix and Marcellus spent the following year performing exhibitions in the military amphitheaters at Legion bases stationed along the Rhine. Today's events were the first in which they'd performed in the building since; during the interim fighting occasionally in the Circus Maximus and in Domitian's stadium on the Campus Martius.

Mannix was thankful for the unusual amount of time off to rest and train – lifting weights and running in the hills – for his body was growing old for his profession. Marcellus, built lighter and less muscled, had aged a bit better physically, his natural sinewy flexibility rebounding more quickly from the punishment. Yet they were both showing signs of strain.

Together the two comrades looked out over the sleeping city, over the terracotta-tiled rooftops of the adjoining Baths of Titus past the great curve of the darkened Amphitheater through the seven meter-long spikes on the crown of the colossal statue of the sun god. The temples topping the hills were lit by massive charcoal braziers placed between the columns running down their flanks. Night-beacons for the troubled masses, Mannix remembered gazing at the wavering lights of these temples as a novice on nights when he couldn't sleep. In the distance, on the Capitoline Hill – the sacred site of Rome for a thousand years – the Temple of Jupiter Optimus Maximus dominated them all, a cyclopean structure befitting the huge marble god enthroned inside. To the north, however, recently erected by Caracalla, the Temple of Serapis ran it a close second in size, its sixty-foot columns wavering in orange light over the Field of Mars atop the cliff-face of the Quirinal.

Symptomatic of the rise in popularity of eastern mystery cults which had begun under the Antonine Dynasty and had become even more widespread under the Severans – though none of the new divinities they represented were members of the traditional Greco-Roman pantheon – their choice not only reflected the Eastern connections and sympathies of the recent dynasties, but moreover the religious confusion of the age. An increasing awareness was spreading across the Mediterranean Basin – the globalization of a world seeking a synthesis between knowledge and faith as it teetered on the verge of great change. The growing trepidation over current events was springing a new kind of need, and the mystery cults evinced the first tentative steps towards fulfilling it.

For certain characteristics of these cults, and particularly their rituals, had begun to exert a pull upon a big-city populace suffering from loneliness and anonymity. Their increased emphasis on the individual – the idea of salvation and a life after death – as well as their sensory-laden liturgies and rituals providing the comfort of the shared meal and the supernatural, offered the attraction of strong feelings and emotions, and provided a sense of belonging devoid in the strictly formalistic worship of the Roman gods, and formerly quenched only in the Amphitheater. The Greeks and Hellenized Easterners had been transporting and adapting eastern gods for two thousand years, making their diffusion and compatibility with the traditional pantheon more flexible. And with the free passage and melding of many different races and cultures – the interchange of men and ideas, fads and sensibilities, all under the protective guise of the 'Pax Romana' – these religious syncretisms had become essential to both peace and commerce. Hence attributes of Egyptian, Syrian and Middle Eastern gods had been carefully studied and matched with those of the traditional Greco-Roman pantheon. In the hands of a Dynasty with sympathies toward them, their overlap with the traditional gods had become ever more disturbing and intense, as evinced by the Temple of Serapis on the Quirinal – a god of healing associated with Jupiter in this age of synthesized iconographies.

The Bestiarius frowned slightly at the thought of these cults, their most recent and powerful manifestation represented by the current Emperor who wanted to combine them all under his own. His eyes moved to the northeastern ledge of the Palatine where, above and beside Hadrian's temple of Venus and Rome, he could see the flank of the so-called Elagaballium, the colossal temple still under construction by the perverse will of the nineteen year-old. He and Marcellus had both heard the stories of what went on up there – the slaughter of bulls and vast quantities of sheep each morning along with, rumor had it, human genitalia and small boys of rare beauty on occasion. Probably lies spread by the aristocracy, Mannix reflected; but still not good.

On the outskirts of the city, in the vast summer estate of the Severans in the suburb of Ad Spem Veterum on the edge of the Esquiline District, the Emperor had built another sanctuary for his god.   Worshipped in the form of a black stone supposedly fallen from the sky, and taken to be a divine image of 'Sol Invictus,' the Invincible Sun, for the last two years at the climax of the Dogstar, Elagabalus had journeyed to this second sanctuary in a grandiose procession, bearing his solar aerolith at the moment in the year when the Sun exerted its maximum intensity.   Mannix and Marcellus, by dint of their profession, fought in the last series of games marking this Sun festival, but avoided the dances and banquets offered the Mob, who lined the processional way as the chariots, attendants, mounted Praetorians and Vestals spreading petals of rose, proceeded to the estate from the Palatine like a huge serpent of ivory and gold.

The Bestiarius remembered with disgust the tens of thousands relishing the angst and the collective orgiastic behavior marked by the Emperor's journey.   The black stone supposedly fallen from the sky was displayed on a chariot sparkling with gold and gems, and   Elagabalus walked backwards in a purple and gold Phoenician robe holding the reins of the horses, his eyes fixed on the stone as his gem-studded slippers leapt and danced along a path scattered with gilded grain.   The Mob ran along on both sides of the chariot waving torches and throwing flowers, and the 'Invincible Sun' was preceded in the procession by statues of all the other gods who were thus reduced to the disgrace of paying homage to Elagabal's supremacy.

Mannix stared at the temple under construction.   He knew that the Empire was changing, and that the old gods were dying.   When no one believed in them anymore, they would have completed their passage into the netherworlds of memory, becoming no more than poetic motifs or ornaments for decorating human solitude and walls, their spirit locked like ghosts inside fragments of marble statuary and architectural ruins.

Change was death. Death was change. When the Empire changed, would it die forever? Or would its death simply transform it, making it imperceptible, yet every bit as alive? He thought of young Demetrius, and pain crept into his eyes.

"Are you all right?" Marcellus asked.

The Bestiarius looked away. "Ah Marcellus," he sighed, "what are we?"

The fellow venator, unused to seeing his friend like this, took a stalling pull from the jug of Falernian in his hand. "We're men, Caius," he replied, lowering the jug. "Men to be damned," he smiled.

"We're whores, Mars," Mannix shook his head softly. "Just whores."

Marcellus cocked his head. "What is it?"

"She sent me a note in the clinic," the Bestiarius said. Staring out into the night, he squinted his eyes.

Marcellus looked up into the clouds drifting before the backdrop of black starry sky. "She can't touch you, Caius. You know that."

The Bestiarius shook his head. "You're missing the point, old friend," he smiled sadly, still looking off into the dark grainy distance. "She already has."

"How's your shoulder?," Marcellus asked, changing the subject and passing him the jug.

"Hurts," Mannix smiled, his face looking old and hard in the light of the moon beginning to rise. "But my ribs hurt worse," he placed his hand to his side and stretched carefully. "I think that bull broke a couple of them."

"Come," Marcellus placed a hand on his friend's corded forearm, "let's wash and sit in the vapors."

XVIII

Inside the huge marbled hall of the frigidarium, the party was in full swing, with gladiators, animal trainers, arena attendants, stage managers, technicians and bestiarii, all relaxing in a subdued state of good humor amongst a plethora of nubile young flesh. Mannix and Marcellus wandered in across the floor of the great communal meeting place of the baths, their thick leather boot sandals sliding pleasantly over the vast expanse of Phrygian marble, its purple veins spreading like a tapestry of wine stains spilled in fanciful rivulets over the slabs. The towering walls of the rectangular space rippled with an incrustation of columns, pediments and entablatures. Fifty-foot Aswan granite monoliths supported the gigantic groin vaults of the ceiling, which arced up and over, caissoned with octagonal coffers inset with gilded rosettes and decorated with white stucco egg-and-dart motif.

High up between the springing vaults rose huge half-moon windows, glass-paned with bronze latticework frames. The night sky outside of them was blackened by the flames from the tripod oil braziers stationed in the corners of the hall, their mellow wavy light undulating across the geometric treatment of the wall surfaces, where temple-fronted niches in columns of green cipollino and pediments of gray-veined Proconnesian alternated between the monolithic Egyptian granite shafts supporting the ceiling vaults. Inside the niches stood ideal representations of the male figure – Roman copies of some of the best Greek originals – discus throwers, athletes with styrils, the great Hercules resting from his labors.

Hailed by a score of voices, the two friends returned greetings and gripped wrists in the Roman manner before proceeding through the dark alcoves into the changing rooms, where they left their grimy garments to the care of the bath slaves. Stained with dirt and sweat and patches of blackly dried blood, the slaves would have the tunics and paenulas washed and dried before the two were ready to leave this evening. Mannix and Marcellus draped towels over their forearms and walked through a coffered archway into the hot baths, where they hung the towels on pegs set in the wall. Mannix removed the ties that held his bandages in place, and dropped the bloody refuse into a trash bin. He stepped stiffly down the marble stairs and carefully waded his naked muscled form into the steaming water, where Marcellus was already floating, luxuriating on his back in the healing vapors.

The Bestiarius ducked his head under and stayed listless in the alternate universe, becoming one with its element, letting the heat salve his aching body and the soft slow motion of the water drift him along on a current of forgetfulness from which a growing part of him would like never to return. His eyes wandered slowly across the mosaic floor of the pool, where dolphins, tritons and sea nymphs beckoned him from silvery depths. After a long while, he grudgingly emerged from the underwater world in a great gasp above its surface, throwing his dark hair back from his forehead to hang long and straight to his shoulders. The amulets of Isis and Serapis on the leather cord around his throat glinted in the light of the oil lamps hanging from chains along the walls as he floated on his back staring up at the mosaic constellations undulating across the ceiling vault, where the bull, the bear and the hunter danced trapping him between their mathematical reality above, and the otherworldly dreams of childhood below. One meant life, the other death; but which wasn't so clear.

After a time, he and Marcellus rose from the hot water, wrapped their towels around their waists, and proceeded down a marbled hallway through an arch into the circular caldarium, where the handsome dome bloomed high above – Apollodorus of Damascus' practice run for the vaulting technique he later perfected in the great Pantheon. The room was full of men mellowed by exhaustion, seated along benches encircling the space where the heated pipes in the walls and the steam conducted up through the floor from the boiler rooms below brought the expiatory release of sweat from their bodies. The two bestiarii took a seat beneath a statue of Dionysus holding the infant Bacchus on his shoulder, a short muscled satyr dancing at his legs with a cluster of grapes. The sculpture group was one of seven spaced around the walls, six in temple-fronted niches – three on either side of the arched entrance leading into the space via the tepidarium. The seventh statue was of the great Trajan himself, in the huge apse opposite the entrance, striding forth in the guise of Jupiter with a golden laurel-leaf crown on his head and a bronze eagle perched atop his staff.

Mannix stared out across the circle and square pattern fanning across the expanse of flooring until the geometric pavement began to buckle and waver in his weary vision through the mist of steam rising gently into the dome. Purple porphyry disks set within yellow-orange squares of Numidian marble alternated with squares of the purple-veined white Phrygian framed in porphyry strips. The colorful marbling of the walls was broken by the white of the statues in their niches, and the colors and the steam mixed and moved in the Bestiarius' eyes with the release of dormant opium in his bloodstream.

"You'd better take this," a voice interrupted his reverie, his eyes refocusing on the boney shoulders and flabby tits of Apicius the Ringmaster, who stood before him with a towel wrapped around his gut and a pensive look on his face, folding another towel into a square and gesturing at his shoulder. Marcellus, who'd been drifting by his side with his eyes closed, came awake as well. Mannix looked down at his upper pectoral to find blood oozing with the heat from the big bruised punctures to run in sweat-diluted rivulets over his shoulder and down his bicep, channeled by the rope vein to gather in the crook where his forearm rested across his thigh, and drip slowly into a watery pink stain in the towel around his waist. He took the squared towel from Apicius and pressed it to his shoulder and upper chest.

"Thanks."

"Bad business with Demetrius and that bull this morning. You did all you could," continued the Ringmaster, nodding. "His ashes are assured a fine amphora in the school's mausoleum."

The side of the Bestiarius' lip twitched involuntarily. He didn't feel much like hearing about the school's mausoleum, a depressing affair outside the Porta Latina in dire need of restoration. Yet he could already picture himself walking out there to burn incense and revere his young friend's grave.

"We're taking you out for the series, Caius," Apicius sighed. "Can't afford to strain you in the first round of games. That shoulder business is no good at all, no good at all."

Mannix felt ice-water flowing down the inside of his torso. He stared off through the vapors, maintaining a blank expression.

"Get some rest," continued the Ringmaster. "Go to Capri; lay in the sun," he nodded. "It's perfect this time of year, and you've got plenty of money. A month off and you'll be eating bears for breakfast."

The Bestiarius didn't respond.

"Well," Apicius put his hand on Mannix's unhurt shoulder. "Good show, son."

The Ringmaster moved off into the vapors, clapping a shoulder here, giving his consternation there.

The Bestiarius' eyes moved to the blossoming dome where the steam rose through its oculus into the night sky. First you started missing acts, next nobody wanted to hear your name.

"Save some of the girls for me, friend," said Marcellus.

Mannix smiled softly, his mind a million miles from girls. He'd never expected to live long enough to have to worry about his career ending.

The two sat in silence and sweated in the steam for a while, occasionally scraping the grime and oil from their skin with styrils. Then they rose and moved into the tepidarium, where they soaped their bodies with horse lard, and plunged into the cool water of the bathing pools. The decoration changed from one of masculinity to one of femininity. Nude Venuses with smooth marble thighs poured a continuous flow of water from urns into the pool under a ceiling frescoed with

132

depictions of the four winds, Aeolus blowing a string of little winged harpies cartwheeling out of his mouth. His torso a matrix of pink scar tissue, Mannix stood with his head under an urn and his arms folded across his chest, letting the cool water tighten his skin and help close the punctures.

Back in the changing rooms, they were handed light tunics of white linen with gold-embroidered Greek key motif running vertically down the sides – courtesy of the Editor of the Games, the young patrician who was also financing the party. Their own tunics and paenulas drying on a grate over a segment of heated pipes with slaves polishing their boot sandals and wide, bronze-studded leather belts, they slipped the party tunics over their heads, and cinched the gold-tasseled rope belts at their waists. Then they slipped their feet into light sandals and tied them at the ankles, and wandered into the large communal hall where low tables laden with greasy viands and exotic delicacies were staged between clusters of banqueting couches.

The bath session having relaxed his senses and opened them to the adventure of the evening, Mannix surveyed the scene, his eyes running across the food. He curled his lip at the silver bowls full of honey-soaked thrushes' tongues, the platters of fried baby mice and the laurel wreaths full of peacock's eggs, settling on a leg of roast partridge, a hunk of cheese and a large goblet of wine. As he took his choices from the table, he was bumped from behind by a huge bull of a man, sloshing wine from his goblet and making his shoulder scream.

He turned to find a smug, sarcastic, good-looking face smiling back at him. "Sorry, old man. Didn't see you."

Marcellus stiffened on the other side of the table.

Mannix stared expressionless at the twenty five year-old favorite of the Emperor and heart-throb of the teenage girls of Rome – the champion gladiator Prixus.

A group of his friends, other young gladiators with names, gathered around snickering and making a few comments that the two bestiarii couldn't quite make out.

"Too bad about today, huh?" smiled Prixus, "heard you're out for the series, old man." He raised an eyebrow and shook his head, "Well," he said mockingly, "get some rest."

His comrades snickered behind him.

Marcellus grit his teeth.

Mannix remained expressionless.

The bigger younger gladiator could smell the wound on him like a pack animal, sense the decline he could capitalize on. There was a deep-seated sense of competition between the two professions, each of which considers itself the nobler. And Prixus, tired of being second-best and stung by the Emperor's comment that morning, knew a fight here would show the entire Arena community, the entire City of Rome, in fact, who was number one. He was fresh, he didn't fight today; and obviously, with Mannix's torn-up shoulder, he would surely win. So he knew that if he could force the Bestiarius' hand and get him to make the first move, he'd have his glory.

Marcellus popped a handful of olives in his mouth and grabbed a silver pitcher of wine. "Come on, friend," he said to Mannix, "let's get some air." He cocked his head toward the door. "The girls are outside. Just little boys in here."

The Bestiarius didn't move. He lifted the leg of roast partridge to his mouth and took a bite, staring all the while at Prixus, who was no longer smiling. One of those rare men with the ability to make even his smallest gestures seem important, he chewed slowly, his blue-green eyes cold, curious, forcing the gladiator to finally blink, and swallow. Mannix smiled softly at him then, and took his time pouring another goblet of wine to the brim. He stepped forward and the big young gladiator involuntarily moved half-a-step to the side as the Bestiarius brushed slowly past him to join Marcellus.

The Editor of the Games having made sure to invite more than a few single young ladies, much of the party had moved out into the gardened grounds of the baths. The two friends wandered through the stragglers and gluttons reclining on the banqueting couches out into the garden scene, where torches lit the low-speed bacchanalia of whispered giggles among the shadow-clad cypresses towering into the backdrop of starry sky. Their sandals slid over a marbled path snaking through the well-sculpted grass, the perfume of rain-freshened oleanders greeting their noses.

Feigning shyness, a covey of young wayward patrician girls overtook them, hurrying coyly by. But men of their profession weren't given to wasting time, and Marcellus corralled two of them around the waist and diverted the group toward a marble exedra across the grass. The girls were careful not to resist too hard.

Another of their number playfully slapped Mannix on the shoulder, smiling seductively. "Tell him to let my friends go!"

The Bestiarius grit his teeth, drawing back with the pain.

The girl shied and raised a hand to her mouth. "I'm sorry, I . . ."

"Forget it," Mannix said softly, walking after Marcellus, who'd made it to the hemicyclical bench, and already subdued his prey with the pitcher of wine and his sandy-blond good looks.

"Ah, this sporting life," he said, as Mannix sidled up and took the silver pitcher. He passed it to the girl, a skinny young patrician with pimples and bad teeth. She took a delicate sip, and then held it up to him in a shy offering. Removing it gently from her hands, he took a long pull. Marcellus had one of her friends in his lap, the other leaning against him. With his arms around both of them, his hands were being playfully slapped away from their milk-white breasts as they toyed with his hair and cooed in his ears.

The girl by his side tried to make conversation, but Mannix wasn't really listening. His mind hollow, his thoughts vaporous, his aquamarine eyes wandered across the garden grounds where the cypresses towered in black silhouette and the ghostly gray statuary of satyrs and nymphs and Greek herms rose amidst the twice-blooming oleanders. The bulk of the baths hovered to his left, the perimeter wall with its shops and libraries, all closed, angling off to his right through the trees. Occasionally a streak of white stoa slipped across his vision trailing a doppler of distant laughter as a young male stumbled in pursuit; and he had a brief memory of his grandmother, sitting by the hearth of their farm of an evening relating the story of Apollo and Daphne, the wood nymph who turned into a tree before the young hot-blooded god could catch her.

He noticed the girl's fingernails whispering across his chest and shoulder, trailing slowly around the stitched puncture wounds, the soft feel of her thigh and breast on his side not unpleasant, only strange after the hard, fast, unforgiving touch of the day. Suddenly he found her hot, garlic-and-wine-musty lips pressed against his, her pointed little tongue exploring his teeth, a small hand running over his whiskers and around his muscled neck under his dark wavy hair. His senses suddenly acute to the texture of her leaning embrace and the feel of her breasts against his chest, he gradually returned her kiss, and she pulled him wearily to his feet. Disoriented with wine-woven fatigue from the day's ordeal, he realized that Marcellus was no longer there.

He stood and half-heartedly returned the girl's embrace, which bespoke of flowers and love letters left on his doorstep in an emotionally complicated future, and then gently disentangled himself from her and kissed her on the forehead. She searched his eyes, looking for a sign, and he smiled softly and looked away. The marble exedra was empty save the two of them, and Marcellus was nowhere in sight. The silver pitcher sat forlorn in the moonlight and he lifted it and turned, leaving the girl staring at his wide back, the roll of trapezius off his neck bunched up and tight, his dark hair curling in strands off it. His powerful hamstrings sloping out of the hem of his party tunic, muscled calves tapering into his slender ankles, Mannix walked alone across the cool dark grass, enjoying its smell. The torches were burning low around the gardens, and the only people in sight were a few scattered couples trying through the drunkenness to have intellectual conversations.

Inside the frigidarium, a slow trickle of guests was filing out, others saying their goodbyes, others still laughing raucously around the banqueting couches. A group of the sailors who worked the awning were chanting bawdy limericks in the corner. The Editor was standing by the huge bronze doors, giving farewells and receiving compliments on what a propitious first day of Games it had been. The Bestiarius slipped inside avoiding people, a drunk girl spinning and falling purposefully into his arms; he righted her and headed for the changing rooms, where a dozen or so gladiators and stage hands were replacing their smocks and tunics. It was close on midnight by the look of the moon, and tomorrow was a work day. A scatter of greetings hailed him as he entered.

"Ave Caius, great show today. You made those tigers look like kittens."

"Thanks boys," the Bestiarius replied, finding his maroon paenula, belt and boot sandals. He noticed that Marcellus' clothes were still there, and he placed the empty silver pitcher on top of his friend's folded tunic as a signifer.

The Editor stopped him on the way out, turning from a conversation. A weak, exhausted-looking young man, he extended his hand. "I've watched you since I was a boy, and always admired you."

Mannix gripped his boney little wrist, his muscled hand nearly encircling it. "Well, that sure makes me feel young," he smiled.

The two shared a laugh, and the Bestiarius excused himself.

XIX

The Amphitheater stood dormant in hulking shadow, the moon bathing its western arcades where the statues materialized ghostly, ethereal, and glowing like pearl in its rays. The Bestiarius left the Baths of Trajan and journeyed down the Clivus Pullius curving around the side of the Oppian Hill toward the valley between it and the Quirinal beyond, where the Suburra – the oldest neighborhood of Rome – stretched its disheveled bulk. Home to such distinguished men as Julius Caesar and Plutarch at early periods in their careers, Mannix made his weary way toward his flat on its main street, the Argiletum.

Like all old neighborhoods with disparate inhabitants, through the centuries the Suburra had accepted with graceful resignation its increasing number of seedy foreign-run taverns and blackmarket businesses, becoming a place where questions were rarely asked and answers never given. Walking down a boulevard lined with dead fig trees and ranked with old, cavernous stone buildings with keystoned portals and ancient bronze statues run green with oxidation, an old bum spotted him from a doorway reeking of urine and sour wine.

"Hey Myth, nice boots, Myth. How about a little something for an old broken-down legionary," he smiled toothlessly.

The Bestiarius stared at the man for a few seconds, laying there in his own stink, a shell left hollowed twenty years ago in the Mesopotamian desert. His medals all lost in an alley-breach loft; his songs and his poems a failure. Bothered by thoughts which had become as tangible as butterflies, his hands continually swatted the air about his face and his ears.

Mannix pulled a denarius out of the small leather coin purse around his neck, wincing with the pain in his shoulder.

"How about a little something for an old broken-down bestiarius," he replied, dropping the coin into the bum's upended claw.

The man smiled his toothless drooling smile and shook his bald weatherbeaten head splotched all over with skin cancer. "You don't need no help," he said. "You're the Myth," staring up at him, his eyes like black holes in the sky. "I knew it . . . soon as I saw them boots . . . you were him."

"I need a lot of help, friend," Mannix said, as he shuffled slowly on his way.

Deciding he had tomorrow to sleep, and needing a stronger drink to dull the throbbing pain in his shoulder, the Bestiarius spotted a tavern down the street, black-shadow figures slipping drunkenly in and out of a wedge of orange light spilling through its doorway with the sounds of the sistra, the flute and tambourine. He put the hood of his paenula up to avoid recognition, and when he reached the entrance, the figures parted for his passage, several whispering his name as he walked through the grimy archway beneath the large, garishly painted wooden sign that read, 'The Cave of Trophonius.'

One of the suspect Levantine bars lamented by Juvenal and established through the commercial aggressiveness of eastern entrepreneurs over the last century – an aggressiveness like that of ants, which first established itself in the ports, then the houses of the wealthy, and was even now whispering in the antechambers, kitchens and offices of the Imperial Palace – the large cavernous space composed the entire ground floor of a five-story apartment block, its storerooms and shop spaces converted into a complex array of rooms defined by the low, wide, bead-curtained archways vaulting between the structural piers. Lined with the typical bar counters of hollowed vats manned by topless barmaids only slightly the worse for wear, the jumble of rooms were crammed with low tables and oriental chairs and dining couches draped with tasteless tapestries, their walls frescoed with representations of Dionysiac, Bacchic, and Orphic mystery cult initiations.

Oil lamps of various shapes and sizes dangled from bronze chains in the vaults, casting a seedy orange glow through the interior crowded with people rank from a day at the Amphitheater. Sprinkled with incense, the lamps in some of the rooms burned fluorescent green, blue or red, turning the girls' lipstick black and their faces to those of drowned corpses as they laughed and threw their heads back on the dining couches to the joggling of their flaccid breasts and the clattering of their elbow bracelets.

Mannix felt the fatigue and the wine begin to rise up in him from the sweet, feral stench of perfume and garlic sweat, the close-up pastiche of passing faces and brushing arms, and the background party roar of indecipherable voices punctuated by sharp bursts of laughter and high-pitched giggles which pricked at his aching nerves. Rejecting dining couches on principle, he stared a few decadent aristocrats away from a choice corner spot. The toga-clad Patricians recognized him and, though they would like to talk shop, could tell by the look in his eyes that it wasn't the time. As they began to rise, one of their drunker and more stupid number still made a try.

"Hail Mannix!" he said. "We were just discussing today's events. Join us. My friend here says a lion is the more dangerous antagonist over a tiger any day. What's your opinion?"

"Beat it, punk," the Bestiarius replied softly without looking at him.

As he slid wearily into a low cushioned arm chair before the quietly vacated table, three Vigiles watched him from a bar counter in an adjoining room. When he returned their gaze through a bead-curtained archway rippling with the chaotic passage of figures and faces, they looked down or away, and he held his stare. The Vigiles rose and walked out, and Mannix's eyes followed them through the crowd until they disappeared behind the topless tavern wench who had materialized before him.

"Grog," he said, and let his eyes, shadowed by the hood of his paenula, wander past her through the vinous shadows to a stage where the music had stopped, and the lyre, flute and tambourine players were making way for another act.

"You have to pay first, big man," replied the surly waitress, her breasts fish-belly blue in the incense light.

The Bestiarius pulled a sestertius out of the coin purse on his belt and held it out to her.

"It's two," the wench sneered, without taking the sestertius. "One for the drink, one for the table."

He pulled another coin out and laid them both on the table where she had to reach, his eyes already dismissing her in favor of the girl taking the stage.

Lit by hundreds of candles ringing its base, the stage was positioned in a central area where it was visible through all the archways in the honeycomb of rooms, from which the barmaids were drawing back the bead curtains. The girl had eyes like a panther, pouting red lips, and a shock of boyishly-short black hair. She wore large Mycenean plate earrings, twice the size of her ears, and her smallish breasts were contained in a shell-and-string top. The filmy gauze skirt around her waist, embroidered with glass beads, pleasantly revealed the thong riding her crevasse and the appealing little space below it between her thighs.

Mannix let his eyes rove over her body, small and hard and lightly oiled, liking the bareness of her neck, unobstructed by hair and almost obscenely emphasized by the earrings. And the way her belly flowed down from the narrow rib cage and widened at the hips that loosely supported a bead chain of fake pearls. As she bent and moved and readied her space, he could make out the rustling sound of the bead chain through the terrific undertone of party noise, the mystery of her furthered by the fine trail of black hairs, slivered in the candlelight, which fanned from the waistband of her gauze skirt to thin around her navel.

Two club employees were carrying a large squat reed basket through the jostling crowd. When they reached the stage, they climbed carefully through the candles and positioned it in the center. African drummers were taking their places in the shadows behind, their faces wavering in the candlelight all white teeth and eyes. A fat Arab in flowing robes and a headdress huffed his girth onto the stage and spread his jewel-

141

bedecked fingers in a gesture of surrender at the mixture of applause, catcalls and whistles he received.

"Ladies and Gentlemen," he announced. "The moment you've been awaiting has arrived." More catcalls, whistles and shouts, which he patted down with his chubby hands. "The Cave of Trophonius is proudly pleased to bring you," turning and gesturing at the girl standing behind him, "with the express permission of their temple at Carrhae," clapping from the audience, "one of the fabled . . . Sisters . . . of the Moon!" . . .

Whistles, shouts and applause, and the barmaids extinguishing the oil lamps around the vaults of the club, leaving a red-orange glow filtering outward from the candles ringing the stage through the archways into the nest of rooms. As the last of the lamps went down, the weird misty glow permeated the empty spaces between the black silhouettes of heads and shoulders applauding on the dining couches, and the whole scene became macabre and livid, like an exhumed graveyard in a burning town.

The grog had materialized without Mannix realizing it, though the topless tavern wench smarted that he didn't notice her, and walked off in a hip-swinging huff in her short leather skirt and red boot sandals. A clear liquid made from aged wine, the mysterious yet famous man with the broad, sloping shoulders brought the cup to his lips and felt its fire go straight up through his molars into his brain.

On stage the girl had reached her long, slender arms toward the ceiling, the bracelets falling from her wrists to above her elbows. Her breasts scrunched together in their little shells, her torso suddenly long and serpentine, she reached first one hand, and then the other, stretching herself, her thighs slightly shifting. The African drummers had begun a slow, broken beat, the tips of their fingers dancing across the rawhide membranes of the various-sized barrels between their legs. The girl's stomach began slowly revolving in time with the rhythm.

An absolute silence fell across the crowd for the first time; nothing save the soft thud of the drums, and the whisper of the bead chain undulating over her hips. And then, the bass drum keeping its beat on the timing of the human pulse, the

142

others began to step up the tempo and the lithe, dusky Armenian, the upper part of her body motionless, arms raised to full extension above her head, gold bracelets winking in the candlelight, began to grind her hips lightly in time.

Some of the people on the dining couches squirmed slightly in discomfort as a collective expectation took possession of the club, the girl's feet shifting now, her shoulders rotating; her body began to move around the basket in the center of the stage, making witching passes over it with her hands. The drums, beating louder, increased their tempo and individual parts her body begin to keep their own time, as if the drums were pulling her in different directions; only her pelvis stayed grounded, sucking and bulging around the basket.

Mannix felt the sweat begin to bead across his forehead, the grog making everything else drop away, the two hundred other people, the place, the day. His vision unnaturally concentrated on the girl, he removed the hood of his paenula, which he'd kept up to avoid recognition, feeling the dampness behind his ears where his mass of dark hair fell heavy and curling.

The girl's pouting red lips pulled back slightly from her sharp little white teeth, her nostrils beginning to flare and her eyes, glinting hotly through the diamond slits in the purple-black mascara, focusing on the large squat reed basket in the center of the whickering candlelight through which her ankle-braceleted bare feet seemed to be moving as if across a pond of fire. The drums thudding faster, a complexity of interlaced rhythms, she suddenly threw her torso forward, contracting at the waist and flinging her long slender arms out to the sides. Her head, perverse and vulnerable without the typical flying hair, began to gyrate in circles, a black ball with the Mycenaean plate earrings jangling and catching and throwing the candlelight sparking through the rooms.

When she raised back up her expression was a grimace, her nostrils seething with breath, eyes rolling upwards to reveal the whites. Her belly moving faster, round and round, in and out, her whole body began to shiver.

143

The crowd gasped as she suddenly leapt forward and straddled the basket with her legs, the flimsy gauze skirt flying outward as her hips began revolving in a wide circle around it, over and over, over and over until they narrowed and narrowed and narrowed into a quivering little grind over the reed-woven top. Then, as if unable to stand it any longer, she ripped the shell from her right breast and threw it into the audience.

A quiet growl rolled across the spectators, no sooner emitted than silenced.

She ripped the other shell and tossed it, the thin cords falling loose and skittering around her maroon-black nipples.

Another growl trailing to silence.

The drums began to crash and roll, sweat flying from the drummers in a fine mist lit by the candlelight, their hands fluttering across the pale membranes, eyes squinting, distant, oblivious of the girl, their heads bent to one side as if listening for the old midnight gods of their ancestors. Over their thrashing an oboe suddenly hit a long piercing wail which sent a chill through the audience as the girl lifted the top of the basket with a precise flick of her toe and the snake's gold and green head rose to the smell of her.

The waitress had refilled Mannix's tall, slender clay cup with grog without him asking for it. She brushed her hip across his arm as she turned away.

The sweat was shining all over the dancer now, mixing with the oil on her skin as if her whole body was a newly minted bronze statue. Her small breasts and belly glistening with it, she broke into great shuddering jerks, the gauze skirt falling away to reveal the thin leather pouch between her legs, the serpent ducking and bobbing and flicking its tongue as the sweat off her body peppered it. Suddenly she threw herself onto her knees before it, reaching her arms out to it as if begging it not to leave, taking hold of it lightly and caressing its slimy throat.

The audience was panting softly, collectively, their drugged eyes bulged and rolling.

Mannix drained the second grog at a draught, feeling it like slivers of ice stabbing through his brain in the feverish, sour-sweet heat of the club.

The girl lifted the long, thick, vile thing tenderly from the basket and draped it over her shoulders, twisting and grinding upward to stand. One hand on its neck turning the snubbed crocodile face around to hers where its forked tongue flickered at her blood-red lips, the oboe lilting insanely over the drums, her other hand guided the serpent's five-foot length down between her breasts and over her torso where its glistening, scaly, yellow-black-and-green sheen downplayed the oily sweat of her skin.

The crowd had begun to murmur and talk to the stage, and the Bestiarius could feel one of his hands gripping the ledge of the table, but as if someone else's, his mouth dry, eyesight tunneled from the grog.

As the girl guided the snake's tail down beneath the leather thong over the bulge of her crevasse, she broke into a thinly controlled shuddering all over her body. Her mouth opened and she screamed softly. The hand guiding the snake trembled and then lost control and tore away the strip of leather thong and, with a childish tempertantrum jerk of her shorn head, threw it into the audience.

The crowd let out a collective grunt.

Still shuddering, the girl pulled the serpent over her neck with her gently trembling hands, its tongue flicking, eyes winking in the candlelight. Her hands guided it past itself to where it framed her navel, the black fan of hairs below all slime and glint now and the crowd beginning to pant and squeal like pigs at the trough. As the snake's ridged throat passed across her vulva, she screamed softly again. And then, one arm outstretched as a balance, she began to lower her body down to the floor and up again. Slowly at first, to the rhythm of the drums, the snake's tongue flicking, its head bobbing as she moved.

The sweat and oil made the area wetter and wetter until the serpent's tail slipped loose and its snout slipped lightly into the puckered pink slit, the crowd gasping and sucking and

145

squealing. She began to move faster now, and faster, the head slipping in and out bumpy and disconcertingly as she thrusted her pelvis forward and back, forward and back, faster and faster until she threw her arm to the rear catching herself on the deck of the stage to keep going.

The crowd shuddered and wallowed on the couches and, as the drummers fell into a hurricane of sexual rhythm, the girl started thrusting faster and faster and faster until she suddenly collapsed forward onto her knees with a loud scream.

She shuddered and jerked straight upward, paused, screamed again and then slowly fell sideways until she hit the stage. On her back in the pond of blurry fire, she began to arc her stomach and raise her boyish head up in tandem, her chin thrust forward, screaming as she rose up and fell back down, up and down, back and forth, the mass of the snake bouncing and hooping and flapping on top of her belly now, her hands clutching its throat between her thighs. Several candles were knocked down as the girl went into a last series of juddering spasms, the candles rolling crazily in different directions over the stage and falling off its rim, black-shadow figures quickly leaping up and extinguishing them.

Gradually the girl fell limp, mewing softly as the drums slowed to a tom-tom beat and then a shuffle, the snake slithering around one of her thighs.

146

XX

Back out into the night, Mannix walked, drunk and depressed down the Clivus Orbius toward his apartment and the grateful death of bed. At this hour the restaurants were closed and the taverns subdued, and very few lights wavered in any of the windows of the high-rise apartment blocks. The Roman day tended to end around sunset, for the snaking tenement streets and alleys of the city were prone to being swept by fire. Most of the old laws passed under Augustus to keep the buildings to five stories, and under Nero to require catwalks for firemen along their facades, had been conveniently forgotten by real estate speculators through the centuries.

Building rickety solutions to the city's growing population problems, the schemers were suppressed under certain dynasties, turned a blind eye to by others, with the overall result that the 'palace-builders,' as they were ironically called, continued to operate. Some of the unsound structures rose to ten stories, their sudden collapse not uncommon, nor was the aftermath of the tragedy that ensued. For after a fire or a collapse, the scavengers were back on the scene buying up the lot to build another tinder box and charge higher rents.

Mannix's building was over a century old, but sound. Lining the main street, most were. It was back in the tight winding alleyways that the speculators were able to bribe building authorities, obtain permits, and throw up their lightless, windowless, airless horrors filled mostly by immigrants and the working poor. From well-established Patrician families that own whole floors of apartment blocks, to flea-bitten Arabs, bewildered Bythinians, confused Circassians and doe-eyed Dacians subdividing single rooms, surfeit and squalor lived just around the corner from each other in the Suburra.

The Bestiarius shuffled wearily down a narrow canyon under a zig-zag of uneven cornices and rickety terraces, the sidewalks cluttered with refuse, his boot sandals rasping lonely on the wet flagstones. The tormented sound of alley cats echoed through the tight streets, and a choleric baby cried somewhere above. He shuddered, and pulled the hood of his paenula up tighter against the chill riding the night air.

At the intersection of the Vicus Sandaliarius, an angle of raking moonlight revealed a worn-out graffito on a corner alleywall, six letters scrawled in flaked and fading paint across the dirty white stucco above a weathered strip of red fresco border. His name didn't register in his memory for a minute. And when it did, it had no more meaning for him than the wall itself.

"The Myth . . ." came a whisper from behind him.

He started and wheeled to find a figure standing in the shadows outside the fall of moonlight beneath an old shrine to Fortuna preserved as an arched inset in the side wall of a government office across the intersection. A small red candle burned before the cracked fresco of the goddess, its tiny flame flickering and surging with the wind.

The figure stepped slowly out of the shadows, a painfully young eastern prostitute turned ghostly and ethereal in the wedge of moonlight. She knew his name but he not hers; and yet he'd seen her before and remarked her for the way her body moved beneath her short-skirted stola as she walked in the daytime up and down the Via Panispernus, Street of the Breadmakers.

A pastiche of her images flickered before his eyes. She was always tan in the summer from off-days at the seaside, but tired-tan; her hopelessly young face ageing around the eyes and mouth in ways that even his hadn't through the years of walking into the jaws of Hell. In the winter her legs looked pitifully cold, the skin translucent like a skim of ice over the network of blue capillaries; her second-hand military paenula cut high to reveal them, and died all over in starburst patterns of red and yellow courtesy of the cheap Nabataean tailors.

She knew his name and she whispered it but it didn't come out throaty and wanton as it should have, but meek and confused. For the look in his eyes frightened her, as he staggered slightly with the weariness and the grog, hesitating though he didn't know why. Not one to frequent prostitutes, still the dancer's sick tickling had become an itch, and he needed a further come-down from the nerve-shock of the day. And he was lonely for something. Lonely for the hills where he was from, lonely for his grandfather and the mystery of death.

The young girl had the kind of dirty-honey skin and slightly oriental eyes that smacked of the steppes northeast of the Black Sea. She also had a room to go to around the corner, a ground-floor hovel with an old fat woman sitting in the alley outside the door in a chair in a shawl like a flea-ridden guard dog. As they went in and closed the door, the Bestiarius felt the depression rise up in him like bile, the ceiling so low he had to duck to avoid its crossing of ancient woodbeams dripping with hooks laden with pots and pans and cooking utensils, the grungy stuccoed walls all too reminiscent of his old cell in the Ludus Matutinus.

The place flickered in grimy candlelight with an old crumbling brick stove in the corner and he wanted to run but he stood mesmerized, watching as she lifted the slatternly paenula over her head and her breasts fell loose and faintly appalling in the candlelight, the nipples swollen and distended. Unable to meet his eyes, she was as nervous of him as if he was the whore and she the first-timer. It made his heart rush out and he placed his hands on her shoulders and thought to kiss her but couldn't manage it; at the last minute simply brushing past her lips with his whiskered cheek.

Wanting to hold someone but it didn't make sense like this, he ran his hand gently over her face and then down over her breasts catching on the rough calloused feel of her nipples and the sickening thought of motherhood. He moved the hand up around her throat, registering and dismissing the faint nerve-twitch in his fingers to crush it, and then around to the back of her neck at the base of her head beneath her dirty oily hair. He trailed it softly and lightly down her spine, his fingertips whispering through the exciting dip where it arced and then flowed into the soft firm buttocks. But it didn't help.

Finally she knelt before him and, though that wasn't much good either, she was patient at it; and shortly he began to run a slightly trembling hand through her greasy hair, tracing a finger around the pitiful little pink volutes of her ear, its nail still speckled with stubbornly dried blood which the bath could not wash off. A minute later the room started to buckle in the candlelight and the visions came. The visions of Demetrius sitting up drunkenly in the sand, his face like a carved pumpkin in the Saturnalia festival, of Delila and the leopard and the snake hooping and thrashing on the big smooth round breasts bursting from Julia Soaemias' black leather bodice before it all swirled and disappeared behind the lightning flares of his orgasm with quick stone glimpses of dancing maidens and drunken centaurs and goats . . . and tambourines . . . and flutes and axes . . . and horny satyrs . . . .

XXI

After leaving more money than he should have on a splintered wooden tabletop, the Bestiarius walked out of the dank hovel past the old dog woman into the alley. Rounding several corners to arrive on the Argiletum, the wider main street was flooded with moonlight, and he angled across it to enter a square doorway between a tavern and a tanner's shop. Climbing slowly the eight flights of stairs, his knee ached. Constant reminder of a boar's tusk years back, a livid pink scar ran the length of his left thigh.

Shuffling dizzily down the dark corridor to his flat, a door opened at an angle across the hall, and a withered apparition stood in a pool of orange candlelight.

"Evening, Erithrea," he said.

"I wanted to make sure you were home," his neighbor replied.

"Thanks," he managed a smile.

"Good night," she said, as she closed her door.

"Night," he replied.

Removing an iron skeleton key from inside his belt, he unlocked his heavy oak-paneled door with the bronze tiger-head knocker, and entered the dark alcove of his apartment. By the light of the moon streaming through the windows of the living area further inside, he chinked the flint and blew on the straw, lighting an ember of incense in the niche in the wall where his small votive statues of the Lares and Penates – the household gods inherited from his parents – stood in weathered nubs of ancient peasant woodcarving. He lit a small oil lamp from the ember and entered the living space, its walls decorated with frescoes a century old. Country scenes with vine-clad trees and birds playing in their leaves undulated in the lamplight as he lit another oil lamp on the opposite side of the room.

Two glass-paned doorways with iron grills gave onto the terrace running the length of the three rooms. Off to one side was the kitchen, and he entered it with the lamp, illuminating a long narrow room with a round brick stove on one side, and a squat toilet facility on the other. He placed the candle on the counter, lifted his tunic and stood over the hole for a good while, listening to the sound of his urine drain the five floors down the lead pipe into the sewage channel beneath the street, which in turn ran down to its intersection with the Cloaca Maxima beneath the Forum. Dreamed up nine hundred years before by some ingenious engineer to drain the marshland of the Forum into the Tiber downstream of the city, the underground channel now formed the main conduit of the city's network of sewer systems – branch channels having been opened off of it with the building of each new neighborhood through the centuries.

Most of Rome's population had no private toilet facilities, and either used the public baths, or the public latrines, where long benches ran beneath arcades lining various streets with a shallow trough of water before them containing horse hair brushes on sticks to clean oneself. The public latrines weren't segregated by sex, but they were functional, and they kept the plague at bay. Mannix had money, however – a decent account in the Basilica Aemilia down the street in the Forum – and his apartment was fully equipped.

He poured water from a terracotta pitcher down the pipe after his urine, and moved to the counter, where he removed the lid on another pitcher and took a long drink of the water he filled fresh at the fountain on the corner this morning courtesy of the Claudian Aqueduct. The kitchen also had its door leading onto the terrace, with its grill for security. His thirst slaked, the Bestiarius moved back through the living space to his bedchamber on the other side, also decorated in fresco. Illusionistic scenes looking into gardens with birds and lemon trees covered on the walls, the frescoes faded and cracked with age. Furniture throughout the flat was sparse – a wooden bedstead on bronze lion-claw legs with a straw-filled mattress and a blanket for sleeping, and a cabinet with knick-knacks in

152

the bedroom. There was a couch of much the same design in the living area and two chairs spaced about a side table. On one wall was a bookshelf, with the leather-bound volumes of Greek philosophy he inherited from Erithrea's dead husband. Mannix was close enough to the old couple, Romans for generations; he had carried the dead man down the stairs to await the funeral cart the morning Erithrea woke him in sobs with the news. She subsequently gave him her husband's books, for she herself could not read.

He undressed in the candlelight, hung his tunic and belt on a peg in the wall, and placed his boot sandals in the corner of the room. A single trunk contained several other tunics, wool socks and a woolen cloak with a hood for winter, and from it he removed a blanket which he draped over his shoulders, the rough feel of it tickling his wound. Spent and exhausted, the pain in his shoulder radiating up into his jaw and down the inside of his torso with the wine wearing off, he unlocked the iron grill and walked out onto the terrace running the length of his apartment.

Standing in the moonlight among a few scattered plants in old vases, he leaned his elbows on the ledge of the terrace and looked down toward the shadowy hulk of the rear of the Temple of Minerva, its weathered bronze roof tiles gleaming softly in the moonlight. A gentle night breeze whispered up the street sending a chill over his achy body, and he pulled the blanket like a robe tighter around him and stared out across the jumbled terracotta rooftops of the sleeping city. The clouds had broken and moved on, and the dusting of stars ran their zenith over the east-west axis of the street. One of them dropped off and fell away, and he felt a strange kinship to it and wondered to himself what could be happening up there.

His grandfather believed in the stars, and on rare occasions would allow him to handle with reverence his collection of stones fallen from the sky. For the old man, the stars and the world itself were all of a piece, and he drew portents from them the same way as he did from clouds, stones and animals – all parts of a magic universe in which were combined the will of the gods, the influence of demons, and the strange lot apportioned to men. On summer nights, Mannix would go with him to the special place on top of the hill to study the heavens. Sitting, gazing upward and turning imperceptibly with the stars, he would invariably drift off to sleep with the cooling smell of the day-sunned grass.

The old man had a rough affection for him, an affection without words, tenderness or visible sign; for his impenetrable hardness came from farther back, and from more ancient times. He was neither uncultivated, nor unlearned, however; Mannix had pried open an old cobwebbed trunk in the shed after his death and found it full of rusty mathematical instruments untouched for fifty years. Still, his grandfather was a man of the tribe, the vestige of a sacred and awe-inspiring world to which his Latin soothsayer ancestors belonged. And his affection for the young boy was the same as he felt for the stones, the clouds and the animals on his farm.

Standing trembling softly in the moonlight, the Bestiarius remembered a summer night when the old man cast his horoscope with sticks, stones and the stars above in the clearing on the hill. He'd fallen asleep on his side in the rough prickly sunburnt grass whose smell brought the dreams, and the old man shook him awake and pulled him to a small fire of roots and leaves and examined his palm, reading some kind of confirmation in its lines with what he'd seen in the sky. Then he announced, with a grumbling severity devoid of any awe, that he would rule the world for a day.

The Bestiarius smiled sadly with the memory. The village folk thought the tall old man who walked bareheaded on horny, unshod feet a wizard, and they tried to avoid his glance. But for Mannix he was just his grandfather. A man who slept on his back on a pine board and breathed from his toes and did not dream. For the world and life itself were all the dream that he needed.

Back inside his apartment, Mannix extinguished the candles, took another long drink of water in the kitchen, and walked back through the pearl rays lancing through the iron latticework of the terrace doors into his room, where he stretched himself slowly and carefully across the bed and pulled the blanket up to his neck. Sleep usually came in an instant for him, for he learned long ago how to shield his mind by emptying his thoughts. Much like when he fought in the arena, the no-mind philosophy of action and reaction devoid of philosophical speculation served his life as it would his death.

But this night he felt unconsciousness wax and wane like the surf in his soul, and as he drifted upon it he was tossed by visions, where the young eastern prostitute transformed into a female body with a jackass head, and the bears in the next room plotted how to acquire his bank account. But, more than any of those, he met over and over the last glance of Demetrius, slowed in the moment before the bull blasted through him, his eyes like those of a child looking at his father as he fell into a well. And he knew, even in the grips of an oncoming, death-like sleep, that today had added another scroll to the library of things he could not get out of his head. Things he could never get out of his head but had to wake up to every morning like a fist to the jaw during that quasi-conscious moment when pangs of youth long lost return and he thought everything might be new again.

XXII

Early morning, her thoughts distracted by the sound of sandals walking down the peristyle toward her, Julia Soaemias looked up to find one of the white-smocked palace clerks bowing as he approached.

"Domina, a message for you."

She took the scrolled parchment and undid its thread.

It took a moment for her eyes to focus on the writing. The oysters from Lucrinus were on schedule, as were the crayfish from the river mouths of Gaul.

"Thank you," she nodded, without looking at the clerk. "And please tell Petricon I wish to see him."

The clerk bowed himself away.

She was taking great pains with the banquet, working closely with the chefs, caterers and entertainers, and taking charge of the decorators personally to ensure that the ambience was as perfect as the food. Several hundred of the Senate and the upper-level aristocracy of Rome would be on hand, and the banquet had been designed to make amends.

It was no secret that things had run amiss. Through the haze of another night's insomnia, she looked through the fluted orange columns of the peristyle. Past the Polyphemus fountain's sparkling after-spray, a statue her of son polluted the place, sixty yards away. The Emperor. The word sounded suddenly funny and she snorted. But then again, she was already nursing a drink.

The sculpture was striding forth from its plinth in the typical guise of a noble Roman conqueror, the Gorgon head on its cuirass flanked by the wolf and the twins on one side and the goddess Roma on the other. She shook her head at the subtle indication – Rome paying homage to the sun god, Elagabal, 'god of the mountain,' a black stone fallen from the sky and

156

thought to be a divine image of Sol Invictus by a bunch of sunstroked camel jockeys a thousand years ago.

She sneered in disgust. The Roman aristocracy wondered at how things had gone so wrong, but the fault was their own, for allowing their servants over time to become their masters. And Julia Soaemias was just as disgusted with it as they, for she was half Roman herself, and that was the only half that ever mattered to her.

But the problem was complicated, at best, and generally indicative of the overflowing wave of immigrants who had established themselves in Rome throughout the previous two centuries. Even as early as the Julio-Claudian Dynasty, the writer Lucan was bemoaning the fact that the city was becoming depopulated of its own citizens and filled with the 'dregs of the universe.' And Nero himself enjoyed mixing with the riffraff of Aramaic courtesans and flute-players who hung around the Circus Maximus. Yet it was these foreigners from the east who adapted themselves to the functional needs of the city, in the vacuum left by the spoiled Roman populace who thus found their way out of jobs such as construction work and repairing public buildings, cleaning the Tiber wharves, clearing the sewers, funeral services and so on.

By this point, however, there were Orientals in the Senate, in the corridors of power with their greasy fingers in the pots of the Imperial domestic scene. From North Africa to the banks of the Rhine and Danube rivers, Commagenians, Emesians, Ituraeans and Palmyrenians served as archers, footsoldiers, and cavalrymen in the Legions. And her cousin Caracalla had gone so far as to confer citizenship upon all inhabitants of tax-paying provinces.

After Macrinus had him assassinated, his mother Julia Domna starved herself rather than face the disgrace of being reduced to the status of a private citizen, expiring in her chair overlooking the stadium garden where the plane trees were again in autumn leaf. But her sister Julia Maesa wasn't about to give up that easily. She immediately set about bringing her wealth to bear on the organization of a rebellion of the Legions stationed in Syria. For these eastern Legions which Caracalla had used in his haphazard Mesopotamian expedition had remained relatively loyal, and Julia Soaemias and her mother did more than buy up the officer corps. They also spread the rumor that her son was in fact the issue of sexual relations with Caracalla, and hence the grandson of Septimius Severus and the rightful heir to the throne.

The boy was given the family name 'Varius Avitus Bassianus.' By the age of seventeen, he was already a priest of Elagabal, from whom he adopted his diminutive pseudonym, Elagabalus. He had, of course, inherited the priesthood from his line just as her sister's son Alexianus had. But, unlike Geta and Caracalla, Elagabalus had decided to assume it.

As she reflected upon it, leaving his upbringing to the Isaic priestesses had probably affected him. For the boy early-on developed a fascination for the occult along with an effeminate and exhibitionistic nature. And yet she couldn't help but remember that it was with no little encouragement from her mother, who seemed to see in it potential with the Mob, for whom the strictly formalistic worship of the classical Western gods had long become emotionally bankrupt. And, in fact, when the officers of the defected Legions found him in a sun-drenched Syrian temple precinct wearing a Phoenician robe of purple and gold, his arms and head studded with jewels, dancing about an altar with a tambourine followed by the citizenry of Emesa, they saw in it just the kind of sensory-laden liturgy that would offer the attraction of strong feelings and emotions, and a sense of belonging to the animalistic and otherwise lonely and anonymous rabble of Rome.

In order to appease the endless fence-riding of the upper classes, however, his grandmother shrewdly had him assume the name of his alleged father – Marcus Aurelius Antoninus; and indeed the accession of Elagabalus was recognized by the Senate and the ever-pragmatic Roman aristocracy moreover due to the fact that Macrinus was of an obscure origin and devoid of the proper political connections. But moreso because Septimius Severus had retrospectively rigged himself legitimate heir of the Antonine Emperors in a process of auto-adoption – and hence Elagabalus (Marcus Aurelius Antoninus), as a Severan, kept things tidy. Julia Soaemias and her mother were both entitled 'Augusta,' Empress, for as far as the Senate and the aristocracy were concerned, the evil they knew was preferable to the evil they didn't; and Macrinus was defeated in battle outside Antioch by the Legions whose defection their wealth had secured. It was made clear that she and her mother were the ones running the show and, in fact, her son wanted to remain a priest. But, as an emperor could truly be so only in Rome (to which she and her mother were both eager to return), he agreed to come only if accompanied by the black stone, which was carried in a processional chariot drawn by four horses, like the quadriga of the Sun.

Julia Soaemias frowned at the memory of the interminably embarrassing journey. Due to frequent stops in various towns where Elagabalus tirelessly attended to the service of his god with gesticulations and sacred orgies performed to the obscene rattling of the timbrels, the journey took an entire year. Neglecting all the affairs of the provinces, he spent the winter in Nicomedia buggering legionaries and the soldiers finally began to regret their choice and turn their thoughts on his cousin Alexianus. She and her mother also began to fear that this strolling strumpet, attired in eastern fashion, ran the risk of making a disastrous impression on the aristocracy of Rome.

Thus, in order to prepare the capital for his priestly entry, they sent the Senate a portrait of Elagabalus in the costume of a sacrificer. The picture was strategically placed in the Senate building above the statue of Victory, at the foot of which each member of the Curia burned incense and poured wine on the altar before each session. From then on it became impossible to accomplish this preliminary rite without technically paying homage to the crowned high priest. And since there were already Orientals in the Senate, in the corridors of power with their fingers in the coffers of Empire, on a technicality the god of Emesa had become invoked before all others.

Looking out across the slaves busying themselves sweeping brown palm fronds loosened by yesterday's rain from

159

the wet-streaks across the blue-veined Pentelic marble pavement, she lifted the glass by her side and drank deeply of its clear, fiery liquid. She had spoiled him. She knew that. She had turned a blind eye to his antics, religious and otherwise.

But he had taken the place of Body there for a while, when Body could no longer get for her what Name desired. And he had been used by her mother, just as she had been. So the boy had become willful and weak, and spoiled just as she had been. But if there was anything her life had taught her it was let youth enjoy itself. For, sooner or later, someone was sure to take it away from them.

If the truth be known, she had never much cared for him, never much cared for children in general and, least of all, the continuation of her line. He bored her, and he had his grandfather's eyes, and she'd pawned him off on the servants and the Isaic priestesses until the little faggot developed on his own into a kind of quiet, living revenge for her. A revenge on her grandfather and the god he represented. A revenge on her mother; a revenge on Name. A revenge on the social pressures that kept her in prison all her life – that would not allow her to leap from the water and take flight. But, more than any of those, a revenge on herself, for losing the light.

'Poor thing,' she thought to herself, casting another look at the sculpture of Elagabalus striding forth with a finger raised. 'He will not do well under the assassin's blade,' she smiled softly. 'No, he will not bear it out well at all in the end.'

She rose a bit unsteadily. The palace slaves were starting their work inside the Banquet Hall and she must dress, and inspect their progress. Everything must be perfect, for the banquet had been designed to make amends. And amends it would make.

XXIII

Mannix's eyes snapped open to a repetitive sound, his consciousness slowly registering it as someone banging on his door. Never good news, his head throbbed, and blood had oozed from his shoulder in the night to coagulate all over the mattress and blanket. He groaned himself into a sitting position and swung his feet over the side of the low bedstead. The doorway onto the terrace blinded him with a mass of liquid gold cut up by the lattices of the iron grill, dust particles rising slowly through the penetrating shafts of sunlight. He stood shakily, dragging the blanket behind him and keeping his head below his shoulders to keep from blacking out. His free hand slapped into walls and doorways, using them to help propel him along.

The rapping continued.

"Hold on, by Mithras!" he yelled over its din as he arrived in the alcove, pulled the boltlock back, and opened the heavy creaking oaken door a few inches into his apartment.

Avidius Lepidus, director of the Ludus Matutinus, stood in the hallway. Tall and thin, with heavy bones and knobby wrists, he looked like a man who knew he'd been something.

"Are you all right?" he said, examining his former charge with his hard, uninterested eyes. Eyes that suited the veined, pitted, but tight-to-the-bone look of his face, which seemed too large, the nose too large, the mouth too large, the cheekbones and gray eyebrows too prominent.

Mannix's own eyes were swollen and pasted with sleep. "What's it look like?" he replied, opening the door and limping back into his apartment.

Lepidus entered the flat like it was his son's bedroom – which it essentially was – his spit-shined boot sandals creaking over the tile floor, leather-strap skirt armor rustling from his thick, iron-studded belt over the blood-red tunic. Sixty-five years old and still tough as hell.

"Sorry about Demetrius," he said. "Boy had a lot of promise."

Mannix stood in the middle of the room with the blanket over his front and his ass bare, blinded in the glare of the sunlight coming through the lattices of the terrace doors. "Not enough, I guess."

Lepidus gazed at his blood-encrusted shoulder and the scar tissue crisscrossing his upper body, and then dismissed it with a flick of his hand, as if swatting a fly away. "What the hell were you doing charging that bull like that?"

The Bestiarius turned aside, knowing what he was in for.

"Son, you can't take anything personally out there. You know that!"

Mannix squinted against the sunlight, still confused from sleep, drink and wounds. The idea of trying to remember the action was ridiculous, just glimpses and reminders that hurt all over his body and brain.

Lepidus put his hands on his hips. "I appreciate your feelings for Demetrius, but it was the work of the Fates. A man with your experience should know that."

The Bestiarius wrapped the blanket around him and walked to the terrace doors, where the raking sunlight filled the sleep-lines and the bloody scratches of frantic foxes and jackals scabbing across his stubbled face.

The Fates . . . he had a strange, dark-cornered vision of lean, long-haired, languidly beautiful women swimming naked in an element of deep green tinged with blackness. An element that was neither water nor air, but something viscid, and in-between.

Lepidus stared at the muscled back of his former charge. "What is it?"

Mannix shook his head, his mass of dark hair beginning to show the first streaks of gray.

Lepidus squinted his eyes.

Sunlight sweltered in the smoky glass panes.

Mannix continued to stare blind at the dust particles, a billion bright ambassadors of morning, dancing slowly before his eyes. He swallowed. "Julia Soaemias sent me a note in the clinic yesterday," he said, his voice deep and cracked with sleep.

Lepidus' face smarted. He began to say something and then stopped. He gripped the handle of the terrace door with his strong, gnarled, leather wrist-banded hand and walked out into the morning. Placing his hands on the railing of the terrace, he leaned out into the sunlight falling in a wedge across the crown of his balding head.

The Bestiarius moved through the doorway, and stood a little way down.

The old director shook his head softly.

"How was I to know it would turn out like this, son?"

"Couldn't you have seen it coming?" Mannix asked quietly, squinting into the deep blue sky.

Lepidus looked up himself. "Perhaps I should have," he nodded.

A gull arced off over the rooftops.

Pursing his lips in thought, the old director shook his head. "But she would have gotten to you anyway." He turned and looked at his former charge. "Sooner or later."

Mannix didn't respond. He knew that Lepidus was not vulnerable and, unlike most people, only death could kill him. The Bestiarius had quite a bit of the man inside of him and knew he would brook no change of attitude from him now, even if he really could not do anything about it. He decided there wasn't any sense showing any. Wasn't any sense in speaking of his growing desire to get out of the noise, confusion and sickness of the city. To return to his grandfather's farm, patch it up and get it working again. Lepidus was too far gone; the roles of surrogate father and son too set in stone.

"Look at this," the director gestured down over the railing of the terrace, changing the subject. Grimacing, his hand moved across the scene like a farmer scattering chaff in the wind.

The Bestiarius looked down. The street below was a congested flow of humanity. He looked back at Lepidus, who returned his gaze with his hard, hawk-like eyes.

"We're not gods, son," the old trainer shook his head. "We're just men," he smiled. And then his face grew serious. "But the Myth is everything."

Mannix glanced aside, clicking his tongue in annoyance.

"If you want to be just like everybody else," Lepidus continued, his voice raising a notch. "Or just like anybody else, for that matter," he shrugged, and then he looked back at Mannix. "If you want that for just one second . . . you're already dead."

The Bestiarius held the blanket around his waist and squinted from the street into the cerulean blue of the sky. 'I am already dead,' he thought to himself. For, despite the fact that Lepidus had taught him to feel his superiority over the Mob as if he stood on the very heights of Olympus itself, in a world of gods and heroes and supermen, a world that the people in the street below couldn't conceive of; and though he had grown daily less and less accessible to fear to the extent that he was no longer really capable of experiencing what fear felt like – for every two thoughts that came into his head, one was of death.

Lepidus turned his cold gaze back to the sea of people clogging the street below, grubbing and haggling and bickering and whining. "How can you do that . . ." he asked rhetorically, "and be alive?"

Mannix glanced down at the confusion and couldn't help but agree. He lived more in one morning in the Arena than most people did in their entire lives. Death was imminent to all; you took what the Fates gave you. But in nourishing the desperate desire necessary to fight in the Amphitheater, the Bestiarius had come to understand what it meant to be as alive as a man can be. To truly live each day as if it were the last.

"Take a break, take a vacation," Lepidus continued, dismissing the matter. "Then come back and help me run the school."

Mannix turned his head and looked at him.

164

The trainer reached for his arm, grasping it above the elbow. "That's right," he nodded. "I want you to take over the school when it's time," he paused, lifting his fist with the signet ring, "to adopt you as my son."

The Bestiarius' eyes moved to a tremendous cumulous cloud, pluming up at an oblique angle over Lepidus' shoulder.

"You don't have to say anything," the director continued. "Just get some rest, boy," Lepidus squeezed his arm, then turned away and squinted against the sunlight, as if trying to find what Mannix was looking for in the sky, but knowing already. Unable to help him there, he turned his thoughts back to the day's business. "Well I'm off," he said, starting for the door. "Pull your chin up, old boy."

The Bestiarius watched him leave. He scratched his head. The skull felt fractured.

Turning back to the terrace, Mannix walked to its western end, where the warm sun stang pleasantly in the fresh scars across his torso. Terracotta rooftops rippled across the hills, a mellow patina of burnished ochre broken occasionally by the surge of temples and basilicas. Over the irregular maze of rooftops, he could see the head and shoulders of the Colossus of Helios rising in age-darkened bronze from the piazza of the Amphitheater, its usual contingent of gulls cruising playfully about its spiked crown. The copper rooftiles of the tremendous Temple of Venus and Rome flanking it wavered like a mirage in the sunlight.

And then his gaze moved to the temple of Elagabal under construction on the knoll of the Palatine a step above it, crawling with ant-like workmen and construction cranes; and he felt the disgust well up inside.

XXIV

The crash of a distant surf punctuated his thoughts, the collective roar from the Amphitheatre trailing off on corridors of sound. He squinted from the multi-colored flow of humanity in the street below up into the sky, where the huge silver cumulous cloud mutated in silence high above, yesterday's lightning buried somewhere deep inside.

Turning back into his apartment, the living area was aflood in sunlight, and he moved through it to the kitchen, where he spent some time clearing a breathing hole in his nasal passages, blowing dried clots of snot and blood from his nose into the drain between great gasps through his mouth. The nose had been broken so many times that the process was a daily ritual. He soaked a rag in some water and carefully dabbed the dried blood from his shoulder, which ached all the way down the inside of his arm. Then he rubbed some bay leaves over his teeth and set about dressing, removing a fresh tunic from the trunk in his bedroom, bending groggily to cinch his boot sandals, buckling his wide black leather belt with the bronze studs, turning the buckle to the back and jerking the tunic straight.

He took up the maroon paenula from yesterday, folded it over his arm and draped his small leather coin purse over his head and tucked it under the neck of the paenula. After locking the terrace doors, he stood pensive in his apartment, looking around him with no one to say goodbye to. Deciding it was better that way, he walked out into the hall, took the skeleton key from inside his belt and locked his door.

"Have you seen Caesar?" the old woman said from her doorway across the hall.

"Afraid not, Erithrea," Mannix said as he turned. "He didn't come in my place last night."

The cat often did, however, climbing from terrace to terrace and entering by the door he left open at night to ventilate his place in the hot months. He'd more than once thought it was a leopard, waking with a start in the night as the little bastard pounced down off his chest and meowed across the floor.

She nodded her head. "Well, if you do see him, will you let me know?"

"I will, Erithrea," he replied, noticing the smell of old people emanating from her apartment and knowing it wasn't so much about the cat as the company of a few shared words in the hallway. "I'll bring him home."

"Are you off to the Amphitheater?" she said, touching the amulets of Isis and Serapis on the cord around his throat.

"No, not today. I'm on holiday," he smiled.

"I'm glad," she nodded. "You should get more rest."

Mannix kissed her withered cheek and gave her hand a squeeze. Then he stepped back and nodded, and turned and walked off down the hall, the old woman watching him with her rheumy eyes.

Carefully down the stairs using the balustrade to help the stiffness in his knee, the Bestiarius emerged from the open doorway of his apartment building into the same kind of madness that made him balk with dread as a fifteen year-old entering the city for the first time. Now it was just reality. And a hazy one at that.

Still swollen-faced and half-blind with sleep, he walked down the sidewalk to the intersection at the corner where he waited his turn at the fountain, leaning with his outstretched hand on the wall and his face buried in his forearm behind some slave girls filling up amphorae with fresh water for their mistresses' morning baths. When they cleared off, he dunked his head full under in the granite basin with the weathered lion's head spout in the wall, and kept it there gurgling in the cold mountain water with the bubbles coming up around his face. Finally emerging, he threw his mass of dark hair back in an arc of water that peppered passers-by, none of whom considered saying anything after a glance at his back and triceps, the bunched trapezius and massive sloping shoulders.

Slicking his hair back off his forehead to fall straight and wet down his neck, he took a long drink from the flow of cold water coursing from the lion's mouth. He brushed the water off his face, smoothed his dark eyebrows, and ran the back of an iron hand across his lips. Finally starting to wake up, he stood at the corner and stretched his limbs like a big cat with the world coming slowly into focus. Looking around, he blinked against the sunlight, cut up by the intersection and the multi-leveled overhang of terracotta-tiled rooftops. The golden light fell in raking angles across the red-bordered white apartment blocks, zig-zagged beneath the hodgepodge of irregular wooden terraces, and bathed the heads, backs and arms of the mobile and very disparate population moving beneath them.

Traders leading donkeys, merchants, mercenaries, adventurers, wandering philosophers and orators, businessmen and exiles, carried with them their hopes, hallowed by a variety of gods, in all directions. Craftsmen plied their trades in the shadows of the ground-floor shop fronts lining the buildings, the sound of hammers and anvils punctuating the surf of voices speaking a mismatch of languages and dialects, with Greek the best bet on meeting someone halfway.

A confluence of currents crisscrossing the Mediterranean, the Rome of the Severans was the result of a series of accumulations and syncretisms which had transformed the Urbs into the Orbs, the City into the Universe. The great political and legal epicenter of the world, cosmopolitan and capricious, Rome was no longer a city properly speaking – it was an idea. A thousand-year old idea that, by this time, no longer worked. For never before in the history of mankind had there been such a density of urban concentration, with the resulting sense of anguish it aroused in the populace.

Cut off from any kind of roots, the tragedy of high-rise housing schemes had demoralized the individual with feelings of dread, oppression, meaninglessness and anonymity. But it had also spoiled him. The relative prosperity enjoyed under the Roman system for the previous two hundred years had gradually decreased his ability to adapt to the general insecurity and feeling of precariousness silently undermining the Roman world since the irreplaceable losses in Germania under Marcus Aurelius, and the unpublicized defensive battle going on every day from Persia to Northern Britannia.

In a sense, the slaughter in the Arena was an ironic metaphor for a situation in which one million Romans ruled over fifty million peoples. For all the blood and death and hell that the Mob surrounded in their little seats in the Amphitheater, is what in reality surrounded them in the 'Real World' out there. Even now, over the noise of the nine hundred and fifty thousand other inhabitants of the city crowding the streets all around him, Mannix could hear the continual rustling sound of the crowd half a mile away.

After ducking into his usual tavern for a morning roll and a cup of grainy Indian tea doled by a ladle from a simmering pot inset in the counter, the Bestiarius was creeping back to life, the blood beginning to course with some confidence again. The rope veins in his arms swelled in the sunlight, and he strode down the Argiletum through the crowds like a wave breaking.

People recognized him and hailed, "Ave Mannix!" "Viva Mannix!" A group of punk kids began chanting "Myth!" and he smiled and raised a fist. An old beggar woman touched him for luck and, down the way, a younger one in a paisley-curtained litter borne by two aged slaves eyed his sculpted girth. The Bestiarius winked and her sea shell-pink eyelids fluttered as she passed.

Over the heads of the people in the street loomed the fifty-foot Porticus Absidata, wet streaks from last night's rain darkening its dedicatory inscription and running the oxidation down its marble facade. A monumental gateway to the rear of the Forum of Nerva – one of the Imperial Forums built off of the Roman Forum proper through the years – the Porticus Absidata formed an arcaded concavity embracing the street of the Argiletum and acting as a re-entrant dynamic to the convex hemicycle of the Forum of Augustus it bordered.

The entire wall system was built with a core of fire-resistant tufa volcanic stone so that it acted as a tremendous fire wall – reaching a hundred and fifteen feet in certain places – that shielded the sacred precincts of the Imperial Forums and the Forum proper from the tinder-box tenement neighborhood of the Suburra behind them. The Argiletum slipped at an angle through one of its arches, and Mannix with it, plunging into the shadowlands beneath the portico.

Like the belly of a ship teeming with rats, the curved arcade was alive with shapes which his eyes didn't immediately adjust to after the brilliant sunlight bathing the street. But gradually they did come into view as shadowy figures of Arabs smoking hookahs, African vendors with their wares spaced on colorful carpets sitting with their backs to the piers, and a group of Palestinian whores lingering in garish makeup and beaded head dresses, hissing and flicking their tongues at him as he passed. One of them brushed her fingernails across his big veined bicep and he shrugged her off with a growl.

"Baahh . . . Sluts."

Once through the portico the world changed, as if the sunlit Suburra was a reality negated by the shadowlands beneath the Porticus Absidata, which in turn formed an intermediate stage between it and the new reality evinced in the light of the Forum of Nerva. The Bestiarius re-emerged into crashing sunlight on the flank of the temple of Minerva, dwarfed by the bulk of the structure rising from its podium on a level ten feet above his head. He underwent a sensory change from the crowded urban quarters just passed, brought upon by the brilliant blue of the sky above, the blinding white of the marble temple cella, and the purple shadow line beneath its roof overhang. A splash of riotous color was thrown into the mix in the form of a flower vendor's booth to the side of the podium on which the temple rose.

He walked through the arch surmounting the narrow passage between the building and one of the hundred-yard-long decorative colonnades lining its retaining walls to emerge into the long and slender space of Nerva's Forum – monochrome in its whiteness, the steam rising around his boot sandals as the sun heated the rain-wet Italic marble. Traversing the hundred yards contained between the colonnades, he glanced through entryways leading into the forums flanking him on either side, seams small enough to both preserve the mystery of each enclosure, as well as exploit the dazzling fascination – the difference in alignment, color and decor – of each new space experienced.

To his left through a large doorway between two of the fluted columns, he could see the groomed garden plots of serene cypress and pinkly blooming oleander in the large square of the Forum of Vespasian next door. He caught a glimpse of the forty-foot pink Aswan granite columns of its Templum Pacis, or Temple of Peace. In the mists of its shadowy interior, the huge bronze Menorah and the silver-bound scrolls of the Talmud taken from the Temple in Jerusalem flickered in the oil braziers lit by its cadre of priests every morning. And indeed, the Flavian Amphitheater in which he fought was largely financed by the gold and silver stripped from Herod's rebuild of Solomon's Temple, and built in part by twelve thousand Jewish prisoners of war, who were subsequently expended in the inaugural games.

As he continued his walk, through a doorway staged in the wall behind the colonnade on his right, the Bestiarius could see the alternating green cipollino and purple marble aggregate squares fanning out across the pavement of the Forum of Augustus, the tops of the eight huge flanking columns of its temple of Mars Ultor rising above the retaining wall. Seeming as child actors on a vast stage set, people clustered in groups scattered near and far across the hundred yards of space. Pigeon sellers hailed their wares to pilgrims making their way to the Capitoline Hill to offer sacrifice, and Mannix could see at an angle up to the right on the northern spur of the hill, on the crest of the old citadel walls, the temple of Juno Moneta presiding over a mass of angular rooftops.

His steps veered across the long slender square, and he exited the Forum of Nerva through the archway at its end, where the Argiletum continued on. To his immediate right he caught a glimpse through the tri-columnar screen leading into

171

the Forum of Julius Caesar, down the green cipollino colonnades flanking its own large rectangular square to the temple of Venus Genetrix. But the glimpse ended just as it began, and he plunged into the shade of the canyon between the precipitous flank of the Senate building towering a hundred feet on his right, and the short axis of the Basilica Aemilia.

The density of people up ahead was becoming greater, people of all kinds, most of them on the make. Armenian merchants lined the porticoes flanking the buildings, opening baskets full of Chinese silk as he passed. There were second-hand clothes for sale, laid out on blankets by poor Romans, leather goods and sandals hawked by Ethiopians in stark white robes, and shamans and amulet sellers all mingled together in a gauntlet of confusing sounds and colorful shapes. And then something amazing happened.

After winding through enclosed vertiginous spaces offering only glimpses of alternate worlds, his sensory perception exploded into the grand open space of the Roman Forum proper, where at once the sense changed from Empire to Epicenter, rendering the Imperial Forums just passed only peripheral outcroppings of a larger idea. Emerging into the space of the Comitium in front of the Senate building, Mannix could see the hallowed black stone pavement of the Lapis Niger marking the tomb of Romulus. Despite the mist of legend surrounding the name, he knew the man was probably one of the kings who ruled Rome eight hundred years ago. To his right, the triple arch of Septimius Severus hovered over the Via Sacra, the triumphal street leading through the Forum and up to the temple of Jupiter on the Capitoline Hill.

Looking out over the vast open space, the white marble of pediments, entablatures, statues and columns, sparkled granular in the sunshine; and the mystical superimposition of forms which the hills and the density of architecture created was as if pushed back by a titan's hands to allow a window opening onto heaven, where the tremendous cumulous cloud he'd been tracking all morning, bigger than the entire city of Rome, plumed up at an angle above the open space of the Forum,

172

framing the deep green of the cypress and pine on the Palatine Hill in jagged silhouette against its sylvan whiteness.

His eyes followed the cloud, blossoming up to touch the tip of the sun. As it broke the diamond radiance of the orb, the cloud's massive bulk was tinted with blue shade. Its edges silvered, it deflected gigantic light beams shooting across the arc of the sky, walking a line of shadow over the Palatine Hill and down into the Forum toward him like a bad omen.

XXV

The Basilica Aemilia – the great banking center of Rome – lined the northeastern side of the Forum square with its prestigious address on the Via Sacra. The interior of the spacious, lofty, softly echoing hall was delineated by double-tiered colonnades, the pillars of the first level of the red-black breccia from the southern coast of Turkey with the green Greek serpentino atop. The entablature running between the levels was carved with episodes from Rome's legendary history – the Rape of the Sabine Women, Lacus Curtius riding to glory, Horatio at the bridge. Between the columns of the second level, which formed a balconied gallery for the offices above the side aisles of the basilica, over-life-size statues of submissive barbarians carved alternately in purple-veined pavonazzetto and Numidian orange marble stared down at the bank's clientele. The entablature atop the second level balcony supported the clerestory windows, through which raking shafts of sunlight lanced to the floor where their bronze latticework patterns were cast in shadow across the variegated slabs of gray Italic, Carystian green and pink Chian marbles. Across the space above the windows stretched the mighty span of the hall – a beautiful open framework of bronze-encased beams with joins in the form of huge palmettos.

The short end walls of the vast rectangular space were apsed, in each of which a large bronze sculpture faced its counterpart down the hundred meter-long center aisle. In one of the forty-foot convex half-domed niches stood a statue of Lucius Aemilius Paullus, who began the basilica almost three hundred years before; in the other his son who completed it. The side walls of the building, apart from their entrances, were paralleled with counters behind which clerks sat. Safes and deposit boxes lined the walls and, at either end of the center aisle, gathered about the pedestals of the statues in their niches, stood the richly-carved oaken tables of the tax officers. Over it all hung the waxen smell of polished marble, the tang of newly-minted coins brought down from the Tabularium under guard, and the grave atmosphere of immense riches.

After taking stock of all of this for the thousandth time while standing in line for half an hour trying to get his drinking money for the evening, with people recognizing him and trying to make small talk while he smiled and tried to be polite, Mannix finally came before the young, bald, quietly professional, clean-fingernailed clerk behind the granite counter who was saying, "But sir, how do we know you're who you say you are?"

"Because I told you," the Bestiarius replied cheerfully.

"But, sir," continued the clerk just as patiently, "you don't have the pass key to your deposit box."

"I forgot it," Mannix shrugged.

The clerk shook his head at the unfortunate situation on both ends. "Well, I don't know," he said. "I'll have to get the manager on duty."

"Look, are you new here?" smiled the Bestiarius.

"He's who he says he is," nodded the bored Praetorian in the silver cuirass sitting on a stool in the shadows picking his nails with his dagger.

And so the clerk, uncomfortable with the breach of procedure, hesitantly processed the transaction, and Mannix finally walked out of the basilica through its fine bronze portals into the massive arcaded portico of Gaius and Lucius fronting the building with its shops and vendors, and its Jewish moneychangers shouting and counting flamboyantly from behind their booths as they dealt with a mixed variety of immigrants and tourists trying to exchange drachmas or gold pieces for denarii and sesterces. As he cinched his replenished coin purse and tucked it beneath the neck of his paenula with the little gypsy pick-pocket beggars touching at his legs, he swore to himself, as he did each time, that he would move to the country tomorrow.

Through the arcade down the steps into the crashing sunlight on the Via Sacra, he was immediately caught up and jostled in a group of worshippers of the Egyptian Isis, wife of Serapis, parading down the street to the sounds of the sistra, their shaven heads bare to the sun, immaculate white robes sparkling. Repressing an urge to flail randomly about him, the Bestiarius grunted, "Out of the way peasants," and continued on, into the thriving multicolored spectacle presented by the cosmopolitanism and religious diversity of his time.

He crossed the Via Sacra and walked across the center of the vast Forum square – a narrowing trapezoid one hundred yards long by fifty and seventy wide, its white travertine pavement glistening with the wet slicks of yesterday's rain. He looked about him as he walked, breathing the energy of the huge open space – the financial, legal, administrative and religious center of the world. Fifty-foot honorific columns with bronze statues of winged victories pirouetting from their tops stretched down the southwestern side of the square in front of him and, sixty yard to his right, the Rostrum, the speaker's platform, faced out over the long axis of the space. Attached in a rank across its long podium, ancient bronze ship prows oxidized lime green in the sunshine, figureheads going back as far as Pompey's defeat of the Cilician pirates three hundred years before.

People were everywhere, coming and going; over it all, the shouts of hawkers and traders, a cacophony of squeaking horn blowers and a roast chestnut seller sitting smiling at the base of one of the victory columns. Eunuchs of Cybele danced in a ring in the square, their bodies undulating to the harsh and doleful noise of the Phrygian aulos. Atop the Rostrum, a disheveled orator protested the world to the laughter and the catcalling of the throngs passing by, flinging his arms and stamping his foot to punctuate his rambling harangue.

Mannix smiled and shook his head, glancing above and behind the Rostrum to the Temple of Titus and Vespasian, and that of Concord behind the Arch of Septimius Severus, standing side by side at a right angle to the temple of Saturn, where all newborn Roman males were registered. Thirty foot bronze doors glowed in the shadowy mist beneath their porches and, above them, the Tabularium – the Treasury, Mint and State Archives – stretched its massive double-arcaded bulk across the saddle between the two spurs of the Capitoline Hill. He could see up above the pediment of the Temple of Saturn to the gigantic Temple of Jupiter, hovering over the city from the western spur. Sacrificial smoke from the charcoal braziers placed at intervals across its porch dispersed into the deep blue sky, and the distant lowing of bulls spoke of the blood of sacrifice. On the other side of the Tabularium, its companion piece, the temple of Juno – Jupiter's wife – faced out from the eastern spur of the hill.

Something stopped him for a moment, and he looked up at the Temple of Jupiter on the Capitoline still sparkling in sunlight, and then back at the cloud and the pine and cypress on the Palatine deepening in shadow with a rustling noise in his ears, as if a strong wind blowing through a plot of oak trees. And he felt beset by a memory of childhood which he could not recall. Then he realized that the noise was that of the crowd in the Amphitheater half a mile away, and he wondered if that was the only place he ever belonged, and if it could really be that bad.

Finding no solution to his feelings, he shrugged them off and continued on, between two of the bases of the victory columns onto the Via Nova lining the southwestern side of the square where the Basilica Giulia, the lawcourts, stretched its massive arcaded bulk. The building's usual contingent of idlers were wiling away the time shooting dice on gameboards cut by their predecessors into the pavement beneath its arcades; and the Bestiarius made his way irritably through a group of itinerant clergy carrying the icon of the Syrian goddess in procession down the Via Nova. Turning into the Vicus Tuscus along the side of the basilica between it and the Temple of Castor and Pollux, he left the open square of the Forum, the window onto heaven, and re-entered the density and spacial complexity of tight metropolitan streets winding through canyons of monumental architecture.

He walked past the huge audience hall built by Domitian in conjunction with his Palace. Behind it, vast ceremonial switchback staircases scaled the Germalus, the western spur of the Palatine. Then the open-fronted shop kiosks lining the ground floor of the Markets of Agrippa – people buying and selling, haggling and yelling, entering and exiting – sausages hung on strings in the shadows of the shops and the smells of fish and fresh bread, oranges and onions hit his nostrils, making his mouth water.

A neighborhood of apartment blocks rose to his right, where perpendicular streets led off the Tuscus into a matrix of tight jumbled tenement alleyways. He passed a train of bulls being led toward the Capitoline for sacrifice, faintly wishing that yesterday's was as docile as these farm bovines. But yesterday's was Spanish, and trained for meanness. He took a deep breath, probing instinctively at the pain in his ribs which caught him up short.

The huge sweep of the Circus Maximus loomed ahead, its white travertine gilded with afternoon sunlight. He turned left on the long street running between the Circus and the southern flank of the Palatine. The standards of the Empire atop one of the triumphal entry gates of the stadium were thrown in jagged shadow across the flagstones, the eagles on their crest warped like gigantic buzzards perched waiting along his path. The 'Circus People' recognized him – the vendors, whores and bums beneath the arcades; they hailed him as he passed and he smiled and waved, took a drink from jug and joined in a song. He enjoyed the Circus atmosphere, the festival quality, the people, but he soon moved on, past the three hundred-meter flank of the stadium stretching huge and honeycombed with arches on his right, and the towering facade of the Palatine Palace on his left.

From the shadowy canyon of the crowded street, he looked up at an angle through the needle-peaks of the black-green cypresses flanking the facade, walking and watching as they broke for the flowing cascade of huge marble staircase emptying into the street with its usual contingent of bored Praetorians milling about a hundred feet beneath the great hemicyclical terrace of the Imperial Palace. As he stared at the rose-marbled colonnades of the terrace glowing warmly in the sun, with their expansive view out over the Circus, Mannix remembered with disgust the grand finale of last summer's Dogstar Climax Ceremony. After the sacrifices at the vast summer estate of the Severans in the suburb of Ad Spem Veterum on the edge of the Esquiline District, Elagabalus returned to the Palatine and banqueted the Mob on the huge staircase and the street beneath while he and his courtiers stood on the terrace above. He had massive amounts of wine and food distributed to the throngs, and then began to throw favors off the terrace – jars of gold and silver and live animals to the Mob, who tore them from one another, trampling themselves, many impaled on the Praetorian's spears in the process.

At the southeastern end of the Circus, Mannix came upon the confluence at the beginning of the Via Appia – a wide, triumphal thoroughfare marked by a huge Egyptian obelisk. To his left in the distance, he could see part of the top of the Flavian Amphitheater down the street through the arches of the Claudian Aqueduct stretching across the narrow valley between the Palatine and Caelian Hills. A rush of crowd noise funneled up the street toward him through the four-storied arches of the aqueduct, and he stopped for a minute on the corner, hesitated, and then turned back and took a long drink from a fountain spigot beneath the tremendous seven-bayed columnar facade of the Septizodium. Built by Severus in conjunction with his new wing of the Palace, like the stage-building of a great theater, the curious false-front screened the Palatine from the traffic coming in off the Appia. Its marble encrusted niches framed colossal statues representing the seven planets – Saturn, Jupiter, Mars, the Sun, Venus, Mercury and the Moon.

Mannix cast a brief glance upward at the fifteen-foot statue of Saturn, under whose sign he was born. An ambiguous god of time and artists represented as a hooded, pensive, powerful figure in Luna marble, the sculpture stared back at him from the light blue shadows of its niche, pigeon shit frosting its shoulders, black streaks of oxidation deepening the folds of its drapery and running down its bearded cheeks from the hollows

179

of its eyes. The Bestiarius squinted, and wiped the water from his lips with the back of his leather-banded wrist. Then he crossed the street and started into the confluence of the Via Appia beneath the vine-draped remains of the old Porta Capena. One of the gates in the Republican walls which had been surpassed by suburbs over the past two centuries, the walls had been dismantled in some parts, in others simply allowed to fall into disrepair or recycled into subsequent structures.

He walked through the dappled sunlight and purple shadows beneath the Appia's border of stately umbrella pines, their canopy tops lime green against the sky. The tremendous bulk of the Baths of Caracalla stretched to his right, a neighborhood of nouveau-riche apartments lining the base of the long side of the Caelian Hill on his left. Half a mile further, he reached the outskirts of the city proper – the greenbelt – where the Via Latina began its slight veer east off the Appia. People were thinning out and he took the Via Latina, and walked in mood-drenched silence beneath the corridor of rampant evergreen boughs hovering high over the thin-bricked walls framing the narrow road.

The walls were clung with ivy and splotched with the worn remnants of white stucco. The gardens of the rich and famous lined either side of them, where the Odes of Horace often rang to the lyres through the cypresses of a candle-lit evening, or under the verandas during an afternoon shower. The oleanders gave off their still-rain-wet-from-yesterday smells of spring and sex and smiles, perfuming the corridor of road; and he donned his paenula against the chill feeling of the fresh air, fitting it over his head careful of the throbbing pain in his shoulder.

With the day of Games nearing time for its main event a mile away, Mannix felt displaced, but content to let the poetry of damp foliage carry him along, soothing his senses and nerves. A third of a mile up the road, the garden walls framing the suburban villas of the greenbelt gave way to the 'disabitato,' the uninhabited no-man's land between them and the outerlying farms, and he spotted the cart of a flower seller positioned at the edge of a grove of silvery-leafed olive trees.

"Ave, Thimbria," he hailed, as he walked toward the cart.

"Hello, Mr. Mannix," smiled a pious, simple man who sat on a stool behind the cart selling votives to the bereaved; one of those rare creatures who brought a smidgen of honor to life in the city.

"Nice rain we had yesterday," continued the Bestiarius, as he picked out a bouquet of wild flowers and a small clay dish of incense.

"Yes indeed," nodded old Thimbria. "Wonderful for the flowers. They open like maidens this time of year. But you must keep them under cover where the drops don't hit them."

"A nice thought, that," said Mannix, pulling a denarius out of the leather purse on his belt and laying it on the worn wooden counting top.

Thimbria shook his head softly, knowingly, and without feigning. "That's too much, Mr. Mannix."

"Keep the change for you and your wife, Thimbria," replied the Bestiarius, not looking at him, letting the old man preserve his dignity. "And give her my regards."

"Thank you sir," the old flower seller nodded humbly. He lit the bowl of incense from the candle kept burning, well-familiar with the routine. "And have a few olives and dates from our humble garden," he said, handing Mannix a small bundle of parchment, wrapped and tied with a string.

"Much obliged, Thimbria," the Bestiarius nodded, remembering that he hadn't eaten since the roll of the morning.

From the 'disabitato,' the highway began its cypress-lined journey into the rolling countryside of Latium, bordered by villas, farms, and the tombs of Rome's elite. The plebs occupied dank slots in the catacombs beneath ground, or in the walls of the suburban columbaria – vast structures composed of adjacent halls containing thousands of niches for urns; all of it in accord with the old Republican law forbidding burial within the city walls. To his right in the distance, Mannix could see the tumulus of Caecilia Metella rearing its drum-shaped bulk above the scattering of trees.

The Mausoleum of the Ludus Matutinus rose in a yellow-grass copse of poplar trees set off the road near the first milestone outside the Porta Latina. The Bestiarius walked down the gray dirt pathway across the snaking purple shadows cast by the treetrunks toward the large, simple, barn-like structure. Typical of many suburban mausolea, the plainness of its architecture was delineated by thin, shallowly-projecting pilaster strips with Corinthian capitals upholding a molded brick entablature lining the base of its gabled rooftop. Its subdued earth tones – the pale pink brickwork of its wall-faces and the deeper burnt-ochre of the pilaster strips with their molded terracotta capitals – contrasted pleasantly with the green of the trees and the sandy blond grass of the glade.

He raised the hood of his maroon paenula in reverence, before   entering the building's shade through the twin-columned portico into the cavernous interior lit by the open rectangle of window above the doorway. Leaving the pine-sap and grass smell of the glade, the inside of the place was dank, chilly, and full of the smell of dead flowers and mildew. Though novices were sent out randomly from the school to sweep and clean it, the mausoleum soon after returned to the ghostly feel of the countryside, with pine needles and leaves finding their way back in on the wind to litter the dark basaltic stones of the floor, and the dust ever-sweltering in the light falling through the large high window over the door.

The walls were inset with small, deep, half-moon niches containing the ash-urns of the deceased. Stuccoed in hexagonal patterns embroidered with fading fresco colors, moveable ladders facilitated access to the ones staged ten and twenty feet high. It took a moment for the Bestiarius' deep aquamarine eyes to adjust to the dimness of the interior. He squinted at the names labeling the niches, far too many of them familiar, others echoing back over a century. A small candle burned before the one freshly inset by hammer and chisel with the words DEMETRIVS VENATOR; and he moved a ladder into position, and climbed it carefully. The old wound in his knee ached, and he balanced the smoking bowl of incense and the bouquet of wild flowers precariously in one hand.

Arriving at the niche, he placed the flowers before the simple red-glazed clay urn containing all that was left of the worldly Demetrius. Then he put the bowl of smoking incense beside the candle, the wax of which had dripped in rippling red tendrils over the lip of the niche to hang from the arch of the niche beneath it. He touched the urn with two fingers, a sudden blinding memory of a boy in a corner wearing a silver dog collar with the sunlight falling through his hair and illuminating the fine net of gold fanning across his spine. And swimming up out of a day-time drunkenness sated with sex amidst the hallucinatory effects of gleaming white plaster wall panels traced in green and golden architectural illusions to find the boy being lightly whipped with rose stems, their thorns drawing little beads of blood which fell among the pink petals littering the cream-colored marble floor.

XXVI

"I want them to fall over this area here," Julia Soaemias shouted to the men far above, her head thrown back with its mane of black hair, the voice out of her husky throat drink-deepened and full of command. In her mind was a strange rare clarity – a curious combination of expectation, the morning's liquor, and the green-powdered contents of the empty amphetamine phial in her hand, which she'd just mixed rather secretively, and chased in a goblet of mineral water. She still had a shred of dignity, even in front of the help.

The morning's long, dreamy wake-up call of alcohol was cut with the pleasant sting of the stimulant, and she was back in a pair of old legionary boot sandals she hadn't worn in years. Her plain white nightgown stola had been exchanged for a short-skirted green Chinese silk robe belted at her waist – which was still surprisingly small – and her big tan breasts joggled loosely as she gestured to the workmen one hundred feet above, beyond the hazy zone of sunlight sweltering in the bronze-framed, thick-glazed window panes of the banquet hall.

The windows were rectangular, and ten feet tall – six across the front, and six each along the lateral sides. But their placement ninety feet high was such that, even on the brightest of days, they emitted only a glaucous glow which never quite reached the floor of an interior much taller than it was broad. A further ten feet beyond the hazy zone of light they gave, the palace slaves were working to string a massive leather tarpaulin beneath the deeply coffered, heavily gilt ceiling. The dark-shadowed, insect-like figures had removed many of the bronze rosette panels insetting the coffers, some of the men harnessed and dangling by ropes from the attic skeleton of massive timbers – hundred-foot beams of Lebanese cedar which had once spanned the roof of the Herodian rebuild of the great Temple of Solomon in Jerusalem.

The side walls of the interior were framed with three super-imposed orders of columns, the lowest level of Numidian orange echoing the peristyle of the great fountain court outside. The middle level were of Phrygian purple, and the uppermost of pink Chian marble, their colors rich and deep in the shadowland of space beneath the veil of warped sunlight in the windows alternately shimmering or receding with the passage of cloud outside. Between the columns of the lowest level, and almost at floor-level, the four-foot thick walls were cut on either side with three large rectangular windows flanked by two doorways. The windows and doorways gave onto small semicircular fountain courts on either side of the building, their twin scalloped fountains surrounded by intimate two-storied peristyles appendaged out from the sides of the hall and connected by spiral staircases. The little side courts enabled guests the ability stroll out with their wine goblets between courses and enjoy the coolness of the water and the adventure of the architecture.

With the tremendous Polyphemus fountain in the center of the great court fronting the hall – which was open through the thirty-foot Egyptian granite monoliths leading in from the peristyle where she took her morning drinks – warm weather banquets were graced by the pleasant gurgling of water on three sides, as well as the cooling flow of air through the columns and windows. And the guests were greeted by vistas of ornamental water and greenery framed in a setting of richly variegated marble which, in the winter months, could be closed off in conjunction with the bronze doors hinged to the granite monoliths when utilizing the hypocaust heating system running beneath the floor.

Her son, who was fond of color-coding his banquets in the summer, often had huge swathes of colored silks hung everywhere about, polluting Rabirius' design of manly baroque pleasantry. As she reflected upon a space in which she had not only dined in grace but even danced with Mannix, Julia Soaemias was aware of how lost on her son and his courtiers was the ingenuity displayed by Domitian's architect, many of whom spent the latter courses of his banquets vomiting in the small scalloped fountains, falling through the open bay windows in tangles of colored silk, or chasing the prostitutes he liked to keep about the fountain court outside.

Yes, she had spoiled him. But as weak and worthless as she knew Elagabalus was, Julia Soaemias had seen him grow into an evil of late – the evil of absolute power.

The demon tempted them all at one time or another; she'd seen it before. Some succumbed to it; some did not. The ones who did all died sooner or later – like Caracalla, who was also spoiled and weak. And so he died in a ditch with his member in his hand and a page-boy's knife in his kidneys at the age of twenty-seven. She shook her head.

At the beginning her son was under the complete control of her and her mother. But now he'd grown out of control, and would obviously have to go. She would have to go with him, of course. Propriety dictated that. But, from the start, the boy on the throne wasn't so much the important thing. Elagabalus was older than his cousin, so it made sense at the time. Now it made sense to advance the thirteen year-old Alexianus. The only important thing for her mother was to maintain the line. In any event, Alexianus would make a better emperor.

"Just over this space here," she said. "So that they funnel into the apse area." She would not want the boy to be hurt. No, she would not want that at all.

Several months before she and her mother tried to persuade Elagabalus to adopt his cousin as his heir and Caesar. They said it would allow him to spend more time with his religious 'duties,' while the thirteen year-old Alexianus stood in for ceremonial obligations. Elagabalus agreed at the time, but his recent plot on his cousin's life was very childish, very foolish. He took it all upon himself without consultation, and it cost her and her mother and sister no small amount to stop both of them from being killed, which would have plunged the Empire into another civil war. For many of the junior officers were supportive of Alexianus, not only for his goodness, but moreover for the money which had begun to be distributed them in secret by his mother Julia Mamaea. She smiled at the wiles of her sister, who she in fact loved very much.

But Elagabalus had a strange kind of power over the lower ranks – many of them still filled with veterans of Severus' legions – not only for the priestly aura he exuded when before them, but also for his god's iconographical connection with Mithraism, the ancient god of the Persians, imported from India – the god of light and wisdom, closely associated with 'Sol Invictus,' the Invincible Sun. Finding its greatest adherents among these eastern legions, whose veterans had imported it to the West over the prior two centuries, Mithras represented the ideal divine comrade and fighter; a fearless antagonist of the powers of darkness who gave to his devotees the hope of immortality.

Julia Soaemias felt only disgust at the superstition of the masses. And yet, since the Antonines, the Empire had become ripe for mysticism. And, thanks in great part to her aunt and uncle Severus, it had finally caught this disease which had been stirring in the bowels of the Mediterranean for centuries. Originating in the East, in Persia, Egypt and pre-Judaic Palestine, the populace of the Roman Empire had been corrupted by a thirst for spirituality. And her son had proven just the right charlatan to stir it up, with his oracles and magic, and his assurance of a life after death.

In any event, through the wiles of her mother, the lesser accomplices in the plot on her nephew were blamed for its greater share (the Emperor had obviously been beguiled by their lies). And they were executed in the Saturnalia Games three months before by being aligned on the torchlit sands of the Circus Maximus one evening and spitted like quail on a single thirty-foot spear, which pierced one's anus and came out of his mouth directly into another's anus and so on and so forth down the line so that 'their deaths were as evil as their lives,' exclaimed Apicius the Ringmaster.

Never mind Elagabalus being fond of his own piercings, the Mob loved it. And, as Julia Soaemias very well knew, that's what counted. Hence the whole affair blew over as far as the city was concerned, with vast sums of bribery money being

187

tossed back and forth behind the scenes, and political Rome sinking lower than a street whore on her knees. Thus things had simmered to a standstill. And the banquet tonight had been designed to show the Senate and the aristocracy that her mother was still in control.

For though Elagabalus' abuses were well known – the religious quackism, the profanation of the Vestal Complex, the debauchery and financial profligacy – it was mainly the Senate and the aristocracy, the old noble Roman families, who were offended by them. The Mob could care less, for Elagabalus' spectacles had been particularly popular, especially the naval battles on the artificial canals flooded from the Tiber while the Amphitheater was under restoration, one of them fought on a canal filled entirely with wine. As with the lower ranks of the Praetorians, the Emperor held a kind of power over the Mob, banqueting them and catering to them as he did with spectacles and religious festivals.

As for the upper classes, as long as the situation was corrected – and the elevation of Alexianus could correct it – the Severan line could remain. For it stretched to the Antonines thanks to her uncle's feat of retrospective auto-adoption. Moreover it could remain because no one wanted another civil war. Rome couldn't afford it with as many difficulties in the provinces and on the frontiers as she already had.

The problem, then, remained the Praetorians – a vast organization originally formed as the Emperor's personal bodyguard, but having become a political entity of their own through the years, with camps and contingents all over Europe and Asia. The nucleus of the Praetorian power structure in Rome was split between her son and his cousin with a possible leaning toward Alexianus. But things could happen – things which could throw the entire Empire into chaos and affect the lives of millions.

Walking between the pearl-inlayed silver dining couches over the floor spiraling outward in red and green complexities of marble intarsia, she passed a life-size bronze of Bacchus and Ampelus, the god's youthful lover – replete with faun and panther – standing dark and gleaming in the shadows.

"Have this removed, please," she raised her voice to Petricon, the steward across the way who was supervising a group of slaves bringing in more dining couches.

The steward looked up nervously. Though the banquet was her mother's design, as Julia Soaemias inhabited the Palace and her mother did not, she was technically its hostess, and was in charge of its food and decor. Outside, behind the shallow convex apse of the hall, in a pleasant little wedge of garden between it and the Latin and Greek libraries, the cherry trees had been cut back for the scaffolding which scaled the rear outer wall of the building since repairs to the roof began some months before. Its original copper tiles were now worn and corroded after a hundred and thirty years, and the massive structural beams of the attic needed checking. The loss of the trees was unfortunate – she had loved them since she was a child – but the scaffolding served her purpose. She had planned things to the last detail.

For the last week ox carts had come in from the Imperial estates outside the city laden beneath their tarps with rose bulbs, which were being hoisted by the sackful up the rigging of the scaffolding behind the hall. She had been meticulous in demanding, through her correspondence with the estates, that the stems be cut precisely, and that no green must show. For the banquet must be perfect. And its theme was the rose.

Though the palace slaves knew her design, they were as loyal to her as their great-great-great-great grandfathers were to Augustus himself. They were a type, a breed; and she was 'Augusta.' And the purges would never touch them, like they would the Guard, the Prefects, and she herself. When all faith was lost, tradition still held sway.

"Petricon," she called. "A word."

The old skinny bald Egyptian steward with black eyeshadow scurried across the floor toward her in a belted red robe. She shook her head. As much as she loved her uncle Severus, and as much as he spoiled her, his religious dilettantism and fascination with Egyptian gods had caused him to fill the ranks of the palace freedmen with two-bit sham artists like this who probably grew up in Roman Alexandria. And his

189

wife, who considered herself a great patron of the arts, liked to keep impossible help anyway. She thought it liberal and avant-garde. 'Too bad Macrinus hadn't enough time to get rid of them all,' Soaemias thought to herself.

"Been avoiding me, have you?" she said to the steward as he arrived.

The Egyptian lowered his ingratiating little chin. "But of course not, my lady."

"I want the old silver," she said, looking up at the ceiling. "The Antonine ware. Do not use any of the new."

"But, Domina," bowed Petricon, "the old is all in storage in the Tiberian wing. It has not been polished in decades."

"Well," she smiled out of one corner of her mouth, "the last I heard we employee six hundred of you here. So get to it."

The steward hesitated, looking strangely at his Empress, his mouth open to protest, but Julia Soaemias slowly lowered her head and met his gaze with her big almond eyes.

"I want all of it removed," she said placidly. "And those statues too. Get it all out," she made a throw-away gesture at a round-plinthed marble of Pan atop a female goat on her back with her legs spread, and then turned her attention back to the ceiling. "I don't care what you have to do. Now get over to the Tiberiana and start digging the silverware out and I'll join you when I'm finished here."

The steward nodded and bowed himself carefully away.

Julia Soaemias sighed, and walked to a table laden with refreshments for the servants, on which she left her green-glass beaker. She lifted a leg of greasy chicken took a bite. Like the idiot he was, her cousin Caracalla sold at public auction much of the Imperial trappings, some of which were Augustan, all of which were priceless, to help finance his ridiculous eastern campaigns. And thus her son, who fancied himself something of a decorator, was left a clean slate. Being a great banqueter, one of the first things Elagabalus did upon taking up court in the Palace was to commission a vast new series of chased silver plate, casseroles, urns and wine vessels, their exquisite craftsmanship exhibiting the lewdest designs that his deviant mind could concoct. He also fancied perverse sculpture groups

190

– never absent in any decent collection, she had to admit; but in bad taste in the banquet hall.

Referred to as the 'Tiberian Wing' because of its connection with the Palace by the cryptoporticus for the servants, the place wasn't a wing at all, but a large palace in its own right built by Tiberius two hundred years before on the opposite spur of the hill – the Germalus – overlooking the Forum below. Quasi-derelict now, some of its wings were partially used as offices for Imperial scribes and quarters for servants, but mainly as a vast storage facility full of the remainder of the old trappings and objects d'art which the emperors' wives had removed from the new palace over the last century in their redecorating campaigns. As such, the place was full of some dust-ridden gems that were very unfortunately passed by through the years.

A colossal Greek bronze of Poseidon with his trident came to mind, fallen over and corroding in age-blackened and green-oxidized bronze in the palace's vast peristyle garden. The garden had gone to seed, and had become a kind of overgrown graveyard full of wonderful old sculptures now in pieces, obscured by vines, and darkened with grime. If she'd had the time and the feeling of being part of something truly worthy, Julia Soaemias would have loved to have catalogued the works, and brought many of the finer ones back to light. But she did not. And it was one of her great regrets.

She lifted the beaker to her lips, finished its contents and perused the ceiling one more time, reminding herself to check with her private physicians to ensure that the unusual amount of belladonna and hemlock had arrived. Satisfied with the progress on the ceiling, she set the glass down and walked out of the building through the gray granite monoliths and then through the parallel rank of Numidian orange columns of the peristyle out onto the Pentelic paving of the great fountain court. She glanced up at the evening sky, and nodded at a group of palace slaves on their way into the hall with supplies.

191

XXVII

Mannix sat on a yellow-grass knoll behind the mausoleum of the Ludus Matutinus, its terracotta-tiled rooftop sloping off to the side, nibbling absently at Thimbria's olives with the breeze blowing through his hair. The peace and the poetry of nature in moments like this were as close to happiness as anything he'd ever known. Cradling his knees with his forearms, he let his eyes follow the rusty tentacle of an aqueduct snaking out over the umber-and-yellow patchwork of landscape toward the blue-distant hills where he was born.

Coming from the west over the sea unobstructed, the sunlight had turned Parnassian, horizontal and raking, and the clouds to marigold mountains just as they did when he was a boy living in the hills on the plot of government land his father had earned as a centurian. Though just fifteen miles distant, the weather in the hills was much different than in Rome below – colder in the winter, cooler in the summer; in the spring and autumn given to extreme storms in which Jupiter hurled his angry bolts. The clouds were mystical then, when he was a boy, just as they still were to him; and he would often watch them travel down over the city to spread their rain or shade, and then return again in the course of a day.

He thought again of the contentment of his youth, when sunrises and sunsets, the first smell of a season, or the deepening of the blue of the sky in autumn gave him a way out, a way to transcend. And though he wished he could have lived longer in his boyhood, those were the things that could still transport him to that time before, when he ploughed in his grandfather's vineyards, and harvested grapes with the workmen. When, of an evening, he would join with the villagers in celebrating the harvest or, in spring, the rites of Pan and Bacchus – that time of welcoming the awakening earth with entrails and incense, the taste of roast lamb and farmer's wine, the singing of the paeans and the dance around the altar in a ring with the unspoiled peasant girls.

After his grandfather died he began to wander at night. Unable to sleep, he would climb to their special place to watch the sun rise, up the ancient lichen-frosted steps to the clearing where his grandfather had baptized him with lightning and where the resonance within him grew taught as a bowstring each time. The altar and its herms had become overgrown, and marked only by wild thorn bushes that flowered in the spring. But there was no need to uncover them for he knew them all by heart.

He would sit up there in the death of darkness just before dawn and watch the stars until the sky paled to lime and the moon slipped massive and cratered and golden into the distant sea. And then, to the east, would come a glow that quivered into a quickening shimmering and the sun would break like a great golden shield over the black outstretch of broken hills. The night's-rain forest smells would lift by his feet as the mist rose with the sun's calling, creeping up the side of the ridge toward him – the last chance for the night spirits as for few golden moments he was completely enshrouded in blinding sunlit moisture. And then it would rise off, and the spirits seep back down under rocks, retreat into caves, osmotize into the trunks of trees, or sink back into the mountain streams to wait out the day.

In the days he would crouch fishing on one of the huge rocks jutting into the glass-smooth surface of the lake, and catch a glimpse of his reflection and wonder if it was really him, and not just something he was locked inside. He stalked the colonies of wild mountain pigs and wonderfully-spotted deer, crouching in the treelines bordering the cool, mist-shrouded surfaces of black water where they drank, his legs double-wrapped with hide against snakebite. Or he would spend the days in the platform shelters he built in the trees, the planks for which he ripped from the old moss-covered hulk of one of the pleasure barges that Caligula had built for weekend excursions two hundred years before.

193

He would wait up in the trees all day, his grandfather's spear poised in hand – an old blade from the iron age fixed to a carven limb – until the wild pig passed beneath and he would drop straight down upon it. Sometimes he would take to the trees for weeks, unaware of the time and for the duration of which he did not speak a human word but simply watched and waited, often staring for an entire day at the large red and green caterpillars that inched infinitely over the thick black branches until he became part of the forest itself, and felt his own life-force to be simply a version of that which moved in the dark, patient torpidity of the plant kingdom. A place devoid of love and conscious life, but filled with instinct and feeling.

He missed his grandfather. His grandfather had understood. Had understood the un-nameable essence behind these things. Had understood the divinity in trees, rivers, rocks and sky. Perhaps Marcellus did too.

Lepidus was too one-sided and women in general too practical and literal-minded. It was no use telling them about trees and clouds and the way sunlight danced across the rocks in a river. Because then they went and tried to read some kind of significance into what he'd said. And there was none.

He thought of Julia Soaemias. How she ever let her son turn out like that was something he would never understand; for Soaemias was smart, smarter than her looks and her loose morals would indicate. She understood things to an extent – things about sunlight and trees and clouds – and she wanted to understand more, but it bored him to talk.

Perhaps he should have, he thought to himself now, in a rare moment of retrospection to which he'd never been given. But what good would it have done? He hated her kind and their lifestyle. Hated the wealth and the waste and the sickness of the power addiction in their blood. They were just more of the same kind of self-aggrandizers who took his father away from him and then became gods when they died. And now her son had become the quintessential manifestation of that lie of divine right.

Yes, he hated Julia Soaemias' kind. And yet he couldn't help remembering how they both shared a fondness for peripheral areas, like where he sat now – forlorn places where streets turned to dirt paths, and houses to huts. It gave them both an essence of childhood which they shared in an unforced, familiar way. He remembered how she used to wait for him in that abandoned old atrium-style house on the vast property of the Gardens of Sallust, back in an overgrown area of towering, brown-leafed palm trees set well away from the villa grounds where her aunt and mother would be organizing one of their interminable functions for the high society. Like two children orchestrating a play of hide-and-seek, he would take his time, enjoying the diffracted sunlight in the gardens before entering the abandoned house through its square doorway molded with a marble entablature of Hellenistic palmettos.

As his eyes adjusted to the shadows of the large atrium, deepened by the shaft of sunlight falling through the large square open space in its roof, he could make out the dust-blackened statues lining the back walls frescoed in deep red and black panels with delicate tracery patterns of gold leaf connecting and framing them. All of it desperately in need of a restoration which would never come, the stately house was over three hundred years old, and hearkened back to the days before the lives of the citizenry were reduced to meaningless numerics. It had no doubt once belonged to someone who was a name, who was an individual – someone who turned certain defeat into stunning victory on the rocky plains of North Africa, or the desert sands of Syria.

Upon entering the old house, he would always take a moment and lean against one of the red-frescoed columns supporting the roof where it drew back over the open space above the impluvium pool, and gaze into the beauty of the reflected sky between the lily pads and the lush oleanders and the elephant ear run riot around the confines of the stagnant, mosquito-infested water. Sometimes she would startle him, and he would look up to see her emerge, ghostly and ethereal on the other side of the shaft of sunlight falling through the roof, staring at him with that look which always made him uncomfortable. And then she would run to wrap her hands about his neck and meet his lips with a kiss.

Or she would play her games and be absent and he would continue on, walking back through the tablinio to emerge in a garden where two cypresses rose above the roof of its surrounding peristyle, a pine tree smiled in the sunlight, and a simple birdbath sat amongst the weeds. The rooms opening off the sides of the peristyle were converted into kitchens at some later date of the house's decrepitude – perhaps for massive picnics of the Plebs in the gardens thrown by some libertine Equestrian – some of their walls torn down for the large, clay-baked bread ovens which were all long-derelict by then as well. He would continue through another short, mosaic-paved hallway to come upon a still-larger peristyle garden with four plots and marble paths between, their cracks grown with waist-high weeds, enjoying the light and shade and the dusty smell of the sun-dried leaves.

She would be waiting for him in the room in the back corner – with the wine and the bed she had had moved in by close-mouthed slaves – a long, lean figure reclining ghostly white in the shadows. In the afternoons when they met and when it came the easiest for both of them, the milky sunlight fell through a high window to illumine a patch of fresco above the bed, a panel of Venus and Adonis set amongst illusionistic architectural caprices in golds and reds, old as the house, their colors subdued with age, cracks spreading slowly across them. He could remember the sight of her as she lay on those long still hot September afternoons on a light blue coverlet in a short but tasteful white stola which left one of her shoulders bare, her dark hair drawn up in a bun behind her head, her bare feet larger than most men's, her hands chunky, clumsy and oversize as well. And yet, much more than her breasts or thighs, it was those things which touched him.

On those late summer afternoons with his stomach all knotted up with expectation for the coming season of Games, she would take it away for a day, with the things she could do. Just like on those winter nights at the Palace when she lit the candle and placed the lock upon the door, and sent her body slave away. But this evening, while sitting on the yellow-grass knoll behind the mausoleum, what he remembered most about

196

Julia Soaemias was a conversation they'd had at the abandoned house during the 'Summer of her Smile,' as she'd called it, with the old clay pitcher and the drinking bowl on the table by their bedside. He'd eased up in bed and accepted its volcanic mystery as she passed it to him, and then handed it back to her and she had taken a sip, exchanging its contents through his lips with a kiss. Then she layed the bowl on the side table and adjusted herself behind him, placing one long thick leg on either side of his hips. Gently massaging his shoulders, neck and head, careful of whatever recent wound he might have had, "Why don't you retire?' she'd asked.

The gods knew he'd thought about it before. Plenty of times. Lepidus would gladly have allowed him a training capacity. But something always held him back, whether the fear of losing what he had – the fame of his name which he pretended to disdain – or simply what Lepidus said this morning about being 'just like everybody else.'

The father he never knew died for Rome, the mother he barely knew died of a combination of grief and influenza shortly thereafter; and his grandfather taught him animals. But he spent more years under the rough care of Lepidus than any of them, and the old director was the closest thing to a father he had left. Which made Rome the only mother he had to prove anything to, and the Mob his only brothers and sisters. He sighed. It was a dysfunctional family; still it was his family.

"You've done it for long enough," she'd continued. "You've got money, you're alive. Why don't we get out of this place . . ." she caught herself, her hands faltering for an instant on his trapezius. It wasn't the first time they'd been over the subject.

He had placed a hand on her leg and squeezed gently in acknowledgement, then let the moment pass. "I'm getting to where I can't get away from it," he said.

"What do you mean?"

He turned his head to the side. "When your kind . . . your mother or your aunt, say, signs an edict sending a political enemy to their death. Do you think they ever feel dirty when it's over?"

The pressure of her hands cooled slightly on his shoulders. She paused, the tone of her voice infinitely changed. "When it's over I suppose they take a bath and feel as clean as ever."

"When it's over for me," he said, "I can't wash it off."

"What do you mean?"

"The Arena . . . it's on the inside . . . I can't get it off."

Her hands grasped him around the chest convulsively and she buried her head in the side of his neck, the warm wetness of her tears on his skin.

"Take me with you," she sobbed. "Let's get out of here. Go to the countryside where you're from." She brought her voice under some control, trying to seem happy and positive. "I can learn how to farm," she said. "We can raise a family, be happy. Be normal people. This city is a lie . . ."

Mannix stilled her and pulled her down by his side. It was the only time she'd ever asked him to take her with him. The other times she'd always asked him to come with her. To Crete or someplace.

"Please . . ." she said.

Later, she snored softly beside him, her head on his chest. The dusty shaft of sunlight had moved from one faded frescoed wall to the other, from Venus and Adonis to Pluto and Persephone. She felt wonderful beside him, long and lean and heavy, the smell of her skin. He felt what it must feel like to have a child. Yet he also felt an aloneness which was much deeper with her by his side than he ever felt when he was alone. He kissed her softly on her dark lavender hair and she woke and looked at him dreamily with her big almond eyes.

"Don't leave."

"I'll come back tomorrow."

"Damn your lies."

Mannix released the memory with a sigh, and pushed himself stiffly from the ground. His foot hurt where the wolf had him by the boot sandal yesterday. Starting on his way to an evening at Milo's tavern out the Via Praenestina, a favorite haunt for the Arena world, he was gladdened by the knowledge that Marcellus would arrive when his work at the Amphitheater was finished.   As he walked down the knoll where the mausoleum rose amongst the trees, he reflected that, in the final analysis, it wouldn't be such a bad place to end up, this austere but handsome building in a pleasant glade of glittering poplars, in a middle ground between the place where he would die and the hills where he was born.   Something like his Self, in life caught amidst the two, finally comes to rest in a peaceful space between.   Whether that Self would detach from his body and move on from there was another matter.   And none of his concern.

XXVIII

The Bestiarius walked northeast through the 'disabitato,' beneath the plane trees rippling in the golden light of evening, his hand tracing the tops of the high grass and the sounds of the cicadas coming up. His muscled calves fell bare beneath the edge of his light-woolen paenula and he thought briefly of vipers, faintly humored by the thought of being bitten and perhaps making it to one of the low piles of stone wall defining a farmer's plot, before expiring to be nuzzled by curious sheep in the following days, licked by the tongues of their shaggy herding dogs, and finally found by some sunburned shepherd with a swathe of red cloth binding his blue-black locks. He smiled to himself. The Fates were capricious.

The sun was at full angle, and raking light bathed a stretch of the old derelict Servian wall, where it was cut up into knife-wedge patterns of light and shadow by the porous grey stone. Mannix walked pensively through the fading afternoon, past the rust-red ruins of ancient tombs. The huge plane trees had a dusty yellow winter look, their fan-sized leaves tired and cracked, the firmament above an infinite arc so vast and deep that he felt dizzy beneath it.

He thought of Julia, her big hands and feet and the way she smelled like heat and the honey-spiced wine the street vendors sold from vats over coals during the winter Saturnalia Festival. Not at all the predictable blood and fish scent of the slave girls he'd known. He had a fleeting glimpse of them swimming together in the deep blue volcanic lake that he used to swim in as a boy. Thinking about those big silly hands and feet, and the way she'd smile sometimes before she tried to tickle him, made him wonder now if he might even have been a little in love with her if he'd really examined his feelings.

200

But he hadn't.   And she was damaged.   And the Bestiarius was no savior, neither of others, nor of himself.

He crossed the Via Tusculana and re-entered the greenbelt, up the gradual rise over the eastern slope of the Caelian Hill, emerging into an area of high-ground where the properties of Imperial-owned garden estates and aristocratic residences bordered a no-man's-land crisscrossed by aqueducts. The barracks and training grounds of the Imperial Horse Guards were visible in the distance, and his boot sandals stepped through the weeds of a ditch past a dead gypsy onto a sandy dirt track of road following the tall, slender, creeper-clad arches of the aqueduct of Nero, as it traveled downhill to where it once fed his House of Gold. A mile and a half down the gentle slope, he could see the top of the Flavian Amphitheater in the valley below, rising from a maze of irregular rooftops.   Its great curving rank of two hundred and forty masts were etched black against the drastic stain of burnt orange sunset, its arcades pulsing with a reddish glow.   His journey from home having taken him in a five-mile arc tracing the southern half of the Amphitheater's oval, like some magnetic sun and he a planet revolving, the roar of the Mob whispered uphill to him through the trilling of the cicadas.

He turned away from the sight and walked the road east, past the mansion of Severus' general Lateranus, and the estate of Domitia Lucilla where Marcus Aurelius was born and raised. The Gardens of Maecenas stretched to his left above their walls through the trees, greens of cypress and pine deepening to silhouette, serrated feathers of palm colored the soft inside of a black olive. Further on, he skirted the edge of the vast summer residence of the Severans; then the tremendous double-arched gateway of the Claudian Aqueduct loomed ahead, rising eighty feet into the sky, the last of the sunset slipping rose off the top of its western facade.

Built two centuries before of rusticated travertine, its twin arches emitted the Via Labicana and the Via Praenestina, two of the highways heading east out of Rome, its attic story bearing conduits of both the Claudian Aqueduct and the Aqua Anio Novus. Handsome commemorative inscriptions spanned the gate's entire length on either side, where the stonemasons carefully chiseled the letters and numerals lauding the Emperor Claudius' great hydraulic gift to the people of Rome – the restoration of an older aqueduct system which daily brought tons of cold fresh mountain water into the capital from reservoirs in the Sabine Hills. Its two arches bustled with humanity passing beneath the frozen stares of the weathered statues of Augustus, Claudius and Caligula standing in the niches of the piers, booths of merchants clustered about selling everything from chickens to Chinese pottery.

Ox carts clopped wearily out of the city through the twenty foot-thick arches they entered by that morning full of fruits and vegetables. The farmers were going home for the day after selling their produce in the squares. Patricians passed them on horseback as they returned to their villas sprawling across the countryside and down the cypress-lined highways.

The Bestiarius entered the bottleneck beneath one of the arches along with a flood of immigrants returning to their collective hovels on the outskirts of town, or bunched around the bases of the great piers of the aqueducts stretching off into the hills, after a day of selling their own goods in the center of the city – cheap pots and cooking utensils, tapestries and clothes. Arab jewelers and Greek weavers and Ethiopian wool-sellers hailed him amidst the squeaking horns of Indian snakecharmers and the confusion of a dozen different languages. The dust from the continual passing of feet, hooves and cart wheels rose slowly into the air until it was lit like pink spray in the last of the sun rays rocketing through the atmosphere.

Outside the gate, Mannix veered left onto the Via Praenestina past the Tomb of the Baker on his way into the 'Wolf's Den,' the most infamous red light district of Rome. The area took its name from its position bordering the vast animal pens that formed a way station for the beasts en route to the Flavian Amphitheater from the government stockyards at Laurentum during any given series of games. The smell of cooking mixed with that of the beasts, Indian curry and the musty scent of Arab sweets, and the Bestiarius stopped to urinate beneath one of the vine-draped arches in the confusion of aqueducts. A huge, cratered, golden moon was rising to the east, and massive coils of purple cirrus trailed off at an oblique angle above behind a patchwork of rainclouds floating like blue ice in the softly glowing dusk. He appreciated the confusion in the sky before continuing on his way, turning down the Street of the Charioteers. The commercial shops were closing for the day, the clack and clatter of chain-worked wooden slat gates echoing up the block as they were pulled shut over the door fronts, their proprietors hurrying to be rid of the neighborhood before sundown, when it gave way to its drunken, dangerous evenings punctuated by the howling of the beasts in the stockyards.

Milo's tavern catered to an eclectic mix of sleazy patricians and burnt-out poets, cut-throats and gladiators; and the Bestiarius walked through its grimy doorway with a thirst for wine, nostalgia, and, ultimately, forgetfulness. When his eyes adjusted to the seedy lamplight of the interior, he noticed old Milo himself sitting at his usual perch behind the stone counter hollowed with vats containing the musty house wine, which the surly barkeep ladled into the cups of his patrons. The better vintages were kept in amphorae on the racks behind him. A tall, thin, take-your-time kind of man in a long-sleeved white tunic with seedy gray hair combed forward over his head, he sat on the back counter before the ranked amphorae of his better wines, his arms so long he could ladle the rotgut on the front counter without standing up. Nobody knew where he came from, though some said he'd been, by turns, a bandit, a smuggler and a mercenary. But Milo could run up a decent steak or plate of pork chops if he was in the mood, and Mannix and he went way back to the Bestiarius' training days in the stockyards.

"I see your arm's still on," the proprietor stated matter-of-factly, folding his own long arms across his chest, neither surprised nor impressed by the presence of the veteran venator. News traveled fast, and the highlights of yesterday's games were known all over Rome by noon.

Mannix smiled despite himself at the sight of an old, if not friend, then definitely a familiar. "By Mithra, I'm thirsty," he said. "What kind of watered-down resin you serving around here?"

"Good enough for the likes of you, bestiarius. They haven't felt sorry enough for you to retire you yet?"

"No," Mannix grinned, "they said they wouldn't sully the citizenry with anyone who drank in this dive."

Milo stood as the Bestiarius approached the bar. They gripped wrists in the customary Roman handshake. Mannix looked about the place, its walls decorated with crude fresco paintings of fighting gladiators and African lion hunts and erotic mythological scenes of satyrs with huge penises and forest nymphs performing fellatio on deer. Racks of horns lined the walls – stags, bulls, antelope, rhino; and some of the old-time gladiators and bestiarii had signed their portraits, inscribing them with knife gouges – 'To my good friend Milo in memory of many a pleasant evening, Carpophorus.'

"Place looks nice," Mannix said, though it hadn't changed in twenty years.

"Hades it does," replied Milo, ladling him a cup of wine. "This one's on me. Compliments of that bear that kissed you yesterday."

Mannix grimaced, not sure whether it was the thought of the bear or the taste of the wine.

"What do you want, twenty year-old Falernian?" The barkeep shrugged. "You're on the wrong side of town."

"There's no doubt of that," the Bestiarius laughed good-naturedly, grabbing old Milo by the shoulder and squeezing affectionately, warming to the harsh taste of the house wine which he used to appease the uncomplicated thirsts of his patrons, for most of whom quantity was more important than quality. Mannix drained the cup at a draught and Milo filled it again.

"Milo, I'm going to need something that will stick to my ribs in order to drink this swill," the Bestiarius chuckled.

The barkeep grinned in understanding and whistled to one of his wenches in the back.

The tavern was filling up, the after-work crowd from the Amphitheater trickling in, most of whom had little or no interest in watching the main event – fifty Jewish zealots armed with daggers pitted against thirty bears – unless their jobs entailed it. Mannix enjoyed the sweaty, vinous smell, the working-class atmosphere. Feeling suddenly on holiday, he looked forward to seeing Marcellus, knowing the fellow venator had a week off after today, and thinking perhaps they could go to the seaside, or camp in the hills.

Before long, a barmaid brought a large platter and set it before him.

"Thanks, Paula."

"Nothing," she smiled.

The Bestiarius set to on the stringy greasy lamb, the spicy Calabrian sausages, the bowl of steamed greens and the hunk of fresh bread. Washing it down with copious amounts of farmer's wine, he glanced around for the unlikely presence of any pretty girls, turning just in time to watch his old friend Pompey walk through the tavern door, fresh from the baths, his ebony skin glistening in the light of the oil lamps.

"Hello there, Mister Caius."

"Hello Pompey," Mannix smiled, standing to grip his wrist.

About forty years old – tall, slim and toughly muscled – the Numidian charioteer spoke Latin with a happy-lilting African accent. He wore a blue-gray tunic with his customary lion's-tooth necklace, and his white teeth gleamed in the gloom of the tavern as he slid onto a stool at the bar next to Mannix. "What's doing?"

"Just you, friend," the Bestiarius replied, resuming his meal.

Milo poured the charioteer a clay cup of wine, which he rolled slowly between his long thin fingers, their skin cracked like the leather of the trace reins he gripped as he whipped his horses in death-defying speeds around the Spina of the Circus Maximus.

Mannix rubbed the African's clean-shaven head affectionately, glad to be in the company of people he could be

205

himself around. "Say Milo," he said, spearing a forkful of greens, "remember those Norsemen that were in here," he smiled. "Had those broken bits of horn that people were saying were from unicorns but it turned out they were from whales?"

Milo smirked despite himself. "Those were some fellows," he replied. "Almost drank me out of business. If that story hadn't gotten around, you could've made a fortune on one of those horns."

The Bestiarius laughed, and swiped grease off his plate with a hunk of bread. Roman trappers had reported seeing unicorns in India, but he could see through the speculations that they were only rhinoceroses. However, it caused a stir. And, fancying himself a showman, it got him worked up as well.

He soon promised an exhibition of unicorns in the arena, which he delivered. But they were really just young African oryx, which he'd been working with since they were calved – bleaching their coats and binding their horns so the soft calcium deposits would grow together to produce one relatively straight horn. People figured out the trick, but it was still a hit that advanced his reputation.

The three men laugh at the story, but just then Apicius the Ringmaster rushed in in a flurry of wizard robes, saw Mannix and shouted, "Where in the fuck have you been! I've been looking all over for you!" Then his face contorted and he stopped dead on the floor amidst the tables filling up and the barmaids moving between them.

The barmaids froze, clay cups and pitchers poised on their trays, and the place fell silent.

Mannix, turned sideways on his stool at the bar, buzzed and faintly humored, says, "What the hell's the matter with . . ." but then he stood up. "What is it?" he hissed between bared teeth, his lips drawn back.

Apicius started and then faltered, his hand raising.

The Bestiarius slammed his hand down gripping the bar, "What is it?" he screamed, though he already knew.

"It's Marcellus," the Ringmaster blurted out, both hands now raised. "That re-enactment of the 'Twelve Labors of Hercules' you were on for," he turned to the side, rubbing his

206

forehead, shocked despite himself. "Lion," he muttered, "young male." He shrugged helplessly, "couldn't have weighed more than three hundred pounds."

His lips parted, his teeth grit, Mannix's face was like a glimpse into Hell before he recovered it. He slowly turned, and settled back onto his stool.

Pompey sat taut as a bowstring beside him, not moving, and Milo slowly filled a cup from an amphora off the back racks.

Apicius walked across the space between, his mouth slightly open, a finger raised. He came and stood at the bar beside the Bestiarius, looking straight ahead. "I'm sorry, Caius."

Mannix didn't seem to hear.

Milo set a cup of his best wine before him, and poured another two for Pompey and Apicius.

The men drank without talking, and Milo filled the cups again.

But their silence was soon interrupted by an uproar in the increasingly crowded tavern. Pompey looked up, and Milo gestured with disgust out across the room where clusters of big swaggering men were singing boisterously, pinching the barmaids, and drowning out the eclectic scene with their domineering laughter.

"It's Prixus and his bunch."

Paula the barmaid censured the huge gladiator under her breath and he jerked her onto his lap, ripped her smock over her dimply white buttocks and slapped them harshly several times.

"Who does that man think he is?" Pompey asked.

"A bully and a cut-throat," Apicius sighed. "Also the new-found favorite of the Emperor. Puts on a hell of a show, though. Real crowd-pleaser." He removed his elbow from the bar for a closer look at the money-makers. "We've got him and his friends there slotted for the grand finale of the series."

"Gladiators?" spat Milo. "If you call slicing up a bunch of blindfolded cripples 'swordsmanship.' In the old days they would've been in a state of shock, I tell you. Antoninus Pius knew his fighting men. He wouldn't have even had this bunch

207

in his novelty acts. They can't compare to the old breed. Boys among men, they'd be."

Pompey looked at the barkeep. He'd seen him come across the bar more than once with a club of hard wood, the offender waking with one hell of a hangover in the alley out back. "Why do you let them act like that in here, Milo?"

"Because, dear boy," Milo sneered, "as Apicius said, he's the darling of our noble Emperor." He shook his head. "He and his bunch get away with whatever they want – murder people in the streets if they look at them wrong, cut up whores. Hell, if I said anything about it they'd burn this place to the ground. And the Vigiles wouldn't do a damn thing about it," he sneered. "Elagabalus protects them, laughs at their abuses like a doting father. I just keep hoping they'll go somewhere else." His voice piped up, "Prixus, knock that crap off if you want to drink in here."

The huge man stopped, raised his head and approached, his arms outspread, one hand gripping an empty wine jug, his tremendous shoulders shrugged in a gesture of mock supplication. "Don't be an old sourpuss, Milo. The boys and I, we're just letting off some steam. Had a hard time up in Verona last week. Those damned Christians are hell, let me tell you. Wear a man's arm right out!" He made a repetitive hacking motion with his arm, the table of gladiators breaking up with laughter, their ringleader roaring loudly at his own sick joke.

Paula spit on the floor and scurried away redfaced, and Milo's lips soured with distaste as several of the patrons found opportunities to escape.

Prixus held the floor, his short black tunic cinched with a gaudy, silver-encrusted belt and matching wristbands. "Fucking sheep won't even put up a fight! They just die!" he shouted. "Ha! Well that's all they're good for."

The tavern fell quiet, its nostalgic atmosphere broken like a fine crystal vase.

The gladiator sidled up to the bar and slammed the clay jug down unnecessarily hard, chipping its bottom on the stone counter. "More wine, you old pisshead!"

Pompey lowered his head, minding his business, but Mannix turned the gladiator a look of cold steel from his blue-green, wolfen eyes.

Prixus, his pride wounded from the Emperor's statement and last night's confrontation in the baths, was taken aback for a minute, but determined not to let it happen again. "You got a problem, Mannix?"

Milo quickly filled the jug of wine with his ladle. "Just settle down, Prixus. He didn't say anything."

The Bestiarius turned slowly back to his drink.

"Hades he didn't," said Prixus. "And don't tell me to settle down, shitbag." The big gladiator turned his attention back to the Bestiarius, sizing him up, the bandages bulging beneath his paenula, the drawn look of his face. "You know, Mannix," he sneered, "you're starting to look a little past it."

Milo slid the newly-filled jug toward the big gladiator. "There you are, Prixus; there's your wine."

The gladiator hesitated a moment, "You're smart, old man," he said, taking the jug and starting to turn. But then he stopped. "Oh and Mannix," he grinned, "sorry about your boyfriend out there today."

Prixus turned to his rowdy drinking companions and broke out in obnoxious laughter, theirs rising up at his cue. He turned back and slapped the Bestiarius hard on his bad shoulder, in mock friendship, little knowing that would be the last proactive move he'd ever make.

The clay wine cup crashed into his face with a ferocity of speed that splintered his nose and lacerated his lips and splattered his face with blood, Milo grabbing for Mannix yelling "NO!" but only catching air as the follow-through with the cup arced Prixus over and down to smash into the floor.

The other gladiators were tripping drunkenly over tables and chairs trying to get to the scene, but they were too late. A few of them slipped in the purple blood fanning alluvial from the back of their friend's head, Mannix sweeping up a barstool and smashing it through the uncoordinated wedge cracking jaws and collarbones, moving like lightning with just the right amount of wine in his blood to make the synapses fire without

209

any hesitation as he cycloned into the cloud of gladiators, beating and stabbing the stool into shards on their arms, kneecaps and skulls until its last leg finally snapped on the side of a caved-in face and then he was biting, gouging and raking with his claws, whipping a chin the wrong way rippling vertebrae and shaking individual victims so violently the others couldn't get a disabling shot in on him.

Six seconds later, four of the toughest gladiators in the Empire lay dead on the floor of Milo's tavern and five others were thwapping sandals down the stones of the Street of the Charioteers trying to get away. And all of it before Milo could bring the hard wooden stick down on Mannix's head and he just let it fall clattering to the floor by his feet.

The Bestiarius bumped into tables walking around trying to catch his breath, his shoulder streaming blood from where he'd ripped the stitches all to hell, the shocked patrons sticking to the walls of the tavern slinking away from him trying to slip out the door.

Apicius, shaking palsy-like, wheeled away from the scene back to the bar. "Somebody should have told them," he spat bitterly, looking at nothing, "you're not in Verona anymore." He slammed his fist down on the counter, hell-to-pay for the loss, the grand finale of the series out the window. "Fucking Assholes," he hissed.

XXIX

The Vigiles were there almost immediately. One of the customers who escaped early must have told them there was trouble. As soon as they saw the bloody heap of dead gladiators they drew swords.

But then their captain exclaimed, "Gods, it's Mannix!" and the four policemen in leather torso armor hesitated, shifting their feet to avoid the widening flow of blood filling the cracks across the tiled floor. City boys whose petty magistrate fathers wheedled them their jobs, used to roughing up drunks, they stepped around and over it like dainty maidens would dogshit. But the problem was that the man who stood across the pool of it from them was Hero of The Mob since they were kids, and three of them even won money on him yesterday. And the real problem was that he still had the craziness in his eyes that sent the piss shivers running down the inside of their stomachs when they looked at him.

And indeed four other men, the same number as them, but much tougher, harder men, lay dead on the floor. Their mouths open, their lips peeled back over shattered teeth, their noses flattened into jellied pulp, one of them's bladder slowly emptied into the small lake of black blood flickering rich ruby-and-gold in the light of the oil lamps, little air bubbles expanding off its surface to pop like mellow lava as it spread.

"Shit!," one of the policemen exclaimed, "it's Prixus!" recognizing the gladiator more for his gaudy silver-encrusted belt and build than for his face.

"Fucking Hell!" blurted the captain, turning his head away and biting his lip and almost slapping his thigh in disdain. There would be hell to pay for this mess, and he'd no doubt be run up in front of somebody, perhaps even the Emperor, to explain. But then the realization hit – Prixus, the toughest gladiator in Rome, lying there with a mask of blackly drying blood covering his nose and mouth, and bits of skull and purple brain ejectiles shot out from the back of his head where it hit the floor. The big man's eyes, beginning to glass, still registered the shock. How the fuck did Mannix do it?

"Milo, you'll lose your license for this," the captain said, trying to regain his composure.

Still staring in disbelief at the heap of twisted limbs littering his tavern, "They slipped on the floor," the grizzled barkeep replied softly.

The Bestiarius stood across the room, breathing deeply through his nose, his paenula twisted up and around his neck, the blood from his shoulder running in rivulets over his striated bicep to channel with the rope vein down his forearm and over his hand where it glooped, and dripped off his fingers.

Apicius leaned against the bar with his head in his hands, and Pompey still hadn't moved.

The Vigiles poke tentatively at the dead bodies, their faces screwed up with distaste at the sight of the brained men flowing blood from their eyes, ears and nostrils. Their captain looked at the floor and then at nothing. He made a confused, throw-away gesture at his men and turned and walked out. The policemen looked at each other and shrugged and shifted their feet. Then they grimaced and began dragging the four bodies out the door by their least-mangled parts to await the cart.

Mannix shuffled stiffly to the bar. In a cracked, toneless voice he said, "Wine."

Milo obeyed, pouring the good stuff, and knowing, by the look in the Bestiarius' eyes, that it wasn't over. He knew Mannix well enough to know that when it came over him like this he couldn't stop it but just had to ride it out until it was gone, hoping he didn't hurt anyone who didn't deserve it, the drunkenness no more than a prop to cover some of the worst of it. And he also knew that he hadn't seen the last of the Vigiles, and would be lucky if the Praetorians weren't on him within the hour.

Behind them, the barmaids were toting buckets of water and pouring it over the blood and sweeping it out the door.

Paula walked over with a clean wet rag and gently dabbed the blood off Mannix's shoulder and arm, leaving the rag across the reopened wound. He didn't seem to notice.

"Caius," Milo said cautiously, "go home." He shook his head. "Or, better yet, don't go home. But go somewhere. Go find Lepidus," he nodded, "go to the school." The barkeep lowered his head and looked up at him under his furrowed brow. "They'll be back, son," he said. "They'll be back and it won't just be four of them."

The Bestiarius didn't seem to hear. He just drank. A vacuous expression in his eyes, like black coals, glazed and dead, he drank again, and then set the empty cup down.

Milo sighed, and filled the cup again, not wanting to think about the rest. "I'll cover for you as best I can," he said, "and you will too, Apicius," he looked at the Ringmaster, who shrugged hopelessly and then nodded slowly in assent.

"They started it," Apicius sighed. And then he looks at the ceiling, "Much good may it do us all."

Milo turned his head back to Mannix. "You've got to try and ride this out," he continued. "And I mean ride it out smart, until it blows over."

The Bestiarius still wasn't listening, though a dangerously interested look had crept into his face with the wine, his eyes not meeting anyone's.

Milo shook his head and rubbed his eyes with his fingertips and then placed the amphora on the counter and went around the bar to spread rags over the wetness on the floor. He knew the news was probably all over the Esquiline District by now, and the entire city would be throbbing with it by morning. The Emperor's favorite . . . nothing good would come of it, and most probably something very bad.

Mannix set his empty cup down, removed the rag from his shoulder and placed it on the bar. "Come on, Pompey," he said to the shocked charioteer, his voice still toneless, "let's go get a real drink. There's a tavern down in the Suburra that's got grog. I can't take anymore of this vile wine."

Pompey, who still hadn't moved or said a word but only kept his eyes down minding his own business, opened his hand on the bar. "Mr. Caius . . ." he shook his head hopelessly, pleadingly, not looking at him, "I . . . I'd best be going."

The Bestiarius nodded grimly in understanding. He tugged his paenula back over his shoulders. Its coarse woolen weave scratched and burned in the opened stitches of his wound. As he turned and walked slowly and unsteadily across the floor and out the door, Milo, Apicius, Pompey and the barmaids looked up quickly to watch his big muscled back disappear in the grainy darkness.

XXX

Built two hundred years ago at the time of Christ by Tiberius, and originally sited well beyond the city limits, the Castra Praetoria – the great barracks of the Praetorian Guard – wasn't more than a mile northeast of Milo's tavern across the disabitato. When the cart came to pick up the bodies of the dead gladiators, the young captain of the watch in charge of the Vigiles of the Esquiline district, in a panic over his situation, ordered his men to spread the word in the checkpoints, and then jumped onto the bench beside the driver and told him to make haste to the Castra forthwith. Trying to avoid the thought of the mangled, bloody bodies jostling behind, the captain betook himself and his situation to the prefect of the guard – a man named Valerius Comazon Eutychianus.

Eutychianus was a former dancer of Syrian descent who had an inconsistent career on the stage in Rome during the reign of Septimius Severus due mainly to the influence of Julia Domna, who felt sorry for him and kept him around as a heel. He had pulled up stakes with the remainder of the Severan court when Macrinus exiled them back to Syria; and while there he worked as a secretary for the mother-daughter team of Maesa and Soaemias in their overthrow of Macrinus. Serving his third term as Praetorian Prefect, he was typical of the nepotism of the regime, as well as its recent degeneracy (Elagabalus having filled many other such posts of distinction with ex-charioteers, barbers, muleteers and prostitutes – all in good fun).

Awakened by the news and not in a good mood – his pasty white curls rancid with unwashed perfume – lifting the stained canvas and staring at the mangled forms of Prixus and several of the emperor's other favorite gladiators didn't help Eutychianus' mood much. He knew full well that Caius Marius Mannix was Hero of the Mob. And if it had been anyone else that the Bestiarius had killed below senatorial rank, he would have had the watch captain flogged for waking him. But Prixus was popular with the Mob as well, and he was moreover the Emperor's favorite.

Eutychianus inwardly cursed the little police captain for dumping the situation in his lap, and forcing him into a position in which he had to act. For having to act was a nasty thing for Eutychianus, unless it was on the stage. Being a prefect, in fact, was a nasty thing to Eutychianus and not an office he'd sought but rather been appointed to by Julia Maesa for his marginal administrative skills. Having to act and holding a public office were especially nasty things, and especially in the capacity of a Praetorian. For they both had an unnerving tendency to get one killed.

The purges within the Praetorian Guard had been almost non-stop over the last twenty years, and they always ran from the top down. Tens of thousands had been killed through the power shifts, starting from when Severus had the entire officer corps executed for their loyalty to Didius Julianus, and his son Caracalla went on to have thousands more killed for their loyalty to his brother Geta. Macrinus, Caracalla's own Praetorian Prefect, killed his share in overthrowing him. And then Maesa and Soaemias three years before with their defected legions fought a pitched battle at Immae in Syria against a Praetorian field army loyal to Macrinus and were victorious. And suddenly there were once again a lot of job vacancies. Hence, Eutychianus the dancer turned secretary woke up one day to the nightmare of his promotion.

But, in fact, he underrated himself a bit. For Eutychianus had not survived three terms as prefect for his light feet. He had an uncanny knack for ending up on whichever side happened not to get beat. And, in this day and time, that was no little feat.

Several months back – during Elagabalus' assassination plot upon his cousin Alexianus – he had narrowly escaped. After his grandmother Maesa and his mother Soaemias persuaded him to adopt Alexianus as his heir and Caesar, Elagabalus smelled a rat and ordered that the boy be removed from his court and that his office be revoked by the Senate. But when this was announced in the lofty chamber aside the Forum square, confusion reigned. For Alexianus was known to be a youth of a rare, chaste and excellent character. So a conundrum followed in the duration of which Elagabalus turned to the guard, plotting with some of the tribunes to kill Alexianus.

The Emperor began by trying to get the guard to refuse to recognize the boy's title of Caesar, and then dispatched hooligans to smear mud and horse dung on his inscriptions and statues throughout the squares. He also sought to bribe the boy's guardians and tutors with rewards and distinctions for killing him any which way they wished – in his bath, by poison, or with the blade. But the conundrum subsequently split the Praetorian camp, for many in the ranks were supportive of Alexianus for the funds distributed them in secret by his mother Julia Mamaea.

After the young boy's statues were desecrated, a contingent of several hundred of the Praetorians were fired with anger and went to the palace, where they placed a guard about Alexianus and his mother. They then proceeded to the gardens of Spes Vetus in the vast summer estate of the Severans on the edge of the Esquiline district, where Elagabalus was awaiting news of his cousin's assassination while driving around in a little gem-studden chariot harnessed to four beautiful buxom Patrician women naked as the day they were born. The women were grunting and squealing and trying to find the game as he quirted their healthy wriggling buttocks and cried, 'Onward, my Vixens!'

A fight with his personal bodyguard ensued in which a total of seventy-two from both sides were killed and, interrupted by the sudden clatter of the soldiers, Elagabalus grabbed Eutychianus – who was conspicuously on hand – and told him to distract the men while he meanwhile withdrew. Eutychianus summoned his stage presence, miraculously controlled the trembling in his knees, climbed atop a terrace and raised his voice over the melee. He admirably reminded the soldiers of their oath of allegiance, and acknowledged that changes needed to be made. No sooner had he stalled them, however, than

Elagabalus arrived, a look of fire in his greenish-brown eyes, in his raised hand the Imperial Genius – the infinitely sacred little silver statue of the female victory with the snake and the eagle before which the aromatic oil had burned nightly in the tent of Marcus Aurelius on the Danube.

Representing not only himself, but moreover the concept of Emperor, the concept of Rome, and the concept of Divine Right, the display of the Genius had a shamanistic effect on the soldiers, no little aided by Elagabalus' own persona. For the young man was surrounded by a kind of aura, like that of a youthful Roman consul making a tour among the barbarian hordes which his grandfather had conquered. He gave a speech on the above concepts interlaced with his claim of divinity not only through them, but through his priesthood of the Sun God, and moreover let them in on the new resolution of their imminent raise in pay.

At the end of the speech, the men cheered him and turned from their designs. Eutychianus was amazed and had couriers dispatched to the Castra Praetoria where the vast bulk of the guard loyal to Alexianus replied to their placations with a unanimous decision that they would spare Elagabalus' life on the condition that he not only send away all of his degenerate courtiers and start on a decent mode of living, but also that Alexianus be kept separate from him, not only for his safety, but so that the young boy could not by chance be corrupted by his cousin's baseness. Thus, through negotiations and compromise and, moreover, in order to keep peace amongst the Praetorians and in the streets – Julia Maesa had the lesser accomplices scapegoated and the affair came to a close. And Eutychianus stayed alive.

But now here he was in another quandary. Yes, being a Praetorian Prefect was a nasty business indeed. And yet something could be made of this. 'Something must be made of this,' he thought to himself, curling his lip and wishing all the while to return to his pillow.

But the winds of change were blowing, and Eutychianus intended to stay abreast of them. He knew full well that Mannix was not popular with the current regime. And he also knew why. Being one of Julia Domna's lackeys ten years before, he slunk around the palace with the other writers, poets and artists she kept about. Her niece's amour with the Bestiarius was no secret on the Palatine in those days, and Eutychianus had been at half a dozen torchlit garden parties where Mannix was present through the years. One time the Bestiarius even threw him into a fountain for making an asininely drunken, overly-aggressive pass at him. But Eutychianus didn't particularly hold that against him.

The problem was that he had to act, to do something. And he had to do it right, or lose his head. For, though Mannix may not have been popular with Elagabalus and Julia Soaemias, due to his popularity with the Mob, the Bestiarius had remained untouchable. But Prixus was popular with the Mob as well, and he was moreover known to be the Emperor's favorite. So now just might be Eutychianus' chance to level the playing field and further ingratiate himself. The problem there was that, as the winds of change were indeed blowing, and Elagabalus was growing increasingly insane, it looked as if grandmother Maesa was about to let the axe fall in favor of her other grandson Alexianus.

Therefore Eutychianus needed, once again, to play both sides. His better judgment told him that Maesa should be told first. But since the news would be all over the city by morning, and since there was plenty in the ranks still loyal to Elagabalus, the only thing to do was to dispatch the word to both parties at the same time. The other necessity was to get Mannix, and get him off the streets before they all had a bloody disaster on their hands.

Standing in the peristyled parade ground of the Castra Praetoria behind the huge gate atop which the standards of the Empire fluttered slowly in the misting drizzle, Eutychianus turned to his adjutant and said, "Call out the guard."

Then he wheeled and started off across the large torchlit parade ground in his nightshirt to his office – overweight and debauched yet his steps still as light as a dancer's in his yellow night slippers – where he proceeded to write a message to be sent by courier to both the Imperial Palace, where the Emperor and his mother Julia Soaemias were residing, and to the gardens of Sallust, where Julia Maesa, Mamaea, and Alexianus were living.

XXXI

The windchimes tinkled in the night breeze that made the oil lamps whicker and the globular bronze incense censures twist on their chains. Forsaking the novel spatial solutions of the Domitianic private wing – corrupted by her son and his courtiers anyway – Julia Soaemias made her apartments in the Severan addition. Terraced out from the southeastern slope of the Palatine upon massive arched substructures with an almost frightening disregard for the disposition of the walls and the vaults beneath, Crantor, its architect, must have been at least as sure as Rabirius was of his materials and technique.

Topping the wing like a tower room, her uncle's former study was deeply marbled, the columns supporting its ceiling of the reddish-purple porphyry from the Claudianus Mons in Egypt, with gilt bronze bases and capitals. The cross-vaults of its ceiling were decorated in rich, varicolored mosaic, and their glass tesserae sparkled in the warm orange light of the oil lamps and reflected in the flooring of gloss-black Lucullan marble from the southwestern coast of Izmir. The room overlooked the city through open bays giving onto terraces on three sides. The bays were hinged with bronze doors, all open, their spacings hung with linen curtains of a golden weave.

Julia Soaemias stood staring northeast through one of the diaphanous drapes licking gently at her ankles as it swayed in the breeze. The long axis of the stadium garden stretched away eighty feet below. The tops of its trees emerged from the water with which it had been purposefully flooded, all of it frosted in the moonlight rippling like milk over the terracotta-tiles roofing its peristyle. Though it was an airish night, Soaemias at age forty-one was still hot-blooded, with the intrinsic warmth of the voluptuary and the drinker. Always a point of difference between her and her sister, Soaemias always preferred air and a view, warming her hands when she had to by the bronze oil braziers spaced burning about the room.

"Thank you, Omphale," she nodded. "I will extinguish the lamps. That's all for tonight."

Standing across the room from her, the old body slave in the plain gray dress who had been with her since she outgrew her wet nurse looked concerned.

"Perhaps mistress would like a hot bath?"

Julia Soaemias smiled softly and shook her head. "Thank you, Omphale. Not tonight."

The ornatrice lowered her chin. "Forgive me, but the mistress has not been herself of late." Her kind had been burned for less, but one does not hand styril and sponge, oil and towel every day for almost forty years without some familiarity.

Soaemias registered it and smiled again thinly. "We've never had a cup of wine together," she casually stated. "Have we, Omphale?"

"Mistress?" The perpendicular furrows of pensiveness deepened between the body slave's eyebrows.

The empress turned. "I've asked much of you, much of your service." She moved across the gloss-black floor in her gold-laced sandals to a table upheld by twin dog-headed figures of the Nile-god Anubis. From it she lifted a silver flagon of exquisite workmanship and poured into a silver cup with matching vine tendrils in relief. She refreshed her own cup, and then turned to face her ornatrice. "I've asked you to maintain a difficult role, Omphale – the difficult role of servant and friend."

The body slave had seen her mistress drunk plenty of times, but she had never seen this before. Like a scroll unraveling, the old ornatrice had a flickering of memories run across the space behind her eyes – memories of holding a little girl as she vomited with the flu or singing her to sleep when she was blue, memories of cleaning up a teenager when she was too hungover to do it herself, memories of massaging her through menstruation and covering for the antics of her and her friends with the Domina Maesa, which often got her whipped. Memories of standing behind a curtain in the doorway with a whispered warning at the ready while some pretty-faced palace slave or some two-bit bestiarius romped with her. If that was something like love, the body slave did not know.

"Yes. It's you, Omphale, and you alone, who have truly known me," Soaemias parted her arms with the cups slightly, her peacock-colored robe open over a tight black linen body suit. She walked to the slave and handed her the silver cup with a nod. Omphale's mouth trembled slightly as her Empress initiated the drinking ceremony of the old kings.

Hooking their arms and bringing the cups to their lips, their eyes locked on each other's for perhaps the first time in their history. And they drank, a lifetime passing through the space loosely chained between. As Soaemias lowered her silver cup glinting in the lamplight, she placed her other hand atop the old woman's. "I want to thank you. It has been an honor and a privilege to have your service."

The body slave, understanding all now, nodded with tears in her eyes.

"Are you clear on your role for tomorrow night, Omphale?"

"Yes, mistress."

"Do not be afraid. You will be fine."

"And you, mistress?"

Julia Soaemias nodded. "I will be all right." And then she turned away, "Don't worry about the lamps, Omphale," she said over her shoulder as she returned to the open bay overlooking the Circus. "I will extinguish them before I retire."

The ornatrice hesitated once more. But her mistress had never been a blue calm sea. She had always been a storm. Then she bowed and turned away, leaving Julia Soeamias alone with the marble busts of Marcus Aurelius, Septimius Severus, Julia Domna and Julia Maesa wavering in the lamplight from a northwesterly breeze off the Aventine which carried with it the fresh funereal smell of the rose gardens around the Temple of Diana and its cults shrines.

She glanced about the open bays as if trying to decide. To the southeast stretched the Caelian hill with the Temple of the Divine Claudius, its massive terraced podium clung with the

223

bunched jumble of darkened high-rise apartment blocks scaling and abutting it like cliff dwellings atop which the serene temple rose in spectral white travertine. The tremendous trail of the Claudian aqueduct coming in to feed the Palatine snaked off around the temple podium to stretch sixty-one kilometers into the blackened distance of the Sabine hills. To the northeast, beyond the stadium garden, she could see the Temple of Elagabal rising above its precinct walls.

She had heard rumors of what went on up there which, if true, made none of them fit to live anymore. She confronted her son over it, but he assured her that they were lies spread by Patricians to blacken his name. And yet he had profaned many of the old temples throughout the city by gathering their cult statues to this 'Elagaballium.' And having not only declared that all other gods were merely the servants of his but, aided and abetted by the continual reinforcement of his courtiers, astrologers and magicians – who danced and sung with him in the precinct in the language of the Bedouins – he had recently further scandalized the Senate and the upper classes of Rome by declaring that he and the god were one and the same.

She shook her head. The worst of it took place last summer when, enraged by the senior vestal's public censure of his behavior, he broke into the sanctuary of Vesta in a fit of hormonal pique demanding that his god should be worshipped everywhere and by all. In an effort to appease his insanity, the senior vestal offered him the holy of holies from the temple in their sanctuary – a large earthenware crock containing the seven most sacred relics of Rome including the Palladium, the small statue of Pallas Athena carried from the flames of Troy by Aeneas, ancestor of Romulus and Remus. But she'd offered him a fake, of which there were several for just such a purpose.

Upon discovering its emptiness, Elagabalus threw it down and smashed it, and then tried to extinguish the sacred flame which burned nonstop inside the temple as a signifer of Rome's immortality. When a courageous young vestal tried to stop him, he proceeded to violate one of – if not the – most sacred statutes of Roman law by having his way with her. Elagabalus was big, and physically strong, and the several

Vestals on hand couldn't stop him but were reduced to watching in horror as he ripped the girl's stola over her back and bent her over an altar. After it was over, he stumbled out of the sanctuary, bloodied and besmirched and frothing with his sated rage; and the whole affair was patched up as well as possible by her and her mother, who made enormous donations to the Vestals.

Her eyes moved beyond the Elagaballium to the Flavian Amphitheater hulking in shadow and the Suburra beyond, stretching up the Esquiline. Something moved in the water below, a lazy heavy shifting which sent a series of moonlit ripples fanning away to break around the trunks and branches of the plane trees. To the southeast and likewise directly beneath her stood the small sanctuary of Isis built by her aunt and uncle, both incorrigible Egyptophiles.

Its courtyard flanked by sphinxes and cynocephali, the monumental gateway to the interior of the sanctuary was centered on an obelisk pointing mystic and burnished toward the misting clouds through breaks in which a yellow moon was visible, hanging cold over the city. Gigantic statues personifying the Tiber, the Nile and Oceanus reclined ghostly in the corners of the courtyard, and through three granite columns, six stairs ascended to the door of the sanctuary with its four-columned, triumphal-arch facade with the bow-shaped pediment framing a relief of Isis galloping sidesaddle on a lion.

Though she could care less for the gods of the Nile or any of these other mystery religions – and the sanctuary's gold-leafed doors had blackened without polish – she did sometimes enjoy simply sitting inside the sanctuary for its seclusion. It had a forlorn, unswept quality of neglect which severely called into question the likes of Petricon and all the other pseudo-Egyptian hangers-on.

She suddenly had a flash of her son as child – a blinding sunlit flash of him running about the courtyard down there with the Isaic priestesses chasing him. Already their god, the spoiled little thing was beautifully endearing, with his olive skin and his curly black hair. He could have gone a hundred different ways from those days but, due to her neglect, he had gone the worst possible one.

She walked to her uncle's massive walnut table desk where the remnants of her half-eaten dinner lay cold on a plate, and glanced over the correspondence regarding the banquet. The last shipment of roses would arrive tomorrow. But she knew, from climbing the scaffolding behind the banquet hall herself yesterday, that there were already enough to do the job. The palace slaves had done well, many of them bedding down for the night and to wait out the day tomorrow in the attic of the hall. She had left a reward for them all. Omphale would be notified of hers as well.

She tried to think if anything had been left undone and, finding none, poured herself another cup of the musty wine from the grapes grown across the black slopes of Vesuvius. She carried the cup across the gloss marble floor through the diaphanous golden drapes swaying between two of the purple porphyry columns out onto the southwestern terrace of the study. With one hand on the ledge of its balcony and the other around her silver cup, the Circus Maximus spread before her in darkness, strange in its moon-shadowed emptiness, its massive, gray-brown track cut by the long reef-like form of its spine.

She took a sip of the wine, her eyes running across the spina's encrustation of colossal statues, winged victories pirouetting from columns, fountains and altars to the gods. At each of its ends stood a Carystian marble column surmounted by a long iron crossbar, on one of which was a string of huge marble eggs – symbols of Castor and Pollux, patron divinities of Rome – on the other a line of life-sized bronze dolphins – symbols of Neptune, patron god of horses. A great gambler in her youth, she knew the symbols well; for each time the chariots lapped the course, an egg and a dolphin were removed so that the crowd could tell how many laps had been run.

The golden globe atop the towering Aswan granite obelisk which Augustus took from Heliopolis and erected at the eastern end of the spina glowed softly in the moonlight along with the copper roof tiles on the small temple below it dedicated to Venus, patron goddess of charioteers. To her right, back,

226

beyond and out of sight, curved the huge rose-marbled double-leveled hemicyclical terrace of Rabirius' original Domitianic design, where she used to watch Mannix train in the Circus below, and with him later stood, and sipped wine, their bodies pressing and close, staring just as she did this evening, what seemed like a lifetime ago.

Perhaps she shouldn't have sent the note, she reflected. Perhaps he never should have known. But when all the gold had lost its luster, and all the jewels had ceased to shine, there was nothing left for her but a girl's love for a boy. And the only thing left undone for Julia Soaemias was to look into his eyes, one last time.

XXXII

Wind had shifted around to the northeast and the air pressure was falling. A slight misting rain had begun to blanket the high-ground of the Esquiline district as Mannix walked down the Clivus Suburanus toward the Suburra. Slickening the black basaltic paving stones, prickling in the torchlight reflections, and floating the city grime snaking in dull rainbow colors in the gutters, the night smelled like a wet dog, and the rain ate damp and aguey into his bones.

He pulled the hood of his paenula over his head, his boot sandals rasping lonely on the wet flagstones. The forlorn clatter of cart traffic echoed in the distance as the merchants, after-hours, brought provisions into the city. New developments of apartment blocks alternated with open ground where weeds grew up to five and six feet in places and ancient shrines grouped along a crumbling, tufa-block stretch of the old Republican city wall. He thought of Marcellus, and a gripping emptiness descended upon him like the net of a Retiarius in the Arena, catching and tripping him – a vacuum of the heart which threatened to explode – and he could not stop the thought of running endlessly in the dark.

Hollow-eyed and swallowing hard, he walked down the Clivus Suburanus into the Argiletum breathing deeply through his nose the closing smell of gray weather. He arrived at his apartment block to find that he could not go home, could not face Erithrea, could not face any of it any more. The streets of the Suburra were empty save a few insomniac old men and a scattering of young hoodlums out avoiding the watch. The Mob had long returned to their homes, drained after the day of games. The curfew was always more-or-less loosely in effect during any given series, and anyone on the streets at this hour was fair game for getting roughed up by the Vigiles just for the fun of it.

An occasional cart clattered past on its return to the mercantile staging areas outside the Porta Viminalis, after offloading its goods in the markets of Trajan up the street. Mannix continued down the Argiletum to the Porticus Absidata, its iron-studded bronze doors all closed, the monumental center cordoned off for the night. Come full circle from the morning with no way back, everything had changed, everything was at an end.

He ascended the Alta Semita up the Quirinal hill along the back of the fire wall behind the forum of Augustus, its blocky tufa volcanic stones glistening blackly with the clinging mist of drizzle. Turning left onto the Via Biberatica into the markets of Trajan — a brilliant complexity of architectural utilitarianism terraced theater-like into the slope of the Quirinal — he stopped at the railing of a lookout point over the Forum of Trajan spreading at the foot of the hill below. His gaze moved across the statues of the Dacian prisoners lining the attic story of the far peristyle flanking the forum square — opaque ghosts ranked in marble darkness, their bearded heads bowed in submission, hands crossed before their characteristic trousers.

Partially visible above the roof of the near peristyle, its wet bronze glowing softly in the grainy darkness, he could see the head, shoulders and outstretched arm of the colossal bronze equestrian statue of Trajan striding forth in the center of the square. The entire complex dedicated to the defeat of a people, the basilica Ulpia stretched its massive bulk across the transverse axis at the end. Behind it, the upper part of the column relating the campaigns in Dacia rose in carved relief like an unevenly wound scroll. Topped by another statue of just another of the self-glorifying men that took his father away from him and then became gods when they died, the pediment of the Temple of the Deified Trajan peaked in the gray mist of shadow behind the column.

His gaze returned across the square to the temple of Venus Genetrix in the forum of Caesar beyond, and then up to the temple of Juno facing out from the rocky northeastern spur of the Capitoline with the oil braziers flickering along its flanks in the cool wet night. In the distance behind it, the temple of Jupiter Optimus Maximus hovered huge from the hill's southwestern spur. The Bestiarius' aquamarine eyes moved down from the Capitoline and out over the Forum proper, the Senate house and the Basilica Giulia and the wet-darkened gray temples jumbled in the blue haze of night. The Palatine hill spread across the southwestern horizon, pinpoints of torchlight surging through the palms in the Imperial garden grounds and he wondered vaguely how he could set fire to it all, like old Nero did, and burn the whole city down.

Turning away, he staggered slightly as he passed beneath a dripping brick archway into the upper-level hemicycle of the markets, the shops lining the concave street all closed. Street people grumbled and wondered at him, shadows shifting from piles of trash adjusted up into the doorways of the shops against the weather. At the end of the Biberatica, he could see the massive new Temple of Serapis looming in the northern middle distance on the apex of the Quirinal, pulsing with firelight. And then the street turned left and he walked down the hill, weaving slightly with the wine and the weariness, flanking the Semo Sancus to arrive at the rear of the Basilica Ulpia's convex apse, its weather-worn marble slickened with wet streaks.

A tomcat crouched in a corner and hissed wickedly as he passed along the base of the towering Temple of Trajan, a forest of fifty-foot Egyptian granite monolithic columns, each weighing a hundred and twenty tons. Turning behind its bulk into a narrow residential street lined with apartment blocks connected by a corridor of weed-hung supporting arches, he arrived on the Via Lata – the straight, broad avenue leading between the northern city gate and the Forum area. As he walked, the whisper of a name passed unconsciously between his grim lips,

"Marcellus."

The wine and the grog and the fatigue and the heartsickness twisting his brain, a soft, subconscious moan escaped him, the cry of a wounded wolf on a moonlit night.

Memories came flooding back through the drunkenness he had tried to kill them with, memories of how they had met at the school, and helped one another along as novices. Memories of those days when Lepidus would give them a free afternoon, and they would wander into the disabitato to nature places where they would compose poetry together, helped along by the red wine and the way the clouds looked and the blue-distant hills. Or how they would spend the day at the seaside, and watch the western sunset.

With a feeling of searing pain in his chest, he remembered a conversation they'd had at the seaside one evening ten years ago . . .

"Makes you believe in the gods, this," Marcellus had gestured at the softly glowing colors in the huge sky.

Mannix nodded, staring at the massive brushstrokes of pink cirrus.

"Do you believe in something, Caius?" his friend had gone on to ask.

There was silence for a moment. "I believe in this," replied the Bestiarius, gesturing at the heavenly spectacle.

"I mean . . . when we die," Marcellus continued, "something."

Mannix shrugged. "Things return . . . grass, trees . . . they die and dissolve into the earth . . . yet something of them remains to aid in the process of new ones coming up." He sighed. "I don't know."

"But what is God?" asked Marcellus. "Where does He come in?"

"God is life," Mannix nodded. "The force of life that's in us, the birds, plants, trees, animals, clouds, water." He looked over at Marcellus. "God is that within a man which makes him keep going even though he knows it can only end one way."

Marcellus had looked at him and smiled, and the two youths swam in the sea, their bodies bronzed by the sun, laughing and charging the waves and seeking a newer man within their souls, one who longed for a new and superior form of life. In any other era they would have been merely minor,

231

fallible gods. In this one they drank raw farmer's wine around a bonfire at night, and danced their love for one another. And, reeling with hot blood and wine, they wrestled and laughed, and rocked playfully with each other until they fell to the ground, stretched out on the pebbles, and fell asleep in one another's arms.

The tears brimmed over his eyes and spilled down his whiskered cheeks, and Mannix began to weep. Like he hadn't in years, like he never had until he was reeling with it, choking and gasping with hot, bitter tears. He laid his head on his forearm against an unknown wall and he cried like a baby, and he screamed like a panther, and he banged his head against the wall and that was when they came at him, five against one.

The first baton caught him in the small of the back a vicious hit that sent a sear of lightning up his spine into his brain. His knees buckled and he dropped, making the second hit aimed for the back of his head miss and crash into the wall gouging fragments of stucco exploding off. Out of the blue and into the black, the pain rage set in and the quickness began and he was moving spider-like and shifting instinctively with the blows and the kicks.

Ripping a foot the wrong way in its boot sandal, the ankle popped like a stick in the night and the scream ricocheted down the deserted street. A blow aimed for his jaw caught him in his hurt shoulder and he roared and spun and corralled one of them around the throat with his forearm jerking him into his chest to immediately crush the trachea and then release to jump back dodging the next arc of baton which smashed into the helmet of the dead Vigile before he dropped. The dead man's baton clattered to the pavement and the Bestiarius lunged to swipe it up.

The policeman with his foot turned behind his leg was screaming and crawling across the middle of the street and the other three backed off and spread out, shifting and circling, trying to get behind him, the sound of their boot sandals yipping and squealing on the wet pavement.

"You're wanted for the murder of Prixus, Mannix!" one of them yelled.

232

The Bestiarius kept his back to the wall, a fiendish grin spreading across his face as he lunged and stutter-stepped at the three Vigiles beginning to lose their nerve. "Hell, boys," he said, "I was just trying to have a little fun."

As he faked at one, another came in with a hacking blow which he dodged, throwing the policeman off balance, Mannix grabbing his red cape fluttering past with one hand. Throwing his weight backwards and around like a shot thrower, he arced the vigile tripping past his fellows to smash drunkenly into the side of the wall, which the policeman no sooner impacted than the Bestiarius shattered his jaw with the baton.

As the third of the vigiles slides limply down the side of the wall, the remaining two dropped their batons and drew swords, Mannix moving frantically to try and get the sword off their comrade at the bottom of the wall but it was beneath him, one of his legs twitching sickeningly as he slipped into a coma.

"Give it up, Mannix," one of them said. "Come easy."

Pretending to bend down and try to take the sword, he looked up with his wolfen eyes. "But boys," he smiled, "I'm just getting started."

As one of the Vigiles moved in he charged, covering the space between in a split-second and uppercutting with his baton knocking the sword out of the policeman's hand, hooking his ankle with his foot and smashing him hard into the pavement. The other one tried to stab him from the side but he was already past and, as the policeman slipped on the wet stone trying to jump over his friend, he planted his foot and cut back and smashed the baton over and over into the two men until the rain-water eased red down the gutters and the Bestiarius gasped for breath through the snot and the tears.

Lights had come on in the windows lining the street, shadowy figures watching from above. The angry clatter of horses echoed through the hard-walled stillness, making it difficult to determine from which direction they came. The Vigile with his foot pointing backwards was screaming for help in a doorway on the opposite sidewalk and Mannix walked across the street and stomped him to silence. He ripped the sword out of the policeman's scabbard and set off at a jog down the Via Lata, trying to calculate how much money he had left in the coin purse around his neck.

He didn't make ten yards before the first mounted horseman rounded a corner up ahead. The street suddenly alight and flickering with torches, a red-caped contingent of mounted Praetorians poured into it. Big, windburned, mean-looking mothers hand-picked from the Legions, the first one flipped his spear butt-end first and smiled, motioning for the others to stay back.

Mannix looked behind him. More horsemen were pouring in. He looked up. The first terrace was too high to jump for. He smiled.

"Bestiarius!" hailed the first Praetorian as he spurred his horse into a charge, "I must have you!"

As the horse began to close and the spear came down into position, Mannix sprinted forward and then slid on the wet paving stones swinging his sword from the side into the horse's forelegs, the beast in its screaming fall throwing its rider driving his spear into the ground snapping loud as a lightning crack pivoting the Praetorian fifteen yards sliding, scraping and stunned.

Mannix was up, wheeling, the sword ripped from his hands; the horse was screaming like a woman, trying to stand – one of its legs a spurting stump, the other not quite severed and flopping like a broken tail.

The fallen guardsman rose to his knees and the Bestiarius started kicking him, hard, ferociously, kicking him in the gut, the back of the legs, kicking his helmet off, crashing his heel down into his kidneys, the leather armor little protection. He smashed his fists into his ears, his head, grabbed him by the back of the hair, kicked him in the face, fast, over and over and oblivious of the terrific drumming sound coming through the ground around him faster, louder, all-encompassing, and then he was blasted flat on his face and stunned.

He couldn't breathe and felt sure his back was broken. The adrenaline raced electrically through his shocked body as he gasped for air, kneeing and scratching and clawing himself upright, flailing for something vertical to cling to, stumbling

234

back onto his knees and then finally up, staggering and reeling, his horizons slowly locking into place.

The horse which came from behind was galloping ahead, its rider standing in the stirrups, the plume of his helmet streaming behind, arms raised in a V, one holding a spear, the butt of which must have floored him for he wasn't run through yet.

The Praetorians seemed to want to make sport of him, one at a time, for they'd blocked the side streets, closing off the thoroughfare. Another horseman pulled away from the group and began his pass.

Mannix roared. Quickly picking up the downed Praetorian's spear, he sprinted forward several steps and javelined it into the chest and face area of the next closing guardsman who flinched like a girl as it caught him in the chin a stunning blow, knocking him off his horse onto the basalt paving stones.

The first rope cast glanced off the side of Mannix's head but the second didn't miss and the Bestiarius was suddenly jerked onto his back with the wind knocked out of him and another Praetorian, a bigger, tougher one, tried his luck as his friend kept the rope cinched around Mannix's neck just loose enough to keep him from blacking out. The Bestiarius scissor-kicked the big man, bringing him down and, before it even registered in the praetorian's mind what had happened, he was crawling and clawing up him like a cliff-face, all over him sticking gluey as a rapist and the confidence was turning to fear, the adrenaline that too much scare brought starting to work against the guardsman now and the weakness spreading through his abdomen and across his chest as Mannix's hands raked at his face, gouged at his eyes, ripped at his trachea and the big Praetorian was smashing his fists into the side of the Bestiarius' head but he couldn't get any force into his blows because Mannix kept wedging his forearms and elbows across his shoulders and biceps and the guardsman was trying to knee him in the gut, somehow get him off, but the Bestiarius had his pelvis locked on his and he started head-butting the big tough Praetorian, biting at his cheek, tearing part of his lip off.

The guardsman had never experienced anything like this before, never fought anybody that wouldn't quit like this, never felt this kind of helplessness, never been up against an animal before. And suddenly it occurred to him that he was going to die. But the kicks were coming into Mannix now, the boots smashing into his ribs, kidneys and head. His neck muscles strained against the rope tightening him to blackness yet still he was pounding his fists into the face of the big Praetorian, already dead now, the limp head snapping loosely on its neck with his blows.

Knowing that this was the end but only formally, for it ended all long ago – the laughter and the soft light, the green grass and the summer nights – the Bestiarius felt the blackness closing in on his consciousness. His eyes slow-blinking and closing like a child, he was running again, through the lance-thrusts of sunlight penetrating the pines, turning lime and limpid green and then darkening with shadow . . . to Jupiter and Saturn . . . Oberon and Miranda . . . Neptune . . . and Titan . . . .

XXXIII

Strapped to a horse with his hands tied behind his back and his arms tight to his sides, with ropes cinched around his stomach, chest and neck, Mannix vomited himself awake. The horse whinnied and sidestepped with the feel of it on its mane and the Bestiarius, choking and gasping and bobbing with the animal's trot, leaned forward to the side and tried to force the rest out with his stomach muscles. The ropes around his neck jerked him back up straight and almost over the horse's rump.

Four extensions of rope trailed off to a like number of Praetorians surrounding him, a central gap in the midst of the column of over a hundred red capes trotting up the long straight wide avenue of the Vicus Patricus between the Esquiline and Quirinal Hills. One of the few truly straight thoroughfares of Rome, the Patricus was lined with huge plane trees which swayed in a ghostly breeze before the tall, exclusive, seven-storied apartment blocks in which families lay safe asleep beneath the cloak of moonlit loneliness enshrouding the city. Mannix coughed up a few chunks of Milo's greasy undigested lamb and spat them onto the pavement, his breath billowing out in dank plumes of steam turned viscid in the rain-wet night air. One of the bilious burning chunks of vomit caught in his sinuses and he gagged miserably.

"What did you say there, hero?" laughed one of the big Praetorians, jerking on the rope tied around the pommel of his saddle leading to Mannix's neck. The rope cut off the circulation to his brain, making the Bestiarius choke and gasp. Seeing stars everywhere, he tried to control his breathing, inhaling through his nose; but the swollen cartilage had filled up with more than its usual quotient of congestion and blood which ran in rivulets over his lips to flicker out like windblown cobwebs as he roared, startling a nightbird busy warbling in a cornice high above.

"Keep your stinking mouth shut," the Praetorian jerked hard again on the rope.

The column of horsemen trotted out of the city proper through the Porta Viminalis, one of the gates in the old derelict Republican walls. An architectural confusion of arches, piers and dilapidated stretches of wall, the Marcian Aqueduct entered the city to the side of the weed-hung portal as if its hooping arcades were legs stepping straight over it. The horses passed through one of its high brick arches to emerge into open ground lifting a covey of grouse flittering off through the high grass with the vast Castra Praetoria looming ahead beneath the tattered remnants of moonlit cloud. Like a city in the distance, the lighted streets of the camp created a faint glow above its tremendous brick walls.

As they neared, sentries atop the western parapets called to the men manning the main gate below, and the huge iron-bolted doors beneath the triumphal arch facade inset with the bronze lettering lauding the building as the work Tiberius Caesar, groaned inward on their massive hinges.

"You assholes!," Eutychianus yelled, standing in the torchlit forecourt wringing his hands like a mother worried sick, "I told you not to rough him up," he whined.

"He killed four Vigiles and two of ours, Praefectus," replied the tribune in charge of the column, "he's dangerous."

Eutychianus, still in his nightrobe and yellow slippers, looked at Mannix slumped in the saddle, the venator's visage wavering in torchlight with streams of black blood traveling downward from his shadow-clad eyesockets. "There's a hundred of you cocksuckers!" the dancer yelled. "You mean to tell me you can't restrain one man without killing him? Assholes! Get him to the clinic," he pointed down an avenue between barracks blocks. "And no more rough stuff!"

"Shit," he whined to himself as the horsemen set off, shaking his head and knowing it was all going to hell in a handbasket – his retirement years which he'd planned to spend engaged in the pleasurable debauches of the Alexandrian Canopus until his heart or his money gave out.

For Mannix, resistance was futile at this point. He knew instinctively that it was better to try to collect some of his energy for whatever was coming; for it was unlikely that he would be meeting his end here. After being cleaned up in the clinic by camp doctors whose sympathy level was roughly half that between Eutychianus' and the guardsmen who apprehended him, the Bestiarius, still roped, was led to the brig, Eutychianus following behind, tripping and cursing in his yellow slippers over the street stones.

The cellars for political undesirables – who may or may not have something to say before they die – with their manacles and their leather-aproned technicians, were quiet tonight, their great travertine-block walls flickering in torchlight. Over the lime and antiseptic scent pervading them, they smelled of two hundred years of mildewed fear, death, and the underworld. The guardsmen led him down a flight of steps into a corridor and down into a large holding room with twenty or thirty shadowy figures lying about the patches of straw littering the cold black basaltic slabs of the floor. They chained his wrists and ankles to iron rings set in the wall which allowed him just enough freedom of movement to sit down. Then they cut the ropes tying him, leaving his hands and arms to take twenty minutes to tingle back into miserable life.

As the Praetorians left, and with them the torchlight, Mannix could just make out the simple outline of a fish carved in the rock with the edge of a manacle. After that, the raspy breathing of the room's inhabitants and the soft scuttling of rats across the stone floor. Then a voice.

"Hey, Myth. Nice boots, Myth."

The Bestiarius groaned and leaned over onto his side. "I don't have any money," he said hoarsely, his coin purse missing after the fight. On the other side of a shaft of weak moonlight streaming down through an iron ventilation grill high above, he could see the old drunk sitting across the room contentedly swatting his butterflies. "What are you doing here?"

The man chuckled. "They needed some extras for the new series of Games," he replied, swatting in indication of the figures lying across the floor.

Mannix squinted through his swollen eyes. He knew that Vigiles often received a little pocket money from the wardens at the Amphitheater for handing over people who wouldn't be missed. People like this. But it seemed a bit low for Praetorians to stoop to.

"Amphitheater's closed tonight, so we get the royal treatment here at the Castra," the old drunk chuckled. "Be open tomorrow, though."

"Sorry bastards," muttered the Bestiarius.

"Ah," shrugged the bum. "I'll miss the drink the most. Could be worse, I suppose."

Mannix chuckled despite himself, somewhat surprised at a coherency from the man which his looks would not belie. "I'd like to see how," he said absently.

"Don't you give up, old boy," smiled the toothless old legionary.

XXXIV

Standing on the moonlit terrace overlooking the Circus, her thoughts were distracted by a soft rustle of bracelets and a disturbing scent of perfume, and Julia Soaemias turned to find her son smiling at her from across the room. Despite herself, a relic of that stinging feeling of fear which Mannix once elicited stung in her bowels. "Well," she smiled at him, "made it off your knees this evening, I see."

Elagabalus, in a peach and jade silk robe studded with jewels and open over his surprisingly muscular torso, smirked. And with a theatrical gesture in which he rounded his mouth and brought his gold-painted fingernails up to cover it, said, "Oh my."

As he walked toward her swinging his hips slightly, the bracelets whispered on his wrists and the gems engraved by famous artists attached to his shoes crunched lightly like gravel underfoot. His salty vinous body scent permeated through the perfume, dominating the rain-fresh smell of the night air as he arrived before her. Tall and well-built, one of those rare young males who were almost fully physically mature at the age of seventeen, now, at nineteen, he had an unnerving presence. As if an aura of Scythian glitter surrounded him such as that detected by the officers of the defected Legions and even before by her mother, his grandmother, who founded and cultivated his god-like ambitions.

"Anything in particular you wanted, little man?" Julia Soaemias raised her chin.

A finger to his full red lips, Elagabalus pondered his mother standing there, her back against the terrace leaning infinitesimally outward, away from him ever so slightly over the hundred and fifty-foot drop to the street beneath running between the Palatine and the Circus Maximus. Though still flushed with the luster of youth, his face was slightly puffy from the night's debauchery, and the perfect, honey-colored skin of his smooth, well-sculpted cheeks was corrupted by garish red rouge. Looking for a resemblance, she could find none, save the hair. He had his father's hair. But he resembled neither of them so much as her grandfather. And though his hair was spoiled by the thin golden diadem of the former Queen of Laodicea, she had to admit that the discreet little golden loop earrings hanging from each of his earlobes matched it rather well.

Elagabalus' large, piercing green pupils were bright with snake-like interest beneath their heavy languorous lids brushed lightly with pearl dust. "Well, mother," he said, his nostrils quivering slightly as he tried to conceal his smile, "pray, guess who's coming for dinner tomorrow night?"

He held up a small scrolled parchment in front of her face. The heavy paper tried to unroll, but merely curled downward and dangled back up with its weight. Then it dropped to the floor before she could take it. Her son did not bend to pick it up.

Julia Soaemias looked at him without expression. Then she bent stiffly to retrieve the unwound scroll. Turning to the moonlight, it took a moment for her eyes to focus on the writing – a message with the seal of the Castra Praetoria, the barracks of the Praetorian Guard. When they did, her lips parted slightly, giving her a suddenly younger, almost girlish look. She unconsciously tucked several loose strands of hair behind an ear, and turned and walked past her son into the lamplight of the room. The stinging feeling of fear was real now, and no longer an echo.

"Need another drink, mother dear?" Elagabalus hissed from behind, his face no longer a sick comic pantomime but hardened with a strangeness that made it difficult to believe that less than an hour ago he was indeed on his knees, squealing in shameful glee and jutting his buttocks backwards at his 'husband' Hierocles – a blond Carian slave whom he arranged to have catch and spank him after offering himself naked to foreign dignitaries in the palace, or occasionally disguising

242

himself as a prostitute and frequenting the city's brothels and taverns.

Replete with golden breastplate and helmet, Hierocles played the role of Paris in the little theater enacted before their choice courtiers and dinner guests, while the Emperor, having dropped his clothing and placed a hand to his breast – the other covering his shaven-haired privates – assumed the role of Helen. With his testicles tied and his entire body depilated, his face was made up along the lines of that with which the queen was typically painted in the frescoes.

His mother had momentarily forgotten him. She looked up, her back to him, her eyes searching for an answer. Seeming without concern, "It will only hurt you further," she replied.

Looking back at the parchment, she re-focused her eyes. Prixus. The reading of his name meant random marble-hard nothingness to her. The mention of his death less than nothing. And yet the rusty cogwheels in her mind began to squeak and turn and she did indeed need another drink to oil them.

Behind her, Elagabalus' lowered his head and raised his eyes, "Hurt me?" he said. The drooping eyelids disappeared leaving the pupils suddenly huge and black against the whites, and lifeless as a doll's eyes, "Or hurt you?" he smiled.

She turned slowly and stared at him without wavering. "You have no idea what can or cannot hurt me," she shook her head slowly. "You have no idea about anything at all."

"And you are an old drunken slut, mother," his smile thinned. And then his eyes grew dreamy and he cocked his head to the side. "And you have no idea how good a time we are all going to have tomorrow night."

"Feeling our oats are we?" she casually turned away, and walked to the massive old walnut table where her uncle labored over the endless death warrants while she and her sister and cousins played through the halls, "Milk and biscuits kept us awake."

"He has killed one of my courtiers," Elagabalus softly replied. "Four," he pursed his lips and examined the rare jewels set in rings of electrum on his fingers, "of my courtiers." He looked up at her. "The entire city will know of it tomorrow."

243

Desperately wanting the wine, she ran her finger down the blade of the ornamental dagger Septimius Severus received upon his elevation to the Equestrian Order fifty years before; and which he subsequently used to cut the ties of incoming correspondence scrolls. "And what of it?" she said. "Prixus was a menace. A bully and a murderer. Not to mention an idiot."

"It is not about Prixus, mother," Elagabalus smiled wickedly.

She felt that sick stinging relic of fear and something else and she raised her eyebrows as she stared at the top of the table. "We've been through this before."

"And if I let him get away with it?" Elagabalus asked. "If I let them see that he can get away with it? What then? What will they say about me tomorrow night?"

"If you harm him," she shook her head, "You will be lucky to live out tomorrow night."

Elagabalus cocked his doll-like head to the other side. "And do you intend to kill me, mother?"

Still looking down at the dagger, "I don't have to," Soaemias replied, "There's an entire city out there that will do it for you."

Her son threw a glance at one of the open bays looking out over the city. A momentary look of confusion crossed his face.

"Your position depends upon how you keep the Mob amused," his mother continued. "It's that simple. You can cross your family, and you can cross the Senate. And you can offend the aristocracy," she looked up at him, "as you have so successfully done. But when you cross the Mob you're through."

"They love me," Elagabalus walked contemptuously to the open bay. "Who gives them their Games? Who lets them run wild? I banqueted ten thousand Plebians on the Field of Mars last month," his voice began to rise.

His mother didn't respond.

Elagabalus turned. "They love me!" he said again.

Julia Soaemias took a deep breath and raised her eyebrows. She turned to face him. "Of course they do, Varius."

"Am I not a god!" he screamed, his voice cracking.

She smiled listlessly, despite herself somewhat genuinely amused, touched even. For the boy was, after all, hers. "Not in the Mob's mythology."

"They love me," he said again, but quietly this time.

"That's right, son," she sighed, bored now and wishing he would go away.

A pause. The tinkling of windchimes, the strangely canted tentacle of smoke from a dangling incense censure.

Elagabalus raised his head slightly to reveal his thick smooth throat. "You love me."

Soaemias looked up quickly. Meeting his stare, she felt ice water rush into her bowels.

"Don't you Mother?"

Her eyelids flickered and she looked down, a hunted animal.

"I used to watch you," Elagabalus whispered. "And him." He walked slowly across the floor toward her.

Soaemias watched him approach, her hand inching infinitely across the ledge of the massive walnut table desk toward the dagger.

"You didn't know it but I did," Elagabalus smiled, his eyes returned to those of a doll's, his face raising another inch on his neck, staring down at her, a full head taller.

"You're sick," she replied in a hoarse whisper.

Elagabalus nodded his head slowly up and down. The windchimes tinkled and the lamplight flickered and the curtains rustled inward on the breeze. "I learned it all . . . from watching you . . ."

She slapped him across the face a loud crack and he grabbed her before she could raise the dagger. One arm around the small of her back pinning her arm to her side, with his free hand Elagabalus grabbed her other arm and held it still. Her eyes at the level of his parted lips, she could smell the wine and

245

the salt tang of semen on his breath, feel the dryness creeping into her own mouth.

He moved his free hand around the back of her head, grabbed a handful of her bountiful black hair and jerked her head back. Her mouth opened and she felt the life run out of her legs. He released her hair and her head lolled limply backwards staring at him.

Moving his hand around to the front, he jerked downward on the neck of her black linen bodysuit, ripping it and pulling her forward off balance, ripping again and again until her breasts burst loose and smooth and quivering in the lamplight. And it all came back to him. The day he walked into her bedchamber to find that the disturbing sound he'd heard while playing outside was none other than the ridiculous and sickening slap of Mannix's muscular thighs against the back of hers, her buttocks bounding and shivering and gods the smell in the hot late summer shaft of sunlit gloom.

He released her roughly and looked at her with disgust, his eyes moving from her breasts to her face. "We shall test this . . . mythology of the Mob," he hissed. And then he wheeled, and strode out of the room, his peach and jade robe trailing away down the long marble corridor.

Soaemias grasped the ledge of the table. She lurched across the floor toward the pitcher of wine and grabbed it and poured into her cup until the black ruby liquid ran over its silver sides and down her fingers like blood. And then she grit her teeth and threw its contents on the floor.

XXXV

Avoiding the early morning traffic heralding another work day in the city, the column of Praetorians escorting the Bestiarius moved due south through the high grass of the Esquiline disabitato. The Marcian Aqueduct angled off before them toward the Sabine Hills, with the smell of cooking fires coming up in a nearby gypsy camp huddled around its piers. Mannix, strapped to a horse again but manacled this time, watched for the steeds of the Sun God to mount the sky.

The bowl of watery oats they gave him at the Castra was beginning to work their bland magic, the energy creeping back into his blood in increments. He only wished he had more water to aid the process. A bit of sleep wouldn't have hurt either; but there would be time enough for that in the grave, he reflected. His eye sockets had stopped bleeding and the blue-green color had come back into his pupils as they watched the molten magenta orb emerge from the black outstretch of the Sabines to his left in the east. As it happened he thought of his father and his grandfather; and the tears stung his swollen eyes.

The column passed beneath one of the rust-red arches of the Marcia in time for him to see the sun's pink rays warm the face of the huge gateway of the Claudian Aqueduct in the right middle distance, before disappearing beneath the iron overcast blanketing the city and the plains of Latium rolling west to the coastline. The eighty-foot travertine gate he passed through last night from the opposite direction was coming back to life, its twin arches bustling again with humanity. The ox and ass-pulled carts of the farmers were clattering back into the city on the Via Praenestina en route to sell their produce in the squares, lines of immigrants and gypsies filing past them on their way to another day of scraping up the dregs of the big city food chain. The booths of the merchants clustered about the gate were opening – the cheap jewelry sellers, weavers and tapestry merchants. The smell of the nearby stockyards mingled with the smoke from the cooking fires and added a tang to the pervading scent of rain-wet spring foliage.

Blocking their path, a line of carts was stalled behind one belonging to an old peasant whose ox had decided to lie down in the road. The farmer was trying to pull him up and the Praetorian Tribune leading the column screamed, "Move that miserable piece of shit!"

The peasant began pitifully pleading with the old beast – a broken-down bovine version of himself – for he hadn't the strength to pull him up by his harness. "Come on then, Argo! Come along, old boy! Argo, please!"

The column of Praetorians burst out with laughter as the frail old man scurried around behind the ox and tried to push him up by the haunches. But their tribune lost patience and unhooked a coil of bullwhip from the side of his saddle. He spurred his mount forward and began lashing the ox and the man and the fruit in the baskets on the little cart, which spilled and scattered and burst all over the road and beneath the hooves of his rearing horse.

The ox rolled its eyes and mooed as the whip carved bloody lacerations across its boney white flanks and caught his master in the face splitting his skin and knocking him on his back on the hard stones. Women screamed, asses brayed, and the drivers of the carts on either end began moving chaotically out of the way. As the column of Praetorians trotted on through the hastily-made space between, the old peasant, staring at his shattered produce and his bloodied ox, rolled over on his side in the gutter and died.

Mannix looked impassively at the dead farmer as the horse bobbed him past. Then he turned his eyes back to the red-caped tribune up ahead, remarking everything about him – his gold-corded white leather headgear with the cocky red plume, his build and his face. And he made a mental note to kill him.

They clopped back into the city past the baker's tomb, down the Via Labicana through that part of the Esquiline District where they rented hotel rooms by the hour, the sound of their hooves echoing loudly on the wet cobblestones. Skirting the northern side of the Gardens of Maecenas, the branches of huge pines leaned out lush and wet and shadowy over a stretch of the high wall bordering the vast estate, and Mannix looked up through their branches at the charcoal-smudge vapor trails crisscrossing the gray sky.

Rome was coming to life, the number of people in the streets increasing, the clatter of chain-worked wooden slat gates rising to their shouts, yawns and greetings. Down the Labicana, the column of red-caped horsemen came upon a long train of caged carts en route to the Amphitheater, which was now rising ominously several hundred yards down the thoroughfare. The column of Praetorians thinned and lengthened as the horsemen moved around the side of the train, which had come from the stockyards with its vast number of attendants walking along beside it. As he trotted past, the Bestiarius remarked an unusual number of 'make lions' in the caged carts – the maneaters they put into the Arena with their untrained fellows. A shortcut to the training process, when the untrained animals saw the make lion attack a human, they soon enough followed suit.

As they passed the side of the Ludus Magnus and came into the square surrounding the Amphitheater, he could see another train of carts disappearing beneath the triumphal arch over the Porta Libitina – named for the Roman goddess of Death. Surmounted by a typical blackened-bronze sculpture of a four-horse chariot driven by a winged victory, arena slaves were unloading the fresh beasts off the carts and sliding the cages down the ramps into the holding pens. The Praetorians curved around the side of the Amphitheater past another triumphal arch with its quadriga marking the Senator's entrance, and Mannix could see the disassembled mock-up of a town laid out across the rain-wet cobbles, with wooden walls painted to look like white stucco, wooden temple columns painted to look like marble, and pieces of painted red roofing. Technicians squatted hammering nails into planks, others carrying sub-assemblies into the Amphitheater; a group of sailors walked past them toward another day at work, hungover and surly and complaining about the rain.

The column of horsemen continued on past the base of the Colossus of Helios, the statue towering into the overcast, the tent kiosks of the merchants clustered beneath its huge green-oxidized bronze toes. Then they turned into the Via Sacra at the fountain of the Meta Sudans, along the side of the massive podium of the Temple of Venus and Rome. The precinct walls of the Elagaballium loomed on the left from the northeastern spur of the Palatine; and they turned left before the Arch of Titus off the Via Sacra onto the Clivus Palatinus leading up the hill, passing the colossal column drums scattered about the unfinished entrance to Elagabal's dark sanctuary.

The smell of spring greeted the Bestiarius' nose through its blood crusted congestion – the smell of the orange trees and the carefully-tended gardens around the small Temple of Jupiter Stator marking the spot where Romulus and his fellows stood their ground in a battle against the Sabines a thousand years ago. The palace complex loomed ahead above the trees, a jumble of heavy cornices and pediments and ochre-stuccoed walls snaking with blooming vines. As they passed through the Praetorian checkpoint beneath the Arch of Domitian, the marble-paved open square of the Area Palatina spread around them before the hundred yard-long portico of Carystian green columns lining the facade of the towering public wing.

Slaves worked quietly about the open square, tending the plants, filling buckets from the various array of fountain spigots which gushed and gurgled about the rain-glossed marble and the green acanthus and the huge plinthed statues of emperors. The column came to a halt before the raised portico with a signal of its leader's hand. Mannix noticed a large presence of Praetorians about – lines of them filing up the side of the public wing in dress armor. The tribune dismounted and drew his sword as he walked down the column of horsemen toward him.

"All right, hero," he yelled. "Get off," he sneered. "And don't get cute. I'd like nothing better than an excuse to stick your ass right here and watch you bleed."

The Bestiarius stayed silent. No smile, no threat; he just gave the man a once-over with his impassive gaze, and then put a leg over the pommel of the saddle and slid off the horse onto the gray-veined marble pavement. With his hands manacled behind his back, one of the big guardsmen grabbed him hard by the arms and jerked him backwards causing his shoulder to start bleeding again while another chained his ankles.

The ankle chains allowed him just enough movement to trip and shuffle along as they shoved and pulled him around the side of the facade and up the steps into its portico, the dismounted Praetorians filing up with him and all around him. They passed the bronze doors of the basilica first and, another forty yards down, arrived at the twenty-foot portal of the throne room.

"Wait here," the tribune said to the men guarding the Bestiarius.

The two silver-cuirassed palace guards flanking the portal pushed one of its huge gilt-bronze doors inward on its well-oiled hinges, and the tribune disappeared in the building's gloom.

Mannix looked out through the green marble columns of the elevated porch over the square and down the cypress-lined Clivus to a slice of the Forum below, where the throngs were flowing through the Arch of Titus, the traffic sounds muted by the distance and the morning birdsong in the trees. A stone's throw to his right stretched the precinct walls of the Elagaballium, the unfinished temple rising above them with the caterwauling of the construction cranes coming to life. To his left, parts of the old Palace of Tiberius rose above the pines of a large area of garden grounds he remembered from years back.

The tribune's harsh voice interrupted his reverie. "All right, bring him in."

Two of the guardsmen walked him through the huge bronze doors with their hands jerking him by the arms. Before his eyes could adjust to the dim light of the interior, they tried to thrust him to his knees on the hard polished marble floor but the Bestiarius did not go down. One of them kicked him in the back of the knees trying to buckle his legs and he wheeled and headbutted him, breaking his nose.

The man emitted a high-pitched scream and the tribune rushed back toward Mannix from somewhere up near the head of the room but a voice raised and said, "Leave him be."

The tribune stopped short and grit his teeth in the Bestiarius' face and Mannix stared impassively back at him.

The Emperor rose off the tiger skin draping the gilt-bronze throne on the raised dais in the apse at the head of the room. Flanked on either side by three giant Nubian bodyguards in white feather head-dresses, "Stay here," he said to them, as he descended the steps out of the apse, its blue and green mosaic winking in the wavering light of the two ten-foot, seven-branched golden candelabra taken by Titus as spoils from the Temple in Jerusalem a century and a half before.

As his red Spanish leather boots came forward across the flooring composed of huge porphyry disks inset alternately within Numidan orange and speckled green squares, the Praetorians bowed low for his approach. The ornate benches for his audiences had been pushed against the walls, which were articulated on either side by four huge projecting niches with fluted purple columns upholding white Luna pediments. The niches contained twelve-foot statues in metallic green Bekhen stone from the eastern desert of Egypt – a massively muscled Hercules, Pan with the infant Bacchus, and a cadre of lesser planetary deities. The walls between the niches were paneled in the purple porphyry, Numidian orange and Thessalian green marbles in geometric patterns which echoed the floor, and were broken on either side by two bronze doors.

Atop the richly decorated, almost-organic stringcourse running above the bays stood a like number of smaller sculptures in rectangular niches between four square windows on either side. Above them sprang the massive coffered barrel vault of the ceiling, arcing to a peak of one hundred and twenty feet above the floor, its coffers decorated in gilt egg-and-dart motif without rosettes. On the front and back walls, tremendous twenty by forty-foot bronze-latticed, glass-paned windows shimmered with a dull crystal glow.

"You can leave now," Elagabalus said to the three Praetorians as he arrived, one of them whimpering and holding his cape to his blood-gushing nose.

"He's dangerous, sire," pleaded the tribune, lusting to torture the Bestiarius.

"I know. We'll be all right," the Emperor nodded, staring at Mannix with his piercing green eyes.

The Bestiarius returned his stare.

"I said you can leave," Elagabalus smiled irritatedly at the guardsmen.

The tribune bowed low, then turned with his men.

"Close the doors," the nineteen year-old said calmly, his voice sonorous in the huge space.

The bronze doors swung silently shut behind them, their closing echoing like a soft drumbeat throughout the vast room.

"I apologize for them," Elagabalus shrugged, turning his attention to Mannix. His hair combed forward in the classical Roman manner, gone was the diadem, the ear rings, the makeup and jewelry; the vinous smell of last night's party scrubbed hastily away in the bath this morning by his body slaves. He wore a simple red subarmilis – a linen military tunic with small square pockets stuffed with woolen padding that acted as an undergarment for legionary battle armor. Standing just a hair's breadth taller than the Bestiarius, though not nearly as densely muscled, the simple tunic showed his physique to be surprisingly well-proportioned, and evident of a natural athleticism.

"I regret the chains as well," he made a throwaway gesture with his fingers. "If I had your word you wouldn't try to kill me, I'd have them removed," he smiled amiably.

Continuing to stare darkly at him, Mannix didn't respond.

"Well," Elagabalus nodded, "in time, then." He placed his hands behind his back and nodded up and down, his face open, honest. "I suppose I should say it's an honor to meet you. But then," he frowned pensively, "I guess we've already met, haven't we?"

The Bestiarius sneered.

253

Elagabalus nodded again. "I didn't make a very good impression on you as a child, did I?"

Mannix raised his chin a fraction. "What do you want twinkle-toes. Or haven't you made up your mind."

Elagabalus shrugged and smiled, "I want you to be my friend," he said, as if it was the most obvious answer in the world.

XXXVI

The news had not only spread throughout the Esquiline district, but the entire city was indeed throbbing with it this morning. The talk of the taverns, it had spread from district to district, throughout all of the fourteen zones, town criers running with it through the streets, the markets abuzz with it, 'Mannix killed Prixus!' in the squares. Some even reported having seen the Bestiarius tied to a horse.

Lepidus had cancelled the morning Venationes, notified the Senate, and called a general strike of bestiarii until Mannix was released. Severely hampering the other venues – most of which relied on bestiarii of one specialty or another, whether hunters, dodgers, tamers, pole-vaulters or handlers – the remaining twenty-eight days of the series inaugurating Elagabalus' restoration of the Amphitheater looked grim indeed. Apicius the Ringmaster was pulling his hair out and kicking arena attendants. The Editor of the Games – whose olive oil conglomerate could potentially go bankrupt over the affair – was in a panic. And a slight collective grumble had begun to roll through the streets.

The disheveled orator atop the Rostrum in the Forum, amidst his rambling harangue about the approaching end of the world, spoke of it as a sign of the times. Not more than fifty yards away, a special session of the Senate had been called together in their lofty chamber, and Avidius Lepidus had been summoned to attend.

The severe old members were in arrival, white togas with red-striped borders filing up the steps and beneath the building's portico. Some gripped the arms of their body slaves to help them along. The slaves would await them throughout the meeting, outside, with their parasols. The twenty-foot bronze doors of the building were open, the Senators' burgundy boot sandals shuffling into the gloom across the floor of purple-veined white marble. Three wide platform steps to either side of the floor accommodated seating for several hundred men. Attached ranks of curved-backed porphyry arm chairs lined the first row; on the latter two, curule fold-out chairs could be established as needed.

Like the banquet hall of the Imperial Palace, the interior of the building was lit by high rectangular windows which in this case were fifteen by twenty feet tall – three across the front, one each along the sides and rear of the four-foot thick walls. Their high placement created the same kind of hazy glow which left the floor and ceiling of the building in a grainy mist of shadow, especially in the gray light of morning outside. Thus attendants were lighting the flammable oil in the bronze tripod braziers staged in the corners of the space to illuminate the shadowland beneath the huge squat opaque rectangles of window sixty feet above.

As the flames began to flicker they enlivened the walls, the two lateral sides each staged with three projecting niches framed in alabaster columns supported on brackets carved with acanthus leaves and eagles and upholding alternating bow and triangular-shaped pediments. The niches contained statues of Caesar, Agrippa, Augustus, Antoninus Pius and Marcus Aurelius; and one of the current Emperor Elagabalus. The walls were veneered in marble for two-thirds of the interior's hundred-foot height, the lowest zone in large panels of Phrygian purple alternating with white Luna. Above it, an elaborate scheme of inlayed architectural illusions with Corinthian columns and pilasters in flat relief framed geometric panel designs in white and gray marbles, and red and green porphyries.

A forty-foot gilt bronze statue of Victory – a huge, beautiful, high-breasted sculpture holding a scepter in one hand and a laurel leaf crown in the other – towered with her wings outspread on a plinth against the back wall. Flanking her, two large bronze doors, both closed, led into the Forum of Caesar behind; at her feet was an altar smoking with incense.

Avidius Lepidus sat on a gray marble visitor's bench to the side of the front door, wearing a black cape over his leather-strap skirt armor with his old lanista's cane poised on the floor. It was neither his first nor his fifth time in the building. He watched as the Senators filed slowly toward the foot of the colossal statue of Victory, where each of them lit a stick of incense and poured a dripping of wine on the altar, the process facilitated by an attendant who handed them the sticks and the simple clay pitcher of wine. The only thing amiss in this four hundred year-old preliminary rite was the tremendous wood-paneled tempera painting hung by steel-banded cords to slope out at a slight angle over the top of the statue, its bottom ledge between the upsweep of her wings – the portrait of Elagabalus in the costume of a sacrificer sent by Julia Maesa three years before.

As the Senators made their invocation, the convex porphyry arm chairs began to fill. When all had finished, the old members sat gossiping in relaxed postures in their white togas with the red-striped borders, the light from the oil braziers rendering their septuagenarian craniums shadow-hollowed and skull-like in the wavering of the flames which flickered across the dark marble accoutrements and the ghostly white statues, and pulsed along the rich colors of the wall paneling. The smell of incense lay heavy and faintly nauseous in the gloom; and the smoke from the braziers rose through the hazy middle zone of light from the windows as it ascended to further blacken the square bronze coffers of the flat ceiling ninety feet above.

The Director of the Ludus Matutinus sat to the side to await his call, his face a stoic mask which concealed his inner agitation. Lepidus was in none too fine a humor this morning, as one of his favorite charges lay on a funeral bier prepped for cremation, and another was incarcerated by the Praetorians. Neither was he pleased with the painting that hung hovering over the venerable space, the sight of which told him that Rome had – perhaps permanently – seen her better days.

He knew the economy was unraveling like a moth-eaten tapestry. The cost of maintaining the gigantic armed forces, equipped with the latest catapults, ballistae and fast war galleys, was bleeding the nation white. In addition, there were the heavy subsidies that had to be paid to the satellite nations dependent on Rome for support, and upon which she had become dependent to levy troops to man the contracting frontiers. The corruption of Roman officials in the northern provinces, who were supposed to supply the barbarians with food until they could gather a harvest, had forced many of the tribes to go to war in order to avoid starvation. And the impoverished government had neither the funds nor the power to stop the coming catastrophe.

Elagabalus, having made many of his freedmen governors and legates, consuls and generals, had subjected the Empire to further bleeding through embezzlement and massive money-laundering schemes, not to mention his own profligacy through which, last month alone, he squandered an amount of public grain equal to one year's tribute in banqueting the Mob. For, due to the foresight of his adoptive grandfather Septimius Severus, Elagabalus inherited a store of grain in the city equal to seven years' tribute; most of which was gone now.

In the midst of this crisis, the Captain of Shipping, who sat fidgeting beside Lepidus, was first called before the harried congregation by the clerk who held a list of the meeting's topics on a scroll. As his name was read aloud, the young Equite rose and walked to the center of the marble floor.

"Honorable members of the Senate. Noble Romans. Hail." His arm stretched out and moved to include both sides of the room. "The merchant fleet is in Egypt awaiting loading," he announced. "As you're aware, the fleet is still at only half-strength due to the riots in Alexandria in which the docks were burned and many of our galleys lost. As a consequence, the ships can either be loaded with the grain for the dole or the special sand used on the track for the chariot races scheduled for the summer opening of the Circus in two months. I regret to admit that the fleet cannot carry both items; and that the thirty-day passage will not allow us enough time to come with the grain and return for the sand and bring it back here in time for the races. I come before you today to ask – which shall it be?"

The Senators mumbled among themselves, leaning toward each other, their arguments a murmur of echoes in the hard-walled tightness of the huge room. Most of the trireme transport ships of the navy had been detailed to evacuate the Severan outposts in Scotland after the Caledonian disaster, and were currently docked in the Metaris Estuary in Britain for bad weather. Private contractors with the proper carrying capacity were difficult to find, especially within the time frame.

Cassius Dio, a short fat choleric man, his gray coiffeured curls framing his sweaty brow, his puffy cheeks shaking with nervous agitation, took the floor, raising a plump arm to silence the congregation. "The answer is clear enough!"

His colleagues seemed contented enough with Dio's voice of authority. They stopped their internal bickering with his gesture.

"Yes, the bread dole for the Mob has almost run out," he nodded. "But the situation here is rapidly growing out of control," he threw an arm out. "The Eastern Legions are on the verge of mutiny; the Praetorians on the verge of civil war." He turned to the captain. "By Jupiter, load the sand, boy! We have to get the people's minds off their troubles!"

A rumble of more or less affirmed assent filled the room, and the Captain of Shipping bowed and left quickly for the port of Ostia.

Lepidus' hard, craggy face remained impassive. He had already sat on the board at the meeting detailing the publicity campaign that would be pushed throughout the city. And he could already envision the hundreds of sign painters attacking the walls with venue announcements, the heralds sprinting through the streets and standing on the lips of the grand fountains in the squares announcing that the finest chariot races on record would be held at the Circus Maximus. As intermission features, hundreds of gladiators would fight to the death, and thousands of condemned criminals would be executed by wild animals. Fights between elephants and rhinos, buffalo and tigers, leopards and wild boars would be staged for betting purposes. Admission to the rear seats, free. Small charge for the first thirty-six tiers.

259

His would be no small task in the matter, and he had already sent word to his trappers in North Africa to initiate more forays into the dark continent; and also to begin emptying the vast overseas holding pens and shipping the beasts to Rome where they would fill the stockyards at Laurentum. Local tribes would be pressed into forced labor, hauling cages, loading and unloading cargo, their fields often stripped to feed the beasts – just one more example of the overweening truth that a human life meant nothing in comparison to the needs and appetites of the Urbs that had become the Orbs, the city that had become the universe.

Those needs required that an immense amount of animal blood be spilled in sacrifice to somewhat capricious and oft-angered gods. For the games were still thrown under the auspices of a religious ceremony. And the Mob loved animals.

XXXVII

"So, you see, Mannix, it's not about Prixus," Elagabalus walked with his hands behind his back beside the Bestiarius over the sprawling marble floor of the throne room beneath the pale crystal light from the windows hovering above. By their builds, height and color, the two could almost be brothers, but for a faint quality difference in their respective walks.

"The witnesses say you were fully in the right for what you did," the young Emperor paused, searching for words. "Prixus was pretty strong, though," he glanced furtively at the Bestiarius. "I wish I could have seen it."

Unchained by the Praetorians the Emperor called back in and then dismissed forthwith, and though not having given his word that he would not kill him, Mannix had accepted Elagabalus' invitation for food and drink. He knew he needed the strength. His eyes calculated the Nubians in the apse. The six bodyguards in cheetah-skin tunics and white feather head-dresses eyed him back hungrily.

"As soon as I heard the news and that you were incarcerated, I had you brought here immediately to personally ensure your safety and condition." Elagabalus turned his head and looked at him sincerely. "I want you to see my doctors. I want you to rest," he nodded. "I want you to be my guest at the banquet tonight. To dine at my table," he added. "By my side."

He offhandedly took the Bestiarius by the arm, nonchalantly – as if escorting a favored visiting prelate – his fingers trembling faintly as they touched the muscled tricep through the woolen fall of the paenula, one of his nails still traced with last night's golden paint. Mannix turned his head for the first time then, and gave him a look that would turn goats' milk to cheese. Elagabalus' fingers faltered, and returned

261

slowly to his side as he walked, no sooner covering the awkwardness with a chuckle.

"Strange this Palace," he shrugged. "Throne room, basilica next door," he threw a thumb to his right in indication of the door leading into the adjoining hall where the emperors sat in judgment over high-level court cases. "Gods," he shook his head, "do you know that by Roman law I'm technically the only man in this city who can sentence a person to death? They make me sit in there sometimes. I never sentence anybody. It's always my grandmother handling the court cases." He pursed his lips. "She's a bit put out with me these days, I'm afraid. But tonight will bring us back together."

"And your mother?" Mannix asked flatly.

Elagabalus' steps shifted slightly. "Oh. She'll be glad to see you, I'm sure." Glancing at him with a raised eyebrow, "Come. I'll show you her preparations for the banquet." He gestured for the Nubians to open the rear doors flanking the apsed throne on his righthand side. "Then you can say hello and we'll have a light brunch. Wouldn't want to spoil your dinner."

As they exited the rear bronze doors held open by the bowing, ebony-muscled bodyguards, Mannix was confronted by a scene of enormous preparation. In the first court with its tremendous Polyphemus fountain he remembered from years back, servants were passing hurriedly to and fro beneath the porticoes, wheeling carts laden with flagons of wine and lobsters on ice, others carrying stacks of curule chairs and various items of decor down the far side of the peristyle toward the banquet hall rising at its end. The servants and slaves bowed low as they passed.

"Did you ever find it curious," Elagabalus asked, as they walked down the orange-columned portico along its marble-paneled back wall, "that the Imperial Office is, again by Roman Law, considered to be a divine institution?"

The Bestiarius smiled humorlessly.

Elagabalus registered it. "Yes," he nodded. "The lararium flanks the throne room on the other side, over there," gesturing behind him to his left. "I'll take you sometime. It's where the Imperial Genius is kept. An exquisite work in silver commissioned by Augustus, it accompanies me wherever I go. Just as it did my official namesake, Marcus Aurelius, on the Danube."

Mannix squinted his eyes with the memory of his father, who died on the Danube.

"When I hold that little statue," Elagabalus continued, "I feel a sense of belonging to something. Something powerful . . . Godlike, even." He turned his head and looked at the Bestiarius. "Do you believe in the gods, Mannix?"

The Bestiarius, eyeing the Praetorian presence about, didn't respond. There was a guardsman in every corner of the square, another standing by each door lining the back wall of the peristyle; and five or six more at the square's entrance through the block of waiting rooms along the opposite side. He could feel the Nubians following quietly several paces behind.

"No, of course you don't," the Emperor smiled. "Man like you? Too independent. Too self-sufficient for that sort of nonsense." He shook his head. "But the people need gods, Mannix," he stopped and turned to face him. "They do," he nodded. "They need something to believe in."

A pause.

"You see," Elagabalus chuckled, "we can't all be like you. Can we, Myth?," he smiled again pleasantly, raising his eyebrows. "But then we're all born to be, and to do, different things," he continued walking, past the bench where his mother sat yesterday morning, slowly approaching the banquet hall. "Those things are never the same."

A guardsman came to attention as they passed.

"You were born to be a hero," Elagabalus turned his head and smiled amiably at him. "I was born to be an Emperor."

"Emperor of what?," hissed the Bestiarius, bored and sickened.

"Of you," Elagabalus chuckled again, not put off in the least. Nineteen years around his grandmother had never been so well-paid. He stared at Mannix with his piercing green eyes, and then raised one of his trimmed eyebrows. "I am your Emperor."

"You're a puppet on a broken string held by two women," the Bestiarius replied without hesitation.

Elagabalus' face smarted for a second and Mannix returned his stare, their eyes level with each other. He felt the guardsman they just passed shift behind him and he saw Elagabalus' eyes dart to him and quickly shake his head. "Perhaps I have been somewhat under their control," the Emperor nodded, recovering his composure. "But that is changing."

Fifteen yards away, Julia Soaemias walked through the gray granite monoliths out of the banquet hall dictating orders to Petricon, who was hurrying along beside her. Though making towards the opposite side of the peristyle, her head turned to Mannix as if drawn by a magnet and she stopped.

The Bestiarius' face emptied with the quickening in his gut and Elagabalus registered it and turned.

"Mother," he called and waved, ever the dutiful son, "Look who's come for a visit," proudly presenting Mannix. "I was hoping you could talk him into staying for dinner."

In her boot sandals and an oversized long-sleeved woolen blue tunic that fell slightly below her knees, Soaemias involuntarily took a step forward and then stood by one of the fluted orange columns trying to control the trembling in her hands. Unbelted at the waist, the tunic made her look fat. And, wearing no makeup, she had dark circles under her big almond eyes. She unconsciously tucked a few loose strands of hair behind an ear.

"Hello Caius."

"Julia," he nodded.

Soaemias had the hunted look of last night. Her eyes flittered across the face of her son trying to judge his intent but knowing it instinctively.

"Well," Elagabalus stood to the side glancing back and forth at both of them and beaming. "What a surprise. Takes the strangest things to bring people back together again."

A Praetorain Tribune interrupted the uncomfortable reunion, bowing and looking harried as he approaches. "Sire?"

"Yes," Elagabalus turned to him, irritated with the interruption.

The tribune's eyes flickered across the Bestiarius.

"Go on, man," the Emperor said.

"Sire, there's trouble at the Amphitheater."

Elagabalus' eyes fluttered for a split-second, but he recovered. "Why?" he asked slowly and with faint exasperation.

"The Venatione has been striked," the tribune replied. "And all of the venues utilizing bestiarii cancelled."

"Pray, by whose order?," Elagabalus raised an eyebrow.

"Avidius Lepidus," blurted the Praetorian. "The director of the Ludus Matutinus."

"I'm well aware of who he is, tribune," the Emperor said. He sighed noisily, "Very well. Get to Eutychianus and tell him to send a cohort from the Castra by my order to supplement the normal security sealing the Patrician seating. Tell him to act as a presence only. No heavy-handedness with the Plebs," he smiled thinly.

"Sire," the tribune bowed. And then he hesitated, looking at Mannix.

"Is something unclear?," Elagabalus asked menacingly.

The tribune bowed again, "No, Sire."

As the man wheeled and set off at a jog down the peristyle, Elagabalus turned to the Bestiarius. "You see, Mannix," he smiled. "We can't all be like you. Can we."

XXXVIII

"Avidius Lepidus!" called the Senate clerk staring at his scrolled list of the day's topics.

The grizzled old bestiarius rose. Cane in hand, he took the floor between the tiered seats of the Senators as the herald announced the case.

"You are hereby called before the Senate and the People of Rome regarding the strike of the morning's Venatione at the Amphitheater," continued the clerk.

Lepidus let the silence in the room brood for a time, and then announced, "Romans. Fathers of your country. I stand before you as your son," he nodded. "More importantly, I stand before you in representation of another of your sons. In my mind, one of the first of your sons in this time of disparate character."

The Senators grumbled and shifted in their seats.

Lepidus raised his voice. "His feats in the Arena are well known, as is his fame with the people of the city for whom the Games are our most popular institution."

A murmur rippled through the august body. Over it, a lanky old skeleton stood up, pointing his withered claw of a finger in outrage.

"Mannix has committed murder. He has subverted the authority of the Emperor, causing us," gesturing to the Senators, "considerable embarrassment and inconvenience. I can only hope that punishment be swift and severe!"

More indecisive murmuring.

Lepidus raised his commanding voice, "The facts of the case are well-known; the witnesses all in agreement. Prixus and his bunch goaded the fight and they received their just deserts."

"Lepidus, it has nothing to do with your idea of right or wrong," the old crow covered him again with his indignant claw, "It's a matter of the law. If we bend the rules for every two-bit hero of the Mob, we'll have an Empire run by Circus Freaks!" the old man sputtered, trying for an insult and catching his mistake too late.

"It's men like him who built this bloody Empire, you old fool," Lepidus roared. "Men like Caius Marius Mannix, and the virtues they represent, who've kept it, and kept you," he raised his old gray eyebrows, "til now, that is," he cast a well-placed glance at the tremendous portrait of Elagabalus on the back wall, "from being run by Circus Freaks!"

The members of the Senate fell into an uproar of argument and assent, some standing and yelling at Lepidus, others standing and yelling at them. The old crow raised his cracked squeaking voice, "I tell you this kind of impertinence is impermissible!"

Lepidus rapped his cane on the floor. "I want that boy freed!" he thundered. "And I want him freed right now! Or I not only guarantee you that the strike will go on and the stockyards follow suit; but moreover that you'll have a bloody riot on your hands," he threw his cane toward the door gesturing at the city outside. "And it'll be your own bloody fault!"

The purple crow was choking with rage as he addressed the room, his hook-like finger upraised, "You have heard him! Not only does he have the audacity to blaspheme against the divine office of the Emperor! He guarantees rebellion! We cannot allow this! I propose the maximum penalty!"

"Now, now, hold on Mucius!," said Cassius Dio, the gouty Senator who spoke in favor of the special sand earlier. "And you too Lepidus!" He winced down the several steps to the floor, sweating profusely, his hand raised in his customary gesture of pacification, the room still in an uproar. Blinking disconcertedly, his voice raised with bored exasperation as if talking to children, "Senators, Senators, will you give me leave? Mucius! Sit Down!"

After the uproar had settled, Cassius Dio raised his finger. "No one here would concede to the fact that Caius Marius Mannix is just another two-bit hero of the Mob. But," turning to Lepidus, "neither can we concede to the economic

267

reverberations of a strike at the Amphitheater." He shook his head. "There has to be a middle-of-the-road solution."

The uproar started again and a high, firm female voice pierced the confusion, "If he's a hero of the populace, we shall let the populace decide."

The uproar trickled down to a murmur, and then silence.

She stood in the blinding wedge of open doorway which threw a shaft of milky light across the Phrygian marble floor, bleaching its purple veins. The porters outside still bowing in her wake, the only woman allowed to enter the Senate since Nero's mother Agrippina – who was made to stand behind a curtain – Julia Maesa at least had the decorousness to cover her head.

Lepidus shook his own at this further indication of the times, for, like himself, this was neither her first, nor her fifth time in the chamber.

"Lepidus," she nodded, as if reading his mind.

"Domina," Lepidus declined his head in reply. 'Old bitch,' he thought to himself. He'd made her sing a few times thirty years back. 'She never had her daughters tits. And I'd hate to see them now,' he thought. 'But I bet she's still got a trick or two to make you go off your head, old boy.'

An awkward moment followed in which the Senators, most of whom were already standing, stayed that way.

"There's nothing to be done now," Julia Maesa continued, her clear, precise Latin diction edged with age, but still smooth as it rung off the marble walls. "If we act, the Guard will split and there will be war in the streets."

As she walked into the room, her features began to clarify – the craggy aquiline face that could never have been more than slightly pretty and that, during sex, Lepidus reflected, had the sneer of the assassin that joys in feeling the death throes of his victim through the blade. He knew she had at least half the Praetorian Guard and most of this room in her pocket. "If you don't act, there will be war in the streets," he stated.

As she arrived to stand before him, he took in her withered cheeks plastered with mauve powder, the red velvet ribbon around her neck helping to conceal its sagging gullet.

The ridiculous volutes of her hair were hidden under her hooded shawl like a sack of potatoes atop her head with one little flax-colored lock fallen gaily loose over her brow. His eyes moved from the beauty mark aside her mouth that was one of the few things that had once excited him about her – but which was grown with sow's bristles now – to her sharp little aquiline eyes. "Give the order to the Castra and get him out of the city," he said.

"He's not at the Castra anymore," Maesa shook her head. "They've had him up on the hill since sunrise along with a cohort of the Guard most loyal to Elagabalus to provide security for tonight's banquet."

The atmosphere in the room shifted, and Lepidus felt a sinking feeling inside. With four hundred and eighty Praetorians sealing off the Palatine, he knew Mannix was finished now.

"Is there any man here who would vote for another civil war?" Julia Maesa raised her voice to drive home her point. In the midst of the general murmur of agreement, she looked Lepidus in the eyes. "If he dies, he dies," she stated, loudly enough for the room to hear.

The old director returned her look with a sneer. "You cunt," he growled back.

Maesa slapped him surprisingly quick, as if planning on it anyway, the crack ricocheting off the walls and drawing a bright little squiggle of blood from his weather-chapped lips. The old bestiarius, as if expecting it anyway, didn't so much as blink.

A slight collective gasp of surprise rolled instantaneously across the several hundred Senators, silencing them. All of them together weren't worth the man and woman standing before them.

Julia Maesa threw the wing of her shawl back over the shoulder of her silver-embroidered stola. "Let the strike at the Amphitheater stand for now. And carry on with the day's business, gentlemen. Mannix's fate is out of our hands." Then she turned and walked toward the door.

"Like hell it is," Lepidus shouted, cane point still on the floor, his voice ringing formidably through the room.

Maesa turned him a look of unspeakable rancor. "You always were too big for your britches, Lepidus," her voice rising to a piercing dagger point on his name. "Since the affair has now become a private one, perhaps we should leave these men to the administration of the Empire, and discuss the sorrows of the Circus life outside this venerable chamber." She wheeled, and walked straight and slender and old and angular into the towering wedge of opaque light where her softly silvered stola sparked for a second, before disappearing through the open wedge of doorway.

The old director's chin jut forth and he tossed his oaken Lanista's cane up and grabbed it in the center and strode out after her, his black cape trailing behind him. The several hundred members of the Senate were dead quiet.

Outside, the old Empress stood stock-still beneath the shade of the columned portico, her Circassian bodyguards lining its sides and steps. A haze of milky white light from the overcast sky lay in a pallor across the Forum square making Lepidus squint after the building's gloom. He arrived at her side, old and angular like her, but two heads taller.

"You old kite," he said, not looking at her.

"I could have you killed for that, Lepidus," she replied, looking straight ahead as well.

"Yes, but you won't, will you old girl?" he smiled.

Julia Maesa's large, beautifully-wrought litter waited to the side of the ancient Comitium by the venerable black stone pavement. Thirty feet long, and of black-stained sandalwood with heavy red curtains and a train of twenty porters standing to the side to man its poles, Septimius Severus purchased it from the Mouseion at Alexandria for an exorbitant sum – an old river barque of Cleopatra's which he'd had converted into a litter for his wife upon coming to Rome.

"Get in," she said, and they walked down the steps together between the bodyguards almost as if they looked like they belonged that way.

270

Inside the old converted barque with its gilt-inlayed hieroglyphics and its smell of two hundred and fifty year-old love, death and decadence, Maesa drew the heavy crimson curtain on her side as the porters hefted and the bodyguards formed in line. As they started off up the Clivus Argentarius which connected with the Via Lata along the side of the Capitoline Hill, "Draw the other side, you old crone," she said.

And Lepidus followed suit.

"You're escorting me to the banquet tonight, you know," Maesa looked at him.

"I ought to crush your scraggly old throat," he grinned back at her.

"Yes, but you won't, will you, old boy," she smiled at him with her little rodent-like teeth. Then she leaned over and sucked the bright squiggle of blood off his lip, running her hand over his wrinkly muscled thigh as she withdrew. "Too big for your britches indeed."

XXXIX

"You're looking well," Mannix interrupted the awkward silence.

"I look like hell," Julia Soaemias glanced aside, "and you know it." She tried to control the faint trembling in her hands, then gave it up and placed them in her lap as a servant filled their wine glasses. "None for me, thank you."

Turning her head back to the Bestiarius, she took in his blood-encrusted paenula and the purple bruises around his eyes. "But you don't look so well either. You need a doctor. And a lot of sleep."

Mannix shrugged. "What else is new?"

They sat at a table inside the beautiful little round Grecian temple which graced the island of the second fountain court. Open through its columns, and hovered over by a tremendous umbrella pine, the Grecian temple centered the island in the large pond from which it rose, where slightly over-life-sized figures of Apollo and a dozen wood nymphs grouped about the bank in frozen marble frolicsomeness amid the gently erupting geysers of the fountain's water and the fat old swans.

Parallel to the first fountain court and separated from it by the office wing, which rose above the flank of its western peristyle, the second court was slightly larger than the first, though more intimate in nature. It fronted the facade of the private wing of the palace in the same way as the first court fronted the banquet hall. But with its grass-and-flower bordered fountain pond, its towering umbrella pine, and the back walls of it peristyle frescoed in illusionistic garden scenes which echoed the carefully-contrived rusticity of its setting, the second court successfully evinced the private character of its respective part of the palace.

The trio no sooner sat at table than Elagabalus excused himself to handle his dwarf's interruption. The two were conferring twenty yards away in the middle of the small bridge leading from the bank to the island. The dwarf hopped from one foot to the other and the Emperor's voice rose and fell, but remained unintelligible for the gurgling of the little geysers about the well-hipped white marble nymphs dancing in dramatic postures, some of the statues up to their knees in the lake, others leaning wildly over the sculpted rock formations as Apollo plucked away on his lyre.

Mannix fingered his fork atop the table, calculating its potential with the Nubian bodyguards standing around the outside of the temple, their eyes never leaving him. He noted the spacing of the Praetorians about the frescoed back wall of the peristyle, and then cast a glance at the Emperor on the bridge. Turning back to Julia Soaemias, the sneer was still evident on his face.

"Why?" he asked incriminatingly.

"Did I let him turn out like this?" she completed his question. "Oh Caius," she sighed. "We can't all be like you."

"That's the same thing he said. I'm getting a little tired of hearing it."

"It didn't have to be like this," she said.

"Is that the threat after the fact?," he returned her look with a twinkle of humor in his swollen, blood-shot eyes.

She glanced down and examined her hands. "I'm sorry about Demetrius."

"So am I. Now Marcellus is gone."

She looked up in time to see the pain cross his face, then looked away just as quickly. She remembered how terribly jealous of Marcellus she was. And she knew Mannix did too.

"Yesterday," he nodded, still staring at her. "Not many of us left anymore, is there."

She reached out her hand and placed it atop his. He let her. The Nubians shifted around the bank.

"Caius you've got to try and make it through tonight," she squeezed his hand. "I beg of you, play along with whatever

273

it is he wants. Just trust me on this. Bluff it out tonight and you'll be safe."

Mannix looked at her with a face that didn't seem to want to play along with anything. "And you? What's going to happen to you?"

She looked down and shook her head quickly. "It doesn't matter." Her son's voice caused her to quickly withdraw her hand.

"Well," Elagabalus said, returning a bit breathlessly, "catching up on old times, are we?" He took up a lemon half to squeeze over Mannix's plate. "How do you like your lobster?"

"I like it the way it is as well as I like it at all," the Bestiarius replied, sickened by the residue of gold paint still speckling the Emperor's fingernail.

Elagabalus paused, and then chuckled. He took a seat between them. Still chuckling, he squeezed the lemon over his own lobster.

The Bestiarius ate, slowly chewing the meat and continually refilling his water glass with the silver pitcher left by the servants, willing the strength to return. He knew he would need the food and the water for whatever was in store.

"So it seems you're missed at the Amphitheater, Mannix," Elagabalus said cheerfully, digging into his lobster with feigned appetite. "Amazing that Mob. Give them everything they want and they still find something to complain about."

"I'm sure they miss you too," the Bestiarius replied sardonically.

"Perhaps," the Emperor reflected. "Maybe it would be different if I were there."

"Why don't you go, Varius?" Soaemias pleaded. "Why don't you both go. Put a stop to this nonsense," she looked down and shook her head.

"Nonsense?" Elagabalus looked at her, feigning surprise. "I can't have one of my subjects as a guest for a day?"

Soaemias had tears in her eyes.

"Mother," Elagabalus seemed humored, "don't worry about the Mob."

"They say old Nero was pretty popular with the Mob," the Bestiarius remarked.

"Good point, Mannix." Elagabalus leaned back in his chair. "Did you know that Nero and I both inherited the purple at the same age?"

"Interesting."

"Seventeen," the Emperor nodded. "And you know I think Suetonius gave him a bit of a bad rap. Admittedly unstable and perhaps unfit for the responsibilities of unbridled power. Still, Nero was a young man of decided artistic tastes and some talent. There's been some interesting revisionist history written recently to the effect that he exemplifies the potential climate of an advanced state in the hands of an enlightened ruler."

"Is that right," Mannix raised an eyebrow.

Julia Soaemias poured herself a glass of wine from the silver pitcher left on the table by the servants.

Elagabalus smiled at him slyly. "I have them in the library here. I'll show you sometime. The gist of it is that Nero rejected conservative restraints and is now seen as embodying many of the forces of a new age irrespective of his personal instability."

"Really?" the Bestiarius returned his look. "I would have thought he was seen as a criminally willful youth who repeatedly violated law and tradition."

The Emperor shook his head, chewing his lobster. "He may have violated outworn conventions, Mannix; but he showed a genuine desire, especially in the first ten years of his reign, to advance not only the Roman World, but in particular its populace."

"I wonder what they'll be saying about Commodus in a hundred years," Mannix reflected.

"Nero began the cutting of a canal through the Isthmus of Corinth," Elagabalus continued, "in order to facilitate rapid transportation with the eastern Mediterranean. I plan to take back up that noble project. As soon as this unpleasantness on the Danube is settled."

The Bestiarius smiled mirthlessly. Julia Soaemias looked ill.

"Consider the sense of purpose Tacitus' gives him in 'Agricola,' Elagabalus gestured with his fork. "And the straightforwardness and practicality recorded by Frontinus in 'Concerning the Aqueducts.' Quite different gauges than the sordid court life focused on by Suetonius."

"And you?," Mannix interjected.

"Nero's ideas for a new Rome," Elagabalus ignored him, "the building of straight streets and fire-resistant apartment blocks, fountains and an increased network of sewage channels – much of which he financed personally and which still benefits our city – are I think more relevant records of the nature of his reign.

"And yours?" pressed the Bestiarius.

"The Sun," Elagabalus turned to him. "Faith, Mannix. As I said earlier, the people need something to believe in. Something new to believe in. We're living in an age which is ripe for it."

"And you're that something?"

"The Empire is being exposed to a religious ferment that has been stirring for centuries in the Mediterranean basin," Elagabalus continued. "The Earth Mother goddess Cybele was the first non-traditional religion to be legitimized in Rome, four hundred years ago during the Punic Wars against Carthage. Symptomatic of six thousand years of Earth Mother-worship in the cradle of civilization, she was followed by the Egyptian gods of fertility and health – Isis and Serapis – in the late Republic. Gods of the Greek East like Zeus-Heliopolitanus and Dolichenus, Adonis and Salambo came with the early Empire. Our Eastern Legions are largely responsible for the importation of some of these cults, most notably Mithraism, which derives from the Persian god of light."

"What's the point?" the Bestiarius asked, laying down his fork.

"Do you know who my great-grandfather was, Mannix?"

"That doesn't recommend you much," the Bestiarius replied.

"Hereditary high priest of the Syrian Sun God, Elagabal," the Emperor nodded. "Or the Roman Jupiter Heliopolitanus, if you prefer. Which priesthood not only I inherited at birth, but my late cousins Geta and Caracalla, and my cousin Alexianus as well. Right mother?" Elagabalus looked at Soaemias.

She blinked . . . she couldn't breathe, holding her down, hand on her face, biting the ground . . .

Her son turned back to the Bestiarius and shook his head. "My great-grandfather was a full-blooded Roman, and part of a breed of colonial officials dating back to the late Republic who were charged with studying the attributes of the native gods of each newly acquired province, and matching them with those of the traditional western pantheon." Elagabalus smiled. "Religious subversion, Mannix, in order to facilitate peace and commerce."

"And now you're doing it the other way around," the Bestiarius stated. "Subverting traditional Roman gods to those of the provinces? I still don't see the point."

"The point is that there is a caesura coming in history which will make Julius Caesar look like a street-side juggler," Elagabalus replied. "That caesura is the advent of one god, and the consolidation of all others under that god. Not simply to facilitate peace and commerce, but to facilitate control."

Mannix shook his head. "It seems to me that a little religious flexibility would be more conducive to control."

"It was at first," acknowledged Elagabalus. "Now what reigns is simply confusion. The old gods fail to satisfy, and the new ones are all a version of the same thing. All of these mystery cults promise a spirituality dazzled by ecstasies, presences and emanations, by demons and angelic hosts. But, moreover," his eyes narrowed, "by salvation after death." Elagabalus paused. "They are all elusive and volatile, diffuse and disjointed. What is needed is their consolidation under one God, one Faith. Political analysts have been pointing toward this since the late Republic."

"And you're that god?" asked the Bestiarius.

"The idea of oneness is the most Roman idea there is, Mannix. One Empire. One World," Elagabalus continued. "We've long known the benefits it would bring to all who are willing to conform to it. Usually it has been tried militarily and commercially. Alexander the Great and Trajan come to mind. But the biggest stumbling block to it has always been religion." He looked at the Bestiarius with his arrogant green eyes. "I plan to remove that stumbling block, Mannix. I plan to add faith to the execution of oneness. The idea not only of one Empire, of one World; but of one God, of one High Priest," he looked at him, "of one Sun."

"And you're that Sun?"

"The divine institution of the Imperial Genius is that Sun. Or will be," Elagabalus replied sincerely. "The consolidation of the cults of the Invincible Sun – Sol Invictus – with those of Mithras, Helios, Jupiter Heliopolitanus and Elagabal. After all, they're all trying to say the same thing. As you're well aware, one of the chief duties of Emperor is that of 'Pontifex Maximus' – High Priest over all religious rites in the city. I'm building a temple," he looked to his left, to the northeast, as if the Bestiarius didn't know, "where all the gods are gradually being assimilated under one." He smiled gravely. "Under the Sun."

The Bestiarius raised his chin. "And you think that robbing the temples of the old gods and subverting their worship – in other words, pissing on Roman tradition – can give the people something to believe in?"

"Worn-out conventions used by the upper classes to hold the people down," Elagabalus shook his head. "They're not helping them progress. The Empire is faced with a tremendously widespread lower class which needs consolidation. They need a sense of belonging to something instead of a sense of being held down by it. Of being held down by birth, and heredity. And the lifeless formalities of a dead religion," he pointed his fork at him, "the so-called 'State Religion' kept in favor here in the capital by a geriatric upper class intent on keeping them down."

"All I've seen you give them a sense of belonging to is sicker Circus venues and drunken orgiastic festivals," Mannix shook his head. "How is throwing camels and sacks of gold off balconies helping them to progress?"

"Spectacles, Mannix," Elagabalus shrugged. "Just like the Arena. All spectacles are devices of control. The idea behind them is what is important. If that idea be noble, the means used to achieve it aren't important. The Mob needs their outlets," Elagabalus nodded patiently, "just as the aristocracy has theirs behind closed doors. It's no different from the Arena. That's quite an outlet for them, not to mention for yourself. When I watched you the other day, it was plain to see that you were the prey of heightened emotions, of blood and furor."

"The Arena is a controlled competition between life and death originally designed to instill courage by example," the Bestiarius stated. "What you're designing is just misbehavior in the streets."

"It's Magic, Mannix," Elagabalus' eyes flickered as he shook his head. "The ability to control people with performance. You do it your way; I do it mine."

"First of all, I don't control anybody, nor do I want to," the Bestiarius replied. "Second of all, in the Arena it's just me out there. With something very real and immediate to lose. I'm not surrounded by bodyguards and Praetorians." He looked around at the Nubians. "It seems to me you need to re-examine where your sense of control truly lies."

Elagabalus blinked with the slight, but continued. "This idea of oneness – of one God, one High Priest, and one Sun – I want you to help me get this across to them, Mannix," he said. "I want you to support this idea. This dream." He shook his head. "Times are changing. The time is ripe to expose this lie that some are born to rule, some are born to serve, and some are born to die."

"You said yourself that you were born to be Emperor," Mannix countered.

"I was," Elagabalus nodded with a slow smile. "But not because of my class, Mannix."

Julia Soaemias stiffened.

"I was born to be Emperor. But not because they made me out to be Caracalla's son. Not because they named me 'Marcus Aurelius Antoninus," he smirked. "No. I was born to be Emperor because I am your son," his green eyes glistened as he looks at him, "Myth."

The Bestiarius, finished with his lunch, poured himself a tall glass of wine and leaned back in his chair. He drank the glass at one go, placed it on the table and raised his arms behind his head, interlacing his fingers. He smiled coolly. And Julia Soaemias let out a soft moan.

XXXX

Occupying the valley between the Pincian and Quirinal Hills, the Gardens of Sallust originally belonged to the historian of the same name. Soon after his death two hundred and fifty years before, the enormous suburban estate became one of the most important Imperial properties in the greenbelt. Both Vespasian and his son Titus used it as the major Imperial residence, preferring it to Nero's Golden House, which had evil associations and was being systematically dismantled at the time. It was not until Vespasian's younger son Domitian inherited the purple that the current palace was built and the emperors moved back in state to the Palatine.

Outside the old Republican wall, well-removed from the noise and congestion of the city yet still less than an hour from the Forum on foot – with its manicured parks and its wildlife reserve, its figural fountains and its mile-long porticoes for strolling – the Horti Sallustiani rivaled any villa in the Empire for beauty and seclusion. Replete with their own bath complex and a basilical hall for conventions, like Hadrian's Villa at Tivoli the gardens had their own thematic zones, such as the Egyptian pavilion built by Caligula with its pink Aswan granite statues of the Ptolemaic kings, and more than a few of his favorite sister Drusilla, with whom he had special, and not altogether appropriate reasons for her being his favorite.

Julia Maesa and Avidius Lepidus sat on the sweeping, open, weathered marble porch of the main three-story orange ochre-stuccoed mansion house, with its thick, beautifully-wrought balustrade staged with statues and its short, wide staircase flowing down into the several-mile vista of staggered, geyser-spurting fountains and towering hedgerow mazes. The pair sat in cushioned curule garden chairs with footstools on either side of a marble sidetable containing the remnants of a light lunch of chicken and lentils. The huge old oaks marking the deer park were just visible in the distance, and the gray sky lent the foliage a beautiful depth of green. The Praetorian presence was discreet, but evident; and as they conversed, they could see the thirteen year-old Alexianus a hundred yards away returning from a walk in the woods with his mastiff.

"If he's got five hundred men on the Palatine loyal to him, why, by the great waterlogged gonads of Neptune, are you going up there tonight with Mamaea and the boy?" asked Lepidus, his legs outstretched, his old down-at-heel boot sandals crossed on his footstool, tapping at them with his cane.

"Because, my dear old Plebian ex-lover and friend," smiled Julia Maesa, "one of the unfortunate aspects of being an empress is that sometimes you're obliged to act like one." She handed him a five hundred year-old black-lacquered Greek drinking bowl full of light red wine. "And," pouring for herself, "because most of the tribunes in command of that cohort are mine. Or soon will be. With brand new suits of golden armor to prove it."

"You old witch," Lepidus grimaced. "Playing toy soldiers again."

"I do my best," Maesa nodded. "And Eutychianus does what he's told. Nice work with the strike, by the way. You orchestrated it to perfection." She raised her bowl slightly, "To old times."

"To Mannix," the old bestiarius replied, his eyes running across the statue of a dying gladiator as he drank, a powerful work in Aegean marble reclining atop the balustrade in poignant grace.

"Yes, well," Maesa smacked her lips and sets down her bowl, "if all goes as planned, all he has to do is survive this night."

"And this day," Lepidus raised an eyebrow.

Maesa shook her head and adjusted the blanket of rabbit fur over her lap. "Elagabalus won't kill him today. He'll want him for a showpiece at the banquet." She took back up her wine bowl. "I don't think he wants to kill him at all, really. He's insanely jealous of his standing with the Mob, and covets that most of all. He's always hated the upper classes," she reflected. "In any event, and in the position he's in now, his only choice to garner favor with the people is to pardon their hero. Exalt him, even." She took a sip of wine. "Which, to be honest with you, Lepidus, will make my job that much harder." She shook her head. "Elagabalus isn't stupid. In fact he's unusually intelligent. Unfortunately."

"Then why get rid of him?" Lepidus asked.

"For just that very reason," she replied absently, as if speaking to herself.

The old bestiarius turned his head and looked at her.

"He has a perceptivity," Maesa continued, squinting her hawk eyes as she stared into the distant depth of shadow-feathered green, "a foresight of what's coming even though he can't see it clearly."

"Just like your father," Lepidus grinned and shook his head fondly at the memory of her younger years, this daughter of the high priest of the Syrian Ba'al, a jovial old drunk whom he'd met on several occasions.

Maesa cast an irritated side-glance at him and then returned to her ruminations. "Why get rid of him?," she shrugged a boney old shoulder. "For the obvious reasons. The religious gig has worn thin. It's not time for the changes he's trying to make. He really believes that nonsense, believes himself divine, which all weak people start to do after years of nobody telling them 'no.' He continues to purposefully offend the aristocracy with his antics, seemingly oblivious of the fact that we rely on their money." She set her wine bowl on the table. "The thing with the Vestals made us enemies no amount of money can buy."

The old bestiarius grimaced at the memory. "The poor girl."

Maesa made a throwaway gesture with her hand. "Ah, we orchestrated a symbolic marriage ceremony between the two and then pensioned her off to a principate in Thrace. Last I heard she was happy as a lark."

Lepidus raised his eyebrows.

Maesa sighed. "Elagabalus has gotten out of hand. It's one thing having palace slave boys stand in line to bugger you, but undergoing a marriage ceremony with one of them?," she shook her head. "They never stop partying up there." She took another sip of wine. "But the major reason is because things aren't going well on the Danube."

Lepidus looked at her as he took a drink.

"We can blame his foreign policy for the lack of a successful conclusion to this second Macromannic War," Maesa continued, "which he started."

"That's arguable," Lepidus raised one of his fuzzy gray eyebrows. "They're coming against us every chance they get. Have been since I was a boy."

"Doesn't matter," Maesa shook her head. "The people need a scapegoat. It has to be someone's fault. We can't have the general public realizing that all empires have to fall sooner or later."

"Then why in the hell didn't you let the Praetorians kill him over the Alexianus thing?" the old bestiarius looked at her exasperatedly.

"Because it would have made me seem out of control," she replied coolly, "and it wouldn't have helped Alexianus' chances any," she nodded at the boy out wrestling with his dog on the lawn. "We'd have had another Praetorian Prefect on the throne and I'd have either been killed or had to start another civil war," she took a sip of wine, "which I can't afford and no one wants anyway."

Their conversation was interrupted by an apologetic Julia Mamaea, one of those strange individuals who could go physically unnoticed almost anywhere they were.

"Excuse me," she said. "Oh, hello Lepidus."

"Hello dear," smiled the old bestiarius amiably. He rose and kissed both of her cheeks. "Not a day older."

Mamaea smiled back. In a plain blue woolen winter stola, the thirty nine year-old's wiry black hair had gone to gray without the hairdresser's dye, her sharp nervous features slowly changing into the craggy, aquiline ones of her mother, to whom she bowed. "Mother, it's time for Alexianus' mathematics tutorial."

"Well, call him in dear," Maesa nodded, with a tone infinitely edged with exasperation, as if responding patiently to a child who continued to ask the same question over and over.

Julia Mamaea nodded back, oblivious of the tone which told Lepidus everything one needed know of their relationship. "Aleee," she called with a wave to the boy, "Aleee, time to come in."

"Yes mother," Alexianus shouted back, ruffling his dog's ears and starting toward them at a trot. The big black mastiff woofed happily and bounded after him in pursuit.

Lepidus remarked the fine-looking, sandy-blond youth in the red tunic belted over leather trousers as he ran up the stairs taking them two at a time. They met eyes and the boy smiled in an open, friendly way that showed his nature.

"Alexander," his grandmother called, come shake wrists with Avidius Lepidus, "an old friend of mine."

Lepidus stood and the boy grasped his corded forearm above its brown leather wristband. "It's a pleasure to meet you, young man," nodded the old bestiarius, the mastiff jumping playfully about the pair.

"I've heard of you," Alexianus said. "You're the Director of the Ludus Matutinus, aren't you?"

"I am, son," Lepidus nodded with severity and pat on the dog. "And your mother and grandmother have called me here today in order to turn you over to my care and start your training."

"Lepidus," Maesa smirked and shook her head. Her daughter Mamaea smiled nervously.

"Really!" grinned Alexianus. "I want to train with Mannix. Can I meet him please?"

The old director smiled and nodded absently, suddenly deeply sad – an unusual emotion for him.

"Lepidus has a wicked sense of humor, Alexander," Maesa said. "Now take the dog and go inside. It's time for your mathematics tutorial. Crito tells me you're a bit behind in geometry. I want to see you come up to par."

285

"Yes, grandmother," Alexianus bowed. He looked back up at Lepidus. "Can I meet him, though."

The old bestiarius smiled gently. "I think so, young man. I hope so."

As Alexianus jogged into the house with his mastiff woofing behind, Julia Mamaea smiled and nodded at him. "Goodbye Lepidus. It's nice to see you."

"Lepidus is coming with us tonight, dear," her mother stated.

"I'm glad," Mamaea smiled thinly. "I'm very sorry about it all."

"The boy doesn't know?," Lepidus asked.

"No," she shook her head and looked at her toes.

He nodded. "For the best. I'll see you this evening, dear."

As Mamaea walked into the mansion, the old bestiarius sat down stiffly in his chair with a sigh and arranged his black cape about him. "Alexianus is a fine boy."

"He'll do," Julia Maesa nodded severely.

"His mother takes after you."

"Certainly hasn't gotten any prettier, has she," Maesa replied wryly.

"That's not what I meant."

"Ah, Lepidus," she smiled thinly. "Ugly people with any character are happier than pretty people with the same amount. From an early age we forsake ourselves and become much more effective, just at different things." She chuckled slightly and looked over at him. "Anyway, you never were much of an Adonis."

Lepidus smiled absently, nonplussed, his eyes running across another of the statues on the balustrade down the way. An antique Greek sculpture of a dying Niobid – a counterpoint to the gladiator – one of the daughters of Niobe shot with an arrow which she was trying to remove. "And Soaemias?" he asked.

Looking out over the deep, black-green hedgerow maze, Maesa shook her head. "I'm sure she's scared." She finished her bowl of wine and did not pour another. "I know Elagabalus and his courtiers browbeat her and maybe worse. She's basically imprisoned up there in Severus' wing. Hardly ever comes out."

As Lepidus leaned to pour himself another bowl, he glanced furtively at her face, surprised to find her eyes glistening. In a moment of realization, he knew which offspring she had the feeling for in her gut despite it all.

Maesa cleared her throat; a passing phase. "Soaemias was always lost," she shrugged a boney shoulder. "Always a dreamer." She poured herself a short drink. "She never had what it took."

The old bestiarius grimaced and shook his head, "Always the affectionate mother, weren't you."

"Don't bore me with sentimentality, Lepidus" she replied. Then she sighed, her eyes out somewhere off in the oaks of the distant deer park. "It doesn't sit well with you, and I don't want to remember." She took another sip of wine, pulling the blanket up around her sagging gullet. "Soaemias is a drunk with a death wish who is losing her looks," she raised two fingers to the side in a half-hearted gesture, "which are all she ever had anyway."

Lepidus raised his fuzzy grey eyebrows with a sigh and poured another bowl of wine.

"What am I to do, keep her around knitting shawls after her son goes?" shaking her head, "It's just not done. She's a weak link, easy prey for conspirators. You can't trust a drunk," she went on. "They don't even trust themselves."

"I'm a drunk and I trust myself," Lepidus frowned.

"You're not a drunk. You're an alcoholic. And don't drink too much," she raised a few fingers at him, "You've got quite a night ahead of you."

Lepidus shrugged and puts down his bowl. "You let her become what she is."

"Partially, yes. But it is one of the great fallacious beliefs of the masses to think that a child necessarily continues or reflects one of our class."

"Mannix changed her," Lepidus said.

"Mannix finished her," Maesa stated. "But if somebody else can finish you, you're finished already."

The old bestiarius turned and looked at her, "Damn, woman, at least you can make up your mind."

She clacked her tongue in annoyance.

"Mannix is my son," Lepidus sat back in his chair. "He continues me. He reflects me."

"He's a man," she nodded in acknowledgement. "Like you," she cocked her head to the side. "And in this day that's a rarity." She took another miserly sip of wine. "But I'm sure he has his moments."

Lepidus turned his head. "What in hell is that supposed to mean?"

She lifted one of her boney shoulders again. "He's smarter than you, Lepidus. Smarter than most," she reflected. "He would have made Soaemias a fine husband. Would have made her a woman. And I don't mean in the bed," she looked over at him.

Lepidus took a surreptitious drink. "You should have let him."

She shook her head. "Such things are also not done. You know that."

"Can't say much for the men in your life," he replied.

"Yes, well," she said. "It's a good thing they all died young."

Lepidus pursed his lips. "Quite."

"There you go again," she shook her head. "People are a species, Lepidus. If anyone should appreciate that it's you. Some are born to rule, some are born to serve," she raised her fingers beneath the blanket. "And, as you know so well, some are born to die."

"And some are born to play God," Lepidus sighed and looked up into the sky from which a light gauze curtain of mist was beginning to descend. "For me it's a job," he shook his head. "For you it's a game."

"Personally," she frowned, "I prefer your types of species to mine. They're more honest. You know right off if an animal likes you or not," she nodded. "But a human . . ."

"Did you ever love anybody?," he asked.

"No," she shook her head absently, as if trying to make sure. "No I didn't," she repeated softly.

He remained staring at her for a moment. Then he poured a pittance of wine in his bowl and sat back, pulling his cape tighter around him. "And Elagabalus," he continued, interrupting her reverie "you made him what he is."

"The people either need a hero or a god, Lepidus," she sniffed. "I couldn't give them the one, so I gave them the other. The time was ripe; a religious revolution is on the way. Gods are no different than men. They all fall when it's time. They're not made to last."

"I gave them one," Lepidus nodded, sick of the wine and the wealth and the filth and Mannix in a hell of a position. "I gave them a god."

Julia Maesa raised her thin flaxen eyebrows, her craggy, aquiline face assuming a rare look of pensiveness. "Let's hope you're right," she said.

Their conversation was interrupted by a Praetorian tribune – the same one Elagabalus sent to Eutychianus – striding forth across the stones of the terrace. "Domina," he bowed.

"There you are, Ariostomachus. What news?"

"The Mob has become unruly in the Amphitheater, Domina. The Emperor has ordered me to tell Eutychianus to send a cohort to seal off the Patrician seating."

"Very well. Carry out the order. And tell Eutychianus to protect the aristocracy but give the Mob room to move. Keep me informed."

"Domina," the tribune bowed, and wheeled to carry the message to the Castra Praetoria, a ten-minute lope on horseback due south over the disabitato.

"And if the Mob burns the city?" Lepidus raised an eyebrow.

"Then they burn it," Maesa shrugged. "Old Nero started over. I can too."

"It's just a game to you, isn't it?" he shook his head.

"Of course," she nodded. "So why not play to win?"

A moment of silence passed and she leaned over and put a hand on his knee.

"There's not much we can do but wait and play it out, old boy. My bodyguards can stop a rush. And, as for the rest, well, are you afraid?"

"Hell no," he looked at her, surprised. "You know that."

She smiled her old thin smile. "Neither am I." And then she gave him that witching look he knew too well. "Why don't we go up and rest awhile before the party tonight."

He grimaced despite himself at the sight of her beauty mark with its sow's bristles. "Damn you, but you haven't changed a bit, have you woman."

"Well," she reflected, "it's not everyday I get called a 'cunt' in front of the Roman Senate."

Lepidus chuckled, "You always liked it when I talked rough."

Julia Maesa threw her head back and laughed.

XXXXI

"So the bill has finally come due," the Bestiarius smiled absently. "A bill for goods I never asked for. A bill I don't owe." He shook his head. "Somehow I always knew it would."

The trio had moved, due to the onset of rain, into the original Domitianic private wing, upstairs into a long, intimate, timber-ceilinged den amidst the hushed silences of great art and the darkened stares of the Nubian bodyguards.

Elagabalus looked back and forth between Mannix and Soaemias, smiling wanly. "Your relationship with each other is well known. No one among the Senate and the aristocracy has forgotten it." He turned to his mother. "Over half the freedmen, servants and slaves employed at the palace then are still here now."

Her back turned, Julia Soaemias stood before a six hundred year-old panel painting in egg tempera by the Athenian Phidias, who designed the Parthenon frieze. She did not respond. Despite the oversized long-sleeved blue tunic which fell just below her knees and made her look fat, her smooth meaty calves tapered neatly into the unlaced legionary boot sandals.

"I walked in on you two nine years ago," Elagabalus tried to laugh. "I was ten years old. Don't tell me you can't remember?!"

"And you're nineteen years old now, Varius," Soaemias replied flatly. "Not ten."

"Oh, but it started long before that," he squinted his heavy, languorous eyelids. "Petricon has told me everything. Told me about Mannix being let up the servants' stairwells. Told me about how you fell in love with him and wouldn't eat. Told me about grandmother marrying you off because you were

291

pregnant with me," his eyes grew cold. "There's no point in carrying on with this charade."

The maids were hard-pressed, and the den still had the faint vinous scent of last night's romp, its couches and zebra-skinned rugs all array and its diamond-patterned red and white marble flooring splotched with wine stains. The small sculpture groups of fornicating fauns and buggering bacchants and humping hermaphrodites on black marble plinths were still riddled with cups and chalices, glasses and drug vials. A twenty-foot horizontal panel of Alexander and Darius at the Battle of Issus had fallen to the floor and been propped up by the maids to await the palace slaves who would re-hang it for the restorers to come in and patch it up again.

"It removes the last stumbling block," Elagabalus nodded. "Don't you see? This is the legitimacy that I need. A legitimacy that the Senate and the aristocracy will have no choice but to respect. Unless they want mayhem in the streets."

Mannix stood at a window aside a porphyry statue of Marsyas commissioned by Hadrian for his villa at Tivoli. The satyr who dared challenge the sun god Apollo to a musical contest and who lost – and whom the sculptor caught in the red marble act of being flayed alive – was still draped with a pair of silken underwear. A glass of wine in his hand, his nerves raw from the beatings, the Bestiarius stared through the thick lead-glass windowpanes over the sunken third fountain court a hundred and twenty feet below.

"I'm not your father," he said, "and even if I was it wouldn't help you."

"But you are, Caius," Soaemias nodded. Through playing, she turned and looked at him with tears running down her cheeks and everything she had left in her big almond eyes trying to will him to play along.

Unfazed, Mannix continued to gaze out of the window down into the third court with its strange fountain of curvilinear shields surrounded by a two-storied peristyle – a world of its own created, like the stadium garden, by cutting back the slope and building up the opposite side to utilize what would otherwise be space lost to the fall-off of the hill.

"The only thing that will help you," he continued, "is to make a public announcement to the effect that you are dismissing your court and abdicating the throne to Alexianus. And either go into exile," he took a sip of wine, "or take your own life."

Elagabalus felt a wincing pain shoot between his naval and his penis and he swallowed it back with pursed lips. "And take yours with it," he raised an eyebrow and managed a smile.

"You've had it," the Bestiarius went on, unimpressed. "You've lost the support of the army due to your lifestyle and the people you surround yourself with. The moneyed elite hates you because you've spit on them and their tradition." He took another sip of wine. "Whatever Praetorian support you still have won't last much longer and the Mob could care less who's on the throne as long as the bread dole and the Games go on."

"That's a lie," Elagabalus raised his voice and pointed at him. "I still have the people. I will always have the people. We'll see who they love."

The Bestiarius shook his head. "You're intelligent. Maybe with the right kind of guidance you could have been something. But, let's face it, without it you've done everything wrong from the start. The religious act was poorly executed. Maybe you've got something there; maybe you don't. But if there is a God, let him play his games; you should have concentrated better on yours. Otherwise you don't believe in what you preach and you're just a fake," he turned his head to the side.

Elagabalus' jaw slackened and his face emptied.

"If you wanted to level the classes," Mannix continued, turning his head back to the window, "offending the upper to gain the lower has done nothing but further entrench the aristocracy in their conservatism. As far as the Mob, their adulation is fickle at best, and the Games and the dole will go on with or without you and they know it."

"I am their Emperor!" Elagabalus shouted, stabbing his thumb in his chest.

The Bestiarius sighed. "Look at this place," opening his hand to the side in indication of the room. "All you are is a two-bit crowned anarchist with no style."

"I'll kill you, you bastard," Elagabalus spit breathlessly, the Nubians stirring along the walls.

"You can kill me and you can kill your family and you can kill the entire Patrician class," Mannix shrugged. "But your generals will march on Rome just like Severus did." He turned. "You've been had, Varius. You've been kept in an insulated world where you can't see reality, never could see it. You've been used and you've been had. And now you've had it."

"I'll have it tortured out of you," Elagabalus tried to smile again.

The Bestiarius turned to him and raised an eyebrow. "Do you really think you and those ass-thumbing monkeys over there could make me sing, little one? And, even if you could, what then? Prop me up on my last legs in front of the world and make my mouth say the words?" He turned back to the window shaking his head softly. "It won't help you."

Elagabalus' lips trembled and his eyes darted. He swallowed hard.

The Praetorian tribune with the white leather headgear emerged hurriedly clattering up the stairs from the archway at the end of the long den which gave onto a glimpse of a vast dark columnar interior.

Elagabalus threw his head to the side. "What is it?!"

The tribune came forward hesitantly. "Sire the cohort you requested has been dispatched but . . ."

"Say it!"

The tribune looked straight ahead. "It is recommended that Caius Marius Mannix be released in order to avert a potential riot in the streets."

Elagabalus smiled softly. "We are having a visit," he replied slowly and patiently. "He is my guest at the Palace," as if dictating. "And he will be with us for tonight's banquet," he looked straight ahead. "Now tell them that!" he shouted and wheeled and threw his glass of wine the twenty feet across the space between where it shattered on the diamond-patterned marble floor amidst the tribune's dancing feet.

The man bowed and rushed away and Elagabalus walked to a dark marble dolphin-legged sidetable where, with trembling hands, he poured a full glass of wine for himself and downed it in one go. He winced and coughed. Then he walked around as if looking for something.

"She always loved you more than me, you know, Mannix," he smirked.

"Varius," said Julia Soaemias, her voice a moan.

"You never loved me, mother," he smiled at her, his nostrils quivering. "That was always obvious."

"Oh, Varius."

"You never loved me!" he screamed.

The Nubian bodyguards shifted again nervously.

"No, I suppose I didn't," she replied softly, raising her chin.

His face was trembling violently now, trying to control the tears. "But why?" he whispered.

"I don't know," she sighed. "Perhaps because I never really loved myself."

Mannix turned away from the window and walked to the side table and poured another glass of wine. He looked hard at Elagabalus and then walked over to Soaemias and handed her the glass without looking at her. Then he returned over the zebra-skinned rugs to the window by the statue of Marsyas.

Taking a long drink, Julia Soaemias thought back, trying to find an answer. "I came from a family where children were not conceived out of love and, I suppose, as a consequence, they weren't born out of it."

"But you love him!" Elagabalus pointed incriminatingly at Mannix. "You've always loved him!"

"I've felt in prison for most of my life, Varius" she replied. "Doing things to hurt myself. Yes, there was a period when I felt free. Felt the potential for freedom," she stared at the Bestiarius' broad back in the stained and torn maroon paenula. "You were named 'Varius' after my husband," she said. "But the joke arose soon after that it was because you sprung from the seed of 'various' men," she smiled sadly.

The Bestiarius turned from the window and looked at her.

"But I didn't," Elagabalus looked at Mannix. "I sprung from you."

Mannix shook his head, staring at Soaemias. "Julia . . . as many men as you had in those days."

"Look at him, Caius," she said, crying softly.

The Bestiarius took him in – the fine build, the green eyes, the better skin not white and pale by nature like his and yet the total lack, the lack of anything that would make the build, eyes and skin anything more than the incarnations of a festival-booth magician.

Elagabalus returned his look hopefully. "If they made Caracalla be my father we can make you be my father, Mannix." He smiled and shrugged. "That bastard used to pinch me and beat me and hang me over the drop to the street between the terrace and the Circus here. Just for the fun of it," he continued. He reached for the Bestiarius' arm. "I want you to be my father, Mannix," he grasped him, "I . . . need you to be my father. I want to make the announcement tonight at the banquet. For us to stand together and make the announcement tonight. To the entire city."

Mannix sighed, but didn't pull his arm away. "I told you . . . I'm not your father. And it won't help you anyway."

"But I . . . need you," Elagabalus' smile trembled. "You're what I need to turn things around. I'll dismiss my court," he nodded sincerely. "I'll start over. I want to start on this dream that I know is right."

"It's too late, Varius," Mannix turned away with a grimace. He looked hard at Soaemias.

"I can announce it without you," Elagabalus tried to maintain his smile.

"Avoid the bloodshed," Mannix shrugged. "Show that you really do have some control. Some control over yourself."

"I shall do it without you," the Emperor nodded unconvincingly.

"Without my consent it would be meaningless, would only turn them against you further," the Bestiarius replied softly. Shaking his head, "They won't believe you, Varius. Credibility comes with character and," he raised his eyebrows at the window, "you don't have it."

Elagabalus' mouth opened and he paused. "But I . . . I want you to help me to have it."

Mannix continued to shake his head. "The only thing you can do now to redeem a little of yourself is what I said – abdicate to Alexianus and die like a man."

Elagabalus' lips trembled and he looked as if he'd been struck. He walked to the window beside Mannix and stared open-mouthed through the milky glow. "How am I supposed to die like a man," he replied softly, "when I was never taught how to live like one?," he turned his head to the Bestiarius with tears in his eyes. "Where . . . where were you . . . when I needed you?"

Mannix stared out the window beside him. "None of that matters now, Varius. The only thing that matters is what you can control right now. And that is yourself."

Elagabalus searched for words, the tears rolling down his honey-colored cheeks. "That isn't fair," he shook his head. "It's not fair."

"Life isn't fair, Varius."

"Will you help me?"

"I am helping you," the Bestiarius nodded, his expression pained. "It's never too late to start doing the right thing. So do it."

"He's right, Varius," Soaemias nodded with tears in her eyes. "The banquet tonight has been designed to make amends. The guests are due to arrive soon. If you make the announcement of your abdication you might be able to change the course of events."

"But we can make amends. We can all make amends. We can all be together again. Will you help me?" Elagabalus pleaded.

Mannix and Soaemias didn't respond.

297

"Will you help me?!" he shouted, his voice cracking, looking straight ahead, truly frightened.

The Bestiarius turned. "You've got three choices, Varius. One, get yourself a muleteer's cap and get out of Rome as quickly as you can and go pick zucchini in Sicily. Two, abdicate to Alexianus and commit suicide – because, in exile, somebody's sure to get you anyway. Or three," he paused and smiled darkly, glancing from Elagabalus to the Nubians. "Heroes and villains are all the same, Varius. Their lives go straight to the mark." Mannix squinted his eyes. "Can you go all the way?"

The Emperor felt urine bite the tip of his penis as he backed up, away from him, his heel catching on one of the zebra-skinned rugs, tripping him. He fell and felt a bit of urine run warm the inside of his thigh. Then he leapt up and kicked over a side table. "It's your fault!" he screamed at Mannix. "All of it!"

The Bestiarius turned back to the window. "It's nobody's fault now but yours, Varius. If you don't take the opportunity that's being given you to do the right thing."

"Please, Varius," Soaemias said hopefully and Elagabalus wheeled and struck his mother a vicious blow on the side of the head, her hair flying wildly as she went down.

"It's your fault you bitch!" he screamed. "You whore!"

One hand still holding his wine glass, Mannix in one fluid motion was across the room and casually backslapped the Emperor like a doll, knocking him off his feet. Then he smashed his glass on a near statue and jammed it into the face of the first Nubian to reach him, the man's white feather head dress jolting as he screamed. The Bestiarius threw himself backwards as the second one swung, going into a roll and heaving the big man in the cheetah-skin tunic across the floor. He kicked upwards into the next one, knocking him back, then scrambled sideways onto his feet with the other three bodyguards all over him and a contingent of Praetorians rushing up the stairs into the room.

Julia Soaemias jumped on the back of one of the Nubians, clawing at his eyes and Elagabalus hit her hard in the kidneys making her cry out and drop to the floor, where he began kicking her viciously in the stomach while Mannix leapt over a couch, his paenula flying, and tipped a small black bronze of a youth picking a thorn from his foot into the way of the Nubians in pursuit. He turned directly into the wave of Praetorians and tried to blast his way through, a helmet rolling, a sword skittering, a man dropping and then another across the hard marble floor but there were too many and the Bestiarius, gang-tackled, was finally subdued.

Elagabalus, standing over his mother, smiled now, though only with his mouth this time, not his eyes. The doll-like stare had crept back into his pupils and he turned his head and looked at the Bestiarius with that faraway smile and those faraway eyes. With knees all over his back, rear and thighs, a baton choking his throat and the manacles clinking locked around his ankles and wrists, Mannix looked up and met his gaze.

"I've collected all of Rome's worn-out idols to myself here on the Palatine," Elagabalus cocked his head to the side. "Now I've got the Myth."

He looked down at his fallen mother curled fetal in pain. "Mother, mother found me on her step. Gracious mother held me to her breasts," he lisped the nursery rhyme. Stepping over her, he kicked her again as he started slowly across the floor toward Mannix. "Stand him up straight!," he screamed at the Praetorians.

Julia Soaemias rolled over on her side and crawled toward Mannix, meeting his eyes.

"Guess we should have gone to Crete after all," he smiled sadly at her.

"I've missed you so much," she said, the tears rolling from her eyes as their son threw his first punch.

XXXXII

The evening sky had torn apart like a shredded garment to reveal towering golden cumulonimbus canting up at oblique angles directly overhead above the sweeping tattered remnants of horizontal gray overcast. Sunlight stabbed intermittently across the Palatine alternating with brief, clatterous episodes of rain which rippled across the little lake of the second fountain court leaving the nuisanced swans fluttering it off their wings. The guests were arriving for the usual sunset spectacle which traditionally graced the banquets of all emperors – whether musical, theatrical, gladiatorial or otherwise. The courts were strewn with violets, lilies and hyacinths, and flung open with musicians and acrobats performing, and tables laden with cups of rich red wine and appetizing viands.

A massive wedge of orange sunlight angled across the smooth façade of the huge banquet hall, glistening like diamonds in the wet streaks running down from its cornice after the day's rain. Beneath its hovering bulk, throngs of Senators and Equestrians, and even a hundred or more choice Plebians squeezed in just for 'padding,' trickled about the first fountain court. The classes were clicky, and the men grouped and fraternized about the grand Polyphemus fountain in their togas and varicolored robes, the women gossiping and promenading in their dress stolas beneath their pastel paper parasols.

Filing down the peristyle holding Lepidus by the crook of his arm – with daughter Mamaea, Alexianus, and their retinue in train – Julia Maesa's craggy aquiline face showed signs of strain. Her lips were pursed, her hawk eyes wary. The tribune Ariostomachus intercepted their caravan on the Via Lata en route thirty minutes ago. Walking his horse alongside her litter, he informed them of Elagabalus' order of an announcement made at the Amphitheater that the main event

300

was changed to thirty teenage Norse girls being raped by baboons in a forest setting – a ploy calculated to distract the Mob's unrest over Mannix.

Then, upon arrival ten minutes before, her Circassian bodyguards were summarily disarmed of their curved scimitars by the overwhelming number of Praetorians in the 'Area Palatina,' the open square before the public wing. And with a flood of several hundred guests filing in around them, she had to play along to avoid a scene. Now, in the great fountain court, though the unusual amount of guardsmen standing about the peristyles also struck a sinister key, the major factor bothering the wily old empress was that, among them all, she could see none wearing the golden cuirasses which were to be a signifer of their wearers' loyalty. Another abnormality was the conspicuous absence of her daughter Soaemias, who should have received her with the other guests.

"It's not looking so good, old girl," Lepidus said grimly, placing his hand atop hers tenderly.

"Put a smile on your face," Maesa replied, smiling herself and nodding in acknowledgement at the white-powdered, beauty-marked visages passing by. "Remember we've got an audience."

Greeted by Senators and bowed before by prelates, she had outfitted the old bestiarius in trousers of light Spanish leather with a belted turquoise tunic and a rich red robe. With her flaxen gray hair bunched like a beehive on top of her head, she herself wore the tastefully exquisite, golden and green shawled stola she took from Julia Domna's closet after her sister starved herself overlooking the stadium garden five years before. Julia Mamaea and Alexianus walked holding hands behind them, the mother her usual nervous nondescript self, the boy in a tunic of green felt over his leather trousers and boots.

Some of the younger members of the Senate were shocked to see Maesa and Lepidus together after the morning's performance in the chamber, though the old ones found it only faintly amusing. They knew that, with the power this old widow held, she no longer kept up appearances, she simply made them.

301

"Well, Dio," she nodded, as they came upon the short fat choleric man with the gray coiffeured curls and the white toga with the red-striped border, "and how is your grand history coming along."

"Augusta," the Senator bowed, his puffy cheeks already reddened with wine, "I'm afraid it's been a bit bleak of late," he replied.

"I've no doubt of it," Maesa said. "And things certainly aren't looking up around here," she raised an eyebrow and looked at him pointedly.

Cassius Dio blinked and looked about him quickly, lowering his voice. "He's switched out the tribunes."

"How do you know?" Maesa hissed.

"I slipped a palace slave a few sesterces. Rumor has it he had the cohort assembled in the garden grounds before the Temple of Apollo to detail their orders for tonight's security. The slave said he had the Imperial Genius. During his speech, he held it up and revealed the gold-cuirassed tribunes as traitors and had them slaughtered by the men."

Julia Maesa smarted with the news, and then recovered herself.

"And Mannix?" asked Lepidus, grasping Dio by the arm.

The seventy two year-old Senator shook his head. "Another rumor, but the slave told me he was seen carried out of the private wing by four guardsmen. Dead."

The old bestiarius' face emptied. First Marcellus and now Caius.

"It might not be true, Lepidus," Dio blinked.

Maesa squeezed Lepidus' arm tenderly. "Stay under control," she said. "And Soaemias?"

"Not a word, I'm afraid."

"What news from Eutychianus?" Maesa probed.

"The messengers say he's running around pulling his hair out as usual," the wart-faced Senator replied. "The gladiators Cordius and Tychicus gave a speech during the mid-day break at the Amphitheater saying they witnessed the fight and that Mannix started it without provocation and stabbed Prixus in the back as he was trying to walk away."

"Gutless bastards!," Lepidus spat. Part of the athletic contingent of Elagabalus' courtiers, more than a few gladiators and charioteers had ingratiated themselves for advancement and easy venue draws.

"Keep your voice down, Lepidus," Maesa smiled and nodded.

"Supposedly the Mob was subdued by the announcement," Dio continued. He looked around, shaking his nervous jowls in agitation at the number of Praetorians standing at attention along the polished-marble back walls of the peristyle. "Elagabalus isn't going down without a fight, it seems."

The director of the Ludus Matutinus grit his teeth. "I'll kill him when I see him."

"Lepidus," Maesa squeezed his arm. "There are ears everywhere. And will be all the night. Serving us at table and everywhere else. We've discussed this already," she patiently explained. Then she took a breath and continued to smile and nod as if involved in polite conversation. "We don't know that Mannix is dead. But if he is and the Mob finds out, we might lose them. You know how fickle they are."

"Then why wouldn't Elagabalus let it leak?" the old bestiarius ground his jaw.

"Because he can't be sure of their reaction," Maesa quickly replied. Turning her head to Cassius Dio, "Ariostomachus met us on the Via Lata," she said. "I gave the order to announce Mannix's unwillful incarceration after the Emperor's courtiers leave the Amphitheater to come here."

"Which is now," Dio frowned, his eyes on Hierocles – Elagabalus' behind-the-scenes husband – who had just emerged from the rear of the throne room, his curly blond locks bouncing as he skipped across the blue-veined Pentelic paving of the court. Replete in a golden silk robe and wearing a phallus-nosed carnival mask, he was followed by an unusual assortment of uppity prostitutes in garishly revealing costumes dancing and spinning like sprites. The girls flashed tambourines and clattered castanets and the old men in white face powder and hair nets, the magicians, occultists, gladiators and charioteers ensued, with the base-born profligates slinking along in train, their unusually large organs packed into tight leather britches. All of the guests stopped their conversations and some even applauded as they watched the frolicking freakshow trailing with shouts and squeals and high-pitched laughter across the square to disappear in the corridor joining the first and second courts, one of the prostitutes lagging behind at the fountain to give a five-second demonstration of fellatio to a white-marble mariner as he helped heft the sharpened log toward the Cyclops' eye.

"We need to get somebody to Milo's Tavern right away," Lepidus said. "Find anybody in there who saw the fight. Find Pompey the Kenyan charioteer; get Milo himself. And get them to the Amphitheater to tell the truth."

Julia Maesa turned to one of her Circassians and barked at the man in his own language.

"No, Augusta," Cassius Dio placed a liver-splotched hand on her arm. "They might not let one of yours through. And if they do, they'll surely follow him. I'll go," he shook his sweaty brow. "I can tell them I'm suffering from an attack of gout. Which is only too true."

"Can you make it, old boy?" Lepidus grasped his pudgy shoulder.

"I suppose I'll have to," Dio smiled. "If I can't I'll make the announcement myself."

"You know what that could mean, Cassius," Maesa inclined her head.

"You know me," the wart-faced Senator winked. "Just an old slave in a toga here." And then he bowed formally and raised his hand and his voice. "Hail, Augusta! Ave, Lepidus!" And then limped hurriedly away down the peristyle.

XXXXIII

The party was livening with the wine and, amidst the jugglers, acrobats and fire-blowers, the guests were being told by heralds to bring their drinks and proceed to the stadium garden where their Emperor would officially receive them. Lepidus and Maesa flowed with the crowd through the marble corridor beneath the four-story office wing. The angular old Empress told Mamaea and Alexianus to stay close, and ordered her Circassian bodyguards to keep on their toes. Having selected her ten best men – for more would be obnoxious in a setting which was social – the guards were well-practiced at their role of both protecting as well as adding a quiet dash of color to their Empress' retinue.

Alexianus took Lepidus by the hand as they walked, surprising him. The old bestiarius was in tremendous pain, his chest closing with sorrow, making it difficult to breathe. He looked down at the sandy-blond boy in the green felt tunic who reminded him so much of Marcellus, and the tears filled his eyes. But he sniffed them back quickly and nodded and winked and, with a strength-giving grin, squeezed the youth's hand with his gnarled old paw.

The boy overheard their conversation with Cassius Dio and now understood all. The fight with Prixus, Elagabalus' insane jealousy of Mannix; it all made disturbing sense now. Throughout his young life, which had been spent predominantly in the company of adults – without friends of his own age, and under the care of tutors rather than schools – Alexianus had learned to listen more than speak, and had developed a premature ability for discernment as a consequence.

Though his mother and grandmother believed they had kept from him his cousin's plot to kill him, with his knack for developing conclusions out of fragments of overheard

305

information, the boy gleaned it almost immediately. And the knowledge hurt him, for he and Varius played together for years, and he could not understand it. He also loved his aunt Soaemias, who always seemed to love him too; from a young age, Alexianus loved her smells and her cushioned breasts, her foot tickles and endless jests.

Adding a painful implication to it all, his tutor Crito had recently expounded to him the theory that people were what they were in all essentials – their likes and dislikes, their particular forms of courage and fear – by the age of ten. And though those traits may not show their boon or bane until later, they were all already present by a person's tenth year. Hence, with no one to cry to after learning of his cousin's plot, and no one with whom to alleviate his fear, through it all, Alexianus' understanding of human nature had taken another poignant step toward a realization of the calculating and devious nature that forever separated man from his mastiff.

Yet this increasing awareness had not caused him to grow cold like he knew it had his grandmother. And it was this combination of perceptivity and sensitivity in the boy which enabled him to discern Lepidus' pain; and, indeed, to feel it himself. He returned the squeeze of the old bestiarius' leather wrist-banded hand, each of their hearts finding strength from the other as they emerged into the dramatic space of the second fountain court fronting the private wing.

The presence of red capes was increasing. With hundreds of guests around them and Julia Maesa still nodding and making small talk as they proceeded along the Phrygian purple columns of the peristyle past the little island with its round temple graced in the golden light of evening, the tribune in the white leather headgear interrupted their walk.

Flanked by armed Praetorians, with many more staged about the peristyles, "Domina Augusta," he bowed, "I am afraid that the number of seats for the spectacle had been calculated precisely, and regret to inform you that there is no room for your additional guests," he nodded in indication of the ten Circassians in the belted black goatskin vests.

"I see," she said, smiling coldly. "You peel away in layers so we can't run off."

"Only for the spectacle, Domina," the tribune shrugged in practiced friendliness. "They may wait in the court here. With us."

Maesa paused, giving the man a withering look. "They shall be here when I return, tribune."

"But of course, Domina Augusta," he replied, feigning surprise.

She turned to her Circassians and barked in their guttural speech. The men shifted uncomfortably, though none raised a complaint. They merely looked at her as one, lifting their bearded chins. Then she turned back to the tribune with a look as if at something warm and wet she picked up in the gutter on her shoe; and the man smiled and bowed and moved aside with his guardsmen still gripping the hilts of their sheathed swords.

At the edge of the court they passed through another corridor, frescoed this time, to emerge onto the mid-point of the upper-level peristyle surrounding the stadium garden, where an appreciative gasp escaped the guests at the sight stretching before them.

Water filled the hundred yard-long space almost up to the tops of the arches of its ground-floor arcade, turning it into a kind of strangely-enclosed lake with a depth of roughly fifteen feet. Due to its original creation by cutting back the slope and building up the other three sides of the hill – with the Claudian Aqueduct going to ground at its northeastern end where the great cisterns stretched along the side of the hill – the work of the palace slaves in flooding the garden consisted of bricking up the stairwells leading down to the ground-floor arcaded peristyle and the little summer dining room beneath the huge apsed semi-dome, and then the re-routing and extending of a myriad of aqueduct pipes.

The water pressure in the Polyphemus fountain of the great first court was rendered a bit low, and the statuary ranked before the pink Chian marble half-columns projecting from the piers of the garden's ground-floor arcade would need re-polishing, but the 'stadium' was quite a spectacle – an aquatic

307

wonder-world with the tops of its trees emerging from the surface of the water and two small islands rising out of it at either end. Not to mention the waterwheel at its southwestern end to which Elagabalus sometimes had one of his courtiers tied and dunked up and down again, calling them his river Ixions.

The huge apsed semi-dome was strung with a thirty-by-forty foot purple banner with the black aerolith of Elagabal superimposed with a golden Imperial Eagle. The banner rippled softly, aflame in the sunset. Beneath it, atop the raised marble dais stood the Emperor himself, in a purple and gold silk robe, his jewel-bedecked hands upraised in faux priestly greeting.

"Grandmother!" he shouted, "Salutas!"

The hundreds of guests filing in stopped their conversations, and Julia Maesa's lips formed a cold smile, her hawk-eyes lifeless. "Hail Caesar," she replied, her voice echoing across the water.

"Ah," Elagabalus playfully shook his fist, as if at some inside joke between them. And then, "Hi Alee!" he waved cheerfully.

Alexianus slowly raised his hand from his side and opened his fingers.

"And who's that with you?" Elagabalus continued, smiling his brilliant white-teeth smile, his voice ringing through the peristyles. "Avidius Lepidus!" he slapped his thigh. "Well, well, what a pleasant surprise."

Lepidus grit his teeth and did not reply.

"I think we have a venue here this evening that you might like," the Emperor spread his hands in indication of the flooded space, over which the guests were gathering at the balustrades at the sighting of a hippopotamus, which had just risen to the surface of the water and blown two shoots of spray, and was currently resubmerging. "So why don't you all come around and join me on the dais."

The peristyle was fifteen feet wide, and seating for hundreds had been established around it, with more drinks and appetizers being served by a myriad of slaves in Egyptianate dress. A small wind and string orchestra began playing in the peristyle beside the apse; and the guests resumed their jovial discourses as they filed in and around and began jostling for front-row positions.

"We're not seriously going to sit up there with him," Lepidus growled.

"It's too late now," Maesa replied, none too excited about it herself. "We have to brass it out."

"Woman, I simply do not understand you . . . ." the old bestiarius began but the Empress cut him off.

"Put some steel in your backbone, boy. If we leave now he wins. And he'll have us killed for sure." She gripped Lepidus' arm with her small boney fingers. "We don't know that he's killed Mannix. What we do know is that he's waiting for us to make a false move. We've nothing left to do but wait him out."

Alexianus, listening to it all and looking desperately for another sighting of the hippo, felt a giddy excitement welling up inside that made his mouth dry. His mother Mamaea put her arms around his chest. She looked at her own mother with fear but followed, as she always had, as Julia Maesa began to walk, erect and proud, down the passage between the seats and the red-black-and-orange-frescoed back wall against which a Praetorian Guardsmen with a lance and a plumed helmet stood every ten paces.

"Gods, all these bastards," said Lepidus, looking with disgust at the Senators in their white togas with the red-striped borders, strolling with their wives down the peristyle, the Equites and Patricians pulling class rank on each other over the seating; the hundreds of voices a low uproar channeled by the acoustics of the huge bandstand-like apse across the way. "They bitch and they whine and they claim to hate him and yet, with five hundred of them here, not one of them will lift a finger."

"You know how they are, old friend," Maesa nodded at a random greeting. "It's always someone else's job. And, besides, with a cohort of Praetorians here, there's almost a guardsmen for every guest," she smiled thinly.

As they turned the corner, Lepidus glanced through the heads of the people standing, sitting, laughing and drinking, out through the Parian marble columns of the portico across the aquatic scene of partially submerged trees with the two mock islands rising from the surface. At the far southwestern end, he could see grated caging emerging from the water line across the arches of the ground-floor arcade. No seats had been established in the peristyle atop it. The gradually filling crowd had now spotted two additional hippopotami, and stood pointing delightedly at the ponderous leviathans walking along the surface of the flooded garden as if on dry land.

"It seems our hope lies with Cassius Dio now," Lepidus said.

"Our hope lies where it always has, bestiarius," she replied. "In the grave." She raised her voice cheerfully. "Hail Crassus and the good lady Matidia."

"Domina Augusta," the couple bowed.

As they rounded the next corner of the peristyle and proceeded toward the Imperial Podium, Elagabalus stood facing their arrival with his hands on his hips and a dangerous smile on his face. The jewel-encrusted priestly robe seemed to increase his height, the belt cinching it emphasizing the breadth of his shoulders. The raised dais was still framed by four speckled green columns with gilded bases and gilt-bronze victories pirouetting from white-marble globes atop their gilded Ionic capitals. The shafts were strung between with fat drooping purple swathes of silk which matched the great banner hanging from the apse.

But it was the smell of the area as they neared it that gained their attention. The silver braziers smoked with costly incense rising in tendrils through the angled sunlight, adding a sickly-sweet tinge to the collective stink of the crude cast of courtiers milling about atop the leopard-skin rugs amidst the griffon-sculpted side tables with their platters of appetizers and flagons of wine – a combined reek of perfume and balsam-oil, of sardines, sweat and surfeit from a long day at the Amphitheater. Hierocles, still wearing his phallus-nosed carnival mask, simpered pondering them behind his Emperor with a finger between his lips.

Elagabalus, in the decadent regalia of his jewel-encrusted Phoenician robe, bowed flamboyantly as they emerged from beneath the roof of the peristyle where it broke at the mid-point of the longitudinal axis of the garden and forfeit its shelter to the huge apsed semi-dome. He made to kiss his grandmother Maesa's hand as she climbed the three steps onto the dais holding up her stola so as not to trip over its hem.

"Where is my daughter?" she said, not extending her hand.

The Emperor, ignoring the slight, "I'm afraid she's a bit under the weather," he replied, pursing his lips.

"Drunk, you mean," Maesa arched a flaxen gray eyebrow.

Elagabalus smiled wanly. "Well, grandmother . . . you know how she is."

"Doubtful she'd be that way tonight."

The Emperor clasped his hands together and nodded reassuringly. "I'm sure she'll join us for dinner."

"Where is Mannix?" Lepidus asked, lifting his chin.

"Ah," Elagabalus raised a finger. "The question of the day it seems. Thanks to you," he added, cocking his head, livid about the strike.

"Don't mix words with me, boy," Lepidus said.

"Watch your tongue, old man," Elagabalus squinted his eyes, already planning how the man would die.

Maesa took Lepidus' arm again, squeezing it; and the old bestiarius stayed silent.

The Emperor glanced around him at his courtiers and out at all of the guests, the last of whom were settling into their seats. All eyes were on him and he forcibly recovered himself. "Don't worry," he smiled, Hierocles giggling behind him, "Mannix will be joining us soon."

Lepidus felt hope leap in his breast despite himself. Julia Maesa kept a tight hold of his arm, her eyes on the guardsmen flanking the corners of the platform and lining the curve of the apse, the men standing at attention but facing them.

"Everybody back please," the Emperor raised his voice, clapping his braceleted hands like a school teacher at his

311

courtiers lingering about the dais drunk and squealing. "You too, I'm afraid," he cooed at Hierocles, who let out a soft whine and then smiled and kissed the top of his finger three times. The blond Carian then wheeled and bounded bouncing his golden locks down the back steps of the dais onto the rich expanse of Numidian orange marble pavement inset with large porphyry disks below the coffered curve of the banner-strung semi-dome, where more of his crass companions were already in various states of misbehavior and the dwarf was dancing atop one of the side tables. The original sculpture groups in their niches framed by pairs of outlandishly-speckled red and black marble columns had been replaced by lewd bronzes with copper genitalia, the prostitutes harassing the Praetorians beneath them, tugging at their leather skirt armor, one of them gyrating in a red-plumed helmet.

"Take a seat, if you please," Elagabalus bowed to Maesa and Lepidus, opening his hand in indication of the ram's-headed marble armchairs positioned across the dais. "Hello aunty," he smiled charmingly at Mamaea. "It's been too long."

The timid wiry-haired woman blinked and nodded and then, "Aleeeeeeeee!!!!" her nephew squealed, ruffling his cousin's sandy-blond hair. "You're growing like a weed!" He danced back shadow boxing playfully before the boy, tickling him with his punches while his grandmother looked on with a frown and cleared her throat and his aunt brought a fragile white hand to her forehead.

Forgiving by nature, Alexianus smiled despite himself, trying to work it out. Maybe Mannix was all right. Maybe it was all a misunderstanding. Maybe everything was all right. But the smell . . .

Elagabalus kissed him hard on the forehead and then turned and clapped his hands at the quietly practiced female servants in the same cheetah-skin tunics as his Nubian bodyguards, who were nowhere to be seen. "Wine," he cried, walking across the leopard skins in his gem-studded yellow shoes, "Women and song" he laughed. "Or something like that."

Maesa took charge of the seating, motioning for Alexianus to sit between Lepidus and her daughter, then seated herself on the other side of the old bestiarius. The girls in the cheetah skins came before them balancing trays laden with wine-filled goblets, others placing cut-glass bowls full of cheese and olives, and garlic-buttered bread crusts on the narrow side tables wedged between their chairs. The olives were large and green, smothered in oil and liberally sprinkled with the sun-dried seeds of fiery-hot Calabrian red peppers which made the wine, cooled by the airish spring evening – red and dry and smooth yet bitter – increasingly welcome.

As they settled in, Elagabalus gestured in indication of them, presenting them to the audience, who began to clap while he stood aside and beamed and then turned to the conductor of the small orchestra in the peristyle on the other side of the apse. With a raise of his hand the music stopped, and the Emperor took up his goblet. The columns of the peristyles flanking the apse glowed rose in the sunset, touched with random hangings of gold, their reflection wavering in the water below along with the volcanic orange cumulonimbus overhead and one of the hippopotami occasionally rising to blow.

After letting the atmosphere settle for a few seconds, his voice rang out across the colorfully rippling space. "We have the five hundred wealthiest people in Rome here this evening," he said. "And I'm sure my grandmother is glad to hear it," turning to Julia Maesa with a smile and a wink.

Polite laughter came from the audience, grunts and claps from his courtiers in the apse. Julia Maesa smiled humorlessly and the Emperor raised his hand, pleased at his own joke. "On a serious note. I know that many of you think that things have run amiss up here. And that we're all at each other's throats." He shook his head sincerely. "We are here this evening to show you that this is simply not the case."

Random scattered clapping came from the crowd.

"My mother has told me to inform you of her regret that she could not be on hand for the spectacle," Elagabalus continued. "We agreed to split the responsibility for the festivities. I, of course, am in charge of the show," he smiled.

"And my mother, the poor dear, is still in the banquet hall busily overseeing the preparations for tonight's grand repast."

Applause and more polite laughter.

"She wants it to be perfect, you see," Elagabalus nodded. "Because she feels the same way as I do." He turned and indicated his grandmother, aunt, and cousin Alexianus. "The same way we all do."

Silence fell across the space and a sneer crept across Maesa's face. The black back of a hippo wallowed up out of the water turned pink and gold by the sunset in the clouds overhead.

"The Severan family has seen its up's and down's. Like all families have," Elagabalus continued. "But we are still together. Still together on this dream. This dream a thousand years old." He spread his arms wide, " This dream . . . called Rome."

A few claps from the audience but mostly whoops from his courtiers in the apse, to whom Elagabalus turned his head adroitly, while pretending to pace and think, and gave them a rabid look with his grit and glaring teeth. Maesa smiled to herself. Hierocles flurried about the apse in his golden silk robe with the bouncing phallus nose and a finger to his lips.

"My ideas for a new Rome," the Emperor raised his voice. "A new way that Rome can solidify her dominion over the world," he lifted a finger in the old Augustan power gesture, "have met with resistance from all of you." He paused. "But I am here this evening to tell you that I understand."

The Senators, Patricians and Equites shifted in their seats. Some leaned forward slightly for a better look at Elagabalus' face. Humility was not the nineteen year-old's forte.

"I have felt . . . and I still feel," he nodded, "that the Sun God is a practicable solution for the religious confusion facing us in this age. This age of great change. This age of ours," he opened his hand.

The audience remained silent as he paused again.

"But I am willing to admit," he continued, "that perhaps I have not gone about this dream in the right way."

314

Some shifting in the seats, and low whispering amongst the five hundred aristocrats.

"And so, this evening," Elagabalus raised his voice, "I herewith announce my sincere desire to take your counsel on these issues. You, the Senate and the aristocracy of Rome. I propose to open the throne room to weekly meetings in which all of you will be able to take part and have a say." He raised his hand. "In order for us to work together toward a solution to this problem which threatens to destabilize the classes, and which has for years created disorder in the provinces."

A slow trickle of applause rippled across the water toward him and Elagabalus raised his finger in acknowledgement.

"The whole world will be different soon. The whole world will be relieved," he smiled. A smile that none of them could see was doll-like in its fixed intensity. With the audience still clapping, "I would like to propose a toast," the Emperor said. "A toast to my grandmother Julia Maesa. To my aunt Julia Mamaea. To my cousin Alexianus. And to my mother Julia Soaemias." He lifted his goblet. "A toast to the Severans. A toast to you all. A toast . . . to Rome."

XXXXIV

Cassius Dio bounced through the gate of the great Claudian Aqueduct cursing the traffic trailing back to the periphery; but moreover the mule he sequestered from the palace livery, which the surly groom informed him was all that was available. The ornery old bowlegged beast had jostled and jolted him along, seeming to pick only the hardest cobblestones, tossing its head and swishing its tail and braying the whole way. Once through the confusion of cheap jewelers, weavers and wool-sellers hailing him amidst the squeaking horns of Indian snakecharmers and the dust from the foot, hoof and cart traffic rising into the sunset like pink spray, Dio cut the ill-tempered beast across traffic onto the Via Praenestina into the 'Wolf's Den,' with its smell of the stockyards, of spices and dung.

By the time the old Senator jerked and kicked and cursed the mule into the Street of the Charioteers, past the chain-worked wooden slat gates closing for the day, his gout was flaring to the extent that, when he arrived at Milo's Tavern, he didn't attempt to dismount but simply leaned over and goaded the beast through the grimy open archway. The atmosphere inside was subdued, the disturbing memory of last-night's fight still heavy in the air. With his eclectic clientele of sleazy Patricians, burnt-out poets, cutthroats, one-armed gladiators and maimed bestiarii mostly heads-down over their cups, Milo looked up from his usual perch behind the counter. Before him sat Pompey the Kenyan charioteer.

"May the gods smile on all here," the Senator hailed.

A few grunts greeted him in return from the patrons, none of whom looked like the gods had smiled on them lately.

"No wives allowed, Dio," the barkeep said, frowning at the mule. "Or can't you read the sign," he nodded in indication of the placard outside designed to dissuade thirsty animal trainers from the stockyards from wandering in with their leopards.

"The old gout's acting up from all your rot-gut I've drunk," the Senator replied.

The mule shuddered and clopped its back hoof.

"And I'm not here to drink, but for a show of Roman honor. A friend in need is a friend indeed," Cassius Dio continued, "and Caius Marius Mannix is he."

Pompey turned on his stool. Paula the barmaid walked out of the kitchen to the smell of pork fat frying, wiping her hands on a towel.

"The gladiators Cordius and Tychicus made an announcement during the mid-day break at the Amphitheater," Dio raised his voice across the murky space, where it rang with senatorial authority off the crudely-frescoed walls lined with racks of horns and gouged with the autographs of old-time gladiators and bestiarii. "They said Mannix started the fight and stabbed Prixus in the back as he tried to walk away."

Milo squinted his eyes, and Pompey drained his cup.

"I'm looking for a few good men of courage and honor to accompany me to the Amphitheater and set the record straight," the Senator nodded.

"It won't help Mannix any," the barkeep shook his head.

"It might help us all plenty," Dio shot back.

"And get us all killed," Milo continued.

"Eutychianus is there," the Senator shook his head. "He's on our side. And, besides, it's a fine-looking evening and will get you out of this hole for a change. So who's with me?"

"I'll go," the charioteer stood.

Milo groaned, and pulled an amphora off the back racks. "A round on the house," he said. "And then we'll all go."

A cheer erupted from the tables, and the barkeep shook his head as he poured. "If we have to die tonight, might as well drink the good stuff."

"Don't mind if I do," Dio nodded. "Paula be a dear and bring me a cup. Make it a good pour, Milo. A good pour."

XXXXV

As Maesa, Mamaea and Alexianus drank the toast along with the five hundred aristocrats about the space, Lepidus – who has been considering the efficaciousness of throwing Elagabalus over the balustrade into the water – quaffed his second goblet in one go. It wouldn't help Mannix any and he knew that Hippos, though aggressive, were not carnivorous by nature. The Emperor would no doubt be pulled out by the Praetorians in time to watch them cut his throat.

"But enough of business on a night designed for pleasure to make amends," Elagabalus lowered his goblet and lifted his hand. "I also know that most of you think I'm a man of neither taste nor culture. Unlike my grandmother Maesa," he turned and indicated her, "and her sister, my great aunt Julia Domna, the honorable Septimius Severus' wife. But what I have for you tonight might just prove you wrong," he smiled his brilliant smile.

"Ladies and gentlemen, our focus this evening is Myth. And a particular favorite of mine. The story of Orpheus, the Thracian minstrel, perfecter of the lyre. Who, by his music and singing was not only able to tame wild beasts, but even draw rocks and trees from their places, and arrest rivers in their course."

"We will go through several key stages of his life," Elagabalus continued. "This child of the Sun and the Muse. Taught and given his lyre by Apollo himself, who had it made by Hermes out of a turtle shell."

He paused while the audience applauded, and then raised his hand to silence them. "The most difficult element was finding the right actor to play the part. And I've taken great pains in finding him," he smiled. "In the end the choice seemed obvious. A man you all know for his brilliance on the stage in

318

Rome under the patronage of my great aunt Domna and my grandmother Maesa, of whom he was a personal favorite. Ladies and gentlemen," he shouted, "a round of applause for my own honorable and esteemed Praetorian Prefect, Valerius Comazon Eutychianus!"

On the island at the northeastern end of the flooded garden, the ex-dancer suddenly appeared stumbling up from beneath the ground tripping over the hem of his white and gold gown fumbling a turtle-shell lyre amidst the delighted applause of the crowd. Julia Maesa went cold inside, her face an immovable mask fixed with its thin smile. As Elagabalus took his seat in the ram's headed marble armchair by her side, "The game goes on, MaeMae," he commented quietly, looking straight ahead and using the pet name by which he called her when he was a child and they used to play chess together on the terrace at Antioch. "Or did you think you could so easily cast me aside?"

"I commend you," Maesa replied. "Still an apt pupil," she turned her head and looked at him, "despite your choice of dress."

Elagabalus turned his own head to meet her gaze.

"It didn't work with the speech," she added. "Like all the rest," inclining her head in indication of his courtiers in the apse.

The Emperor's nostrils quivered slightly, and he forced a laugh.

"But did I not also teach you," she continued, "that it is he who laughs last . . . who wins?"

On the island below them, Eutychianus looked terrified. An oldish forty-five, he was only passable at the lyre, due to his career on the stage and his cross-training in the arts. But it would have to do; and he began plucking on cue, tripping and wincing around the lemon trees and golden broom, the scarlet poppies and oleander bushes planted haphazardly in the sand-trap. 'Fucking bastards!,' he screamed in his mind, but there was nothing left for him to do but hope that that old witch Maesa would somehow come through.

319

They took him at the Amphitheater after the discovery of the gold-cuirassed tribunes, one of whom exposed him before he died. Now Elagabalus had countered his order to protect the upper class seating and give the Mob room, and ordered a tremendous amount of pitch and flammable oil taken to the Amphitheater in case they moved.

"Standing . . . by my window," he began to sing in his liquor-rusty falsetto voice, ". . . breathing summer breeze . . . ." Suddenly a lion emerged from the same spot as he did and the crowd let out a gasp of surprise, lurching forward in their seats. Then another came out, both of them panting, overfed and lazy. Eutychianus, still singing, "saw a figure . . . floating . . ." tripped nervously around the side of a fake boulder away from them and the lions trotted following behind, swinging their haunches like two playful pups.

Part of the small contingent of beasts Elagabalus kept stalled in the little summer dining rooms around the low-lying third fountain court, the lions were tame as house cats; and he sometimes let them up on his dining couches during dessert in the banquet hall, or surprised his overnight guests by letting them into the rooms where they lay sleeping – once promoting the untimely demise by heart attack of an ambassador from Moesia. A lioness walked out next, and then a leopard. Then a beautiful black panther, its sleek muscles rippling in the golden light of evening.

"She asked me . . . if I . . . loved her," Eutychianus continued, his voice squeaking, terrified of the sluggish beasts and finding it harder to keep away from them. He climbed up on the boulder trying to seem nonchalant, "I said I didn't know . . . ." One of the lions came around behind him and licked his ankle and he screamed and dropped the lyre.

The crowd burst out laughing, most of them feeling more than a little effect from the wine they'd been drinking for the last hour. They didn't quite understand the situation. But as long as it wasn't them out there, why not enjoy the fun.

On the dais, Elagabalus roared heartily as well, clapping his braceleted hands. He leaned toward his grandmother and whispered, "All I ask is your support."

"Where is my daughter?"

"Hopefully putting her makeup on," he replied. "You will see her in the banquet hall. She has agreed to go along."

"What, did you give her Mannix?" Maesa raised an eyebrow.

Elagabalus' face hardened and his smile curled into a sneer as he stood. "She rejected him in the end."

He turned and gestured to the twenty odd prostitutes in the apse, who began moving on his cue into the peristyle behind the orchestra, where they proceeded down to its southwestern end and across the short axis above the flooded arcades blocked by grated caging. Buzzed and giggling, the girls had difficulty concealing their excitement. They stutter-stepped as they filed in line past the Parian columns, pushing and pinching each other.

Lepidus couldn't make out the exchange between Elagabalus and Maesa, but he knew there was nothing he could do now but wait. He poured another goblet of wine from the table by his side and watched Eutychianus' ridiculous antics with a resigned, irritated boredom, more interested in the hippos than the fat old lions. The dancer had tumbled off the rock and stumbled around it to run head on into the leopard, who playfully pounced its paws up on the terrified man, its claws catching in his gown.

The prostitutes disappeared in a stairwell on the opposite end of the peristyle, and Elagabalus, still standing, walked to the center of the dais and addressed the increasingly boisterous crowd. "As you can see, ladies and gentlemen. These ferocious beasts have been rendered quite harmless by the talents of 'valorous' Valerius."

More laughter and applause from the audience, slaves scurrying back and forth among them with flagons of wine.

"And now," Elagabalus continued, raising his hand, "for the second major stage in Orpheus' life – his journey with Jason and the Argonauts!

Cheers and clapping.

"Chiron told Jason that only with the aid of Orpheus would he be able to pass the island of the Sirens unscathed," the

Emperor continued. "As you may know, when ships passed them out to sea, the Sirens lured the unfortunate sailors to their island with beautiful songs. And then ate them!"

The Nubian bodyguards in their cheetah-skin tunics and white feather head dresses appeared on the island hustling a small skiff up out of the ground. They threw it down on the bank with two oars before disappearing back the way they came. Eutychianus stumbled shakily about the shore sweating profusely. The animals had lost interest in him and he kicked the lyre and stubbed his toe. "Cocksuckers!" he yelled at no one in particular, and the crowd split their sides.

Darkness was closing in, the last shades of rose slipping off the tops of the clouds now hovering like gigantic icebergs over the Alban Hills on the western horizon. Dozens of slaves were climbing atop the roof of the peristyle fixing and lighting phosphorescent torches in brackets which began to blacken the sky and illuminate the watery scene. One of them screamed as a patch of tiles came loose and he scrambled clawing desperately to hold on but the other tiles around him gave too and the audience gasped as he slid off the roof and fell forty feet down into a great splash in the water amidst a rain of terracotta.

With no way up he began to swim feverishly for the island rising from the flooded garden's southwestern end, bumping a random surfacing hippo as he did. The slave floundered desperately over its back startling and irritating the hippo, and the disgruntled creature's jaws parted in an audible groan and swung round in a rush of torch-lit foam to plunge their blunt stubby tusks into the man's body crunching through his clavicle and breaking his spinal cord. Worth less than the jewels on one of the Patrician women's hands who were excitedly watching him, the slave died with a gargling scream and Elagabalus, raising a finger, said, "These Nile hippopotami of mine are by no means the big, good-natured herbivores they seem. They're all bulls and quite aggressive. So you swimmers," he smiled and wagged his finger, "be careful."

His courtiers laughed obnoxiously, many of them now gathered at the balustrade of the peristyle flanking the apse. One of the old men in white face powder and hair nets vomited drunkenly over the side and a buzz of excitement emitted from the talkative crowd as they marveled at the limp white forearm of the dead slave disappearing in the watery vortex left by the submerging hippo.

"Back to business, ladies and gentlemen," the Emperor raised his hand. "The role of Jason was also a specially deliberated one. But in the end I believe I've found the right man. A veteran at the art of survival. A true hero in his own right. Without further ado, and with warm thanks to Avidius Lepidus, director of the Bestiarii School," he turned and gestured in indication of the sneering old trainer, "I bring you . . . not the Sun God but the Mob's God . . . I bring you Mannix the Myth!"

At their cue on the word 'myth,' the Nubian bodyguards forced the Bestiarius at spear-point up the ramp of the cramped, dripping low tunnel built before the garden was flooded of brick and pitch and leading from the third fountain court of the private wing to the mock island rising from the surface of the water where Eutychianus emerged.

The crowd let out another gasp, straining forward in their seats at the sight of Mannix, who wore only the short-skirt bottom half of his torn-off tunic held in place by his broad, black, bronze-studded leather belt. His dark wavy hair fell to his shoulders, his massive muscles glowing in the torchlight, the ruby and azure amulets winking on their cord around his throat. The stitches in his shoulder were ripped and frayed and blood, both dried and fresh, ran in streaks down his arm and over his pectoral. He looked up at the Imperial Podium, his eyesockets blackened with shadow.

"Give them Hell, boy!" Lepidus shouted, leaping up and raising his fist.

A Praetorian Guardsman stepped quickly up onto the dais behind them and Maesa leaned forward and took hold of the back of Lepidus' robe, pulling him gently into his seat.

"If you act up again," Elagabalus smiled softly at them, "you die. Immediately."

323

Alexianus, hearing it and seeing Mannix, knew now that nothing was all right. His lips parted and his mother took his hand.

Confused by the surprise, the audience gradually applauded. Mannix killing Prixus was the talk of the town, and they all knew of his incarceration. But they could only guess at the situation and, anyway, at least it was not them out there.

The prostitutes began emerging from a like tunnel on the island at the southern end near the flooded grating across the ground floor peristyle, naked save slender thongs. The flutes and trumpets of the orchestra started, and the girls began clattering their castanets and rustling their tambourines, warming into a torchlit bacchanalian scene.

"By the brass balls of Jupiter, am I glad to see you!" Eutychianus shouted at Mannix, his golden slippers tip-toeing hurriedly through the yawning lions.

"Get in, asshole," Mannix hissed, already preparing to shove off.

"What, in that thing?!" the ex-prefect shouted. "Have you seen those giant fucking water-pigs out there?"

"There are two make-lions coming up that tunnel," Mannix pointed. "They should be here . . . right about now," he said, as one of the big cats slunk out with a growl.

Eutychianus was in the boat in three leaps just as the lion, attracted by his nimble feet, charged across the sand. The Bestiarius heaved the boat and himself out and the cat hit the water right behind with a guttural roar and a raucous splash silvered in the phosphorescent torches.

Missing Mannix by inches, the lion snarled and jumped and thrust itself backwards out of the irritating, unfamiliar element.

"What the fuck are we supposed to do out here?" Eutychianus yelled, as the Bestiarius climbed in with a groan and took up one of the oars lying in the bottom of the boat.

"You mean you don't know?" Mannix grinned, turning his head to the side. "You're the actor. Don't you have the script?"

"Hell No," the dancer kicked the side of the boat, "Ouch! Fucking Cocksuckers!"

"We're supposed to stay alive," Mannix growled back. "So why don't you start by taking this sword here and throwing it through your little friend up there," he jerked his head in indication of the Imperial Podium, where Elagabalus, in a flamboyant flutter of purple and gold, had just leaned out over the balustrade and tossed a laurel-leaf crown down into the boat.

Eutychianus watched it hit the deck and saw the sword Mannix indicated and another, along with two harpoons affixed with lengths of chain bolted to the sides of the boat. "He's not my friend," he shouted back. "The little Cocksucker!"

"We have one coming up in front," the Bestiarius said.

"Have one what?!" the ex-prefect yelled, looking frantically around him.

"A giant water-pig," Mannix replied, pulling up the oar and placing it softly down and rising nimbly and quietly off the bench and taking up one of the chained harpoons. "Take up that oar and turn us away from him."

The Bestiarius watched the hippo, its nostrils and eyes glistening, its huge bulk just visible above the surface. He hoped it wouldn't take an interest in them but Eutychianus rocked the boat, clattering and knocking its sides with the oar. Irritated by the noise and the taste of the dead slave's blood, the hippo thrust its head and shoulders up out of the water opening its mouth and crashing its blunt tusks down over the gunwale. Its weight tipped the front of the skiff under water and it thrashed its head to the side, splintering several planks and knocking Mannix off balance onto his knees, from which the Bestiarius plunged the chained harpoon into the base of its skull.

The two-ton beast lurched in a watery bellow, letting go of its hold and jerking the harpoon out of Mannix's hands as it trailed away. Grabbing the chain and jerking it back, "Row, asshole!" he yelled at Eutychianus, who was frantically slapping at the water with his oar to little avail.

The prostitutes on their island had begun performing their role as Sirens, clustering about the shore singing, oblivious to the water level slowly rising from the valve-worked aqueduct pipes which had been pouring from beneath the flooded ground-floor arcades since before the guests arrived. Mannix and Eutychianus changed places, the Bestiarius rowing in the back of the boat while the dancer balanced himself with one knee on the bench at the prow. Heartened by the presence of the Bestiarius and not one to be upstaged by a pack of two-bit whores, Eutychianus couldn't resist picking up the laurel-leaf crown and adjusting it atop his head. He placed his hands to his breast and raised his voice to the crowd. "O Nymphs and Graces . . . with your girdles loose . . ."

Meanwhile slaves atop the short southwestern axis of the peristyle were pulling up the grated caging blocking the arcades below with ropes, which they tied off around the columns of the upper story. Within seconds, shouts of surprise came from the audience at the sight of the long slithery shadows emerging across the surface of the water where the phosphorescent torchlight rippled over their wet ridged backs.

XXXXVI

The statue-lined arcades of the Flavian Amphitheater towered overhead with a witching glow as the motley crew from Milo's arrived in the square below. Clustered about their ass-mounted leader with the crusty old barkeep and the Kenyan charioteer, they came upon hundreds of Praetorians stationed around the stadium with lances at the ready. The guardsmen stared up at the arcades through which the noise of the Mob ebbed and flowed like the roar of the surf in a gigantic conch shell. Wooden barricades had been established across many of the ground-floor arches, and burning cauldrons of pitch flickered in the square. Cassius Dio goaded the mule up to the triumphal arch with its quadriga-mount marking the Senatorial entrance and Milo and Pompey helped the gout-ridden epicure off the beast while he grunted and winced.

An officer in charge of the contingent of soldiers guarding the arch walked toward them shaking his head and waving them back. "No more inside tonight."

The wily old Senator dropped his jowls and looked up bugging his eyes and assuming his best drunk-act. Pulling his coin purse out of the neck of his toga, "Cassius Dio's the name," he slurred. "It's written on my chair in the senatorial seating," nodding through the arch. "Here for the main event, my friends and I," he threw his pudgy arm out in indication of the group of barflies. "Heard there were some girls on hand tonight."

The marble-jawed officer shook his head again. "Full house I'm afraid, sir."

"What's that you say, boy-o?" Dio reeled slightly, squinting his eyes.

"No more spectators allowed inside, Senator," the officer replied patiently, for Cassius Dio's was no little name.

"Now . . . Who . . . says?"

"The Emperor, sir. The gates are closed for the evening."

"The Emperor?" Dio squinted his eyes. "Well," he jerked his jowls up, "we were just up . . . over there . . . at the Emperor's party," he pointed his chubby finger, reeling as he tried to get his bearings. Giving it up, he turned back to the officer, "And I told him that . . . his spectacle . . . was a two-bit-third-rate-flop-with-no-girls," he hiccupped.

"I have my orders, sir," the Praetorian continued to shake his head.

"And he says to me, he says, 'then Dio my boy," the Senator continued rambling as if he hadn't heard, "go on down to the Arena for the real stuff." He raised a chubby finger, "But be sure . . . to make it back . . . by suppertime." Burp. "So here we are," he smiled, his head shaking palsiedly. "You have your orders," hiccup, "and I have mine."

"Senator," the leather-cuirassed Praetorian sighed, pained at the sight and looking around him taking in the broken-down barflies, "you can understand my position."

"Well of course I can understand it, my boy," Dio nodded sincerely, bugging out his eyes and fumbling in his coin purse. "And that is why" he winked, "I am here to," hiccup, "give a little something toward its cause." He pulled out a handful of silver sesterces, dropping several. Pretending to bend down and try to pick them up, he poured the rest clattering across the travertine pavement. While he wavered back and forth trying to pick up the coins and seeming as if about to fall, the red-caped officer licked his lips and looked around him.

"Here, sir," the man bent down impatiently, "let me help you."

"Good lad," Dio burped, rising up and stumbling on, past the confused guardsmen flanking the towering shadow-clad arch, its inward surfaces flickering faintly with the witching glow emitting from the building's interior. "And see to my mule there," he shouted back over his shoulder, waving at Milo, Pompey and the barflies to follow along.

328

Hurrying quickly beneath the stucco-decorated arcades hovering massively above – cursing the gout which made his ankles, knees and hips feel as if they had broken glass ground into their joints – Dio and crew passed between lateral arches blocked by the heavy wooden grating which kept the general public from accessing the senatorial seating. With carved-ivory ticketing for the upper class – minus some of the bigger-name Senators like Dio himself, whose names were inscribed on their platform precincts – the Flavian Amphitheater's seventy-six numbered entrances corresponded with a system of radiating ramps and staircases, lateral passageways and ambulatory corridors, all of which belay its architect's successful answer to the problem of handling a vast and potentially unruly crowd. The overall result was that the Plebs and the Mob had no access to the upper class seating, and their movement could be further controlled by heavy wooden barriers. As it was this night.

Through the diamond-patterned wedges of the latticed wooden grating they could see the torchlit throngs clotting the 'under the stands' world accessed by the Plebians – the world of fortune tellers, astrologers, fruit and amulet sellers, sausage and sweetmeat vendors. Fat prostitutes sat on stools munching feed apples with their thighs spread before the tattered curtains drawn across the wedge-shaped chambers terracing the stands above. With the noise of the crowd inside increasing with every step, the wincing Senator led the group straight up the ramp and out the 'vomitoria' where the ovoid bowl of the Amphitheater exploded around them and the insane screaming of fifty-five thousand people hit them like a wave in the chest.

The barflies' jaws dropped as they looked out across the Arena where a forest of uprooted trees rose from the dirt and sand masking their supports. High above, the myriad of huge silver stars dangled from the catwalks, twisting and twinkling in the multi-colored light of the incense torches in their brackets staged between the statuary niches around the horizontal band dividing the Patrician from the Plebian seating. Among the trees carefully defoliated to increase visibility, the Nordic teenagers were getting the worst of it from the baboons, one of the nubile young blonds trying to climb a tree, her smock ripped off, little white hands bloody as they clawed at the bark. The Mob howled their support as one of the screeching satyr-like creatures swung quickly from limb to limb, its erect banana-shaped penis bouncing as it dropped to grab and bend, and start humping away at her rabidly.

Sweating and blinking, Dio continued on down the ambulatory aisle backing the first concentric ring of Senatorial seating making straight for the Ringmaster's box beside the huge empty blackened-bronze one of the Emperor. Apicius sat slumped and brooding in his chair in his white-marble cubicle, his blue satin wizard's robe disheveled, his face in a sneer. Depressed about the lie spread by Cordius and Tychicus at the mid-day break, and resentful that the main event had been taken out of his hands, he'd given in to a fit of melancholy and been drinking heavily, the large pitcher of wine almost empty on the little round table by his side.

Placing his pudgy forearms on the back ledge of the small box, "Call off this child's play," Cassius Dio shouted over the roar, gesturing in disgust out at the primates raping the Nordic girls. "We're here to set the record straight."

"Good luck!," the Ringmaster yelled back, knowing which record he meant right away. "Look at this fucking place," he stomped his feet, thrusting his hand from its yawning sleeve in indication of the hundreds of Praetorians lining the marbled wall backing the Patrician seating, their caped and helmeted shadows leaping in the torchlight beneath the temple-fronted statuary niches.

"Where is Eutychianus?" Dio shouted back.

"They got him," Apicius shook his head.

"What do you mean they got him?!"

"Trouble Apicius?" a tribune interrupted, pacing nonchalantly down the ambulatory aisle with his hands clasping a baton behind his back.

The Ringmaster looked over his other shoulder and then turned back shaking his head dejectedly.

"Anything I can do for you, Senator?" the tribune continued, raising an eyebrow.

And Cassius Dio smiled at the sight of Ariostomachus.

XXXXVII

Mannix was watching the water for hippos and glancing back at the island from which he emerged, where the make lions had started fighting with the tame beasts, one of them biting viciously at the panther's back while the black cat hissed wildly and snapped at the air. He felt water tickling his feet through the straps of his boot sandals and looked down to notice that the boat had been perforated to create a slow leak.

"And life . . . so uncongenial without you," sang Eutychianus over the Sirens, whose single high-pitched wailing notes were suddenly interrupted by a piercing scream as one of the girls turned to see a fifteen-foot crocodile crawling up the bank behind them. They all turned and spread out and began backing away from it, pointing at it and shouting up at the Imperial Podium that there had been a terrible mistake.

Elagabalus rose from his chair with his goblet in hand, and raised his voice over the crowd's excited uproar. "Ladies and gentlemen," he shouted. "As you can see, the talents of Orpheus have again succeeded, rendering these Sirens quite harmless. They've obviously lost their appetite," he gestured down at their island near the grated caging, where a small flotilla of the long glistening shapes were gathering. "But, friends, I'm afraid it's eat or be eaten at the banquet tonight," he smiled, turning a look on his grandmother Julia Maesa and then back to face the crowd, "and perhaps my crocodiles, not having eaten for a week, can help them get the hang of it." He gestured to the conductor of the orchestra, and the flutes, lyres and water organ began to play.

As the prostitutes scurried frantically around the island, one of the girls tripped, falling on her thonged bottom directly in front of another of the nervous saurians curiously testing the bank. Scrambling to get to her feet, she came face to face with

331

its long grinning snout emerging from the water. The quick movement agitated the croc and its snake eyes blinked and it shot at the fallen girl as she shrieked, its jaws snapping closed around her head.

Mannix, watching grimly, knew what would happen next. Crocodiles, like any wild animals, were nervous of people. But when the killing started, they became frenzied. With a whiplash of its huge torso, the croc tore the girl's head off.

Eutychianus squeaked, seeing the plume of purple blood spurt from the neck and the decapitated body convulse on the bank, the sandy buttocks thrashing up and down and then quivering into lifelessness.

"I've got worse news for you," the Bestiarius shouted. "We're leaking."

Eutychianus looked down. "Cocksuckers!" he lost his head, pointing and ranting at the crowd and the Imperial Podium. "You're all no-good dirty money-grubbing Cocksuckers!"

Elagabalus' courtiers choked with laughter and sprayed wine out of their mouths. Their Emperor's own laughter seemed more forced, his eyes continually watching Mannix. It was all Lepidus could do to remain in his seat and keep from diving in to help his former charge. But he knew that, even if he made it, the boat wasn't big enough and he'd simply get them all killed. Alexianus sat mystified, feeling the pull of the frantic naked girls and the shouting of the crowd, while his mother Mamaea had lowered her head and placed a hand to her brow. Julia Maesa remained impassive, her eyes dead-center, not watching, her mind continuously calculating.

"What do we do?! . . . what do we do now?!" Eutychianus yelled.

"Pick up that harpoon and get ready to use it," Mannix said, torn between trying to save the girls and using what time the boat had left afloat to get back to the other island, where they still had a decent chance to fight their way through the cats. The panther and one of the tame lions were already dead; one of the make lions wounded. He looked back and forth trying to decide and then cursed and started rowing toward the southwestern island. Staged lower in elevation than the one with the lions, the panicking prostitutes were splashing in ankle-deep water around its shrinking bank with three big crocs already claiming its still-dry center space.

Eutychianus, seeing their chance to potentially escape, looked frantically back at him. "Why are we going over there!?" he screamed.

"Whore's have hearts too," the Bestiarius growled. "And, besides, I might get a free lay off of one of them when all of this is through."

"A FREE LAY!!??" the dancer ripped at his pasty white curls. "The hell with those sluts; let's get out of here!"

"Pick up that harpoon," Mannix said, just as two tons of enraged hippopotamus reared out of the water throwing its massive block of head smashing into the skiff knocking Eutychianus over the side in a splash and a scream and then came bellowing back crashing its top-jaw over the already-splintered gunwale, from where it started worrying the small vessel like a terrier shaking a rat. Thrown forward and almost overboard, the Bestiarius felt two grunting shoots of the animal's stinking exhale hit him in the face and he lunged back to his bleeding knees, jerked a harpoon into his hands by its chain and plunged it through the hippo's eye socket into its brain.

The crowd was on their feet now, transfixed by the bloody scene. The men were shouting at each new development, the women's mouths parted in sneers of fascination. On the island rising from the northeastern end, the tame lions and the leopard were fighting with the make lions, and the panther lay dead on its side with a streak of black blood painting the sandy bank.

Out of their minds with terror, two of the prostitutes had stumbled out into the water and started to swim frantically for the skiff, Mannix yelling "NO!" and waving them back. Eutychianus had his arms and one of his legs over the side and the Bestiarius leaned over with his good arm, grabbed him around his flabby torso and rolled him in.

"Cocksuckers!" the dancer screamed, coughing and choking and picking up the chained harpoon awash in the water flooding the boat.

The whores on the island were tripping and stumbling over each other as they looked back and forth, turning their heads in every direction, their screams much more than merely ones of facing death, but rather of insane, teeth-gnashing primal terror at the glistening, wet-stinking, mindless hissing horrors beginning to thrash their huge tails with excitement at the blood smell and snap at one another when they got too close. Sensing the fright and the helplessness of the humanoids, a twenty footer that must have weighed over a ton scurried toward the group on its clumsy waddling legs and the girls scattered like birds, their oiled breasts bouncing pitifully. One of them went down in a tail swipe and two crocs grabbed her with jaw snaps audible above her cries.

The orchestra played on, the gurgling of the organ and the lilting of the flutes; and, of the two girls still swimming toward Mannix and Eutychianus, one suddenly disappeared with a cut-off shriek under the glinting black surface of the water. Then she shot back up again like a buoy, screaming and flailing her fists as the white bellies flashed around her and the water churned to bloody foam. Sliding up in the boat, the Bestiarius plunged downward with his harpoon through a hard crust of green calcinate armor sending a blurp of oily black out of the croc's back, while Eutychianus stabbed desperately at another one. Mannix grabbed the girl by an arm and pulled her limp body up the side of the boat, only to find that both of her legs were gone below the waist. He squinted in pain and let the high-breasted Siren slip away.

On the island, the downed girl suddenly sat up screaming gutturally with an arm off at the shoulder; and one of the crocs behind had her limp-wristed hand dangling out the side of its mouth with a cheap costume-jewelry ring winking on one of its fingers. Tossing its head, the saurian snapped and swallowed it down, the other one still locked onto the girl's legs biting and shaking repetitively as she screamed and shifted on the sand.

334

Suddenly one of the Senators' wives leapt up thrashing her head from side to side and began drumming her fists on the back of the white toga in front of her screaming "KILL! KILL! KILL!" The impotent drooling helpless man who had voted against Aurelius' campaigns forty years before squealed and pulled his head into the fleshy folds of his neck like a turtle as the lady's husband tried to pull her back. With the woman kicking her feet and tearing at her hair, and the Plebians shouting and standing, only some of the connoisseurs in the front row remained calm, commenting on the girls' figures and the behavior of the crocs.

On the Imperial Podium, Elagabalus dropped his goblet of wine, spilling its dregs across a leopard-skin rug. He stood and walked slowly to the balustrade. Watching Mannix choose the whores made the fear tickle his gut. For he knew without a doubt that he would not have tried to save the slaves; yet buried deep down, he felt a flicker of something inside of him that would have liked to have been the kind of man who would.

Eutychianus screamed as two hands slapped down on the ledge of the skiff and the other prostitute who swam out clawed choking and gasping and scrambling to get in the boat. Mannix grabbed her by the hair and pulled her up with Eutychianus hefting her by a thigh. As she collapsed on the deck between, she looked up at the Bestiarius with her faintly oriental eyes; and he recognized the pitiful eastern prostitute from two nights before. But just then a fifteen-foot leviathan reared sideways out of the water and crashed down over the boat snapping its jaws from side to side.

With the girl's screaming muffled beneath the croc's stinking belly, the Bestiarius stuck it in quick jabs, Eutychianus following suit from the other side, screaming mindlessly all the while. The boat was finished, but they were almost to the shore; and Mannix, with one hand on the harpoon stuck in the side of the croc's jaw, shifted carefully down to the deck and grabbed one of the swords. He flipped it, catching the grip, and thrust the blade deep into the saurian's head going for its pea-sized brain. The beast whiplashed its torso violently, knocking him five feet over the side onto the bank, then curled crazily in its death throes, its six-foot tail rising like a hugely erecting phallus. Then it flipped off the side of the half-sunken boat, Eutychianus and the girl stumbling and splashing out of the skiff around the thrashing beast, lunging and pulling each other to the shrinking shore.

"The swords!," Mannix yelled, leaping up and running with high knees back into the water. Stomping his boot sandal down on the saurian's back, he ripped the blade out of its quivering head. "Here!" he shouted, tossing the sword back to Eutychianus on the bank.

Glinting in the torchlight, the dancer took the weapon in his trembling hands, watching the slow advance of horrible toothy smiles and slithering calcinate armor with the bodies of mutilated prostitutes being drug and shaken behind. The low, flat island was almost completely submerged, only a patch of sand on its center still dry. Four of the remaining girls, driven out of their minds, sprinted splashing through the crocodiles from the other side. One went down and the other three dashed screaming past the ex-prefect into the water where they began swimming frantically for the opposite island, one diving straight into the erupting mouth a hippopotamus floating in approach, excited by the hysterical noise. The hippo blasted the girl backward, her buttocks and legs flailing two feet above the surface as it slammed its tusks shut.

Mannix was pulling and jerking the ruined boat ashore, yelling with the pain in his shoulder. When he got it to the shallows, he grabbed the other sword from the deck and began hacking the chains off the harpoons, tossing the first one that came loose to the girl. As he turned back to start on the second one, another Hippo charged the wreck and he stabbed wildly at its snout, driving it back in a bellow of spray and rage.

Pulling the remainder of the skiff ashore, he saw the fallen prostitute claw at the flooding sand as a croc took her leg off at the knee. She scrambled upward into a jerky crawl and another one hit her from the side, its jaws snapping down around her little torso, cutting off her scream and sending a gout of red hurling from her mouth. Eutychianus was dancing backward before one of the hissing saurians; the eastern prostitute crying and jabbing at another one with the harpoon.

The crowd was out of control, one of the Patrician women digging furrows in her cheeks with her manicured fingernails; the Praetorians brandishing lances at a group of fistfighting Plebians. The two swimming girls had reached the northeastern island. Collapsing and coughing up water on the shore, they were promptly mauled by the make lions, crazed by the sweet scent of blood from their wounds.

On the southwestern island, the Bestiarius rushed splashing to the fray with the harpoon in one hand and the sword in his other. Hurdling through the space between Eutychianus and the girl with the two crocodiles throwing their heads toward him, he jammed the harpoon through the back of one, pinning it; then cut back and hacked a wedge through the head of the other, leaving the saurians tail-thrashing on the sand. "Throw me the harpoon!" he yelled at the girl, while Eutychianus stabbed at the dying crocs.

From the peristyle above the caged arcades, a woman suddenly appeared holding a torch in an elegant black dress that hugged her neck and left her long arms bare. The audience gasped with surprise as "Caius!" Julia Soaemias shouted, throwing the torch cartwheeling out to fall on the island amidst the hissing and scurrying of three agitated crocodiles, one of which wiggled off into the water.

Elagabalus stood gripping the balustrade watching open-mouthed as the Bestiarius took up the torch and began driving the remaining saurians back. His mother was in obvious pain, limping stiffly from his earlier kicking as she walked down the peristyle. Julia Maesa, Mamaea, Alexianus and Lepidus were at the balustrade as well, the old trainer roaring advice. The Praetorians around the dais looked back and forth at each other and their Emperor, waiting for an order, unsure of what to do.

Holding off the crocodiles while the nine remaining prostitutes scattered around the side of the island behind him, Mannix hacked the tail off one with the sword, then thrust the torch into the jaws of another coming at him from the side. He jogged back to the floating skiff and tried desperately to light the random parts of its wood that were still dry. Glancing at the other island set higher in the water, "We have to swim for it," he shouted, the crocs gradually gaining courage again on the opposite bank.

"I can't swim!" one of the prostitute's shrieked.

Mannix looked at her and blinked. "Get that robe off, Eutychianus."

The dancer ripped his wet soiled gown off and stood in his golden slippers in his loincloth with his flabby gut and his still-lithe legs.

"You'll have to bring up the rear," Mannix said. "And swim holding this torch out of the water."

Eutychianus took the torch with trembling hands. He gulped and nodded and became brave for the first time in his life. The Bestiarius quickly gathered the swords and harpoons and dropped them into the infrequently burning wreck of the boat, then shoved it carefully into the water. He went to his knees and said, "Hold on to my shoulders and lay on my back," to the girl who couldn't swim. "Everybody follow behind."

Pushing the skiff into the water, the pitiful little prostitute clawed at his shoulder with shaking hands, Mannix gritting his teeth against her nails digging into the bear-wound. They set off and he began frog-kicking with everything he had left, shoving the burning skiff ahead and using his hands to swim in the same movement. The remaining prostitutes started in after them, Eutychianus wading in petrified with the torch behind.

The crowd was shouting for them to make it the forty yards to the other island, Julia Soaemias trailing a shaking hand along the rail of the balustrade, limping, watching, and praying to a god she hoped might listen. The orchestra had stopped playing and the musicians stood shouting along with the crowd lining the opposite side. Making her way behind them, she stepped up onto the dais, where her son met her large almond eyes. He grit his teeth and then wheeled back to the scene, his face trembling, his nostrils quivering.

Weak with exhaustion, the girl's weight threatened to sink Mannix, choking as he took in water, his hair singed by the fire dying on the boat. The eastern prostitute swam by his side, glancing at him and helping push the skiff. Half-way to the island, the fat black back of a hippo surfaced behind them in the midst of the swimming girls, all of them screaming and splashing as they tried to get away from it. As the huge water beast thrashed around, Eutychianus, choking and spitting, kicked himself forward with his springy legs and thrust the torch into its eyes, making its pig-like ears tweak as it sank away.

On the island, one of the make lions was fighting with the tame lioness; the wounded one in a snarling stand-off with the leopard. As the boat began to scrape along the shore, their attention was distracted by the humans and they hissed and roared, the sound drowned out by the crowd noise. With Eutychianus and the girls clawing frantically to get on the bank, "Stay behind me!" Mannix yelled, grabbing the harpoons and the sword.

The flames were dowsed on the wreck and so was the dancer's torch. Thrusting one of the harpoons in the sand, the Bestiarius came slowly out of the water in a crouch with the other one in his right hand and the sword in his left. Throwing caution to the winds, he rushed forward and hurled the harpoon through the ribcage of the wounded make lion biting at the tame lioness, and then dropped the sword and switched the other harpoon to his side, turning and planting his foot in time to receive the charge of the second one. He dropped to his knees as the maneater leapt, lunging forward running the harpoon through its chest. The cat bowled over him as it died, baptizing him in a warm font of arterial blood.

Eutychianus helped pull him out from under the shuddering flanks of the beast, the nine remaining prostitutes crawling ashore. One of them screamed as a crocodile shot out of the water, clamped down on her legs and pulled her backward thrashing its head from side to side. Mannix rolled desperately for the sword and threw himself toward the girl, meeting her eyes for a split-second as she was pulled off the ledge of the steep bank. He roared and turned back stalking the remaining cats, but they were retreating, and scurrying away from him, the panther and one of the tame male lions dead, the lioness mortally wounded. The other tame male limped behind the fake boulder casting growling glances back at him, the leopard biting and clawing at the grate closing the mouth of the tunnel.

Realizing that it was over, Mannix stopped short and stood heaving great gasps. The girls were huddled crying on the bank and the crowd had gone deathly silent, watching his every movement. His chest and torso glistening blackly with the lion's blood, he walked over and pulled the harpoon out of the big cat and limped slowly toward the whores. "Move away from the bank," he said with a trembling voice.

Eutychianus stood sodden and drained in his sagging loincloth and his golden slippers. He stared at the Bestiarius with wildly blinking eyes. And then he collapsed to his knees and began weeping.

Over the thunderstruck silence of the crowd, with even Elagabalus' courtiers and the Praetorians staring open-mouthed down at the island littered with the carcasses of the panther and the three lions and the mauled bodies of the two dead girls who swam to it before – the phosphorescent torchlight casting it all in a haunting sylvan glow – a whispered rustling noise traveled across the top of the peristyles. Curious as it came, indecipherable and barely perceptible and then the first syllables came into earshot like the sound of a million branches swaying in the wind as – at the Amphitheater half a mile away as the crow flies – fifty-five thousand voices chanted "Mann . . . nixxx . . . Mann . . . nixxx . . . Mann . . . nixxx . . . Mann . . . nixx . . . ."

Elagabalus was in shock. Gone was the false bravado, gone the doll-like stare. His lip parted wetly and his eyes look drugged.

Julia Soaemias raised her throaty voice to the silent crowd, in awe as they listened to the rush of distant sound. "It was always a custom of Septimius Severus . . . the founder of the Severan line and a great sportsman himself . . . to invite the victors of his spectacles to his banquets." She turned and looked at her son.

340

The Emperor returned her gaze speechlessly, and then turned his head and looked down at the island where the Bestiarius stood shakily with his hand placed gently atop the head of a crying whore. Mannix looked up and met his eyes and Elagabalus blinked and swallowed. "I salute you," he shouted forcefully, his voice cracking. "You and yours shall indeed dine with us tonight. At my table. By my side."

XXXXVIII

Filing out of the stadium garden drained and drawn, the hundreds of guests made their way back through the second court toward the banquet hall. Streaming into the first court over the flowers littering its peristyle – rustling through them ankle-deep in some places – their ears were all cocked to the sound swirling above the marbled walls. A sound like rain though, despite the veins of lightning dancing in the darkened clouds, none fell.

The violets, lilies and hyacinths flooding the court spilled through the thirty-foot granite columns into the vast dining hall, their odor mingling with the Indian perfumes burning in bronze braziers throughout the space, where the hundreds of subdued Senators and anxious aristocrats began taking up places on the pearl-inlayed silver dining couches. The couches had golden coverlets of Persian weave, their fabric glittering in the lamplight along with the silver dust strewn across the floor of red and green porphyry disks inset within Numidian orange squares. The warm light glowed across the marbles of the walls, bathing their super-imposed columns of purple, pink and peach, and glimmering a hundred feet above across the enormous leather tarpaulin bulging beneath the ceiling. Audible over the low murmuring of the guests, the pleasant gurgling of the twin scalloped fountains in the small courts flanking the hall was punctuated by the delicate sound of spring thunder, which occasionally rumbled above.

"Our next move?" Lepidus asked, walking beside Julia Maesa down the center of the hall over the silver dust and the trampled lilies.

"We don't have one," she smiled thinly. "He's doing it all for us." Followed by Mamaea and the ten disarmed Circassians, "Things are looking up."

342

"We have Caius to thank for that," the trainer said, holding Alexianus by the hand as they walked passing a row of short thick palms staged in gilt-bronze pots.

"And, I think, Julia Soaemias," Maesa nodded at a group of addled aristocrats. Choosing dining couches near enough for her to keep a close watch on the apse, the aquiline old Empress in the gold and green shawled stola officiated over her retinue's placings. "And it sounds as if friend Dio made it to the Amphitheater after all."

"Elagabalus could still have Mannix killed," Lepidus stated grimly, taking a seat with Alexianus on one of the couches.

"It's too late for that now," Maesa shook her head. "He's just tried. And failed."

The low tables were laden with lobsters, crayfish, oysters and squills, and Lepidus took up an urn and poured a silver cup full of wine. Handing it to Maesa, he poured another for Julia Mamaea, and a splash for Alexianus befitting his size. Looking out across the hundreds of Patricians jostling nervously in the huge room, the men's togas disheveled, the women's curls fallen loose, "He certainly didn't win them with the spectacle," he said, pouring for himself.

"No," Maesa agreed. "And it subverted his speech."

As the dining couches gradually filled, Alexianus began to discern a disconcerting smell – a phenomonic compost of greed, fear and nervous tension. His senses untarnished by the years, over the plethora of odoriferous emanations from the food and the burning perfumes, the boy's nostrils dilated with the scent of the violence-sated Patricians. Murmuring uncomfortably among themselves, their nerves frayed by the spectacle, a fanfare of trumpets turned their heads and their voices trickled down to silence.

The Emperor entered the hall with his court and the five hundred rose to receive him. Alexianus could see that his cousin was shaken. Flanked by Praetorians, the nineteen year-old walked ashen-faced down the center of the room toward the fifty-foot apse at its head. Young dancers scurried backwards before him scattering gold dust in his path and Hierocles and the

343

old faced-powdered queens – the occultists, gutless gladiators and base-born profligates – traipsed drunkenly in his wake.

After hurriedly traversing the floor, Elagabalus climbed the steps onto the dais filling the apse. Draped haphazardly with tiger-skins and staged with candles in thin bronze stands and marble-topped tables heaped with exotic viands, ten of his Nubian bodyguards stood along the concave back wall paneled in cipollino and alabaster. His raucous courtiers stumbled up behind him and began plopping down upon the huge cushions stuffed with rabbit-fur and partridge feathers.

"We welcome all here to our grand repast," the Emperor announced, his voice unnaturally loud to cover its shaking. "My mother will join us shortly to give the toast. But please begin. The first courses are on the tables," he gestured out at the buffets heaped with the viscera of mullets, with flamingo-brains, partridge-eggs and thrush-brains; also the heads of parrots, pheasants and peacocks creatively arrayed. Clapping his hands, a line of gold-smocked slaves filed through the doors flanking the apse. Bearing trays full of camels' heels and nightingales' tongues, as well as coxcombs pulled from the living birds, the slaves moved among the couches proffering them to the guests.

The beards of the mullets were so large that they were brought out separately and announced by chimes, and the casseroles and bowls, urns and wine vessels were all of chased silver, their exquisite craftsmanship commissioned sixty years before by the Antonines. There were mountains of cress and parsley, pickled beans and fenugreek. Of the variety of wines, some were honeyed, some seasoned with mastic; there was also rose-wine fragranced with pulverized pine cones.

The small wind and string ensemble arrived and took up places in a corner of the room, where they began a pleasant, calmative tune strangely subverted by the ominous pulsing of lightning in the windows ninety feet above.

Lepidus leaned toward Maesa. Breaking a crust of bread and scooping up some of the creamed chickpea dip filling a cured camel's heel, "And if he decides to take the boy on his way down?" he said in her ear, so that Alexianus could not hear.

Spearing a wild sow's udder with a silver prong, "Look closely at those guardsmen," she nodded in indication of the leather-cuirassed Praetorians lining the walls.

Shifty-eyed and sweating, they seemed confused; the old trainer registered it as he chewed.

"My Circassians can take those Nubians with or without weapons," Maesa continued, angling her head at the ten walrus-mustachioed men in the black goatskin vests on the couches behind her, who were eating very little and drinking none. Then a cymbal crash made her turn. The wily old Empress watched the tribune in the white leather headgear slow to a fast walk down the center aisle after running through the granite monoliths directly into a gold-smocked slave, knocking the youth down and spilling the contents of his tray.

Quickly covering the forty yards of space, the tribune ascended the three steps of the dais where Elagabalus stood to meet him, sneering wildly.

"Sire, the Mob is chanting Mannix's name at the Amphitheater!"

"We heard them, you ass; the question is why?!"

"Cassius Dio interrupted the main event!" the tribune breathlessly replied. "He gave a speech with witnesses saying that Mannix was innocent in the killing of Prixus."

"How did he get through?!" the Emperor bared his teeth.

"He must have bribed the tribunes!"

"Mutinous bastards! Take half the cohort and bring me their heads," Elagabalus spit. "And Dio's too!"

"But Sire, the Mob is on the move!"

"The fires! Start the fires!" the Emperor shouted, shoving the man. "Blockade the exits and set fire to the blasted place!"

Hierocles giggled as the tribune tripped and fell and Elagabalus wheeled and struck him, knocking his phallus-nosed carnival mask off. The curly-blond went down in a squeal and a flutter of golden silk; and the tribune leapt up and ran out one of the side doors flanking the apse.

The hall had fallen deathly still.

Elagabalus looked up slowly with the realization that the guests had stopped their conversations and heard his every word. His eyelids fluttered and his nostrils quivered and his face contorted with rage. "I said eat!" he screamed.

Trying to recover his composure, he cleared his throat and lowered his voice and opened his trembling hand. "Please," he added, looking down.

Alexianus noticed a sudden shift in the scent of the room. As the first pincers of panic began to nibble at the edges of the atmosphere with the mention of fire and the Mob on the move, a sickly-sweet secretion began to permeate through the body oil and stale perfume. The sandy blond boy in the green felt tunic would later recall the smell on the battlefield, though in this instance it was devoid of the reassuring tang of leather and sweat, and made the more disturbing by its feminine element.

His mother Julia Mamaea sat pale as a Luna marble statue by his side. She took his hand, irritating him though he wasn't sure why. Fascinated by the tension, and tasting copper coins in his mouth, the thirteen year-old watched his cousin suddenly shift on the dais. A flicker of candlelight across his purple-and-gold-silk robe, Elagabalus' head rose and his lips parted and he jerked as if struck in the chest by an invisible blow.

The musical ensemble stopped their playing, the lyres trickling into discordancy, the flutes trailing off. Lightning whitened the windows ninety feet above and Alexianus and Mamaea, Lepidus and Maesa and the five hundred aristocrats, turned to see Julia Soaemias standing in her full-length black dress in the entrance portico of granite columns. Mannix stood by her side, washed and bandaged. He wore a deep burgundy robe embroidered with saffron which had belonged to Septimius Severus. The robe was belted at the waist and open over his muscled chest. Eutychianus and the girls were with them as well, also washed and dressed – the prostitutes from Soaemias' own closet.

She took the Bestiarius by the arm, their eyes fixed on the dais as they started down the center aisle of the room.

Elagabalus watched them come, watched them as if two ghosts returned from the shadows of a marbled bedchamber on an autumn afternoon. His pupils grew huge and piercing-green against the whites, and the nineteen year-old sensed something from the pair for the first time in his life. Something that he had always missed and which had left a gaping hole in his breast the day he wandered into that room after playing in the sun-lemoned grass outside and hearing a disconcerting sound emitting from its gloom.

Unable to hold their stare, his eyes flickered to his grandmother only to meet her own stare and those sickly thin lips creased with their sickly thin smile. The same smile she used to look up at him with when they played chess when he was a child and she had him under checkmate. The same smile which still gave him nightmares and that said as it always did, 'There is no way out . . . . You can scream and you can shout . . . . but it is too late now . . . .'

And Elagabalus was afraid. Like he always was. Afraid of Mannix and his mother, of grandmother MaeMae and of his kind. A fear that formerly attention from the Mob could assuage; but that now he realized only death truly could.

As Julia Soaemias neared the apse, she nodded at Omphale. Standing in the doorway of the small fountain court on the hall's left side, the faithful ornatrice motioned behind her and a line of cheetah skin-clad slave girls bearing silver pitchers flowed out and filed up the steps onto the dais, where they began serving the Emperor's lounging parasites. Soaemias stopped before her mother, and Maesa took her by the hands. Her daughter looked into her eyes, and then nodded and broke away.

Lepidus tearfully embraced Mannix, and Soaemias moved past them and kissed her sister and nephew Alexianus. She bent over the table and filled three cups with wine. Through the makeup on her face, the deep bruise along its side was apparent; and she continually glanced at the Bestiarius with her large almond eyes.

Phantoms of their former selves beneath the urn of a marble sea nymph, Soaemias handed him two of the cups, then

347

turned to face her son.   The long black dress elegantly emphasized her voluptuous form, flowing beautifully as she walked past philodendron stalks and fingered leaves over the floor of red and green porphyries, across the open space before the apse while the silence deepened in the hall.   In the rich burgundy robe which fell to the ankles of his black leather boot sandals, Mannix walked by her side and even the Emperor's crass courtiers grew quiet as the pair ascended the three steps to arrive atop the dais.

The five hundred aristocrats watched closely as Julia Soaemias nodded at Elagabalus, and Mannix handed him a cup. The Emperor reached slowly and took it with trembling fingers, staring at his mother as she turned to face the crowd. The black dress collared her thick smooth throat, Mannix's ruby and azure amulets winking in the candlelight where her breasts began to slope. Her mane of black hair was pulled up in a swirl atop her head, and delicate golden spiral chains dangled from the lobes of each of her ears. Above the elbow of one of her long honey-colored arms, an entwining golden snake bracelet glinted through the smoke rising in tendrils off the perfume braziers.

Raising her chin slightly over her thick throat, "This banquet is for Rome," she said.

She looked at Julia Maesa, who stood beside Lepidus, "And for you, mother," she nodded, her eyes moving slowly to Mamaea and Alexianus, with Eutychianus and the surviving prostitutes standing behind. "And you, sister," she nodded again. "And you, nephew," she smiled kindly.

She raised her cup and her family and the five hundred aristocrats – as well as Mannix and Elagabalus and the courtiers in the apse – all drank the toast. After they lowered their cups, Julia Soaemias turned her head to the side. "Perhaps my son has something to add."

With his eyes darting to and fro beneath their heavy languorous lids, the Emperor looked like a cornered rat. His green and black pupils moved from his mother to the Bestiarius, blinking rapidly.

Mannix returned his look impassively, with neither sympathy nor scorn; and Elagabalus swallowed, and turned his face away. "This man is," he hesitated. Clearing his throat, "This man is my . . ." he started again, his mouth open, his voice weak.

The hundreds of guests glanced at one another and shifted their slippered feet.

Elagabalus turned his head back to Mannix, who looked at him in volcanic shades of aquamarine.

"Heroes and villains are all the same, Varius," the Bestiarius repeated. "Their lives go straight to the mark."

Candlelight heliographed off of a swathe of the Emperor's purple-and-gold silk robe and the Senators and Equites leaned forward slightly, watching close.

"Can you go all the way?" Mannix asked quietly.

Elagabalus shifted again. His lips trembled and his nostrils quivered and he turned his head to the audience. "This man is the champion of my spectacle," he quickly stated. "I salute him." He raised his cup. "To Caius Marius Mannix . . ." he loudly proclaimed.

Then he turned his head to the woman in black, "and to my mother . . . Julia Soaemias."

The aristocrats paused, puzzled, and only gradually raised their cups to drink. But just then a collective gasp of surprise rolled across them as a section of the huge leather tarpaulin gave way. Falling loose to swoop ninety feet above the apse, a great rush of air fanned downward making the palm trees in the bronze pots sway. Forty yards wide, the massive leather tongue swung slowly backwards to curl and flap, causing the heaps of curls atop the women's heads to flatten.

Then, after a pause of frightened anticipation, something bizarre happened.

XLIX

With all five hundred heads looking up, at first they look liked butterflies – a billion red, white and pink butterflies – fluttering down through the shadows above into the glimmering lamplight bathing the marbled walls. Then the gasps of surprise turned to ones of delight as the distracted crowd recognized the loosened petals flittering off. Lightning flickered in the windows and thunder crackled across the sky; and the courtiers on the dais stared wide-eyed in wonder at the rose petals fluttering down around them.

Julia Soaemias watched them fall. Just as she had watched the hundreds of ox carts from the Imperial Estates throughout Latium; watched the bulbs they carried hoisted by the sackfull up the scaffolding behind the hall. Her orders assiduously followed, their stems thoroughly cut, a steady stream of roses funneled directly into the apse with cluster-patterns of lamplit petals trailing out over the guests like spray from a waterfall.

As their rich odor began to blanket that of the burning perfumes, the food and the nervy aristocrats, the oblivious courtiers on the dais shouted and clapped; all save Hierocles, who was pouting from Elagabalus' blow. Blinking tearfully and taking surly little sips of wine as the roses pattered softly on the tabletops around him, the curly blond Carian watched the dwarf begin to dance and hop about, scooping up stubby armfuls of the petals and throwing them up like snow. But suddenly one of the old face-powdered occultists dropped his silver cup. The cup clattered on a slab of marble paving not covered by a tiger-skin rug; and the sound drew Elagabalus' attention and he turned.

The man's head lolled back on his rabbit-fur cushion and the Emperor squinted his eyes as he watched his courtier's bloated form slide slowly downward to crumple on the floor, his yellow robe pulled up over his fish-white belly to reveal his flaccid thighs and sagging loins. The occultist's hair net came to rest on the edge of the couch, his fleshy white-powdered face with its little black beauty mark pointing upward. Then his thin pink lips peeled back and his mouth opened in a silent shout, and the drifting red petals began to fill his wine-dribbling mouth.

The dwarf abruptly doubled, and fell to his pudgy knees. All lips and nose and eyebrows and cheeks, his face screwed up like a Greek theater mask and he squealed like a pig. One of the large-organed profligates walked across the tiger skins laughing obnoxiously at him but then stopped short, as if hearing a strange noise. The base-born wavered once and then his eyes rolled and he dropped catching his chin on the corner of a marble tabletop slamming his teeth shut severing the tip of his tongue, his muted scream bursting crimson over a cut-glass bowl.

Elagabalus' lips parted as he watched the dwarf draw slowly up into a silent fetal curl.

"It's over Varius," Mannix said softly, the rose petals catching in his dark mass of hair.

The nineteen year-old turned his head and blinked at the Bestiarius, then turned back as another of his courtiers fell across a tabletop upsetting a bowl full of pears. The body rolled off the table to collapse on the floor and then the hemlock and the belladonna began to work on them all, another choking as he stood, only to spin and fall.

Captivated, nervous, wine-befuddled and unaware, the five hundred aristocrats were wandering absently about the hall, bumping gently into one another as they watched the florid phantasmagoria fluttering down overhead. Meanwhile on the dais, Elagabalus' eyes darted as the drugged astrologers, actors, dancers and charioteers suffocated in a flood of aromatic petals; Hierocles already buried up to his ears.

The Emperor looked up, open-mouthed, his piercing green pupils mirroring the hundreds of thousands of roses.

Roses en masse, roses alone; he lowered his head and he looked at his mother and he realized that she was their thorn.

"There is still time, Varius," Julia Soaemias said.

Her son licked his fear-dried lips and glanced out at the guests. Jostling his way through them, the tribune in the gold-corded white leather headgear rushed again over the forty yards of space. Seeing him come, Elagabalus grit his teeth and clinched his fist and swatted at a stream of rose petals drifting in front of his face.

"There's war at the Amphitheater, sire!" the tribune shouted as he arrived before the dais.

"And the fires?!" the Emperor yelled, descending the three steps and grabbing him by the armholes of his cuirass. "The cohort?!" he screamed.

"Most of the cohort revolted after Cassius Dio's speech," the man gasped, his face blackened with smoke, his cape stained. "And much of the Mob broke through!"

Elagabalus' nostrils quivered and he looked out at his grandmother, who stared back at him with her hawk-eyes and her thin smile.

"They're demanding Mannix!" the tribune continued.

"He's here!" the Emperor yelled, throwing a finger in indication of the Bestiarius standing on the dais.

The tribune saw Mannix and his eyes widened with fear.

Elagabalus gripped him harder. "Hold them in the square of the Amphitheater and I'll come and speak!"

"We're holding them in the Area Palatina!," the bewildered man replied. "It's too late!"

"What!?" the wild-eyed Emperor screamed, shaking him by the breastplate.

"The Mob!" shouted the tribune, "They're here!"

Over the silence which had suddenly fallen in the hall, the rushing sound became audible. A sound like rain, or wind through distant trees; lightning flared again in the windows and an Equestrian's wife screamed. Her husband chased after her as she scurried out through the thirty-foot granite monoliths and then the panic took hold of them all, the Praetorians sidestepping along the walls as the hundreds of aristocrats

352

began running frantically out of the hall, knocking over tables, tripping on the hems of their stolas and togas, slipping on the silver dust and falling in clouds of rose petals.

With Elagabalus and the tribune staring out in shock at the pandemonium, the Bestiarius slowly descended the steps of the dais, his boot sandals rustling through the pink white and red flood. Moving past the Emperor, he grabbed the tribune by the throat as he turned. The bully's eyes bulged as Mannix's fingers slowly collapsed his trachea, his hands clawing feverishly at the Bestiarius' leather wrist band.

"Remember that farmer you killed this morning?" Mannix asked calmly, angling his head.

Shifting down into a squat, he threw his forearm upward between the tribune's legs, the man's scream no more than a high-pitched whistle as he fell helplessly across the Bestiarius' shoulders. Grimacing with the strain, Mannix stood and jostled and pressed the big tribune over his head. His arms shaking with the weight, he turned to the side and met eyes with Elagabalus. Then he drove the tribune headfirst onto the marble pavement. The body flipped once like a fish, and the purple-red brain blood welled up syrupy and stark against the white leather of his headgear.

"Shall we stop it now?" Mannix nodded at Elagabalus, "Together?"

The Emperor glanced at his bodyguards. The Nubians stood knee-deep in the roses continuing to fall, watching, their eyes as white as their feathered head dresses. Two of the magicians were gagging and clawing at an alabaster panel on the apse wall. The bodyguards looked back and forth between Elagabalus and the Bestiarius and Julia Maesa's ten massive Circassians moving slowly into the space before the dais. Then one of them slinked off down the steps and the rest began to follow, slipping through the side doors flanking the apse.

Elagabalus looked out in search of the Praetorians formerly lining the walls, only to find that the guardsmen were also gone. He turned his head to his mother, the petals frosting her shoulders and hair and the slope of her full breasts in the long black dress with Mannix's ruby and azure amulets winking on their leather thong. Turning back to watch the last of the Senators, Patricians and Equites pushing and trampling each other to get out of the hall, the Emperor's body finally relaxed. His face emptied and his eyes returned to those of a doll's.

In his purple and gold priestly robe, for a moment the Scythian glitter returned and the bacchic vacuity bathed his form. "They've come to me," he smiled. "The people," he nodded, the rose petals falling all around. "They've come to us," he turned to the Bestiarius. "Just as it should be."

Mannix opened his hand in indication of the granite-columned entryway and Elagabalus raised his chin. The nineteen year-old looked at him for a moment and then turned and set off, the Bestiarius turning with him and Julia Soaemias descending the rose-flooded steps holding up the hem of her dress to follow. Lepidus and Maesa, Mamaea and Alexianus and the ten Circassians brought up the rear, with Eutychianus and the remaining prostitutes trailing along fearfully.

The group moved out through the Egyptian granite monoliths beneath the Numidian peristyle into the freshness of the night leaving the smell of incense, rich food and roses behind. In the open space of the first fountain court, they could hear the rushing sound much louder now, though still muffled by the looming surge of the public wing. His silk robe whispering as he walked, Elagabalus strode straight across the court backlit by the yellow lamplight filtering through the columns of the banquet hall.

The torches had been extinguished around the peristyle, and the square was bathed in a pale blue pallor. Frightened serving slaves huddled watching from the shadows. As the Imperial Family passed the Polyphemus fountain, lightning veined the sky and a clatter of Praetorian guardsmen running down the opposite column line punctuated the atmosphere of siege blanketing the Palatine.

Bottlenecked beneath the peristyle at the northern end of the court, hundreds of frightened Senators and Equites were being herded through the throne room's rear doors. As Elagabalus and Mannix approached, the Patricians parted and the Praetorians moved, but without bowing before their

Emperor. And they moved slowly, looking to Julia Maesa for a sign; but the aquiline old Empress shook her head.

Entering the throne room through one of the side doors flanking its apse, Alexianus noticed the sickly-sweet smell, but moreso now, without the confusion of incense and food, and devoid of ventilated air. As he followed the group across the huge porphyry disks insetting the orange and green-speckled squares, the thirteen year-old found himself avoiding his mother's hand. Straying from Lepidus and Maesa as well, Alexianus could feel the presence of the Praetorians, and begin to discern their stares. His eyes wandered with contempt through the terrified aristocrats to the small side door connecting the throne room with the lararium, the chapel where the Imperial Genius was kept.

The hastily-arranged lamplight flickered across the white togas and stolas and the shins of the twelve-foot metallic-green Bekhen-stone statues, then gradually faded out in the huge projecting niches in which they stood, leaving the deeply-marbled wall-space above clad in the darkness descending from the hundred and twenty-foot barrel vault. As Elagabalus and Mannix neared the twenty-foot portal of the building, lightning brightened the huge bronze-latticed windows on the front and back walls, and illuminated the smaller sculptures framed in rectangular insets above the richly-decorated stringcourse.

"Open the doors," the Emperor nodded to the Praetorians standing in a group arguing before the portal.

Again the hesitation and the wavering stares.

"You heard him," Mannix said.

Elagabalus turned and looked amiably at the Bestiarius. "Well, I suppose it's finally time to test this . . . Mythology of the Mob," he said.

Sickened and depressed, the Bestiarius squinted his eyes and shook his head.

L

As the Praetorians pulled the huge bronze doors slowly open, the sound and the fury rushed in tangibly as wind and almost bowled them over. Mannix stepped forward into the deafening roar and the nineteen year-old followed, their robes rustling in the storm of noise. Over the caped backs and the plumed helmets of the Praetorians jogging to and fro along the raised portico – out through its Carystian-green columns – an infernal panorama spread before them.

Twelve feet below, in the Area Palatina spreading from the base of the colonnaded porch, tens of thousands of people were barely held at bay by the spears of the guardsmen. Seething like the line of the surf in a storm, only the myriads of screaming faces in the front rows were visible in the hellish glow cast by the torches burning in brackets on the back wall of the portico. The stairstep ends of the hundred yard-long porch had been blockaded with hastily-erected flaming barricades. Their conflagrations further blackened the shifting shapes of the throngs packing the square, where many of the Mob in their frenzy were being thrown forward onto the wall of Praetorian spears.

The dead lay trampled across the white marble pavement along with scores of guardsmen crushed against the base of the portico by random surges in the mindless human wave that stretched back like a plague of dark rippling insects. Dozens of them dangled from the huge plinthed statues of emperors decorating the square, and hundreds of them hung from the Arch of Domitian spanning the Clivus Victoriae leading up to the palace from the Forum. Thousands of them choked the cypress-lined street, some seeking footholds in the precinct walls of the unfinished Elagaballium. Clutching at one another's legs, they climbed the derelict arcades marking a flank of the old Palace of Tiberius, and crawled like cockroaches across the roof of the Temple of Jupiter Stator.

But it was as much the sound of the Mob as their sight which struck terror. For all of them were screaming . . . "MANN...IXX! . . . MANN...IXX! . . . . . . MANN...IXX! . . . . . . MANN...IXX! . . . ."

Rocks and firebrands sailed forward out of the darkness to impact the façade wall of the public wing beneath the portico, Elagabalus ducking as one of the homemade incendiaries glanced exploding off a Carystian column. The Bestiarius moved impatiently through the torchlit confusion, cuffing one of the Praetorians who bumped him. Arriving to stand between two of the columns at the ledge of the platform, several improvisational missiles barely missed him before a collective sound of awe escaped from the front ranks pressing the portico.

As their recognition of him spread, the furor of the Mob gradually ebbed. A serpentine retreat like the surfline in withdrawal; their chanting came to a stop and their pushing trailed off. Subdued by the sight of their hero, a hush descended, and the smoke-blackened Praetorians on the ground turned their heads.

Julia Soaemias stood watching from the portal of the throne room with tears in her eyes as their son walked forward to stand by his father's side. From the rear, both of them in their long robes seemed painfully similar, despite the Bestiarius' shoulder-length wavy hair. Her mother, sister and Lepidus stood watching behind her; the harrowed aristocrats listening intently through the open doors. Eutychianus and the surviving prostitutes grouped together beside the massive marble molding framing the twenty-foot portal.

Thunder crackled across overhead and, in the strange pause which followed, the nineteen year-old licked his fear-dried lips and affected his customary smile. "Behold . . . the Myth!" he shouted, throwing his arm out flamboyantly to the side, where the Bestiarius stood staring at the Mob with black coals in his eyes.

The fires burning half a mile away at the Flavian Amphitheater pulsed redly in the night sky, and the constellations turned imperceptibly above breaks in the clouds.

"Well, here he is!" Elagabalus yelled, opening both arms. "I have delivered him to you!"

The Praetorian Guardsmen had stopped moving and begun to align along the wall beneath the portico, their eyes shifting, their swords drawn.

"Is this not what you came for?!" the Emperor's voice broke as he raised it. "Is not this your savior?!"

A slight murmur rippled across the Mob; a disgruntled, herd-like noise. Angered and embarrassed by their lack of response, Elagabalus' face changed.

"Did he pay for your banquets?!" he shouted, flecks of saliva caught in the torchlight as they flew from his mouth. "Was it he who floated you in wine?!"

Mannix glanced aside and noticed tears welling in the nineteen year-old's eyes.

"Did he sponsor your beloved spectacles?!" he continued. And then he paused, as if for breath, and brought a fist up to his chest. "He's just a man!" Elagabalus yelled, forcibly recovering himself. "Just . . . one . . . man!" his voice rang out across the throngs.

After another pause and still no response from the Mob, the Emperor turned his face to Mannix as if to ask for help. Finding none, he grit his teeth and threw it back to the thousands packing the square. "What did I teach you?!" he shouted.

But the Mob no longer cared.

"I am the Sun of New Rome . . ." he started, trying for the old smile and the flourish of his arms. "I am . . . Alpha Number One!"

He waited again for something that did not come.

"The Sen . . . the Senate are slaves in Togas and the Patri . . . the Patricians and Equites a Joke!"

The silence dug in like claws; nothing but the crackling of the flaming barricades at the ends of the portico and the whispering of the wind in the cypress trees flanking the Clivus Victoriae.

"I am the . . ." Elagabalus began again, his face empty, his voice weak. "I am the . . . son . . ." he said, and then stopped. He turned his face back to Mannix and the tears ran down his cheeks.

Subdued and confused, the crowd stared mutely as their Emperor faltered. Then, sitting astride his donkey rising from their midst, Cassius Dio shouted . . . "MYTH!"

The word cracked the silence like a rock thrown through glass and, as the chanting started, Elagabalus smiled tearfully at the Bestiarius. "I am the son of New Rome," he said.

"Heroes and villains are all the same," Mannix shook his head. "It was all I could give you."

"Their lives go straight to the mark," the Emperor nodded as the thousands of voices locked.

"MYTH! . . . . . . MYTH! . . . . . . MYTH! . . . ." their forearms hammering, fists clenched, "MYTH! . . . . MYTH! . . . . . . MYTH!"

Held back originally on the advice of Cassius Dio, Ariostomachus and his tribunes began moving up through the chanting Mob toward the portico. Watching them come, Elagabalus smiled. And then his body jerked wildly as it took the first knife.

Mannix wheeled in his burgundy robe. Blinded by the torchlight, he saw only the shapes of the Praetorian Guardsmen shifting stealthily behind and – out of the corner of his eye – the glint of the golden dagger Elagabalus was alacritously producing from the folds of his silk robe. Slashing out at the nearest guard, the Emperor lunged off in a flurry of purple and gold.

"The Genius!" he yelled, as he took another blow. His head thrown to the side like an animal snarling at the pain, he ran straight into his mother.

Julia Soaemias did not scream. But for a second, everyone, even the Praetorians, froze.

Staring in shock, Elagabalus' lips parted, and he looked into his mother's large almond eyes to find her staring back at him with all of her heart. Then a glancing blow hit him from the side and he spun off, thrusting past Lepidus, Maesa and Mamaea into the throne room.

Too fast for the surprised Circassians, the powerful youth flattened two of them and scattered a group of hapless Equites as he sprinted frantically through the flickering lamplight toward the door of the lararium, his robe fluttering like wings behind. The guardsmen rushed after him, the Circassians arriving a second too late as Elagabalus slammed the door shut and bolted it from the inside.

While the Praetorians hammered ineffectually on the small blackened-bronze door with the butts of their swords, Lepidus helped Julia Maesa off the floor. "Are you hurt, old girl?"

"Come on," the Empress snarled, throwing the shawl back over her stola and hurrying toward the door.

Amidst the confusion and the shouting aristocrats, Julia Mamaea suddenly screamed "Alexianus!" Her hands flew to her wiry hair and she looked desperately from side to side, "Where is he?!" she cried.

Ariostomachus and his tribunes had reached the portico outside. With the guardsmen in the square holding the chanting Mob at bay, the tribunes rushed to the stairstep ends and began breaking through the flaming barricades. As they flowed up onto the portico and began to pour through the door of the throne room, two of them stopped at the ledge of the platform and lifted Cassius Dio off his mule.

"Pull me, boys! Pull me!," the portly old Senator yelled, his burgundy boots kicking at the saddle of the braying ass as the straining officers hefted him beneath the armpits.

Shoved back by the guardsmen on the ground – their voices drowned in the chanting – Milo, Pompey and the tavern barflies were cheering and waving at Mannix. Walking slowly down the platform with his head lowered and a hand on his hip and his massive slope of trapezius muscle bunched up in the burgundy robe, the Bestiarius stopped and extended his other arm and placed his hand against a column of the portico. The surviving prostitutes crouched a few yards down on the opposite side of the portal in a huddled group with their backs turned and Eutychianus knelt in their midst like a dice player ready to shoot.

Limping across the portico wincing with his gout, "Are you all right, boy?" Cassius Dio shouted.

The Bestiarius slowly turned his head and looked at him.

"You'll get a chapter in my history for this, Mannix," the warty old Senator said. And then he blinked as he registered the Bestiarius' expression. "So be it," Dio nodded, "I understand." He placed a liver-splotched hand on Mannix's shoulder and then limped quickly through the portal of the throne room.

Inside, several big Praetorians were running across the floor with pickaxes. Their boot sandals driving hard on the marble paving, they knocked down two aristocrats and never missed a step. Taking charge beneath the huge-vaulted gloom, Ariostomachus ordered his men to form a line and keep the Patricians back. Their confidence had returned and some of the Senators and Equites were calling for wine.

As the Praetorians arrived at the lararium door, the other guardsmen parted and the men began swinging their pickaxes into the bronze. Under their rabid hacks the bolt was smashed and, within seconds, the door kicked open. Julia Maesa entered immediately behind the Praetorians, her hawk eyes thirsty, barking at the big men to let her through.

A small, sacrosanct space, the chapel walls were frescoed in rectangular fields of rich red, black and yellow, the panels inset with scenes from the battles of Octavian. A fabulously-speckled marble altar stood at the back, on a white Luna step above the multi-colored mosaic of the floor. On the single shelf behind it, the lamp had been lit with the aromatic oil, its smell pungent in the low-ceilinged space. Beside the small golden chalice in which it burned, the little silver statue of the female victory with the eagle and the snake wavered in the smoke of the liquid flames. After establishing that the only thing missing was the ceremonial knife, Maesa's eyes moved to what they had already seen.

At the foot of a bust of Augustus on a slender four-foot plinth set against a side wall near the altar, Elagabalus lay in a confusion of purple and gold silk with a verdigris slipper sticking out. A bright glistening swathe of crimson bloodspray across the saffron-yellow panel of a third-style fresco painting marked the severing of an arterial vein, the blood dripping downward in hundreds of tiny rivulets from its arc. His bloody handprints showed stark as red leaves against the pristine white marble of the pedestal, four fingertip streaks trailing downward in a last loosening grasp of death.

Maesa's eyes followed the pool of her grandson's blood as it spread. Flowing slowly across the tiny mosaic tesserae of the floor, pinking the whites and blackening the reds, the blood purpled the yellows and greened the blues as it moved toward a heavy black-and-gold brocade beneath which two little leather boots protruded. The aquiline old Empress squinted her eyes as she watched the crimson tide break around the toe caps of the little leather boots. Then her gaze moved slowly above them to the rich velvet curtain used to screen the altar when the ceremonies were through. Walking slowly across the mosaic floor, she reached out and quickly drew back the brocade.

The sandy blond boy in the green felt tunic looked wild-eyed from side to side for a way of escape. His nostrils flared with the blood, the aromatic oil and his grandmother's old woman smell, and his eyes saw nothing but big men in red capes. As his grandmother smoothed his hair, wetted two fingers with her cracked gray tongue and wiped the speckles of blood from his face, Alexianus could still feel the death contractions of his cousin trembling through the blade.

Maesa swatted his hand, and the thirteen year-old dropped the gore-clad silver ceremonial knife. The knife clanked loudly on the mosaic floor and his grandmother turned and nodded at Ariostomachus, who had just ducked into the room minding the plume of his helmet beneath the low door. Glancing at the heap of purple and gold silk with the blood spreading obscenely, the new Praetorian Prefect thrust forth his fist and shouted, "Hail Caesar!" and the guardsmen in the room bowed with their hands sweeping the floor.

362

"Take your men out and return with my daughter Mamaea," Maesa commanded.

"Domina Augusta," the prefect nodded, and then left; the guardsmen following after him. In a moment he returned with Julia Mamaea, one hand in her hair, the other over her mouth.

As she rushed forward to embrace her son, her mother asked, "Where is Julia Soaemias?"

Mamaea shook her head, "I do not know," her hands on Alexianus' face, "we were separated," she said.

Maesa sneered, and turned her glance on Ariostomachus. "Have her found." Then she looked at her dead grandson on the ground. "And have the body drug through the Circus tomorrow and then the city streets."

Alexianus felt his sphincter tighten as the prefect bowed.

"Before you dispose of it," his grandmother added. Then she nodded at the door, "Very well," pulling his mother to her side and positioning him before her, "prepare the floor," she said to the Praetorian, Alexianus feeling her arthritic fingers like claws on his shoulders. "I shall count to fifty."

Ariostomachus saluted and walked out; and Julia Maesa began the count – silently and to herself – ignoring the warm liquid seeping through the slits in her dress sandals. Her daughter looked down and gave a small shriek; and Alexianus vomited upon seeing the huge blackish-red flood of his cousin's blood spreading slowly about their feet. Without losing the count, Maesa bent over and irritatedly wiped the pink flecks from the sides of her grandson's mouth.

Outside the lararium, Ariostomachus had aligned his tribunes to either side the door. As the women walked Alexianus out, the Praetorians shouted, "Hail Caesar!;" and the five hundred aristocrats in the throne room fell into a joyous uproar.

Her hawk-eyes wary, the wily old Empress looked out through the confusion of cheering Patricians with a frown. She knew that the Mob was what counted; and the infrequent lamplight reflecting in the marbled walls made it impossible to discern anything of her daughter Soaemias' whereabouts.

363

Standing with Lepidus near the lararium door, Cassius Dio shouted, "Hail, Augusta!" raising his hand and his voice, "Ave, Augustus Imperator!"

"Well, Dio," Maesa smiled thinly, "another chapter for your history."

"And a better one, Empress," he nodded at the boy standing glassy-eyed and trembling before her.

"Thanks to you," she said.

"And yet I think more thanks are due to a man standing out there," the jowly old Senator gestured through the portal of the throne room.

"Come along then," Julia Maesa said to him, "and we shall thank him." She looked at Lepidus and raised an eyebrow.

Ariostomachus ordered his tribunes to dress ranks across the floor. As the men smartly extended their line to the portal, their cuirasses heliographing in the lamplight, the hundreds of Senators and Equites flowed behind, jostling for positions and applauding primly as Maesa, Mamaea, Cassius Dio and Avidius Lepidus walked the thirteen year-old Emperor toward the door.

The newly-revised Imperial Family emerged onto the portico into the torchlight and Ariostomachus raised his voice, "Ave Augustus Imperator!"

Julia Maesa goaded Alexianus forth and the guardsmen on the ground turned.

"Hail Caesar! . . . Hail Caesar! . . . Hail Caesar!" the men cheered, lifting their spears each time.

But the Mob filling the square merely stared.

An awkward pause followed during which Julia Maesa adopted an expression of Olympian calm and the throngs, seeing her grandson, only murmured. Lightning blossomed in the clouds and, as the matriarch opened her mouth, a drunken tanner atop the Temple of Jupiter Stator sprayed wine out of his own and shouted, "Hail MANNIX!"

The Mob broke out in a cacophony of laughter.

The aquiline old Empress' thin lips bent slowly into a frown and Julia Mamaea brought a hand to her forehead. Her mother looked at Ariostomachus. The prefect wheeled to his tribunes and shouted the command and the hundred or more officers lining the back wall of the portico initiated the official proclamation.

Beating their shields in time with their swords . . . "Ave Augustus . . . Imperator!" they chanted, "Ave Augustus . . . Imperator!"

The Mob fell into a furious uproar. No longer laughing, they took it as a challenge and, within seconds, quickly crushed the traditional salute in a volume thrice-doubled from before as they chanted . . . "MANN....IXXX!! . . . MANN....IXXX!!! . . . MANN....IXXX!!!! . . . MANN....IXXX!!!!"

The Praetorians on the ground lost their heads, sidestepping over their own dead and brandishing their swords as the human wave began to roil. Eddying darkly around the Temple of Jupiter Stator and the huge plinthed statues of seated emperors, the pushing started and the thousands of unemployed began to seethe again like the stormy surf, the myriads of their front-row faces rabid in the torches. Then the panic started and the Patrician women began shrieking in the throne room and the tribunes shifted along back wall of the portico.

Mannix stood twenty yards down with his head still lowered and his hand posted on a column for support.

Lepidus and Cassius Dio broke off from the Imperial Family and began walking down the portico toward him. "They're calling you, son," the old trainer said gently over his shoulder.

The Bestiarius turned his head.

"Will you help us, Caius?" Dio nodded, sweat soaking through his toga. "There's a lad."

Mannix's aquamarine eyes ran across the face of the Senator who rode a donkey across town and then the surrogate father who taught him how to drown in blood, death and noise and call it sport. Then he looked at the boy in the green felt tunic.

Alexianus stared mesmerized as the Bestiarius slowly pushed off the column and began to shuffle toward him; the Mob intensifying their uproar . . . "MANNIX! . . . . MANNIX! . . . . MANNIX! . . . ."

Sickened by it all and shaking his head, "Do better than this," Mannix said as he approached.

Transfixed by the dark drawn face, Alexianus wanted to say, 'Take me away . . . Take me with you . . . Take me anywhere but here.' But the thirteen year-old could only nod.

"Do something better than this," the Bestiarius said again as he neared, angling his head in indication of the square, the guards, the Mob, the blood on the boy's boots and especially his grandmother. Then he stopped by his side and turned to face the Mob. And his look silenced the throngs.

"Enough of this," Mannix raised his deep exhausted voice. "Go home," he shook his head. "Go home."

Again the wind and the smell of the tendrils of smoke trailing off the smoldering barricades.

"Go home," the Bestiarius raised his hand slightly now, as if unwilling to say it again. "Go away."

After a long pause the Mob slowly started to obey, a vast herd-like shuffling beginning in the square.

"How does it feel to rule the world for a day?" Julia Maesa asked, as the thousands turned and began to walk away.

The Bestiarius' look made her blink. "Where is Soaemias?" he then asked.

"We don't know," she responded.

Mannix looked at her. "What do you mean you don't know?" Pushing past them, "Julia?!" he shouted, "Julia?!"

A tribune tried to block him and the man's helmet was knocked off.

"Julia!" he roared.

Finally there came a weak response. "Caius?"

Several yards to the left of the portal, Mannix saw the huddled troop of surviving prostitutes part. Eutychianus turned and looked at him with tears in his eyes and the Bestiarius rushed forward.

Julia Soaemias came into his view – strangely small, as if returned to little girl – sitting with her back to the wall in the middle of the group. "I love you," she smiled, and Mannix's eyes went wide as he saw Elagabalus' golden dagger stuck in her abdomen up to the hilt.

Some of the suspicious Mob turned back with his movement and started again to chant, "MYTH!!!! . . . . MYTH!!!! . . . . MYTH!!!! . . . ."

"Julia?" he said softly, kneeling down.

"I love you," she leaned forward. "It's such a gift."

"Don't talk," Mannix put his fingers to her lips. He sat beside her and took her gently in his arms. "Somebody get a doctor," he shouted.

"No doctor," Julia Soaemias shook her head. "Just you."

The Bestiarius gently positioned her against the massive marble molding framing the portal. Running his hand tenderly over her hair flecked with rose petals, "Gather around us, girls," he said to the prostitutes, who closed back in shielding them from view.

Cradling her tenderly in one arm, Mannix grabbed Eutychianus' robe desperately with his other hand, "Find a doctor!" he said, though he knew she was through.

The dancer stood up and rushed into the throne room.

Soaemias looked down at her hands holding her abdomen, her black dress glistening with blood. Then she looked up at Mannix, embarrassed. "I would have liked to have left you with something more," she smiled.

He saw the shape of her legs through the long black dress . . . a patch of fresco above the bed, sunlight through a high window . . . a panel of Venus and Adonis set amongst illusionistic architectural caprices in golds and reds . . . "Julia."

"I have to say goodbye my friend," she touched his face. "My love. My life."

He saw her blood-covered hands, chunky, clumsy and oversize. "No," he said, the tears spilling from his eyes.

"I loved you from the start," she nodded.

"Please be still," he shook his head.

"But I've never . . . been a blue calm sea . . ."

Holding her in his arms, the tears running down his weatherbeaten cheeks, "Don't go."

"I have always . . ." she touched his lips, "been a . . . storm . . ."

"I love you," he said, leaning down to kiss her.

Julia Soaemias breathed her last breath into his mouth while, back in the banquet hall, nothing but the fall of roses, which trickled down in silence onto the mountain of loosened petals filling the apse.

LI

A shaft of dusty sunlight fell through the open rectangle of window above the entryway, and pine needles and leaves littered the dark basalt stones of the floor. As his deep aquamarine eyes adjusted to the dimness of the interior, he squinted at the names labeling the half-moon niches, too many of them familiar. Then he found the one with a small candle burning before it that had been freshly chiseled.

MARCELLVS VENATOR

The hood of his gray woolen paenula raised in reverence, Mannix stood staring at the niche for a long time. Then he moved one of the ladders into position and began the painful climb. The nineteen year-old boar wound in his knee ached, and he balanced the smoking dish of incense and the bouquet of wild flowers precariously in one hand.

Thimbria cried when he gave him a thousand denarii at his flower cart outside the Porta Latina and told him to keep the change for him and his wife. He gave much of his money to Erithrea and the eastern prostitute of two nights ago; and much of the rest to the eight other surviving whores. He said goodbye to Lepidus at the school, and gave some more toward the upkeep of the mausoleum. He even gave a little to Eutychianus for his retirement in Alexandria; for Mannix knew he wouldn't need much where he was going.

Arriving at the niche, he set the flowers before the simple red-glazed clay urn and positioned the bowl of smoking incense beside it. Then he put two fingers to each of his windburned whiskered cheeks, and pulled them back and touched the urn with his tears.

"Keep her company for me, old friend."

369

He stiffly descended the ladder and walked out of the shadowy interior through its twin-columned entryway, leaving the dank scent of dead flowers and mildew and entering the pine-sap and grass smell of the glade. Walking over to a poplar sapling near the open twin columns of the mausoleum, he took from his pack an old iron windchime which hung for years on his terrace in the Suburra. His grandmother had owned it, and it was as old as the hills.

He tied the windchime to one of the poplar's limbs and it tinkled slightly in the breeze as he walked away down the path, his muscled calves falling bare beneath the hem of his paenula. The morning sun cast the tree trunks in blue-gray snaking shadows across the golden-green grass of spring, and he enjoyed the poetry of their shapes.

Emerging from the glade near the first milestone outside the city gate, he set off down the Via Latina toward the blue-distant hills where he was born; not looking for any place in particular, simply enjoying the feelings of a man returning home after many years. In the distances the simple villages of whitewashed buildings with faded red-tiled roofs set on the sides of the rocky hills made him smile. He enjoyed the old ways of the peasants, their simple sacrifices, their rustic gods. He stopped for water at a farmhouse, and casually placed a bit of cheese from his pack in the small offering bowl set out for the household spirits of the Lares and Penates.

That evening, at the hour of Venus, he heard the trilling of flutes and the sweet sound of singing. Following the sound to a grove of olive trees set in a small glade, he laid down his pack, and walked slowly up to where he could make out the singers. Maidens with wreaths of spring flowers in their hair danced in a circle around a stone herm so old that its features were no more than shadows.

A sheep had been sacrificed and an old man was reading the entrails for his village, telling the future secrets of the coming seasons. Wine was flowing freely to the singing of the paeans. It was the spring rite of Pan and Bacchus, a time of welcoming the awakening earth, and preparing her for the planting of new life.

For a minute the music and the voices stopped as Mannix walked into the circle toward the altar. He removed the hood of his paenula and slowly filled a cup with wine from an open jar. He poured a libation to the spirits of the old ones and then drained one himself. The music and laughter returned.

Soon he was dancing in the circle with an olive wreath around his brow. The words of the ancient songs came back to his tongue without conscious bidding; and it was the first time he had truly laughed in years. He felt something lift as he danced – the sickness of the city – sloughing off like a snake shedding its skin. And he thought of Marcellus and of Julia Soaemias, and he felt that they were there with him.

The next morning he rose early off the dew-wet grass with leaves knotted in his dark mass of hair. After a breakfast of a few dates and a handful of olives, he helped the peasants of the small village hoe in their hillside fields, where the labor of a thousand years had cleared terraces for their orchards and vineyards. He enjoyed the work and the sweat, the pleasant dullness of his hangover and the sun on his bare skin.

They asked him to stay and he thanked them, and told them he had to move on but that he would come back from time to time. So the old man who told the fortune for his village the night before told him that, sunshine or thunder, a man will always wonder where the fair wind blows. And they killed for him a spring lamb and gave him a skin of farmer's wine, and wished him well in the hills.

Mannix walked all day with the lamb over his shoulder until in the late afternoon the volcanic lake spread before him in deep shades of aquamarine blue. He stripped to the skin on a huge boulder and dove in, swimming for a time and then floating on his back beneath the towering stone pines watching the huge cumulonimbus plume up into the deep blue sky. Afterwards, he walked on beneath the trees through the dappled golden sunshine playing beneath his feet to the far side of the lake. There he struck the ancient trail, overgrown and invisible to all save he and his grandfather. He wound gradually up through the oaks and the pines until he reached the ancient lichen-frosted steps, remembering how his grandfather used to pull him off his feet and over them when he was a boy.

In the special place, the altar and its herms were overgrown by flowering thorn bushes. He took a long pull from the skin of wine the peasants gave him and looked around the place, feeling its resonance within him increase. Then he set about making a circle of rocks and gathering some limbs and brush. Taking his flint and his iron from his pack, he started a fire and skinned the spring lamb and then spit it over the fire. Then he sat and drank the farmer's wine, turning the lamb occasionally as he watched the sun sink into the distant sea.

After a time the lamb was ready and he began to slice off juicy portions with his knife and chew them slowly, drinking the wine as the stars spread above him a black marble mystery world of crystal and flame. Cradling his knees with his forearms, he sat there late into the night, letting the fire go down and watching the stars as if he was turning with them. One of them dropped away and the Bestiarius felt a strange kinship with it, and wondered to himself what could be happening up there.

HISTORICAL NOTE

Elagabalus and his mother Julia Soaemias were both assassinated on or about the night of March 11, 222 at the instigation of Julia Maesa, who found them growing increasingly out of control. Fell upon and slain by the Praetorian Guard, Elagabalus was beheaded, drug through the Circus Maximus behind a chariot, then through the city streets. Kicked, thrust and stomped into a sewer but finally found to be too big to fit, the nineteen year-old's body was ultimately thrown into the Tiber off the Aemilian Bridge. What became of Julia Soaemias' body is contested.

Maesa's other daughter Julia Mamaea was proclaimed empress and her son Alexianus became Emperor Alexander Severus. Julia Maesa died peacefully in the Gardens of Sallust in 226, and was deified by the Senate. Known to be of a rare, chaste and excellent character, Alexander Severus went on to rule for fourteen successful years until he and his mother were murdered during a mutiny of the troops at Mainz, Germany in 235. Their deaths brought the Severan dynasty to a close and plunged the Roman Empire into chaos for the next sixty years.

The primary source for the reign of Elagabalus (A.D. 219-222) is book LXXX of Cassius Dio's 'Roman History.' The secondary source is the 'Scriptores Historiae Augustae,' a largely anecdotal and sensationalist document written two hundred years after the emperor's death by one Aelius Lampridius. Gibbon's 'Decline and Fall of the Roman Empire' captures the general flavor of both of these documents, which is largely the same; and concentrates mainly on Elagabalus' character, sexual excesses, and subsequent catalogue of scandals.

The 'Writers of the Augustan History' speaks of the young emperor as having offered his physicians enormous sums if they could find a way to turn him into a woman, as having raped a Vestal Virgin, and as having undergone a marriage ceremony with his blond Carian slave Hierocles. They go on to have him filling the court with men picked from the public baths for their unusually large organs; and of his mother Julia Soaemias as having 'lived like a harlot and practiced all manner of lewdness in the Palace.' The popular nineteenth-century view of the young emperor was thus largely based upon the responses of scholars and writers to the political corruption, cruelty, licentiousness and extravagance contained in the 'Scriptores,' which mentions, among many other fantastic incidents, that 'In a banqueting room with a reversible ceiling he once overwhelmed his parasites with violets and other flowers, so that some of them were actually smothered to death being unable to crawl out to the top.'

The great Victorian painter Lawrence Alma-Tadema chose the above episode for one of his better known paintings, 'The Roses of Heliogabalus' (sic). His choice of roses rather than the 'violets and other flowers' mentioned in the Scriptores probably indicates their contemporary English association with beauty, decadence and sensuous love; as in the opening sentence of Oscar Wilde's 'The picture of Dorian Gray' – 'The studio was filled with the rich odor of roses.' Ironically, the homosexual Wilde was captivated enough upon seeing the portrait bust of Elagabalus in the Capitoline Museum at Rome that he wrote to his publisher: 'I saw the other day in the museum here the bust of a young man of grave, somewhat severe beauty, and the most delicate refinement of type, rather like a young Oxonian of a very charming kind, the expression of pride and ennui. On referring to the catalogue I found that it was the Emperor Heliogabalus; it was most curious and has filled me with a desire to write his life.'

The bust shows a short-haired, full-cheeked youth with large eyes beneath languorous lids and a thin whispy moustache. He does in fact seem to be suffering from that most nineteenth-century of maladies – ennui; all of which may indeed have complied with 'fin de siècle' conceptions of beauty. What follows is that someone of his age with absolute power would most probably have sought to alleviate his boredom with the most extreme of diversions. Hence, the notion of Elagabalus as a consummate voluptuary was popularized in the second half of the nineteenth century by writers across Europe such as J.K. Huysmans, who describes him as 'treading in silver dust and sand of gold, his head crowned with a tiara and his clothes studded with jewels.'

What is somewhat less sensational but perhaps more interesting is that Elagabalus is recorded in both Cassius Dio and the 'Scriptores Historiae Augustae' as having tried to consolidate all gods and religions under the Sun God – a cult which would initially have the favor of the first so-called Christian emperor, Constantine, as well as the last pagan emperor, Julian the Apostate. As for the great temple in which this was designed to take place over a century before it did, the 'Elagaballium' was dedicated to Jupiter Ultor by Alexander Severus. Its foundations are partly excavated beside and beneath the church of San Sebastiano al Palatino, and its platform – upon which the little church rises – is still a prominent landmark on the northeastern side of the Palatine Hill in Rome.

When the foliage has dropped and the claws of winter-barren trees scratch at the deep blue sky, from the Area Palatina – now a pleasant slope of green grass with the podium of the Temple of Jupiter Stator still visible – you can picnic with a cold chicken and a bottle of wine and see the platform of Elagabalus' 'Temple of the Sun' quite well. You can also see one of the Carystian green columns of the portico of the Public Wing of the palace, as well as the ruins of its basilica, throne room, lararium and banquet hall. Not long ago, in fact, one used to be able to sit under the umbrella pines of a summer evening and hear symphony concerts played in the Stadium Garden.

You can still imagine the imperial palace rich with many-colored marbles and bright with paintings and gilding, as you wander in the dappled light among oleander and lemon trees, golden broom and scarlet poppies, admiring how the mellow brick glows rose in the late afternoon sun. And you can appreciate the mood of the Romantics for whom all of Rome had this dreamlike quality. You can argue that their attitude may not have been scientific, but did produce the classical revival in architecture.

But if you want to truly understand Ancient Rome, the choice is clear. Sentiment is not a Roman quality. The atmosphere of much of Imperial Rome was not dream but nightmare. The natural beauty of the Palatine is attractive but the essence of the place is of another kind – starker, grander, and darker than a nineteenth-century canvas by Alma-Tadema. Behind it looms always the shadow of violence. And the melancholy of the antique world.